SKY GOLD

Stars On Fire

The Sable Riders - Book 1

This book was professionally typeset on Reedsy.
Find out more at reedsy.com

Contents

Epigraph

"I was the one, I who could
Pull in all the stars above, lay them on your feet
And I gave you my love, you are the one that got me started
You could have let me love anyone but I only wanted you
So why did you make me cry? Why didn't you come get me one
last time?
You'll always know the reason why. We could've had the moon
and the sky. You'll always know the reason why this love ain't
gonna let you go."

'The Moon and the Sky'
— Sade —
You can find 'The Moon and the Sky' on Spotify

Prologue

Embers, flames and wildfire

SELENE

'How is this my life?' Selene muttered under her breath as she stepped from her fly-cab at the gates of an ornate palace.

She took in the view and sighed. *This is so not my scene,* she thought.

Fashionable ensembles glittered, neo-mod threads glistened, and designer-drenched beauties tottered past.

The night was warm, so bronzed upper arms, necks, and long legs were on display, as well as artistic pieces sculpted to perfection by genetic engineering and the latest surgical implants.

Squaring her shoulders, the slight, dark-haired, honey-skinned woman skirted the hordes of fashion swans jostling for camera cameos.

She tried to push through rivers of diamonds and sequins

as she was carried along in a wave of swarming party-goers.

When she broke free, her eyes widened at the sight of the gardens that the planet's most eminent landscapers had transformed into a gilded tropical oasis for the extraordinary affair.

At the center was the palace's famous bioluminescent gold ginkgo tree, whose rich saffron leaves fell into a lacquered pile on the palace grounds throughout the year.

The platinum fronds floated around Selene's heels as she walked past, giving the sensation she was wading through an ocean of aurous spray.

Ahead, lush vines adorned the entryway, where servers greeted visitors with glowing mango daiquiris and champagne on ice upon arrival.

She nabbed a glass of bubbly and sipped it to cool herself off before plunging deeper into the festivities.

Selene navigated the night's thick crowd, winding her way up a candlelit staircase that lured guests to the welcome table, shrouded with mountains of gilded lotus, lilies, and amaryllis flowers.

A host checked her name and title, comparing it to a list at the entrance. She joined the obligatory royal greeting line as cork-popping and effervescent DJing throbbed through the dazzling multi-level palace.

She shuffled further in the queue, fighting a yawn.

It won the battle she'd been waging against it.

She tried gritting her teeth to stop it, but it escaped, and she masked her parting lips with her clutch bag.

Mercy.

Clutches of dignitaries and society darlings crowded ahead of her, and she groaned at the thought of the long wait.

After many more minutes came an announcement.

'Selene Munene, Undersecretary to The Prime of Dunia.'

Holy Dunia, about time!

She stepped forward and curtsied before the royal family.

First, to Prince Occaro, the host of the night and the reason for the most desirable party in Enia City.

Also, one of the King of Rhesia's three brothers.

He was a tall man with dark brown hair who'd once been handsome but was now trying to clutch on to his youth and good looks.

He'd dabbled in one too many face-freezing injectibles over the years and paid for a blinding set of veneers.

He used them to give her a diplomatic smile that didn't quite reach his eyes, for they were busy darting around the rest of the room at the more glittering, beautiful beings within.

He ignored her.

As did his wife, Princess Ameli, a nip-tucked creature of indeterminate age.

Nonplussed, Selene moved on to Prince Emian, a studious-looking man with a heavy brow and cold, measured eyes.

They flicked over her old-fashioned dress with a touch of disdain.

His wife, Princess Zanza, timid and retiring, barely glanced at Selene, extending a limp hand for acknowledgment.

Selene didn't waste time moving along to Prince Torran.

Aged in his late thirties, he was the youngest of the Rhesian royal brothers.

He cut a dashing figure in typical suaveness.

He grinned, revealing glimmering teeth set in a symmetrical face.

Leaning in, he leered at her, his eyes lingering on her cleavage.

She gave him a tight smile and moved away lest he thought she was receptive to his 'magnetism'.

It was rumored that he was the royal playboy.

No wonder, with his baby blue eyes and messy blonde hair.

He'd women swooning over him throughout the Pegasi System, hoping to become his Princess.

She'd no such plans, Selene thought.

She presented herself to the royal couple - King Auban VI and Queen Sanjana of the Rhesian Realm of Nations - who contrasted with their surly and checked-out family members.

She dipped for them, for she was a secret fan.

The most beloved and loved-up regal duo in all Pegasi smiled back in greeting.

He was tall, broad-chested, and handsome; she was a vision of beauty and elegance.

Their images graced the society holos to no end, and unlike their siblings, the welcoming picture they painted was everything desired throughout the System.

Dazzled, Selene kissed the Queen's slim, perfumed hand as custom dictated.

Without warning, she stumbled, her heel caught on a carpet's edge.

She flailed for a second, trying to find her balance.

To her dismay, Queen Sanjana reached a hand out to steady her.

Selene had no choice but to grab onto the jeweled sleeve.

'Thank you, Your Highness,' she breathed.

The regal woman pulled Selene close as she helped her upright.

'I spotted your face on the line,' she whispered. 'These occasions can be so dismal, gorgeous. Keep your head up. And leave at your very first chance.'

Selene's eyes widened, but the banquet organizers were already ushering her along by then.

Not before Selene noted a devilish twinkle in the Queen's eye. Which whisked away some embarrassment at her near faux pas after she caught a few mortified looks from some of the guests and staff nearby.

Selene gave a quick apologetic smile and shame-sidled away, easing into the crowded banquet hall.

It was a typical Rhesian affair.

Lavish. Extra in all ways possible. Over. The. Top.

A grand and elaborate proceeding filled with glamour, sophistication, and elegance.

A dazzling, gem-studded gathering attended by the System's glamour elite, royalty, dignitaries, and influential individuals.

The palace banquet hall she walked into was ornate with high ceilings, chandeliers, and intricate architectural details. It featured champagne towers and chocolate fountains.

Aerial silk choreographers and dancers floated past.

A never-ending stream of cocktails accompanied an indulgent food bar.

Twas an event designed to thrill even the most cynical of party-goers.

The fabulous women and men in the room jostled to see and be seen in the latest Rhesian fashion.

Their accessories and shoes were the showiest and flashiest possible. And they all dripped with jewelry.

Except for Selene. She was all about keeping it simple.

She'd brought out her old striped ebony and white floor-length dress that had never let her down.

It hugged her curves in the right places, accentuating the suitable amount of skin without sacrificing her cleavage.

Paired with a pair of sensible black heels, it was the perfect ensemble for a Government Undersecretary attending a banquet at the Enian residence of Prince Occaro.

The second-oldest royal brother was a persuasive individual.

As Foreign Minister of the Rhesian Realm of Nations, Prince Occaro had perfected the art of quid pro quo and atonement.

So when he sent out birthday party invitations, no member of the ton, diplomatic corps, or establishment could refuse him.

Selene could not wriggle out of the obligatory appearance, no matter how much she'd protested.

She had zero tolerance for parties, small talk, and flattery, even though they were a significant prerequisite of her working life.

As a result, she often escaped from the endless rounds of formal festivities, and her visit to Rhesia was more of the same.

Yet her father, the Prime Leader of Dunia, had insisted on her presence. Stating that a renegotiated xentium supply treaty with Rhesus was paramount.

It all depended on her bargaining skills and showing up this evening. It would help secure the funds needed for their planet's future development.

He'd been unable to attend, for he'd had to remain in Dunia to deal with a few vital policy votes in his own Parliament. Crucial ballots that could not be delayed.

Thus, Selene's reluctant attendance.

Once the ball got underway, the guests waltzed to the music of a live band before servers led them to the most oversized table Selene had ever seen.

Sandwiched between a dour Countess and a simpering Minister from Falasia, Selene tucked into a feast of eclectic dishes and desserts, served on fine china and silverware, accompanied by the System's finest wine and beverages.

She shook hands, answered questions, and made the requisite promises on deals yet to be signed.

She clapped for the dancers whirling above them on silken ropes as they ate, watching to ensure none would tumble from the air and onto her plate.

Likewise, she joined the rounds of applause when the Prince was presented with his birthday cake.

As soon as she nabbed a slice, Selene escaped.

Her head ached, and she wanted out, not of the event but of its suffocating atmosphere.

However, departing the party this early would be a diplomatic misstep.

No one dared take their leave before the royal family.

So she stayed, wandering alone to the only place she could find peace and solace within the grand house.

The deserted terrace outside.

She slipped through the expansive doors to the quiet mezzanine surrounding the banquet hall and the neo-Rhesian palace.

Breathing in the fresh air as she leaned on the edge of a balustrade, she wished to transport herself back to her planet, Dunia.

A week of glad-handing and endless meetings with her

Rhesian counterparts had been draining.

That said, the sphere was beautiful, Enia even more so.

For the first time that evening, Selene relaxed, taking in the views of the extravagant city laid out before her.

The capital took pride in being Pegasi's bauble.

It shone, from its self-illuminating walls, sky glows, giant panels of strobed surfaces, and radiant orbs, to its genetically modified trees and plants that glowed at night with biofluorescence.

Almost twenty million people lived in this metropolis that glimmered from space, appearing as a vast mirror ball on the planet's luminescent emerald surface.

Yet despite all of its bright lights and big dreams, Rhesia was an empire in decline. Overextended, its resources and its energy reserves were stretched.

The state coffers were also dwindling fast. As a result, its imperial, strongman image was eroding.

Moreover, from what she'd read between the lines at recent negotiations, Selene sensed that Rhesia was beginning to get alarmed by their contenders, seen or unseen.

The old empire was vulnerable to the other ascending planets in the System.

Grand and over-the-top events like this party attempted to embody the realm's self-perceived values.

Yet they did little to avert the inevitable. Novel powers were rising in the System, and trailblazing leaders were taking hold of the social order.

The underclass was making its mark. And Rhesia was being left behind in moon dust.

She shivered. She was at the precipice of a historic moment - the dusky end of one empire and the dawn of a new era.

Enia's light-scape punched through her thoughts and riveted her attention. It was like no other. In this city, every street was alive with radiance.

Bio-luminous plants lined the sidewalks, their leaves gleaming in the darkness.

Visitors and residents meandered tree-shaded avenues, surrounded by a verdant glow as if strolling through a magical forest.

Above, the buildings towered into the sky, their windows and balconies illuminated.

At the city's heart was an immense park filled with bright lanterns, a popular gathering place for locals and travelers.

Selene turned her head to marvel at the glowing maglev trains that floated across the skyline, ferrying hordes of people to the city's best attractions.

The light shows, for one, were legendary, featuring millions of flashing LEDs choreographed to sound.

The Fountains of The Gods, which she could see from the deck, was a must-see spectacle. The showcase sprayed wild-colored jets of spray sky-high, twisting and swaying, coordinated with music and giant displays.

If the tourists didn't come for the dancing water and lights, they thronged to the city's hot spots and parties.

Most were held in the vast array of live entertainment and multi-level venues, where sculpted synth droids and genetically enhanced hosts served visitors every pleasure imaginable.

Selene remembered attending an open terrace party at NeoStar, a System-famous establishment on Enia with incredible panoramic views of the city and the surrounding areas.

She and her friends had danced all night, fueled by cocktails, trays of never-ending delicious food, and spine-tingling DJ sets, with a spectacular view of the lit city.

She'd never forgotten the sensation of being carefree and alive as the lights became brighter, the music louder, and the energy more vibrant.

Yet she now missed the simplicity of Dunia's clear, dark skies, pristine and unencumbered from light pollution.

The vast canvas of distant galaxies, nebulae, meteorites, and shooting stars had always left her in awe. She often went stargazing on the beach outside her father's official residence, lying on her back looking up at the heavens as she lost herself in their rich, ancient, mysterious beauty.

For a moment, she longed to return to the utter liberation, deep peace, and sheer joy that Dunia's night sky always imbued.

With another sigh, she yielded to her current circumstance. She bent over the edge of the railing to get a better view of the fireworks in the distance when she froze.

Holy Dunia!

Every nerve under her skin lit up when, a little way along the terrace, she thought she caught movement at the corner of her eye.

She stared.

Something had vaulted from thin air onto the handrail.

A silhouette. One that moved once more to land noiselessly on the balcony's marbled floor.

Selene's heart rate raced.

She glimpsed a man—massive, hulking, and cloaked. His profile stood out against Enia's bright lights.

He turned his head, and she tagged a flash of sapphire-tinged flames from within his hood's confines.

Impossible.

Then he was gone. He'd disappeared into a doorway further down the terrace.

Blood still pounding in her ears, she took deep breaths to calm down. Behind her, the noise of the party rose and fell.

Music played, and voices clashed. Below, Enia's nightlife continued without missing a beat.

Up here, on the mezzanine, however, an uncanny silence settled.

Selene toed off her heels.

She set them down on the ground and crept barefoot along the wall, staying well within the shadows.

After a few tense moments, she reached the doorway where she thought she'd seen the figure slip into.

It led into a dark corridor.

A mysterious pull consumed her, so she took another step forward—quietly, as her years of reserve military training had taught her.

Damn you, woman, her sensible inner voice said. *This is 'raise the alarm and alert the security guards' level shit.*

She fought the logic, debating with herself. *You've trained for this. First, find the threat, if any. Then, notify the guards. Otherwise, you'll look silly if nothing comes of this. One count of embarrassing yourself is all you get this evening.*

Her latter thinking won. She was soon creeping along a wall, past paintings and sculptures of exquisite artistry, towards where voices rumbled.

She approached as soundlessly as possible. Then froze at the sound of a whisper.

'You crossed the wrong people, Occaro.'

The murmur, timbred and sonorous, reverberated against the walls.

'*Fokk* you,' came a strangled utterance.

'You didn't let it go,' the deep voice continued. 'And many lost their lives as a result.'

An incoherent, unintelligible response ensued.

The timbred rumble was unwavering. 'I hope all your affairs are in good nick. I regret it had to come to this, but 'tis the only way of maintaining order in the System.'

A long silence fell.

The script in Selene's head played out a scenario she imagined would outwork itself in the next few moments. *She'd leap forward, confront the intruder, and stop whatever diabolical activity she was eavesdropping on.*

She jumped when she heard crackling.

Followed by the sound of exploding matter and a fiery conflagration.

She flinched.

Someone was in that room, and they most likely needed her help NOW.

Unable to wait longer, she slid closer and leaned in to look inside.

A fire raged within, the flames consuming the space. Her eyes fell on a dense mass of glowing embers and light particles dancing together. Bright against the background of the lit walls.

The swirling, flaming cloud rose from a blaze of fumes and ashes.

A heap of ignited matter remained on the ground as the presence above it merged into a titanic, burning silhouette.

She tried to shrink away from the colossal apparition.

It turned, and she gulped. Her cognition freaked out for the next steps. All she got was a blank mental picture. Even her limbs froze, welded to the floor below.

She must have made a noise because the fire-shrouded creature shifted and moved toward her.

She panicked, sucking in a series of low-key breaths.

Her mind was so consumed by the sparking mass heading her way that she didn't even notice the acrid scent of smoke.

A blaze licked at the walls, engulfing the room and the corridor. She scanned around, trying to find a way out, but none was visible.

She tried to move her feet again, but they refused to obey her commands. Alarms clanged throughout the mansion, but they seemed so far away.

Yet, as soon as a wisp of smoke and flames touched her, she relaxed for some wild, unimaginable reason. She almost melted into it, her fear evaporating.

Instead, the warmth and energy of the creature scorched the air.

Then, it encircled her, sliding up her limbs.

It slipped under her dermis and roared into her core.

She twisted and turned, any inhibitions dissolving into an impossible need as the flaming inferno swept over her body, yet no burn erupted on her skin.

Conversely, it washed over her with the sweetest agonizing heat that snaked all over her.

She wanted more.

Ached for more.

Longed for more.

A loud crack sounded out.

The world imploded, and she fell.

However, strong arms caught her before she hit the floor.

She fluttered her eyes open, trying to focus, but all she tagged was a man's outline against a bright gold incandescence.

The presence moved. It gently lifted and carried Selene away, its unusual inferno not burning her dress or skin.

Then she was back on the terrace where she'd started her small adventure, on the ground, next to her pair of sensible, black heels.

The entity retreated.

She reached out an arm in a futile effort to return to its fiery embrace.

Inexplicably, the silhouette shattered before her in a fountain of embers, flames, and wildfire.

She was beset with an incredible loss.

Tears flowed as she lost consciousness, slipping further away from the flaming, dying inferno.

Darkness took over.

She woke, choking at the splash of water on her face.

'Undersecretary Selene?'

Hovering above her prostrate form was a woman.

Gazing down at her from reddened eyes inset in a furrowed brow.

Higher still was a set of sprinklers dripping with moisture.

Selene's eyes dilated and perplexed, slow-blinked as they receded into the roofline.

She flailed to a seated position, disoriented. 'Where am I?'

'At Prince Occaro's home. On the terrace. A terrible fire just broke out,' the woman said.

Selene noted the terror on the young woman's face.

Followed by a vague recollection of who she was - one of the royal assistants who'd checked her name on the guest list at the front doors earlier that evening.

'When the blaze started, the Queen asked us to look around for any stragglers,' the woman continued, frazzled. 'We found you here on the floor, unconscious, just outside the banquet hall. I've sent for medics.'

Selene glanced down at herself, checking for any signs of damage. She seemed unharmed, except for a slight scorch mark on her favorite ball gown.

'I don't need a medic,' she said. 'I'm OK.'

'We have a duty of care to our guests,' the Rhesian woman implored, wringing her hands. 'I've comm'd for an air ambulance, and they're on their way.'

Selene surrendered to the urging, sinking back to lean against the stone wall, casting furtive glances at the smoke still billowing from the mezzanine beyond.

Soon, a team of efficient-looking emergency caregivers was at the scene.

Selene stated again that she was fine.

But they insisted harder on checking her over. And declared she was, indeed, fine.

'You probably fainted after the fiery explosion and resulting blaze,' one of the medics told her. 'You can leave, but please seek medical help should you feel dizzy or nauseous. You could have a concussion.'

They helped her to her feet and escorted her through the now-empty banquet room.

'Where's everyone else?' Selene asked, still dazed and barefoot, her sensible shoes clutched in one hand.

'The ball ended once the fire alarms sounded,' the assistant said by Selene's side. 'All the royals left in armored flyers, except for Princess Ameli who was rushed to hospital - because she fainted - but her husband, the Prince -!'

Unable to finish her words, the assistant's lip trembled, and she placed a shaking hand over her mouth.

With a sob, she turned and fled out of the reception hall.

Selene wasn't far behind. She stumbled out into the night to join the other horrified guests.

They congregated outside, around the bioluminescent gold ginkgo tree, clutching shawls and steaming drinks as they all stared and whispered.

Pointing to the charred remains of the Prince's office balcony, firefighters directed flame-detecting drones through the burnt and smoking rooms.

A few investigators milled about, asking each of the guests pointed questions.

They soon came to Selene, seated at the back of an air ambulance, sipping a hot *kahawa* to calm her nerves.

She was still processing the night's events and remained speechless as they probed her memory of it.

Once they got word from the medics, the detectives concluded she'd been in the wrong place at the wrong time and was too frazzled to help any further.

Soon, they cleared her to leave.

She extracted herself from the melee, rushing into a fly-cab back to her hotel room, where she lay on her bed for hours, pondering the high-octane incidents of the night.

Had she imagined the mysterious figure? Would anyone believe her if she told them she'd seen a man who'd turned into an otherworldly creature enter Prince Occaro's study? Or that the burning silhouette had carried her out of harm's way? If she told a soul, what level of sensation would her announcement cause, given her position in the Dunian government?

After much tossing and turning, she kept the strange encounter to herself.

Besides, not one of Rhesia's investigators reached out to her again.

Still somewhat shaken, she booked passage back to Dunia the next day.

Later, back home, Selene followed a holographic news interview featuring Rhesian authorities, who claimed they'd found the origin of the vicious fire that had consumed Prince Occaro's study.

According to witnesses, the royal had retrieved a new laser gun he'd wanted to show off to his friends and fans at the party.

The weapon itself was reported to be a rare, handcrafted piece that retailed for hundreds of thousands of schills.

It'd been shipped from Iccythria by a dear friend of the Prince as a birthday gift.

The experts said the firearm must have misfired due to the Prince's mishandling. Its energy cartridge had exploded, causing the blaze.

However, a contradictory top-secret report crossed her desk a few weeks later. One she'd requested from the Dunian

Security Intelligence Office after debating with herself about coming clean about the events of that fateful night.

The brief outlined how Prince Occaro's pleasant public facade had hidden a violent temper. Interviews with anonymous sources uncovered rumors that he'd assaulted more than one noblewoman and gotten another pregnant.

Operatives suggested it'd been Lady Sarita, the wayward daughter of Duke Faustian, one of King Auban's close friends.

Worse still, credible evidence found that Occaro had been behind a plot to assassinate Prince Naveen, the King's first son, and his nephew.

The plan hatched a few years ago was a bid to thrust himself closer to the throne's ascension line.

The conspiracy - an attack on a spaceliner the young Prince had been traveling on - had failed. It turned out the King's heir had not been on board.

However, faceless perpetrators had rigged it with explosives. As a result, it blew up, killing thousands.

Fathers, mothers, children. Many had been refugees from various parts of Pegasi, relocating to the moon station Eden II in the skies above Dunia.

It seemed someone wanted Prince Occaro to pay for some or all of his sins—with his life, no less.

She read the analysis with great outrage.

If the intel was accurate, the flaming vigilante had delivered the best possible justice, Selene thought.

She reached a few conclusions and multiple conjectures, which led her to a single hypothesis.

That this affair, while disturbing, was none of her business.

So she locked the report in her office safe and left it alone.

For her home planet, Dunia had enough problems of its

own.

I

Don't set sail on someone else's star.

1

When Souls Fall Into Pools Of Molten Gold

AN UNIDENTIFIED SHIP ABOVE DUNIA

The Proxima Technocracy would have prevailed if it hadn't been for their vast underestimation of Dunia's sentient powers and its unwavering guardianship over its precious ecology and inhabitants.

One day, the twin suns shone over the magnificent planet, and the air teemed with optimism and possibility.

The next day, torrential rain, howling storms, and waves of relentless hurricanes pummeled the ground.

It was more severe on the southern continent where the interlopers had first landed, for what they thought was a sure-fire invasion.

Massive plate-sized salvos of hail flung from drenched skies slammed into every obstacle in their way. They obliterated power suits with such force that they sheared off armor and turned the surface beneath into a never-ending boggy swamp.

The storm reduced visibility to zero; radio comms turned to static and bionic musculature to mush.

The Technocracy's invincible interceptors and rattlers became weak as gnats against the prevailing gusts and devastating lightning, crashing into prismatic mountainsides in massive explosions that lit up the nightmare scenes.

Even the far north desert tundra fell victim to the high gale that whipped sand into sheets of devastation. The few creatures that made up the arid biosphere retreated into caves and holes carved into the ancient rock.

Despite their firepower and metal might, the invaders' soldiers, also called the crats, crashed in the thousands.

Then, fleeing the planet's endless salvos, the interceptors pulled back from the planet and docked with the armada.

In the stratospheric space above Dunia, The Technocracy's flotilla streaked away one by one into FTL flight. They vanished with a wink as they raced back to the Omega IAZL System and their gleaming silver-plated habitat that hovered around the vibrating exoplanet HD 638974 b.

However, not all of The Technocracy crafts left the region. Three capital cruisers remained, hovering in orbit.

A pair of eyes tracked the partial departure of the crat squadron from well within the confines of an indiscernible spacecraft tucked behind the shadow of a slow-revolving asteroid.

'Looks like they got their asses served to them,' a rumbled

voice said. 'They're standing down to a fractional retreat.'

'So a blockade then?' a melodic tone asked.

'Tis. Two ships are positioned over Dunia's spaceport and cargo facilities,' the rumbling timbre grunted.

'One just headed to the other side of the planet, over Rambasa,' the sing-song lilt said.

'That's close to the xentium ore mines and industrial trade center,' came the measured observation. 'It would seem The Technocracy is digging in their heels over Dunia. They must be desperate.'

'What's our play?'

The conversation paused for a beat.

'We slip into Dunia and retrieve our asset,' the timbred voice said. 'But first, launch a couple of spy drones. Ensure they ease past that blockade and watch Dunia from a guarded distance. Please send me all surveillance and telemetry regarding The Technocracy's actions on the planet. Once we're certain it's safe, we go in.'

'*Naam, khosi.*'

Moments later, the craft's thrusters engaged, and the ship's sylphlike nose turned and shot out of its bolthole.

Heading away from Eden II, a vast, irregularly shaped moon that shone in the dark sky, towards the jade jewel that was Dunia.

SELENE

The Enclave, a garrison deep within the forests of Zaalalum, was located in a sheltered valley shadowed and screened from aerial view by a series of gigantic altiphytes.

Its popular moniker was 'Zulu One'.

The fortified military fortress sat at the center of Dunia's massive Arumba continent.

On a planet chosen centuries ago to harbor humans fleeing a climate-challenged existence.

The wind and mist whipped about the landing pad high above the base, cutting straight to the bone and extremities.

Typical Dunia.

The world was still annoyed at what had transpired in recent days.

Selene looked up at the roiling, dark, empty sky and cursed, kicking at the duffle bag at her feet.

It was cold.

Windy. Wet. Miserable.

This was not her jam.

It didn't help that she was still exhausted and irritable.

'Rina, where is this transport?' she sighed into her wrist comm.

'It should be there anytime now. Patience, woman. We sent a coded request for assistance last night, and a contact on Eden II responded. Fast, might I add. But it's taking time. Remember, they needed to dodge the crats' blockade. Plus, avoid being spotted by the spaceport's orbital defense systems. On that note, they told me they'd be sending a -'

Selene interrupted her friend. 'Is there any way you can please ask them about their ETA?'

'Can't handle a little cold and precipitation? When did you grow so soft?'

'Ri,' I hate you!'

'And I love you back, Sel.'

'But can you inquire, kindly? I've been waiting for ages.'

'When did I become your assistant?' Selene's best friend clapped back. 'You've just gotten too used to the good life as the Prime's daughter and right-hand advisor, with staff at your disposal. It's a new world now, woman. No personnel, zero fakery. Your diplomatic BS does not fly with me.'

Selene was about to clap back when, without warning, the atmosphere in front of her shifted—like, freakin' moved.

Instinct kicked in, and her hand shot to her waist to retrieve her blaster from its holster. Her eyes whipped and darted around, searching for purchase. When she found none, her pulse raced.

Then the empty air before her shimmered and flickered, revealing a dark, sleek Corvette crossed with a fighter set down on the landing pad for a while.

It was like nothing she'd seen: a faceted and streamlined neo-steel structure with armored turrets and rail guns, the entire surface coated in what seemed to be a matte radar-absorbing skin.

Stealth, she concluded.

It wasn't any Technocracy ship design she was apprised of, nor did it resemble any of the Pegasi system aircraft she'd studied at the Academy.

This was new, lethal, and here, on Dunia.

Heart hammering, she eased a foot to the left and froze.

A doorway had materialized on the outer surface of the Corvette. It slid open, and a metal air bridge with neo-steel stairs arced toward the ground.

Stepping down the ramp of the sleek fighter was a figure.

A HUGE man. So extensive, so broad, his deltoids blocked all internal views of his ship.

He was taller than anyone she'd ever seen before.

He was also more muscled than most, with massive, robust, thick limbs twice as expansive as hers.

Clad in a matte black, short-sleeved jumpsuit molded to every inch of his gigantic frame, he sported muscled shoulders, slim power-driven hips, and enormous thighs that eased into gigantic booted feet.

He'd strapped a contoured blaster to his hip, and she saw the outline of throwing knives tucked into his boots.

His skin was a light, lustrous caramel.

His solid neck, broad upper arms, and hands were covered by a series of stunning gilded and azure tattoos in the shape of an evocative nebula, marks he seemed to wear like a badge of honor.

She slow-blinked twice in disbelief.

Yet his magnificence kept giving.

A long, messy mane of inky locks crowned his head.

They were shot with highlights of sapphire and gold with silver at the temples and trailed lush and glossy down past his shoulders.

The same iridescent sapphire, gold, and metallic hues flashed on his beard, squared jaw, and mustache.

His lips were full, his cheekbones high, and his nose prominent and flaring as he paused to draw in Zaalalum's pure forest air.

His forehead was a wall unto itself, the brows dense and unyielding, but it was his eyes that stopped the wind, halted her breath, and stilled all sound around her.

Holy Dunia, she thought, as her gaze and her entire freakin' soul fell into pools of molten gold flecked with flashes of electric sapphire.

Each spark in his deep-set eyes was charged with a blue energy band and pulsed with charged centers that graduated in color and frequency, glowing as they seemed to flow from his corneas toward her.

His life force washed over her in waves, and she broke into a hot flush that traveled over her skin and spine.

The sensation was almost familiar.

That thought alone threw her off.

She took a tentative step back and nearly lost her balance, but recovered before losing her dignity.

He kept coming towards her, lifting a sizable palm. Not in greeting, but a cool command to drop her weapon.

He was, hands down, the most lethal man she'd ever seen or met.

She flicked her gun at him. 'Stay.'

He arched an eyebrow and paused, his sapphire and gold eyes assessing her with glacial coolness as he stopped.

At that moment, she was hit with the awareness that firing her handheld piece would be like hitting him with plastic pellets—zero effectiveness.

Still, she kept it trained on him.

His lips twitched. Then he crossed his massive arms across his chest and jerked his chin towards the Corvette behind him.

'Your transport awaits, *Excellency*.'

Selene blinked in surprise. 'You know who I am?'

'I do.'

His voice was a combination of deep raging waters and a rough, gravelly growl echoing with a lingering melody that roused a stir in her innermost being.

She tamped down the sudden stab of *whatever-the-fokk-it-was* that almost took her breath away. 'You're my ride?'

He lifted a dark eyebrow, and his sapphire-flecked eyes glimmered, his mind leaping in desire-laden bounds.

A flash of heat washed over her. *Straight to her core, dammit.*

To his credit, he didn't indulge the thought further.

'*Naam.* I'm your *pilot.*'

He spoke with an accented lilt. She couldn't quite place it, but his Standard was fluent.

'What were you expecting?' he continued.

'Maybe less of a sneaky fly-in and more of an obvious and on-time announcement of your arrival?' she snarked.

He shrugged his massive shoulders. 'I was on time. To be exact, I was here before the agreed time. Pure precaution, of course. I didn't know what I'd be walking into.'

She had to lean back her petite frame to look up at him, even though he stood a few feet away. 'Well, neither do I, so excuse me as I check in with my people.'

His lips quirked once more as he stepped back to give her privacy.

She kept one hand on her weapon and tapped her wrist comm, turning away from the stranger.

The holo screen popped up, and Rina grinned at her. 'Still here!'

Selene cursed under her breath and whispered. 'Of course you are. Can you confirm that my ride to Eden II is a stealth fighter slash corvette piloted by an unidentified lethal-looking colossus?'

Her best friend nodded.

'Sounds about right,' Rina said, dropping her voice to a

whisper as she peered at the view behind Selene. 'And what a ride, might I add? And I'm not talking about the ship.'

Selene gave her mate a withering look. 'Really, Colonel? Get a grip,' she hissed. 'Why didn't you tell me what to expect?'

Rina sobered up at her friend's glare. 'Like I was trying to tell you earlier before you interrupted me, Excellency, the Edenites agreed to help by secreting you off Dunia. The only way they could exfiltrate you was with a stealth craft. They also reassured me that the pilot they would send would have all the required security clearances and is trustworthy. I didn't know he was already on planet, but I'm taking notes of his skills at sneaking past our sec drones without us having any notion. All that said, jump on that damn ship and talk to them.'

'Are you sure about this?' Selene asked, concern lacing her voice.

'I am,' Rina insisted. 'I'm sorry I didn't brief you in detail before you left this morning. No sleep in 48 hours, last dibs on hot water, and zero hammocks to spare mean I've been off my game. Plus, I had no clue who they'd send. No idea it'd be HIM. Whoever His Magnificence is.'

Selene sighed. 'You're out of control, woman. It also sounds like there's no alternative. I'll do what I need to. Stay safe, Ri'. I'll reach out to you when I get a chance. As soon as possible.'

She tapped off her comm and cocked her head up at the mountain of a man standing a short distance away, lowering her weapon. 'OK, then, pilot. Please take me to your leader.'

2

Clean, windswept, smoky with a hint of musk

SELENE

The sleek Corvette had a name.

Mirage.

And with it, a dulcet-toned AI of the same appellation welcomed her on board.

Selene raised her eyebrows at the unexpected voice, then wondered who these Eden II folk were.

So far, they were challenging all her preconceptions.

First of all, sentient AI tech was hideously expensive, she thought. So, whoever owned this bird had plenty of cash to spare.

Secondly, their stealth kit rocked, something she knew little about from her stint in the army and the time spent with her friend and all-around geek, Harlow.

While she'd already seen evidence of its cloaking capability, what was even more fascinating was that the ship had a radar-absorbing hull.

Designed to deflect most sensor scans and arrays, it cost a bomb.

Whomever they were, they also had *fokkin'* great style.

She craned her head, scanning with curious eyes as she stepped into the airlock above the drive cone, reactor, and engineering.

It opened out to a cargo and storage bay. Every plate and bulkhead was well crafted, with seams expertly sealed, joined, and galvanized.

Everything gleamed and shone from exceptional upkeep, and she'd even seen a series of intricate paintings on the walls.

The air was redolent with metal alloy, leather, and wood, plus the lingering scent of brewed rich kahawa.

While storing her bags in a locker, she spotted one floor dedicated to a compact mess, cabins, and a medbay.

Then she followed the mysterious hulking navigator up a flight of stairs past the galley level, into the control bridge, and into the pilot's seat.

He motioned towards a 360° swivel crash couch that would give her maximum support during a full burn.

'Strap in,' he grunted.

'*Sante*,' she said, thanking him and reverting to Standard, evidence of her nerves.

She acquiesced as he sank into his navigator's pivot chair and began messing with the controls.

Above him were several large multi-holo screens showing

various maps, security feeds, plus a virtual 3D overlay of the external landscape.

The sleek craft's command deck was clean, tidy, and roomy for a vessel of its magnitude.

She supposed it needed the space to accommodate the pilot and about four chairs designed for other people of his immense size.

However, for this short hop, the aviator was alone.

Except, of course, for Mirage.

The AI piped up. 'Does our passenger care for a refreshment?'

Selene was too jittery to drink or eat. 'No, thank you,' she confirmed.

The helmsman focused on his nav holo screens. 'Mirage, prep us for preflight.'

'Preflight sequence initiated,' the AI intoned.

Selene's eyebrows rose as the cockpit reoriented itself, displays and all, so the seats faced up, ready to boost into space.

The pilot conversed with the AI, pausing to cock his head, his eyes glazing over like he was speaking subvocally.

She assumed he was patched into a reconfigurable high-tech control panel and virtual HUD.

Wrapped up in the comfort of her chair, Selene pretended to fuss about on her handheld comm while taking surreptitious glances at the man.

His large hands moved so fast over the controls and key-board that they almost blurred her vision.

She gave up her amateur spying attempt when his eyes sliced over to her and caught her staring at him.

He turned to face her, the glowing irises between the long

lashes fixed on her. Her heart lurched in a massive kick.

'Ready?'

Her traitorous body twitched in response to his deep timbre.

'Nervous?'

She narrowed her eyes at him, and his lips curled.

'I'll get you to Eden II safe and sound, *Excellency*.'

His low, soft voice sent a powerful energy ripple through her small frame.

Little did he know it was not so much the safety of the flight but his presence setting off all her senses.

She forced herself to hold his gaze. In some part, to contain the potency that seemed to emanate from him. Which was somehow flowing over her again. It overwhelmed her, and she restrained her reaction.

'Please don't call me *Excellency*,' she murmured, not wanting to create any distinction between her and the pilot.

His stare intensified, and he leaned back into his chair like he owned the place, his long mane settling on his shoulders in silken ropes.

'Then what may I call you? I ought to know your name to be your pilot.'

She studied him, noting the fine lines around his eyes and the silvery gray flecks in his thick hair at his temples.

This was not a young, unsophisticated man.

He was a full-fledged creature in his beautiful, wild prime.

She needed to be on her A-game.

After a beat, she replied. 'Selene.'

'Selene,' he rasped slowly as if committing it to a cherished memory.

Her heart lurched at the sensuous treatment of her name.

He leaned forward, and suddenly, the spacious cabin was too small.

His scent wafted into her nostrils. It was clean, windswept, yet smoky, with an unexpected hint of forest pine and musk. Enticing.

His eyes dropped to the crux of her neck, where her pulse hammered against its apex.

He turned his oversized maleness away from her.

Silence filled the deck.

Moments later, he spoke again, in a low inflection. 'Call me Kainan.'

His words slid over her like warm, thick, dark honey. *Who was this man, and why was he affecting her so much?*

She'd served in Dunia's nascent military force and dealt with senators, leaders, and representatives from far-flung worlds.

She'd handled the most iron-hearted manipulators and put them in place.

She'd even met a few lawless barons in her time and holo-film celebrities with faces that entranced entire planets. Yet no one had ever affected her as the man beside her did.

She glanced again at him, unable to keep her eyes off him.

His massive body inhabited the space. It crowded her senses and did strange things to her core.

He was dangerous, but just how, she wasn't sure.

Stop it! she chastised herself, turning her head away to look out of the viewport.

This was no time to indulge her fantasies.

Instead, she needed to block out the beautiful specimen of a man at the controls from her mind.

Like she'd done for the many meetings, negotiations, and

parliamentary sittings she'd fronted with her father, she focused on the task ahead of her.

She stepped into her role as a politician and diplomat. She had a mission to fulfill, and mooning over a mere pilot would not help retake Dunia.

The flight went faster than she'd expected.

In complete stealth mode, Kainan piloted the ship while Mirage managed to evade Dunia's planetary security drones, satellites, and The Technocracy's three-ship cordon.

At first, Selene was a mass of nerves, glancing at the holo screen's external view as they ghosted between the surveillance machines and ships.

The Edenite craft nimbly moved past the dragnet using thrusters.

Relief hit when they pulled away from the blockade, and soon, they were speeding away, heading to their destination, far from detection.

The burn from then on was hardcore, and Selene was molded to her crash couch as the craft raced towards the lunar rock.

Lulled by the quiet engines and Kainan's calm energy, she allowed herself to lean back into the deep confines of her chair.

As Dunia receded from view, its green forests lit up by its

twin suns to glow like a jade jewel in space.

For the first time in many days, the band of anxiety inside her released for a brief period.

She'd tried to regulate every aspect of her experience of recent happenings, feeling that if she didn't, she would shatter.

Yet now, she was letting someone else take control.

Having Kainan guide the ship to Eden II was relaxing, even though a thread of mystery and menace surrounded his presence, which she was working triple time to disregard.

What was hard to ignore was the fact that a series of horrific events had precipitated Selene's urgent flight from Dunia.

Starting with a close escape from a burning, rioting city where her name had ratcheted to number one on a 'wanted dead or even more dead' hit list.

It all began when Rina woke Selene, with some urgency, from a deep sleep a few nights ago.

Rina, AKA Colonel R. Mendi, was a senior member of the Planetary Security Council and her best friend.

So, her assessment that Selene was in imminent danger was credible.

The sound of distant explosions further helped justify the dramatic nature of the sudden awakening.

Selene sat up in bed, speechless, as her closest confidant

settled beside her, took her hand, and gave her a rundown of the worst news she had yet to process.

'Darling heart, it's your father. He's been shot dead.'

Selene stared at her mate, disbelieving.

'What the hell?'

Rina nodded. 'I must use formal language, seeing you're his heir, honey. A few hours ago, Kei'Lano Munene III, The Prime and Sovereign Leader of the planet and peoples of Dunia, was murdered by his own Minister of Defense.'

Selene's blood ran cold. 'Tell me everything.'

'At 1030, my Security team informed me of a skirmish at Parliament House. I also received numerous reports of a coup unfolding throughout Dunia, one masterminded by Massimo and underwritten by the Pegasi System's worst nightmare— The Proxima Technocracy.'

'The crats?'

'Yes, they're here.'

Selene shivered as she pictured the race of intelligent beings battling for supremacy in the universe and going about it with a scorched earth policy.

Rina continued. 'They landed interceptors and rattlers supported by an armada of their capital cruisers in orbit. New Malindi's defenses were soon overrun by two large battalions of their crat soldiers, fighting alongside a coalition of fighters given over to the coup.'

Selene held onto her friend's arm. 'Massimo? How did he —'

'He and his militia stormed Parliament. They'd muscled their way, killed a handful of trusted bodyguards, and barreled into the Prime's office, where Kei'Lano had been working late. According to Rina, Massimo had fired a hail of bullets into his chest. The traitor and his entourage had then left to announce their takeover from the steps of the Senate, a few blocks away. Leaving Kei'Lano alone in his final moments.'

Selene's face collapsed as tears streamed down.

Rina gave her a concerned look. 'Shall I stop?'

Selene shook her head. 'No. Please go on.'

'Summoned by one of the Prime's loyal guards who'd survived the attack, I raced to the Prime's office. Only to find Kei'Lano on the floor in a pool of his blood. I tried to administer first aid, but it was too late. So I declared his death and arranged the secret transport of his body to the State Morgue. Followed by a dash across town at midnight to spirit you fokkin' out and away from any possible harm.'

'Thank you.'

'You are not under any obligation to thank me, honey. What you need to do right now is gather everything you can and get out of here, out of the city.'

Shaken, Selene slipped from her bed and dressed at Rina's urging, having no time to process her feelings because, as she'd just been informed, her enemies were hunting her down.

Rina then locked down the Prime residence with fast efficiency so that no one entered it unbidden, activating a powerful perimeter force field.

The pair had sneaked out of the grand house with just minutes to spare.

All they'd managed to retrieve was a file of critical documents, Selene's comm tab, and some clothing stuffed into a single duffle bag.

Soon, the boundary of the stately residence was swarming

with Massimo's guards. Searching for the woman who was now the Prime in Waiting.

However, they were unable to get past its security shield and sensors.

A few avenues away, Rina bundled Selene into a two-person flyer on standby in the dark of night, and they winged their way to the walls of the domed city.

They abandoned the craft and proceeded on foot because the tiny vessel was useless against the raging planetoid storm that had formed over the capital's atmosphere.

In hours, New Malindi, Rambasa, and Paris Minor had fallen to the One Dunia Coalition and militia with the aid of The Technocracy.

The loyalists had managed to keep the enemy away from Axuma, Isacchar, Gisania, and most of Arumba.

General McKenzie, an army leader loyal to Kei'Lano, was doing a great job coordinating the clean-up of any hostiles there.

The blockade hadn't helped, either.

The One Dunia Coalition had sent a planet-wide message prohibiting all unauthorized vessels from entering or leaving the planet.

Massimo Makori, the traitor, fronted the holo comm announcement.

Selene bit back a sigh. She wondered how she, along with the rest of the government and her father, had been suckered in.

By Massimo's wicked charm, sense of humor, and larger-than-life voice and passions.

They'd imagined him to be a genuine, passionate, and loyal citizen.

The ex-Army major had dedicated himself to serving his country in the Ministry of Defense.

His commitment to Dunia's strategic security and military issues made him a darling of the military and the cabinet.

So much so that Kei'Lano, her father, The Prime, had swept aside the growing rumors of Massimo's corruption, bullying, and manipulation.

She also blamed their busy schedule.

In recent months, the Prime and Selene, in her capacity as his Under Secretary, had been focused elsewhere.

On social causes, scientific research, and preserving Dunia's ecology. They'd let Massimo and his largesse have excessive say and sway in Parliament and beyond.

When they'd been given concrete evidence of his betrayal by one of his ex-aides, they'd confronted him, but it was too late.

He'd already made backroom deals to gain upper and lower house support. He'd even had articles of impeachment against Selene's father drawn up.

With the help of a rogue battalion of military soldiers, Massimo stormed Parliament in the heart of New Malindi's city center.

He'd waited for nightfall and killed the Prime, kickstarting a coup.

All so he'd have control of the manufacture and export of xentium.

She'd kicked herself, overwhelmed with guilt at her naïveté.

Then again, the insurrection was never imagined for a planet considered the friendliest in the Pegasi system.

Days later, Selene still didn't have a handle on her sudden, novel reality. She was exhausted and saddened to the core.

Her heart was a mass of emotion, and her mind churned.

Yet all she allowed her spirit to do was push forward and find the help her people needed.

3

Jagged Flashes and Sweet Memories

SELENE

Eden II loomed in view as the stealth craft drew closer to the notorious lunar scape that glinted diamond-like in the light of the System's twin suns.

It was considered a giant moon in actual size, and its immensity surprised her.

She'd read all sorts of stories about the place.

Some said it was a den of iniquity.

Packed with tunneled caverns that hid a litany of gambling casinos, gaming arcades, whore houses, and seedy hotels catering to every vice in the System.

News reports and rumors said that each street corner had its watering hole, complete with gangs that controlled the distribution of alcohol, the coveted synth drug koko, and the sale of illicit weapons.

She had no idea what to expect, and a frisson of fear wandered up her thigh for the first time since she and Rina had concocted their plan.

'Selene?'

The sonorous rumble dragged her away from her thoughts and back into the space she now inhabited.

Kainan jerked his chin in her direction. 'We'll be landing in about ten minutes.'

She inclined her head and sat up in readiness.

Looking at the holo screen, she thought she detected an orbital station in the skies, hiding in the moon's shadow.

She also glimpsed silhouettes of gigantic hyperspace cruisers attached to its nodes, but she couldn't be sure.

Her display was filled with a vision of the port. She spotted a sprawling terminus with plenty of full berths, myriad miniature flyers milling about, and a general sense of bustling busyness.

A multitude of ships, small and behemoth, had called into the pier.

The majority were in the simple, streamlined style favored by Allorian and Dunian merchants and traders who could not afford the sleek Rhesian yachts.

Porters in space suits scurried into the concourse from the pier and air bridges outside the vault, transferring bulky goods onto smaller passenger boats, pushing out toward the moon's massive dome.

The dock was gleaming and shining, brand-new, adding to the mystery of this not-so-rabble-rousing moon and how they afforded their technology.

In the distance, she spotted a set of secluded yards where a host of dark ships were moored. For a moment, she wondered whether this was where Eden II parked its mercenary armada. *Most likely*, she thought.

Mirage's engines powered down, easing from their previous high-grav push.

Thrusters fired in cadence, and the ship slowed. Then, grapples groaned, and there was a slight jolt as Mirage slid into her berth and latched onto the spaceport.

Selene sensed the vessel matched its gravitational pull force to the port's standard g's.

The weight of gravity returned, anchoring her to the floor.

A green light flashed throughout the cabin, indicating a successful docking.

The propulsion rumbled and then cut off smoothly.

Kainan stood his feet and jerked his chin at Selene.

'After me.'

A man of few words, Selene thought, rising.

They retrieved her duffle bag from storage. She flung it over her shoulder while Kainan slid on a jacket and swung a cross-body pack over his broad form.

He ushered her out of the airlock.

It opened to a climate-controlled air bridge that led down a corridor to an auto gate.

There, Kainan lifted his hand and waved the thick bracelet that encircled his even wider wrist over a scanner on the portal.

It beeped green and let them through onto a concourse teeming with life, sounds, smells, and color.

'Welcome to Eden II, where mortal men walk on streets paved with treasure and reside in palaces of emerald and ivory, dancing in the shadows of the moon, where once immortal gods tread.'

Selene started at the sound of the voice and glanced down to see a wizened woman smiling at her, thrusting a tray of baked goods into her face.

'Oh, hello,' Selene called out, her stomach lurching as a delicious scent wafted into her nostrils.

The woman grinned, revealing empty gums. She pushed one of her treats into Selene's hand.

As soon as Selene's hand wrapped around the sugary goodness, the woman's face turned icy, and she hissed, 'Two schills, Dunian!'

Kainan stepped forward, pulling the bun out of Selene's hands and handing it back to the hawker. 'Fili, *nada*. I'd appreciate it if you left my guest alone unless you're giving her the best of your selection.'

The seller's eyes widened at the sight of Selene's massive companion.

She ducked her head and was about to lower her body as if in a bow when Kainan extended a hand and pulled her upright. 'Give me fourfold of your buns, for they are legendary in all of Eden.'

'*Khosi?*' The woman croaked, confused.

'Four fresh ones, *sante* Fili,' he murmured, swiping his comm bracelet in her direction. The hawker woman's hand-held device beeped.

She gaped at the screen, where, given her awed reaction, she must have seen a generous amount of schills transfer.

'To go,' Kainan prompted.

'*Naam, khosi,*' the trader said, fulfilling the order. She discarded her initial staler bun that she'd tried to push into Selene's hands.

Instead, she packed the steaming hot treats in clean to-go bags and thanked the man looming by Selene's side. '*Sante khosi*, so kind-hearted -.'

Selene gazed at the pair, trying to understand the hawker's puzzling behavior toward the hulking man beside her.

He thrust two of the buns into her grip, and the smell of fragrant baked bread, spices, and sticky, nutty sweetness overtook her senses.

'Thank you,' Selene said, still surprised. Her tummy rumbled, and she bit into the snacks before following the colossal man.

He'd since thrown his jacket's hood over his head, obscuring his striking features.

He surged forward, ushering Selene close before him, leaving behind the female trader and her obvious adoration of the now-hooded pilot.

She took in the sights as they strode along, filling her mouth with tasty morsels.

Past shopfronts stacked with sacks and merchandise that lined the concourse. Tradespeople scuttled in and out of an open-air market on the floor below them, exchanging goods extracted from the valuable loads of cargo deposited on Eden II's front door.

At the same time, the cries of stall and kiosk owners clamored with those of roving hawkers to draw attention to their wares.

An extensive range of commodities was offered, from precious jewels to the latest Rhesian fashion. Food stalls were packed with hungry crowds, who availed themselves of spicy, colorful fare.

More displays advertised tech and droid parts that rivaled

the Technocracy's own.

The people milling in the markets hailed from all ends of the System. She spotted Rhesian traders in their luxurious robes that trailed the ground behind them.

Allorian workmen and women swept past, their elongated frames, distinctive tattoos, and flowing dark hair standing out in the throng.

And the Edenites. Even taller, more muscular, and built.

There were a few of them, but she picked them out now that she'd met one of them. They stood out with their strange luminous eyes, patterned skin designs, and forceful strides.

Yet Kainan still loomed over them all.

As they moved past the stalls, the mountainous Edenite escort and his visitor drew curious glances.

He was one of the tallest men under the dome, and his sheer magnetism meant their path cleared much more quickly than most.

Beyond the undercover market was a well-organized metropolis of maglev highways, grav trains, expansive buildings, and vast, spacious, pedestrian-centered urban spaces with busy walkways that weaved in and out of stunning gardens. Everything appeared ordered and neat as a pin.

Selene's wonder at the advanced technology and economy of the moon's metro grew with every minute, her presumptions shifting again.

She even thought she recognized a Falasian chieftain and his entourage dashing past on an open flyer.

She'd hosted his trade delegation a few months ago, and now he was on Eden II. This meant the moon was now considered more than a barbaric outpost worthy of critical foreign relationships.

Even while the new sights of Eden II entranced her, Selene's thoughts strayed to the negotiations yet to come.

From a diplomatic perspective, she'd never transacted with an Edenite before, so she had no context to work with. She'd need to think on her feet and make it up as she went, something she loathed to do.

On the other hand, she didn't have much to bargain with or use to strong-arm the Edenites into helping her cause.

All she had was her father's promise, a few hundred million schills, and one secret advantage up her sleeve, and she hoped against all hope that it would be enough.

A silver missile streaked through Selene's field of view, swooping in from behind her.

On closer inspection, the projectile became a streamlined creature with unusual metallic and shimmering gray plumage dancing through the air, then landing on Kainan's right shoulder.

The hooded man turned to the sleek gyrfalcon, stroking its feathers. He seemed to communicate subvocally with it.

Then he took the gyrfalcon's platinum talons and thrust the bird into the air, where it hovered for a while.

It gazed down on the Edenite with enormous coal-black eyes before driving its mighty pinions forward, its silver wings flashing against the concourse's high transparent roof.

'What was that?' Selene said, awed by the encounter.

He shrugged. 'My eyes and ears.'

'Impressive,' she said. 'A cybernetic robot?'

'Tis,' Kainan muttered.

'Are they going to alert your leader that I'm here?'

His sapphire-gold eyes slid to her, sending a ripple down

her back.

He spoke in a hushed and deep rasp. 'Something like that. Stay near, Selene. These hordes are fodder for pickpockets.'

Selene clutched her bags and sidled closer to her guide.

The crowds thickened, and even though Kainan's size made way for them, he still had to fight through the milieu with his elbows, cursing under his breath when his progress was slowed by the masses of bodies thronging the dome's central passageways.

They wended their way from the milling people, taking a left into a deserted alleyway. Selene gulped in the fresh air after the sense of growing suffocation in the teeming passages behind them.

Kainan steered her into a sleek-looking subterranean maglev lift. Its doors closed, and it moved away from its berth.

He was silent and stoic throughout the journey while Selene took in the flashing lights and shadowy recesses that materialized outside the plex windows.

The elevator stopped at an opening to an underground alley. He used a hand to indicate she step off, which she did.

He took the lead down a dizzying array of twists and turns that led deeper into looming darkness until they arrived at a dead-end where a small light flickered above a single dark door.

Next to it was a high-tech security panel.

It appeared to be the back entrance leading to a gleaming building that soared more than fifty stories over their heads.

Kainan waved his wrist comm over the display, which flashed bright blue. With a click, the door opened.

Taking a last furtive look behind them, Kainan ushered

Selene into the doorway. The door shut after them with a hiss.

They stepped into a corridor lit with dim, warm sconces set at intervals.

Voices, music, and the clink of cutlery and utensils echoed.

The air was redolent with the rich, malty scent of brew and aged liquor.

'A bar?'

Kainan pushed his hood back away from his face. He ran his eyes down the length of her body and again to her face. 'I assumed you'd like to eat, freshen up, and relax before your meeting.'

'That well may be,' Selene said. 'But I'll find it hard to consume much when I know I've got a planet in dire need of aid. It's a generous offer, but please forget about my needs. I just want to meet your boss.'

He raised his eyebrow and gave her a keen look. 'The head honcho will be ready when they say they're ready. Also, one thing you should know about Eden II, *Excellency*, is that we take our time with important matters such as food and nourishment. So, relax, enjoy the hospitality.'

His voice carried an inflection, and she knew then that she'd mistakenly believed he was a mere pilot.

This man was not to be underestimated.

Yet she couldn't figure out where he stood in the grand scheme. Perhaps a senior henchman or even an adjutant. That said, she cautioned herself to be more careful with him.

'This way, *Excellency*,' he rasped.

Kainan directed her a few feet into the corridor, unlocking a second doorway that led to a flight of stairs.

Dim-lit like the rest of the building, they led into a spacious central room.

It featured a series of comfortable couches and chairs arranged around an enormous holo screen.

Behind the sitting area was a generous dining area and bar. A sideboard against one wall held food and drinks of every variety.

'I told you I don't want anything,' Selene sighed.

'Not even I can turn down Edenite bounty,' the massive man rumbled, his tattoos glowing on his skin. 'Eat, drink. It's the least you can do. One should never negotiate on an empty stomach.'

Selene dumped her bag on the floor.

'Does he or she or whatever know that I'm here?'

'They're well aware, *Excellency,*' Kainan rasped, circling the buffet and heaping food on his plate.

Kainan paid her no attention, and she exhaled, giving in to the inevitable. She wandered to the board to fill a dish with colorful fruits, sliced meats, rich cheeses, spiced and fresh vegetables, and hunks of enticing warm flatbread.

Selene took it over to the couch across from the hulking man, and they both ate, with nigh a word between them.

The fare was delicious and necessary, she admitted a few minutes later, licking her fingers, feeling much more energized and refreshed.

She thumbed through her comm tab as Kainan crossed a thick thigh over his other leg and worked on his larger pad while he ingested his meal.

Selene glanced at him and tried to peer at what he was doing. She spotted intricate sketches and drawings on his screen of various aeronautical components and mechanical illustrations, beautifully detailed and precise.

Was he some designer, as well as a pilot? she wondered.

He raised his chin and tagged her curious study of him. He lifted a curved brow, and she flushed, looking away.

The sounds of laughter, clinking glasses, and a crooning singer with an appealing voice wafted up the stairs, and Selene longed to wander down and indulge in all the hilarity and good times. Eden II was beginning to draw her in.

After he'd finished eating, Kainan rose to his feet.

She caught his eye, lifted her hands, and questioned the wait, but all he did was shrug those broad, massive shoulders.

He put his plate away and returned to the couch, where he threw his hood back over his head, stretched his form on the oversized settee, and flung a pillow over his eyes.

'How much longer?' she ventured.

He rumbled from under the cushion. 'As long as it takes, *Excellency.*'

Selene fell back against the divan, and she cursed beneath her breath.

She remembered her father speaking of the Edenites.

He'd described how laid-back the moon's residents could be, which aligned with what Kainan had also told her. Perhaps that was the reason for how slowly things were progressing.

She glanced at the massive man on the davenport, at the rise and fall of his chest.

Heat flushed in her face. *Damn! He was a beautiful man.*

She dragged her eyes away from him.

Minutes passed, and still nobody.

Meanwhile, Kainan seemed to have drifted off to sleep. Restless, Selene got up to her feet and circled the room several times before deciding to read up some more on the people she was meeting.

Rina had sent her a report and a list of links for some background reading.

Resigned to waiting, Selene sat on the couch, tabbing through several pages, and noticed a side note and link Rina had added to the file. She clicked on it. The memo outlined what the author, Laila Dexora, a prominent Rhesian researcher, had written in a paper a couple of months ago analyzing the latest research and innovation in the Pegasi System's security sector.

She'd stated that after an in-depth investigation, she'd found that the true power of Eden II was not the Chamber of Elders but a council of shadowy individuals called The Sable Group.

Confirming what Rina had told her, Selene thought.

Selene sat back, recalling their conversation that had led to her presence on Eden II.

It took place a few days earlier at Enclave Zulu One.

She and Rina had been having breakfast when Selene slumped back in her chair and blew out her frustration from her lips. 'So what do we need to take back our cities?'

Rina thought for a moment. 'Some major firepower, a dreadnought or two, corvettes, a spaceport, soldiers who know what they're doing, and a hell of a lot of luck. Not too much to ask, hey?'

The two friends fell silent, their minds searching for answers.

'There might be a way,' Selene said, lowering her voice in the busy mess tent. 'The night before Massimo stormed the Parliament, Father and I sensed all was not well. We guessed Massimo might make a move against us, but only from a resource perspective. We just had no idea how or when he'd do it. We thought he might twist arms in Parliament to get jurisdiction of Dunia's funds and xentium production. So we managed to transfer all key accounts - our personal finances and government - into my control with secure codes. Now Makori can't access the coffers even though he wants to. From what I last heard, he's in desperate need of funds. So he's used most of his family's wealth to finance the internal coup.'

Rina cocked an eyebrow. 'How much cash do we have?'

'A few hundred million,' Selene confirmed. 'Enough to rent several corvettes, maybe even buy one and ammo.'

Rina shook her head. 'The problem is from whom? Rhesus, our closest allied planet, is a skip-jump away, and we can't access hyperspace or any transfer portals without an interplanetary warship.'

Selene dragged her hands over her face in frustration. 'Even if they wanted to, the Rhesian Realm of Nations, I believe, doesn't have the means to help us. They're dealing with their shit right now.'

Rina sighed. 'Aren't we all? We also can't send any tight beam comms beyond the system to Galicia.'

The two women fell back into their seats and lapsed into silence.

All of a sudden, Rina's eyes lit up.

'What?' Selene said, probing her friend's reaction.

'You won't like it, but hear me out. We may need to go rogue to win against Makori.'

Selene blinked. 'What do you mean?'

'Let me show you.' Rina grabbed her pal's forearm and pulled her out of the mess tent. Then she pointed upward to a round, silver orb hanging high in the sky.

'That's who we talk to,' she declared with a smug smirk.

Selene laughed out loud. 'Eden II? You can't be serious.'

'Dead.'

'Oh *fokk* no!'

'Why not?'

'Are you suggesting that we reach out to the most rabble-rousing, uncouth individuals in the system to assist us in taking back our planet?' Selene scoffed, shaking her head in disbelief.

A group of privates jogging past stared at the squabbling pair.

Rina threw up her arms in frustration. 'Uncouth? Who uses the word? I'd describe them as more anti-heroes, less rabble-rousers. They have a strong honor code and are notorious for standing by their promises. We've no choice, given that we can't ask anyone else but them for help.'

Selene nailed Rina with a glower. 'Convince me why we should consider reaching out to mercs and ex-cons on a hunk of floating rock and ice.'

Rina met Selene's scowl with a cool glance of her own. 'Remember how your father, many years ago, signed an agreement with the kingpins of Eden II?'

'I have a vague recollection. Remind me of the details.'

Rina obliged. 'It was, in essence, a quid pro quo. When

the civil war in the Allorian world broke out, and we faced thousands of refugees that our planet could not home here, we struck a deal with Eden II. They would welcome the asylum seekers, and in turn, we would furnish them with xentium to bolster their biomes, build ships, and add tech to their security. They'd taken in evacuees from their original Earth domicile, Eden City and Alloria. We also consented to provide them with regular food drops, raw materials, and necessary planetary resources. In essence, your father wanted to help legitimize a lawless lunar settlement while stabilizing the balance of power in the sector.'

'Sounds about right,' Selene concurred. 'It all went down about twenty years ago when I was still a teen. Father involved me in writing out the details of that deal. He started training me on the role and responsibilities of a Prime, even when I was that young. But I haven't kept up to date with what's been happening with Eden II since then. That was father's domain.'

'Then let me catch you up. Subsequently, Kei'Lano added a few more provisions to that agreement. One was an SOS clause, which he shared with the security council, now the Free Dunia movement, which is why I know about it. If Dunia ever required Eden II's aid, they would be obliged to help us in whatever way they had in their means. We've never pushed for it because we've never needed to. Until now.'

'Interesting,' Selene said. 'But what do they have that would even come close to helping us out?'

Rina smiled. 'I've got the intel. While you've been flitting across the System on social justice and foreign diplomacy jaunts, some of us have been doing the heavy-duty lifting regarding our planet's protection.'

'Do you recall all those times you've bragged about things I don't care about? Yeah, this is one of them,' Selene snarked back to her friend.

Rina shook her head in mock annoyance. 'Hang tight, woman. I'm going somewhere with this. Remember I'm a Security slash Free Dunia Council member?' she said. 'Which means I get intelligence reports on defense-related manufacturing, critical technologies, unusual deployments, and clandestine activity across the entire Pegasi system.'

'I knew that,' Selene quipped.

'Did you also know the briefings include Eden II?' Rina asked with a gleam in her eye.

'I do,' Selene crabbed. 'Get on with it!'

Rina gave her friend a mock salute. 'As you wish, Your Excellency. The analysis has shown that since your father's intervention, Eden II has built and amassed a considerable armada, including support craft, patrol ships, fighter corvettes, bombers, and carriers. All of them are multi-mission with FTL capability. In terms of fleet power, they've grown more than any other entity in the Pegasi system. And all because of one corporation on the rock. The Sable Group.'

Selene cocked an eyebrow. 'But don't they manufacture luxury flyers and racing pinnaces?'

'They do. But they have a major side hustle. In weapons, armed vessels, and tech.'

'Why have I never been privy to this aspect of them before?'

'Because they want it that way. From what I understand, they're quiet. Keep to themselves. They're like ghosts, wraiths. Shadows. It is rare, if ever, that they talk about their enterprise. While there's a Ruling Council on Eden II, The Sable Group runs the rock. No one can set foot inside its spaceport unless one of them has OK'd it. And if a ship tries to land elsewhere on Eden II without their approval, it is tossed across the moon's desert in a vexing pile of rubble. They're lethal players in business and firepower. They don't advertise it. I like their style. As someone said, a true badass never needs to announce it, and the scariest men I've met are often the most humble.'

Selene raised an eyebrow. 'Color me surprised. And what have they been doing with all this capability?'

'Making money and hiring out and selling their vessels for profit. Eden II is the number one destination for private armed ships, gear, armor, and trained militia in Pegasi and beyond. You can buy your army for a coup if you can afford it.'

Selene's brow wrinkled with worry. 'What stops them from using all that firepower then against us?'

Rina shook her head. 'That was one of the key stipulations that your father built into the contract with Eden II. They can't use any of their capabilities in opposition to Dunia lest our pact falls apart. And, so far, they've been loyal to us. I don't believe they would do anything to harm our understanding, given how much they depend on us for our resources.'

'Won't giving us help break the agreement not to turn their weapons on Dunia?'

'Ideally, they won't harm us. Instead, we'll pay them to help us overcome Massimo's coup. Plus, they had a great relationship with your father. That might be enough to sway them.'

Selene stared up at the silver moon. 'I can't wrap my head around it,' she said. 'All this time flying in and out of Dunia on missions to Rhesus, Galicia, and Alloria, I never gave a second thought to Eden II when we whizzed by. They seemed so small. Insignificant.'

'They may still be small, but I think they pack a mighty punch,' Rina stated dryly.

Selene assented. 'So you're saying we feel out The Sable Group and see whether they'll help?'

Rina nodded. 'It's not like we have many other options.'

'True,' Selene groused. 'How do we even begin to reach out to them?'

'I can send a secure, tight beam using a cipher that your father shared with Eden II,' Rina said. 'They'll respond if they're as smart or, better still, honorable as their reputation says they can be. And if they want to keep to their contract. We should get word from them soon enough. What do you think?'

Selene considered the idea. 'Perhaps, maybe.'

'In any case, I don't imagine Massimo Makori is honoring any of our agreed exports to the rock. Xentium is of particular interest to the Edenites Group. So there's a definite reason for them to hear us out,' Rina added.

Selene reached out her hand to grab her friend's arm as a thought came to her. 'I might even have another bargaining chip up our sleeve if push comes to shove.'

'What's that?'

'Harlow,' was all Selene proffered.

Rina raised an eyebrow. 'Really? Is she ready?'

'Last time I checked, she was 99% there.'

'Where is she?'

'Safe, I hope, in Axuma, where she's so lost in her research work that she's no idea Dunia is under martial law.'

'Harlow and her research are a good carrot to dangle. If the Edenites are as savvy as the grapevine states, then what she's got going on should tip the odds from unlikely to very likely.'

'But if they respond, I'm going,' Selene stated.

Rina whipped her head around to stare at her friend. 'No way! You're the Prime in waiting. We can't put you in danger.'

Selene shook her head. 'We can't risk any more soldiers, and I need you here to oversee our people here and the revolt, if we can even call it that.'

'How about a sentinel or two to accompany you?' Rina suggested.

'Nope, I can handle myself. Our resources are too stretched for guard duty. I'm a big girl.'

'Not on Eden II, you're not.'

Selene lifted an eyebrow in disbelief. 'I'm no babe in the woods, Ri.'

Rina sucked her teeth. 'You haven't met the uncouth rabble-rousing mercs of the moon rock yet. Even though you're a sophisticated, experienced, well-traveled diplomat and negotiator, imagine them as mammoth dracula hawks. They'll suck off all your blood and pick apart your bones if you can't cut it with them. Well, maybe not quite, but they're ruthless. Not to be underestimated.'

'Consider me scared,' Selene huffed. She shifted her view to the sky and the silver orb sitting fat in the heavens. 'Let's do it, Rina. We've nothing to lose.'

Now, here she was, in the lion's den, at the mercy of the rabble-rousing mercs of Eden II.

Intrigued to learn more about them, Selene read the detailed report on her comm tab. Laila Dexora had found that The Sable Group and its leaders from Eden City operated the best shipbuilding facility in the Pegasi system and beyond.

Holo film actors, racing pilots, and entire armies ordered the mysterious enterprise's fastest, sleekest fighters, interceptors, gunships, and pinnaces.

Their builds were legendary and renowned.

Selene even recognized a few of their mentioned airship designs as those commissioned by Dunia's official interstellar line in a recent deal. The paper alluded to The Sable Group's ownership of manufacturing plants, supply chains, and extensive asteroid mining facilities.

Their reach stretched past Pegasi with shipping lines that extended even to the farthest systems of Segundo.

They'd brought legitimacy to Eden II by employing its people and keeping tight control of the economy.

They were erasing their reputation as a crime-riddled, poverty-stricken backwater and improving the lives of its residents.

The Sable Group had also helped to quash piracy from the region. They'd established a security wing of their corporation to protect their ships and those of Eden II's traders from raiders.

They'd rid the territory's airspace of the spate of attacks, murders, and widespread atrocities. These had been regular for Pegasi a decade ago along its System's fringe, on the borders close to Alloria.

Reading between the lines, Selene could tell they were revered and respected by Edenites, foreign states, and planets alike.

Of more importance, Laila Dexora's research found that while they were the true power of Eden II, they avoided the public eye, never showing their faces and leaving all civic-facing duties to the Elders.

Then, nestled deep within the long paper was a link to a handful of images on Sysnet that purported to have captured the profiles of the shadowy leaders of The Sable Group.

She tabbed through the grainy, unclear shots until she stopped with a gasp at a captioned image with a name she recognized, followed by the identity of the group's chief lead.

Her mind spun and dipped, groping the past scant hours for sense and reason.

She glanced up with shock.

HIM?

A rush of blood heated her face. She tossed her comm tab aside and surged to her feet.

Stepping around the coffee table, she snatched away the pillow resting on the slumbering man's face. She leaned over and tapped his muscled chest with a finger.

'You?!'

He opened a sapphire gold eye and peered up at her with a cocked brow.

'*Naam*. Me,' he drawled after a beat.

It took everything she had not to kick him in the balls. She

44

was furious.

'All this time?'

'Took you long enough,' he murmured, knifing upright to swing his feet to the floor.

She realized she was standing between his thick thighs and stepped back. Their eyes met in a clash of heat, which did that snaking thing again straight to her core.

She wrestled her mind back to present reality. 'You're The Sable Group's leader?'

'We say '*khosi*' here on Eden II,' he replied, inclining back into the cushions and stretching his muscled arms above his head, his jacked chest flexing with movement.

She shook her head, aggravated. 'Why didn't you say so earlier?'

'You didn't ask who you'd be seeing. Instead, you asked when and where you'd be seeing them.'

His lips quirked as Selene glared at him. 'Besides, we both needed some rest,' he rumbled. 'And you seemed a little on edge.'

She couldn't further argue, so she took a different tack. 'So why did the *khosi*, you, need to be my pilot?'

Kainan shrugged his massive shoulders. 'I had a free day. I wanted to study who I'd be dealing with. At close quarters.'

She lifted an eyebrow. 'Really?'

'*Naam*.'

'So you brought me here and watched me work out who you were as a test?'

His lips twitched in a half smile.

'And what conclusion did you come to?' she continued.

'You'll do,' was all Kainan offered after a momentary pause.

Selene wasn't convinced. 'Most leaders send their assistants to fetch their allies for meetings. Why go to so much personal trouble?'

'Because I feel the mission warrants my attention,' came the quiet reply.

'And why was that?'

The gold eyes deepened with intensity. 'Because your father was a good man, we worked well together, and I respected him. So he and Dunia deserve nothing less than my full focus.'

Tears rushed to her eyes, and she sat heavily in a chair across from him. 'You collaborated with my father - the Prime?'

Kainan leaned towards her, reaching out a hand that he placed on her shaking shoulder.

'*Naam*, I dealt with him on many missions. We will all miss him. My deepest sympathies.'

She flicked away the tears, memories flooding her like jagged flashes.

Kainan's hand remained steady, hot, throbbing, and potent until the waves of grief slowly ebbed away.

Composed, she glanced up, and he leaned back. But then, his hand fell away, and she shivered, feeling its absence.

'Thank you for your kind words,' she murmured. 'I do appreciate them.'

He inclined his head in acknowledgment.

She touched the back of his hand before snatching it away. 'And apologies for not knowing who you were earlier. I should have been more tuned in.'

'*De nada*. Don't give yourself a hard time. It takes courage and grit to go to a foreign place to ask for the assistance you need.'

'So will you help, please? Even though I insulted you by calling you a mere pilot and almost stabbed you with my finger?'

He lifted a thick brow. 'I like it when my allies stand up to me, as long as they don't do it too often.'

Selene stiffened. 'I'm unlike any other ally you've worked with.'

'Don't I know it,' he drawled.

'I don't give up, and I don't hold back.'

'Is that right?' he probed, his eyes heating up.

Looking into those blazing eyes made her breathless.

In just a few hours, this man had gained the power to rock her emotions from dizzying grief to a deep physical need in seconds.

There was a sort of sorcery in his ability to shift her sentiment with such swiftness, and it was like she was standing on a precipice of something she couldn't quite articulate.

She stilled her heart once more and focused on the problem at hand.

'There's got to be more of a reason why you're considering helping us, more than mere sentiment,' she said, unconvinced.

Kainan raised both hands, hooking them behind his dark-haired head and giving her a long look, this time less heated. 'I'm sure you've gathered by now that we have a symbiotic relationship with your planet. We buy Dunia's xentium to build ships that bank us all a lot of schill coins. Which makes Massimo Makori a massive pain in our collective Edenite ass.'

'So you're on board?'

He nodded. 'I'm committed to hearing you out.'

She fell back deeper into her chair with relief. 'I thought I would have to use more persuasion to get you to listen to me.'

'That's just me, *khamila*,' he rasped. 'Now you've got to convince the rest of the Riders.'

Selene was thrown. 'The who?'

'The Sable Riders, my brothers. We're not blood, but they're my family. I don't make any final decisions without their say-so.'

Selene threw back her head and took in a few deep breaths. Then she righted herself and pierced Kainan with a pointed look. 'When can I see them?'

The man gave her a slow, lingering look, assessing her. 'When did you last sleep? And for how long?'

'Sleep is for the weak,' she retorted.

'Are you always this amped up?'

Selene pulled at her curls, turning one into a knot. 'Maybe. It's heightened because my people need me.'

'Would they rather you were fresh and on your game or exhausted and making mistakes when negotiating their future?'

Selene sucked in air.

'You'll meet them soon enough, Selene,' he rasped. 'You must be tired. I'll take you to a safe space where you can rest until I convene my brothers.'

4

Pure Edenite Pleasure

SELENE

Kainan stashed her in an apartment a few lifts, corridors, and levels away from the spacious dining room they'd been in.

The space was artfully furnished. The holo screens were state-of-the-art, the lighting exquisite, and the couches were top-of-the-line, molding to the spine.

The sprawling bed was covered in silken bedding.

Beside it was an expansive dressing room that opened into a workout gym and a generous bathroom on the other side.

The head was roomy, and Kainan informed her that the showers ran with temperature-controlled water.

The fridge was full of platters of delicious-looking food and sparkling drinks, and the kitchen counters overflowed with trays of fresh fruit and vegetables.

A vase of swan orchids intertwined with tiger moon proteas floated in a white cloud above the sleek coffee table.

All in all, she found nothing wanting.

He prowled the room like a meko panther, checking gadgets and security controls before waving his wrist comm over the door panel. It slid open, and he stepped out, turning to face Selene.

'I'll be back,' he said in his deep timbre. 'This door is paired to my comm for your safety. You can't leave the apartment without my auth. I'll arrange all meals, drinks, and any groceries or toiletries you require. One of our sec droids will deliver them to you. Just send me a list.'

'So I can't go exploring Eden II?' she pushed.

He sliced a sober, narrowed look her way. 'Despite our current veneer of civility and commerce, this rock is still, without a shadow of a doubt, one of the most dangerous places in Pegasi. Given your strategic importance, we must preserve and limit all movement. We'll also travel when we need to in an armored flyer to safeguard you.'

He tapped his wrist device and swiped a file to her own, which pinged in receipt. 'That's my comm sign. Message me if you need anything. I'll fetch you as soon as possible to meet the Riders.'

'So I can only leave this suite with your say-so?'

'It's for your safety, Selene,' he replied after a short silence. 'You're on a wanted list, and Massimo Makori is desperate. We can't take any chances.'

Her face fell. 'How will he know that I'm here, on Eden II? We tried to be discreet, and our flight here was cloaked.'

The man looming over her leveled his gaze on her. 'Anything's feasible. So we ought to keep playing it safe. This apartment is fortified. So you've nothing to fear, *khamila*.'

That word again. *Khamila*. She wondered for a moment what it meant.

'What if I desire to speak to my people?'

Kainan leaned back on his heels in thought. 'I'll set up a secure channel between you and Colonel Rina on one of our drone satellites and patch it to your comm. Give it a try in about an hour.'

Selene didn't know what more to say, so she said what was necessary. '*Sante*. For everything.'

Kainan's blue-gold eyes glowed with a rare emotion she couldn't nail. 'Don't thank me quite yet. Not until we can help Dunia out of this mess.'

He stepped away from the door, and it slid shut.

'I'll come back soon,' he promised as it closed on him, his timbre deep and commanding.

Except that on Day One, he didn't come.

On Day 2, he still hadn't appeared.

On Day 3, he hadn't shown up, and she was about to murder someone.

She'd resisted messaging him because her pride wouldn't let her beg him. Besides, pleading for his return would be a diplomatically weak position to begin their negotiations.

All Selene could do was work out in the suite's gym and eat, and because the secure channel now worked and the connection to Sysnet was lightning fast, she comm'd Rina to complain.

Thank Dunia for her best friend.

She glanced at the woman on the holo screen. She couldn't remember when she'd first met her lean, strong, opinionated woman.

They'd gone to high school together, bonded over boys, books, and a love for Raider bands. The ones who trawled pirate space cruisers and uploaded raucous and haunting percussive cloud trap tunes to the System's rogue airwaves that went on for hours.

They'd applied to the same university, been selected in the identical sorority, and held similar poor-paying jobs to pay their way.

They'd double-dated, double-dipped, and lived like sisters for most of their lives. Now, here they were, attempting to reverse a deadly coup together.

Rina gave her updates on the situation in Dunia. Such as how General McKenzie and the Special Ops Command Force stationed at Rambasa and loyal to the True Prime had retaken control of the critical western front city.

The victory was a significant step forward because Rambasa lay in the Neo Valley, the source of Dunia's rich deposits of xentium, yielding trillions of tonnes annually from its vast ore body, the largest of its kind in the universe.

Rambasa was also where the planet's publicly owned mining company, Dunia Xentium Corp, the DXC, had built its HQ. From this seat, it managed all mineral rights to xentium production in the glen, on the southern continent of Wadi, and the archipelago on the western coast of Usmina.

'It's all well and good, but we need better defenses to face a relentless enemy that is desperate for those xentium mines,' Selene said, biting her lip.

'We don't have much, but my, the planet came to our aid - it went wild, defending it against the Technocracy's first salvo. Outside the domed cities, their air assault was eviscerated before they made it back to their orbital blockade in retreat or to replenish their reserves. Sel, I've seen holos of trees, rocks, plants, and wildlife whipping their ass! Which means only two squadrons of their soldiers got into New Malindi and one or two more in Paris Minor and Rambasa.'

'Fascinating,' Selene half smiled.

Rina shook her head. 'What intrigues me is how Dunia decided to get in on the action. Was it asked? Or did it just sense we needed its help?'

Selene blinked at her friend's rapid-fire questions, then shrugged. 'I don't know.'

Rina gave her a long look. 'Did you summon it?'

'Hell no! I don't even know how!'

'But don't you have the so-called whisperer *talent*? Doesn't it run in your family?'

'Ri,' you know my father talked to the planet. But Dunia has not revealed itself to me yet, so I can't say for sure. One only gets a revelation when its consciousness decides the time is right. Until then, I assume I don't have "the gift". It hasn't been given to me.'

Rina leaned in. 'But don't the Munene heirs inherit it?'

Selene sighed. 'Not always. It's skipped a generation in the past. You must prove yourself worthy before it considers speaking to or with you.'

'Then forget it, Sel, even I know you're unworthy!' her friend laughed.

'Haha, funny.'

The two women exchanged quick smiles. It was clear their bond had weathered plenty, and their connection ran deep.

'What else do we have?' Selene said, sipping from a cup of steaming kahawa.

Rina scrolled through her comm tab. 'Not much. As I said, we're under blockade. We can't even defend ourselves against those three capital ships even if we want to. Hell, we don't have the forces or weapons to fight Makori's militia, who now control the spaceport and have The Technocracy to back them up from the atmosphere.'

Selene grimaced. 'It sucks that we never invested enough in the defenses needed to protect our planet. And that father was a pacifist who moved too slow on decisions about planetary security.'

'We were getting there,' Rina huffed. 'Until Massimo waged his little war. *Fokk* xentium! *Fokk* politicians and their greed! And *Fokk* Massimo Makori in particular. Rumor has it he's upped the reward money and placed a bigger bounty on your head.'

Pacing the spacious apartment, Selene peered at her friend's face on her tab screen.

'How much?' she asked.

'Millions.'

'Dead or alive?'

'Alive. Massimo wants to get you in his grasp so he can strong-arm you into giving back control of the ore fields.'

Selene shook her head. 'I can't believe that I never detected his bull fakery!'

'Who?' Rina asked, raising an eyebrow.

'Massimo. He was always so charming. He never seemed to do anything wrong. If you listen to the stories about him, it's like everyone thought he was a Paladian saint who walked on water and summoned lightning at will.'

'I never liked him,' Rina confessed. 'Too slimy for my palate. He reeked of a man trying too hard for affirmation so it'd hide his scheming and evil under all his couture robes and sweet cologne.'

Selene rolled her eyes. 'So dramatic. Do you think he'll find me?'

'If you're not careful, he will. The Makori Dynasty has a long reach. We're hoping the folks on Eden II are trustworthy, but we can't be sure of all of them. Anyone is capable of spilling the beans on your location in exchange for a few million schill.'

Selene fell into a hushed silence. Maybe she'd been too quick to trust Kainan. He'd disappeared. Yet regular deliveries of steaming, delicious food, wine, and hot brewed kahawa had arrived at the apartment's door—courtesy of a faceless two-legged silver bot droid with zero interaction skills.

Rina interrupted her train of thought. 'You're speculating if Kainan Sable has sold you down the river?'

'Mhmmm,' Selene murmured. 'But then again, every conversation I've had with the man has made me rethink my view of Eden II as a backwater teeming with backstabbing rogues, pirates, and ex-cons. Annoying though he may be, he's smart, and his op here must be run by people with some significant tactical and strategic brains. I'm wondering why Father let me think so little of them.'

'Perhaps he thought if you had a clue that his colleagues

are as gorgeous and intriguing as Kainan seems, you'd have fled to hunt them down,' Rina chuckled.

'Never!' Selene said, shaking her head. 'I was not and have never been a pimply-faced teenager with a sad crush.'

'Girl, I beg to differ!' Rina smirked. 'I'll concede that you were always more earnest and considered than I was in high school, never letting your hair down. But when you crushed on someone, you fell. Hard.'

'True,' Selene conceded.

'Regardless, you're now a woman who needs to be loved. You've got a generous heart that gives as much as it wants to get back. What's more, you haven't had sex in years. You've been married to your job for too long, and you need to get down and dirty with a good, hard, *fokk* fest. Delivered at the hands of a mountainous sensual god with desire tattooed all over him.'

Selene choked and squeezed her eyes closed, trying to unsee the erotic scene Rina had just set off in her mind. 'Stop it! You're being ridiculous, woman.'

Rina sized up her friend. 'So he does affect you -.'

'*Nada*!' Selene shook her head, rejecting her friend's assessment.

'Oh yes, he does. Remember, I know you all too well. *Eyes tight shut* is your tell for when you're flustered. It takes quite the man for this hella reaction from you. Seriously though, what's he like?' Rina ventured, leaning forward on-screen.

Scary, thrilling, arousing, exasperating, daunting. A larger-than-life enigma who inflamed her body and infuriated her mind, Selene thought.

'Like no one I've ever met before,' she said. 'He's unusual. He's even given me a distinct name. *Khamila*.'

Rina's eyes flicked to her left as she accessed a screen on her end. '*Khamila.* It means beautiful, in Edenite.' She glanced back at Selene. 'Well, well, my friend, it would seem your mountainous sex god, your *khaji* – the term for a male lover in his lingua – may want you as much as you want him.'

Selene scoffed. 'Me? Want him? Ri', I don't have time for all of that. And don't be presumptuous! He's no deity. Most people on this rock are human. But, that said, I sense something different about him.'

'I concur,' said Rina. 'He's not your everyday mortal. That's why I took a clearer picture of him, better than the one we had on file when he picked you up at the Enclave,' Rina said with a smirk.

'You didn't?'

'Did so! I ran it through all our available databases. In particular, the University of New Malindi's xeno-archaeological servers. Despite his obvious Edenite features, no civilization, aliens, or biology in this System match his unique eyes and bio pattern. So he's different, all right. Maybe he's a –.'

Rina's face fell. She paused her patter, and her eyes widened, fixed on a point beyond Selene's shoulder.

Selene whirled around, and sure enough, *he* stood behind her.

His massive form filled the apartment's bedroom, dominating the space.

He wore a close-fitting navy and gold jumpsuit with a white crest on one bicep. His sapphire aureate-flecked eyes glowed in the dimly lit room, piercing her to the core.

'How did you –?' she murmured, heart pounding.

'I have my ways,' Kainan said, his rumble deep and amused.

'How long have you –?' she asked, dreading that he might

57

have caught her conversation with Rina.

His lips twitched. 'Long enough.'

She breathed heavy, tamping down the tension of waiting three days and not knowing when he'd return pouring out of her. 'You took your time.'

'Seems you needed it to study up on me,' he quipped with a straight face.

She shook her head at him, exasperated, and he responded with a phantom smile.

'You meant it when you said things take a while on Eden II.'

'Apologies, *khamila*,' Kainan said, dipping his head with genuine feeling. 'Some matters take time. Several of my brothers had to leave their duties elsewhere in the System to meet with you. Their travel back took a few days. We've also had to juggle our logistics to manage a new rush of traffic from all the ships that now can't land on Dunia. So it's been a little busy, to say the least.'

That's when she noticed deep creases on his brow and a haggardness around his eyes, which only meant a lack of sleep. A stab of guilt hit at her misplaced assumptions.

'Have you slept and eaten?' she asked, concern for him rising out of her with unexpected emotion.

His golden eyes intensified even further, and his voice dropped lower. 'You're worried about me, Selene?'

His timbre reverberated, and her heart started hammering again.

She gave him a wry smile to mask the significant jolts cascading over her. 'I'm just wondering if you'd rather be rested on your game or exhausted and making mistakes when negotiating with me?'

His lips quirked once more.

'Well played, but let's park that for a later discussion. Come,' Kainan commanded. 'The Sable Riders are ready for you.'

Selene turned to Rina, exasperated. 'I have to go. I'll be in touch.'

'Good luck ... *khamila*!' her friend said with a cheeky grin before the holo screen winked out.

Selene just had time to throw on a decent pair of boots, shrug her shoulders into a knee-length cape, and grab her communication tab and bag before Kainan rushed her out of the apartment.

He now strode alongside her on their way to goodness-knew-where.

She longed to ask, but she doubted he'd volunteer any intel, so she pumped her legs and lengthened her stride to keep up with his fast, panther-like prowl.

He led her through a dizzying maze of corridors, stopping in front of a nondescript gray doorway. He punched a code into a keypad beside the door and used his wrist comm once more for further authentication. The input device gave a soft beep, and the portal slid open.

He gestured, ushering her in before him.

She stepped into an expansive room dominated by a huge

table. Thick, textured walls surrounded the room on three sides. One solid partition was covered in backlit shelves of books, artifacts, and antique pieces from all over the System.

The fourth was fashioned from what she guessed was high-density anti-ballistic glass, overlooking an extensive area on the floor below that appeared to be an empty bar and dining club.

She spotted a plex elevator in a nook, which she assumed traveled between both levels and beyond.

Two figures sat at the sprawling workspace, which was made of dark, textured altiphyte wood polished to a mirror sheen, and a second pair of men huddled in a corner.

The sleek gyrfalcon scanned the room on a perch next to the table.

The four men studied her.

Kainan's voice rumbled behind her. 'Selene Munene, meet the Sable Riders, referred to in our official capacity as The Sable Group.'

She stepped closer to and gazed at her new acquaintances.

The one closest to her was just as significant in size as Kainan, a hulking figure with a mass of short jet-black hair with blue streaks, a bushy, inky beard, and silver gray eyes, with a stubborn chin and a swathe of jagged scars down one side of his face.

His massive feet were slung up and crossed on top of the table.

The man beside him was tall, with angular, dark features, a roughly shaven jaw, stubble, and penetrating eyes with hazel irises ringed with glowing sapphire flecks. He leaned back in his oversized chair to study her.

Kainan pointed to the scar-faced man. 'This is Kage, call

name *Shadow*. He's our ship designer, tech head, and all-around maestro. He runs our mini armada. Next to him is Xion, call name *Phoenix* - head of internal security on Eden II, overseeing law and order on the rock.'

Two other men glanced at her from the other side of the room.

One sported a magnificent sheath of dead-straight ivory and silver hair that fell to his back in an extended, smooth sheet with a braid over one shoulder.

His skin was pale, and so were his white irised eyes that he seemed a ghoul, albeit an exceedingly handsome one.

He wore a close-fitted black jumpsuit with the same crest on his shoulder as Kainan. She assumed this was The Sable Group's insignia.

He jerked his chin to her, his light eyes raking her face.

Next to him was a lean, towering, striking, and muscled man in an exquisite suit. He had dark, thick hair with silver highlights, a neat mustache, and a beard with piercing blue eyes.

His elegant presence contrasted with his more casual-dressed companions. He nodded to her cordially.

'At the far back is Riv, call name *Wraith*. He runs our armories. He moonlights as the head of our secret surveillance ops and militia, and on his off days, he dallies as a bounty hunter. With him is Zane, call name *Phantom*. Our business and financial controller. He oversees our sales, logistics, private equity, and finance division.'

Selene nodded her head in acknowledgment, unable to speak.

The presence of these five devastating and mighty men had snatched her breath from her lungs.

'MIA is Kisan, call name *Witchman*, medic extraordinaire, currently on a mercy relief mission.'

She spotted sleek blasters strapped to their muscled thighs and hips and imagined other weapons in unseen places. There were no Boy Scouts she was dealing with.

'You remember Mirage,' Kainan added, gesturing toward the gyrfalcon with silver wings and feet.

Selene's eyebrow rose. 'Really?'

'It is indeed, Selene,' said the avifauna in the AI's harmonious tone. 'As a nano-engineered AI, I can take multiple forms, but this is the one I tend to prefer when I'm off Kainan's ship. But, of course, I'm also still on the vessel due to my split consciousness and various remote capabilities.'

'Mirage is our eyes and ears across the rock, and she oversees all AI on all our ships and holdings,' Kainan explained.

'I'm also taking an encrypted recording of these proceedings,' Mirage piped up. 'This will be shared with all your comm tabs after the meeting and will only be accessible with your bio authentication.'

Kainan inclined his head. 'As you can see, she's a valued member of The Sable Riders.'

'I see,' Selene exclaimed, astonished. 'Incredible.'

The gyrfalcon bent her sleek silver head in a bow.

'Sit,' Kainan ordered Selene, pulling out a plush chair.

'What's your call name?' she managed to ask him as she sat down.

He paused for a moment.

'*Chimera*,' he rasped.

Fitting, she thought, given the strange ability he had to switch her feelings from hot to cold in seconds.

The two men on the other side of the room strolled to the

table while Kainan stalked to a long cabinet behind her and plucked a few items in his hands.

She observed, perplexed, until he returned to the work surface and thumped an exquisite crystal decanter swirling with a rich honey liquor and six shot glasses onto the center.

The room fell into a hush as he poured the decadent liquid into each glass and handed one to all persons present.

Kainan then raised his crystal tumbler into the air. 'We pay our respects to Kei'Lano Munene III, the True Prime of Dunia, friend, father, and wise leader,' he murmured, his expression somber, his golden eyes flickering with a spellbinding light.

'Our deepest sympathies,' added the handsome Riv, his eyes slicing over to Selene as the group rose and lifted their glasses.

All five men and Mirage intoned together. '*Inuka!*'

'Though he has fallen, he shall still rise in our hearts,' Kainan rasped.

The Riders downed the liquid, slamming their tumblers on the polished table.

Selene blinked back tears and followed suit.

The smooth, well-aged whiskey slid over her tongue and lit a fire in her belly, leaving behind mellow charcoal, vanilla, and spice notes.

This was not some cheap gag-inducing grog from the bottom of a nasty chlorinated flask.

Instead, it tasted like one of the vintage, small-batch handcrafted whiskeys her father loved when he was alive.

'Is this a Galician Aurora Barrel Select?' she asked Kainan, fighting her emotions.

He jerked his chin in confirmation. 'Tis. After one of our meetings, the Prime was considerate enough to leave a bottle with me. So I only thought it fair to share it with you today.'

She gave him a shaky smile, overwhelmed at the kind gesture and appreciative. Their eyes locked, and the air sparked between them. '*Sante*, that means the world to me.'

Kainan broke the silence and their heated gaze. 'Shall we begin? Selene, you have the room.'

He settled himself into the chair at the head, and the group followed suit.

Selene noted he'd placed her next to him instead of the opposite, which was the norm in negotiations—perhaps signaling to his fellow brothers that he was somewhat partial to her requests, which she appreciated.

Ripples of heat emanated from him, and out of the corner of her eye, she spied the loose collar of his jumpsuit.

It revealed a corded neck and muscled chest covered in beautiful skin art that seemed to move with his breath. Her core clenched with an unexpected rush of desire.

What in the actual?

She willed her body back into control, took a deep inhale, and gathered herself together, gazing at each individual at the table.

'Thank you for your hospitality so far, your acknowledgment of my father, and for making yourselves available to negotiate with me. I hear some of you have come from afar, so please know I appreciate your effort.'

Platitudes out of the way, she dove into the order of business.

'The situation in Dunia is dire. We've lost military dominance of three principal cities, including the capital, New Malindi. The self-proclaimed, self-appointed Prime, Massimo Makori, has declared a state of martial law. He was the ex-defense Minister, and he had the support of several of the most influential dynasties, senators, and even generals in the DUA, including the Dunia Union Army and the Navy. Together with his militia, they're calling themselves the One Dunia Coalition. As of now, The Coalition controls the spaceport and has locked down all communications on and off the planet.'

'What's the good news?' Zane rasped in a hushed voice.

'We - the Free Dunia Council - have control of two of the planet's key cities plus Rambasa, the location of our chief source of xentium on Dunia,' Selene replied.

'Thank *fokk* for that,' grated Kage, the dark-haired, scar-faced man.

'Who makes up the Council?' Riv asked.

'Apart from the traitor, Massimo, all members of my father's cabinet, which includes the Justice, Commerce, Education, Energy, and Health Ministers and various Interior and Treasury Heads, are on our side. We still have a section of the army and navy loyal to the cause of the True Prime and a good number of dynasties and senators,' she continued.

'So what do you need from us?' This time, it was Xion who'd spoken up.

Selene met his gaze. 'Air power, firepower, and manpower.'

'Tis a lot to ask for,' Zane murmured.

'A lot is at stake,' Selene replied. 'I can confirm Massimo engaged with The Technocracy a few days ago, just before their core fleet left the System. What we don't know is what they discussed or agreed on. It's not only the production and distribution of xentium that's on the line. It's millions of innocent lives. I fear that the Technocracy will return if Massimo gets control of the entire planet. We know what happens when the crats get hold of any world in our System.'

65

The five men and Mirage exchanged glances and nodded to each other.

Clearly, The Sable Riders had a shared opinion of the Technocracy.

Selene swore they were communicating subvocally among themselves, but she couldn't be sure.

'I have a few hundred million schills at my disposal,' she offered, speaking into the pause. 'Potentially, we can rent corvettes from you, maybe even buy some, and purchase the ammunition we need with that.'

'Financing a war takes over way more than that sum,' Kainan stated. 'To go against Makori's militia and perhaps even The Technocracy means that we'll be shelling out a whole lot more than that.'

'And taking quite a hit on our bottom line,' Zane added. 'Which impacts the work we do in our community.'

Selene's curiosity got the better of her. 'What kind?'

'Re-homing refugees across the System, but you already know this from our agreements with your father,' Kainan murmured. 'We also fund raider patrols on the lookout for pirate ships. We'd had a spate of attacks here and along the system's fringes, especially on the borders close to Alloria. But we've managed to contain much of that activity now. However, we remain vigilant. In addition, we run a lower-income housing organization, plus a few youth off-the-street initiatives for those living in the tunnels. If we didn't, law and order would go amok on and off the rock.'

'So your profits go into these programs?'

Zane nodded. 'Most of them do. The Riders only keep what we require to live and enjoy a good life, as is our right, then bestow the rest away. We dabbled in community work when

66

we first landed here. We're not monks; we just wanted to help the place that welcomed us. Years later, our commitment remains unchanged. Helping those in distress from a position of strength. We make good bank, and we give back.'

Kainan assented to his fellow Rider's words and spoke in a rumbling timbre. 'Lest we become the same darkness that has sucked so much light from so many people across the System.'

Selene nodded in understanding. 'Thank you for that. Given that you don't want to bleed your pots, I'm open to renegotiating Dunia's original deal with Eden II. We can increase the amount of xentium we sell to you once we regain control of the spaceport and air travel. We can also reduce our prices until you recover your investment.'

The room fell into a laconic pause at her words, and again, she sensed they were talking offline to each other.

A short while later, Zane spoke up as the money man in the room. 'With all due respect, this might still set us back even with your capital. We've worked hard to get The Sable Group and Eden II to where we are now, and I'm not sure we can take the risk. Is anything else on the table to make this more of a confident bet for us?'

Selene had one more card to play and drew a ragged breath, hoping against all hope it would find purchase.

She announced, 'I'm also willing to share a new hybrid fuel FTL technology that my father and I were championing. '

'Is that right?' Kage said, sitting upright and piercing her with his silver eyes.

Selene turned to Kainan. 'None of what I'm about to say can leave this room.'

He jerked his chin in confirmation. 'It won't. We have

quantum jamming sensors around the perimeter of this room. Mirage also monitors and conducts continuous security sweeps of the building. So you can speak without prejudice.'

'Thank you,' Selene said. She swiveled to face the five men and Mirage, choosing her words while meeting each of their gazes. 'One of our scientists, Harlow Meridien, has been developing a hybrid fuel by mixing refined xentium with elentium. The result is a rare fusion that generates unprecedented levels of anti-grav propulsion. It outputs more energy than anything we've seen before - even better than nuclear power and antimatter. However, it must be well tested, and a suitable propulsion system has to be built. If not, using it warps the space around ships and severely damages entire vessels or planets, which is why she's also hoping to find a partner to co-design a fitting drive and engine for this hybrid fuel. Nonetheless, she assures me that when handled with care, the fusion mix is stable and sustainable; a little goes a long way. In addition, she's got a system that can recycle elentium and is working to do the same for refined xentium. This power supply technology will double the price and demand for xentium, as it can act as a hard alloy in starship hulls and a reliable, effective, renewable energy source. And I can confirm on behalf of Harlow and the government of Dunia that we're willing to share this with you and maybe work with you to develop it further.'

'*Fokkin*' hell!' Kage breathed, snapping forward from his former back lean. He turned to Kainan. 'You're across this, *khosi*?'

'*Nada*. First, I've caught wind of it,' his leader said, his deep voice dipping even lower. 'She's full of surprises,' he added, his eyes flashing with emotion and a fair portion of respect as he stared at Selene.

Kage sat up straighter and fixed his intense gaze on her. 'This'll make our cruisers even faster and give our corvettes long-range strike capabilities.'

'I know,' she agreed.

'And make our cargo runs and skips superior in terms of time and reach,' stated Xion.

'*Naam.* Plus, help cut costs and possibly double revenue,' Zane said, with a calculating look on his face.

'And grant us a strong advantage from a system-wide security perspective while improving our defense infrastructure,' Mirage intoned from her perch.

'Absolutely all of that,' Selene said. 'It's a significant leg up, and I'm mindful of the responsibility that comes with it. My father and I sponsored Harlow's research because we believed it would assist us in investing more in transport facilities. This will allow our people to find work and opportunities beyond Dunia, which has a limited population capacity, and increase our people's economic and social opportunities. In addition, we want this technology utilized for good and less for war. That would be one of our clear stipulations.'

'Then it cannot fall into the wrong hands,' Kage rasped.

'You've roused the lion, Selene,' Riv said to Selene, casting an affectionate eye at his fellow Rider. 'Now that he's learned about this new fusion tech, Kage will protect it with his life. As shall we all.'

Riv's words had the desired effect on Selene, and she relaxed.

Kainan rapped a hand on the table. 'Riders, we also owe Kei'Lano for all the aid he rendered us over the years. Without him believing in Eden II, we'd have remained a wasteland of

69

depravity. We wouldn't have become who we are today.'

'Well said,' Zane agreed.

The five men and the gyrfalcon did that sub-vocal talking thing again.

After some moments, Kainan turned to face Selene. 'We've all concurred in principle, so far, to consider your offer. Pending our internal discussions.'

Selene closed her eyes for a moment, relief rushing through her body. 'Shall we then look in detail at the existing agreement?' She ventured.

'*Naam,*' Kainan said. 'Mirage, please pull it up on the holo screen. Let's see if we can't make this as efficient as possible, for all our sakes.'

5

A Landslide Of The Heart

SELENE

Selene's negotiations with The Sable Riders wound down after hours of haggling and moving around one too many numbers, concepts, and arguments.

They had a rough deal in place. First, the Riders pledged to discuss it later among themselves that night.

Then, once they were all pleased with it, they promised Selene they'd entrust it to Mirage, who'd send it via a secure, tight beam to Rina and the Free Dunia Council members, who were waiting for their feedback.

'Shall we adjourn?' Kainan suggested. 'Perhaps a meal and drink to relax after that stretch?'

Selene turned her tired eyes towards him. Her tummy rumbled, and hunger won against her limb-numbing exhaustion.

'Yes, please.'

He rose and extended a hand toward her chair to pull it out. With his help, she got to her feet and slipped her jacket on.

She missed the amused glances his Sable Riders brothers sent their way. Instead, she glanced up to find Kainan glaring at them.

His head tilted as he aphonically spoke to them.

'Let's get out of here,' he grunted as if he'd been annoyed by something one of them said.

They walked away from the entertained quartet into the glass-walled elevator at the corner of the vast meeting room.

The lift slid to the floor below, and they stepped off into a sumptuous dining and lounge area.

'Welcome to The Osirian,' Kainan announced, leading her into the luxurious space.

'What is this place?' Selene asked, looking around at the indulgent parquet, the tessellated tiles, metal detailing, padded velvet booths and banquettes, adjustable lighting, and plush upholstered seating, deep, cozy, and private enough to encourage customers to linger all night.

'One of The Sable Group's establishments, Zane's baby, to be precise,' he said, guiding her to a sprawling bar with an onyx and rare mineral bench top and a mirrored splash-back, where a dozen bartenders hovered over the multiplying number of patrons.

'Are we still in the same building as the apartment?'

'Not quite. One property over. We own the whole block,' came the quiet response. 'And a few more throughout the city.'

She raised an eyebrow. Her measure of respect for the Sable Riders kept growing. These Edenites were strong, a brute

72

force.

Still, they were also strategic, brilliant thinkers and wise investors hiding behind a veneer of mercenary thuggery.

At the same time, they were expanding in their domination of an entire system from the shadows of the stars.

He settled her into a plush, high-backed bar stool at the bar and summoned an Allorian bartender with a flick of his finger.

The barman's eyebrows rose in recognition of the sapphire and gold tattooed man leaning against the counter, and he rushed over.

'What can I get you, *khosi*?'

'A *Zindawa* for me, and the lady -?' Kainan said turning to Selene.

She leaned forward. 'What do you have for a girl, a moon away from her planet and negotiating for the lives of millions?'

The mixologist's eyes widened even further.

'Surprise me,' Selene added.

Kainan's lips quirked with amusement. 'What about one of your infamous moon dust cocktails, Jarok? Perhaps Eden's Mist?'

'What's in it?' Selene asked, intrigued by the name.

The barman grinned, proud of what he was about to proffer. 'Amaretto from the hills of Lasigonia on Dunia, Curacao oranges, distilled kaokao from Tansin, and a touch of silver moon dust from our northern lunar mountains. The sweetness of the amaretto mellows the tartness of the orange without dulling the citrus notes too much. The result is pure Edenite pleasure.'

Selene nodded. 'Sounds sublime. I'll have one, thank you.'

The bartender inclined his shaven dome and made her cocktail with keen relish. He whirled and twirled bottles and glasses before setting down a tall vial of iridescent liquid in front of Selene with theatrical panache.

Selene took a sip of her silver-dusted cocktail and sighed with happiness.

The flavor was like nothing she'd ever had - syrupy with marzipan, macaroon, vanilla, and orange undertones, which left a tingling on her tongue and taste buds.

She took another drink, savoring the sheer decadence, and closed her eyes, almost moaning as the delicious heat snaked to her belly.

Then, she opened her eyes to clash with an intense gold sapphire gaze.

'Acceptable?'

'Better than,' she whispered, the temperature rising under her skin. Her cheeks flushed, and she dipped her head.

Damn, it was getting hot in here.

His lips flexed, and taking hold of his beer, he swigged it back, revealing his corded, thick neck and muscled chin.

Selene tore her eyes away from his beauty and lifted her glass, staring at it instead, captivated by the swirling silver iridescence dancing in the sunset and crimson liquid.

Her eyes caught movement at the lifts. The crystal elevator disgorged the rest of The Sable Riders. The four men strode and approached the bar, slowing down to exchange more sustained looks with their *khosi* and communicate aphonically with him before stalking past and sitting on a table nearby.

'Do you know how annoying that is?' Selene blurted.

Kainan swiveled his head in her direction. 'What is?'

'That silent thing you guys do. How you *talk* to each other.'

His head reared back in surprise, and his voice fell to a husky timbre. 'My apologies, *khamila*, it's an ingrained habit. We forget how it seems to those around us without the same abilities. We only do it in public - when we need to be careful who might hear us.'

'Apology accepted. What are those proficiencies anyway?'

He gave her a long, considered look. 'A sophisticated neural node network. We all have a vertex connection and can do more than speak to each other. We can link our brains with external tech and even AI like Mirage, free from needing a physical connection.'

Selene was fascinated. 'Do all Edenites have one or just The Sable Riders?'

'Just us Riders,' came the clipped reply. It was clear he didn't want to discuss it further.

However, her curiosity still needed to be sated. 'Why do you call yourselves The Sable Riders? How is it different from your public persona, The Sable Group?'

Kainan took a deep breath, his glowing eyes assessing her. He seemed to come to a conclusion. 'I suppose I can share some of our secrets as you have yours. We're retired Kubai warriors. We served together many years ago in the Sable Battalion. Thus the *Sable Riders*.'

'The Kubai warriors? What does that mean?'

'The elite topmost warrior class of the Kwavi people.'

'The Kwavi?'

'My people - the residents of Eden City, a floating metropolis above Planet Earth, located in the adjacent universe also called the Backbone of Night.'

Selene smiled. 'Dunians are likewise descendants from the same world.'

75

Her ancestors were civil engineers who moonlighted as spiritual leaders in Zanzibar circa 5078. After their tiny island home went underwater due to Earth's rising sea levels, they were sold on the benefits of a fresh life in a new galaxy. They'd had no problem signing on the dotted line, boarding a generation ship, and stepping into life pods that ferried them across a universe.

On Dunia, Silas Munene had transitioned from cleric to municipal leader, making a name for himself as a peaceful and caring first Prime.

Hundreds of years later, Selene's father, Kei'Lano, had tried his best to live up to that legacy. He'd promoted peace and harmony throughout Dunia and rejected calls to build expensive orbital planetary security systems, hoping the planet's sentient over-protectiveness would be enough.

Yet he'd seen the writing on the wall and built-in fail-safes because humans were always going to be humans, greedy for resources such as Dunia's xentium.

'I see you know your history,' said Kainan.

'I wouldn't be a competent diplomat if I didn't,' Selene said. 'Our forefathers left Earth on an Ark Ship, fleeing the climate crisis that engulfed the planet. They were lucky to have found this galaxy where they established Dunia as their home.'

She paused mid-thought. 'Why didn't your people come to Dunia or the other Pegasi planets in the Ark Ships?'

He gave her an enigmatic look. 'They couldn't afford it, Selene. They were too poor to fork out the fees required for the passage, so they stayed behind. And ended up as guardians of whoever else was remaining on Earth. Over time, my ancestors bolstered their technology and smarts, and in time, they built space-faring vessels of their own.'

'So, how did *you* find your way here?'

'My battalion - made up of Kubai militants, some of whom include The Sable Riders today - left Eden City over twenty-five standard years ago on a mission for the Eden Guards and Eden City's government. After that was over, we landed here, and with the help of our home administration, we established a Kwavi commerce base in the Pegasi system, which is why this rock is called Eden II. We're an offshoot of our original citadel.'

'Are you still warriors?'

Kainan's mouth twitched. 'Most times, we're business-men.'

Selene studied him for a beat, then shook her head, unconvinced. 'I don't buy that for a minute. There's more to The Sable Group than meets the eye. Soldiers and trade? All cloak and dagger if you asked me.'

Kainan's eyes flashed with a sudden blue and gold energy spike, then narrowed.

She took a long sip of her drink. 'Do all your eyes glow when you're annoyed?'

Kainan smirked at her rather keen observation. 'In varying degrees.'

'May I ask why?'

'You're full of many questions, *Excellency*.'

He was baiting her with her title, and she focused her eyes on his teasing smile.

'I just want to know whom I'm negotiating with,' Selene said. 'For the security of my planet.'

He gave her a prolonged look. 'Fair enough,' he conceded. 'Centuries ago, our human DNA was transformed by rogue cells after a nuclear explosion on Earth during the Great Suffering. We developed metanoids, nanoscale, self-propelled fission-powered cells operating in our bloodstream. Their reactions have some degree of autonomy that we can control and reproduce. When those responses occur, they emit light. Our eyes glow as a result, our most identifiable feature as metahumans.'

Selene's eyebrows lifted. 'Fascinating. And what was the Great Suffering?'

'The evillest of times on Earth. It occurred a few years after the last Ark Ships departed, leaving Earth's poor behind. They were unable to fight the planetary climate-driven collapse that followed. This led to an all-out and terrible war that killed millions and destroyed entire continents.'

'I'm so sorry to hear,' she said, moved by the devastation of what a painful period of his and, in truth, her people's history had been.

A hush fell. She twirled a curacao stem between her lips. His eyes dropped to her mouth, and she jolted at the heightened electricity between them.

Pulling the stalk from her lips, she tried to deflect his attention, pointing to his neck and shoulder. 'What do your markings mean?'

His gaze traveled back to her eyes. 'They're called glyphs. As I said, our metanoids can perform certain functions beyond normal human capabilities; they glow and emit radiating ink under the dermis. So, my people found a way to use them to mark our skin, individuality, and identity. The glyphs tell the stories of our origins and often change form according to our thoughts.'

'What else do the metanoids do?'

'They can deliver a thousand times more oxygen to the

body's tissues. They're also a thousandfold swifter than antibiotic-assisted white blood cells, with no chance of developing multiple drug resistance. They can treat infections in the respiratory apparatus and throughout the neural, spine, and blood network. Additionally, our clottocyte response time is 100-1000 times faster than the natural homeostatic system to reduce clotting time and hemorrhaging.'

'Impressive.'

He kept going, noting her riveted attention. 'Here on Eden II, we pushed our metanoids further. We developed the ability to harvest them from our blood and reproduce them in significant quantities. We can apply our tech to them and alter them as we wish. Some of our ships' surfaces are coated with the same self-replicating 'noids, tweaked to provide them with a unique stealth capability.'

Selene's eyes shone, fascinated by his revelations. 'So any Edenite across the galaxies could, for argument's sake, collect their metanoids and use them for covert warfare or weapons?'

He shook his head slowly. '*Nada.* Just The Sable Group.'

Selene raised an eyebrow. 'Why is that? Do you and the other Riders have proprietary tech?'

Kainan's expression shifted to stone. 'I think I've said enough.'

She studied him, regretting the wall he'd just slammed between them.

Perhaps she'd get her answers somewhere else. Selene turned to check the four other Riders settling into their table.

Then, she leaned forward and into Kainan's space.

'Should we join them?' she asked.

Kainan shook his head, his hair shimmering in the dim

bar light. 'They won't spill any secrets either, Selene. Please give it up. Besides, they have business to discuss among themselves. I'll keep you company.'

Selene blushed at Kainan's spot-on assessment. 'Not if you don't want to. I can take care of myself.'

The gold flecks in his eyes glowed with intensity, and he tilted towards her, a lean finger touching her forearm. 'But I want to.'

Their eyes locked again, and she was caught up in a whirlpool, and she could not escape even if she tried.

Jarok delivered a platter of fare with a flourish, breaking the tension that had leaped up between them.

Following came a pair of servers placing bowls of scrumptious-looking entrées, fried bread, sauces, fruits, and nuts.

The two women, beautiful Falasians with lengthy necks and flowing hair, flashed smiles and giggled behind their trays as they served the food, captivated by Kainan.

He ignored their dancing eyes and seductive smirks, reaching for the snacks on the deep counter.

Selene followed suit, using the delicious bites as a well-needed distraction.

She sensed him gaze at her as she ate and resisted meeting those mesmerizing eyes again.

Instead, she surveyed the room, taking in the atmosphere.

From the crooning Tansinian singer on stage wooing the punters with her haunting voice to the prowling dancers in rainbow-hued Walia peacock tail feathers well placed on their nubile bodies, the place was a fascinating, extravagant establishment.

She peeked back at Kainan and found him doodling.

He'd plucked a drawing tool and napkin from the bar and was now covering it in an illustration she couldn't work out.

His pencil made quick contours and shadows on the paper.

He glanced up for a beat and gave her a wry nod before looking down and continuing his art.

Her gaze shifted back to the mesmerizing room and its occupants.

Servers and busmen darted between tables, delivering banquets of food and trays of kaleidoscopic drinks and cocktails, and the patrons seemed to lap it up.

What would her father have thought of it?

Kei'Lano had always urged Selene to seek the simple joys in life, the company of intimate friends, an excellent repast, and fine wine.

She was sure he'd have enjoyed visiting The Osirian.

They'd have sat at one of the banquettes and discussed politics, science, and social justice until the last crooner left the building and the lights came up at closing time.

Her eyes misted over.

The man beside her stirred. 'Do you want to talk about it?' he murmured.

'What?' she asked, looking up, torn away from her memories.

'Your father. And what happened to him.'

Her face fell, and he reached out a warm hand to cover her cold one on the counter.

'I'm not pushing you, Selene,' he rasped. 'I'm just saying I'm willing to listen when you're ready. I know that sharing how you feel may help to process the awfulness of it all.'

She didn't know what to say, so she dropped into a static pause and pulled away her hand, mulling over his words and keen perception.

It took a moment before she spoke in a whisper. 'Father was the best man I've ever encountered. I'm not quite willing yet to speak, but thank you. It's generous of you. I'll keep your offer in mind.'

'Please do, *khamila*.'

They exchanged a glance, and her heart warmed at the depth of his sincerity.

'In all honesty, he was the closest thing to a father I had,' Kainan confessed to her surprise. 'It would be an honor to help however I can.'

Overwhelmed, Selene scrambled for a way to retain control. 'Why do you call me *khamila*?' she said.

Kainan's brows rose, and then he ran his eyes over her face, features, hair, and mouth.

'Do you know the meaning?' he asked.

She nodded.

'Then know this. I call it as I see it.'

Her heart kicked again, and heat hammered every cell in her body.

He handed her the napkin he'd been drawing on, and she drew in her breath.

He'd captured her and her father in a portrait. Not just their faces but their shared love, their essence, and their full, happy smiles.

The unexpected gesture touched her. 'How did you-? Wow, this is amazing. No one has ever drawn my father, and I like this. I don't know what to say.'

'Say *sante*, *khamila*. That's all I need.'

'Thank you,' she whispered. 'This means more than you know.'

He inclined his head and gave her a small smile as she tucked the drawing into her bag, handling it like it was her most precious object.

They fell into a tranquil stillness, yet she was electrified and aware of his presence.

He'd somehow shifted his chair with one oversized boot planted on the lower rail stretcher of her bar stool and his thick thighs encompassing her body.

It was either a possessive stance or a protective one. She wasn't sure and didn't have the balls to ask.

'Tell me more about your friends,' she said, eager to shift the deep emotion welling up inside her.

'What do you want to know?' Kainan replied, leaning back to pop a breaded morsel into his mouth.

'How and when did you all meet?'

His eyes darkened, and he glanced at the table to his right, where the other Sable Riders sat. 'We've been in each other's lives since we were young. We met when we served our city as members of the Eden Guards *Kubai*. We became close friends. We endured some bad shit together. We joined forces and survived. Then we landed here on Eden II, where we scrapped and worked hard to get where we are today. We're closer than many blood families. We consider ourselves brothers, so we took the same last name. We've always had each other's backs. We'll even kill for and with one another when needed.'

His concluding statement was fierce, and she thought she caught a flicker of pure flames behind his otherworldly eyes. She was sure he meant every word without a shadow of a doubt.

Selene sensed more to the story, but he didn't embellish it further, perhaps unwilling to divulge too much. She was about to insist on more when a voice rang out nearby.

'Kainan! I thought it was you.'

A body inserted itself between them.

A long arm accompanied by thin, painted fingers trailed across Kainan's chest.

At the same time, a rich cloud of blossomed perfume slammed into their shared space.

Selene reared in surprise just as Kainan's face fell into stony hardness.

'Uba,' he said through gritted teeth, using his strong hands to extricate the woman from his neck.

She was, without a doubt, a stunningly beautiful woman— a Rhesian brunette with gleaming black hair flowing down her stunning backside.

Behind her stood two figures with bowed heads, conceivably her entourage or assistants.

'It's been too long, lover,' the woman crooned.

A stab of complex, dark emotion hit Selene.

Jealousy? she thought, horrified at the idea. She had no claim on this man, yet it pained her to see the groping arms travel over Kainan's body with a familiarity she would never know herself.

'I remember when you couldn't have enough of my bed, lover, don't you?' Uba continued, stroking an extended finger over Kainan's muscled arm.

Kainan's square jaw ticked as he pulled away the woman's trailing hand. 'You and I have different memories of the past. I'm busy. Please leave now.'

'Too busy for me?' the brunette whined, her eyes flashing with hurt.

'Every time you ask,' Kainan grounded out.

The woman pouted. 'What could keep you so occupied?'

'Matters beyond your comprehension,' the Edenite growled, a tic appearing along his strong chin.

The dark-haired woman stepped back and turned to look at Selene.

She gave her a long, sweeping look from the top of Selene's wild curls to her understated boots. 'This?' she sneered, pointing an elongated painted claw at Selene. '*This* is not past my perception, lover. It is below it.'

Kainan surged to his feet, pushing Uba away, his massive body looming over her.

His eyes blazed, and Selene swore his skin pulsed with light.

Then he lowered his dark-haired head and spoke, his words dripping with menace.

'Just because your father is the head of one of the most influential families in Rhesus doesn't give you any right to stalk me or speak the way you want about my guests or myself. You've insulted an honored ally of Eden II and an important diplomatic attaché. If you know what's advantageous for you, leave. Now!'

'You can't order me around like that!' the woman whined, not used to boundaries. 'It's like you don't remember that we had such a fun time.'

'What I know is that I've lived to regret it since then,'

Kainan growled, his growl clipped with rage.

The woman's face churned with chaos. 'Where do you get the balls, Sable? You loved it when it was happening. Now you're denying it! You're an entitled and *fokked* up excuse of an Edenite.'

The patrons nearby stared as the scorned lover's drama played out.

His Rider brothers noted the confrontation and half rose to their feet.

Kainan glanced at them and lifted a hand, turning down their assistance.

The enraged brunette whipped her head around to Selene. 'Watch out for him. He's a magnet for all the beauties across this System. Know this: they're falling over for him from Rhesia and Falasia to Galicia. And he takes full advantage of this. What he does is make you feel valued and cherished. First, he'll seduce you and make sweet promises using wild meta magic. Then he'll eat you for breakfast, toss you over for brunch, and spit you out before lunch.'

Selene's eyes widened at the crude words.

Kainan stepped between her and the snarling Rhesian woman. He leaned into the enraged face and spoke, emphasizing every syllable. 'You know what else, princess? Your little display of petulant rudeness just earned you a ban for life at The Osirian and on Eden II. Return or speak to me, my guests, or any member of The Sable Riders ever again, and I'll deal with you myself. And not in the polite way I'm speaking with you now.'

'*Fokk* you, Kainan,' she spat. 'You're banning me? Threatening me with your so-called fabled chimerion?'

Kainan's voice fell lower to a sinister whisper. 'Try me, and you may get an exclusive demonstration.'

The threat must have hit home because the Rhesian woman reared back, fear and rage contorting her beautiful features.

'I don't believe you!' she ventured. 'You wouldn't dare. I'll tell my father that –'

Kainan cut her off. 'Tell Daddy dearest that I've had enough of you. Take your little entourage and get the *fokk* out of our establishment and off this rock!' he stated, his timbre vibrating with controlled menace.

The woman stared aghast, her face burning up with embarrassment.

'You'll live to regret this!' she hissed at Kainan.

'You too,' she spat at Selene before flouncing away, her hips swinging, flicking up an arm to summon her retinue.

With their eyes fixed on the irate woman's exit, Selene and Kainan failed to notice the sneaky look on the face of one of the exiting companions. Who lifted her wrist comm, which clicked, then hurried away after her mistress.

'Well, that was unexpected,' Selene said, leaning back into her chair.

Kainan sank onto the seat beside her and scrubbed one of his palms across his face, sinking it into his hair. 'Fokk, I need a drink,' he declared.

Selene waved Jarok over and ordered a second round.

'You OK?' she asked Kainan after giving him a breather to compose himself.

He shook his head, granting her an abashed look. 'I'm sorry you had to witness that. She's something else.' He paused for a moment. 'But she was never important.'

Selene smiled in reassurance. 'You don't have to justify anything to me. We all have our fair share of embarrassing skeletons in the cupboard.'

'What would yours be?' he said, baiting her with a straight face.

'Not telling. You'll have to strive harder than that to get my secrets.'

Selene's skin flushed as she realized she was enjoying flirting a little too much with this mysterious man who lit her up from within.

'To hard work,' he rumbled, lifting his beer to her glass.

'To hard work,' she agreed with a little smile.

Their meal arrived, and the incident was soon forgotten, swept away by the zest of delicious spices and ingredients that melted on her tongue and filled her belly with goodness.

They spent the rest of the evening talking.

Selene's imagination soared as he regaled her with tales of life growing up on the far-off floating city above Planet Earth and the adventures he and his brothers had indulged in over the years.

To Selene, it was like the world around them - the bar, the restaurant, the servers, and even the lights - faded away, leaving them in a cocoon of their own making.

It was like she could talk all night.

She'd never felt so alive in her entire life.

The retelling of his prior capers and sins made them sound as harebrained as they were brazen.

His dry humor provoked her laughter to the point of tears, and his heated gaze left her with a buzz of euphoria that she hadn't experienced in years.

Hours later, he glanced at his wrist comm and raised an eyebrow.

'It's way past your bedtime, young lady,' he drawled.

'I'm not sleepy, though,' she protested.

'Are we having this conversation again, Selene?'

'Which one's that?'

'The one about your utter disregard for slumber and rest?'

'I take it you're a lover of sleep yourself?' she teased.

'I'm an admirer of the things I treasure the most.'

Selene held his gaze and thought for a moment about its dangerous promise.

He wasn't flirting with her.

He had an intensity about him that made flirting sound like mere child's play.

He was transcendental, cerebral, almost spiritual.

The fierceness in him was as potent as a planetwide tsunami.

Was he as precarious as nature's uncontrollable forces?

And was she even ready for this? *Was he anything she had the time to explore, and was this the right time to probe it further? What would be the repercussions?*

'Don't overthink it, *khamila*,' Kainan rasped, cutting into her train of thought. 'Don't worry about what may or may not happen, for when it comes, it'll have enough worries of its own.'

Selene was amazed once more at his mysterious ability to perceive her deepest thoughts.

He jerked his chin at her and rose to his feet. 'I'm calling it. It's late, and we've got a heavy day ahead of finessing our deal, so I'm taking you back. To your room.'

She smiled at his specific reference, took a deep breath, and nodded, gathering her bag and comm tab.

He took her elbow and led her through The Osirian's still-packed floors to a new elevator near the bar's primary doors.

The lift ascended ten levels before stopping on her floor, where he stalked beside her back to her suite.

Swiping in, he proceeded into the apartment in front of her.

Satisfied, he returned to the open doorway, where she waited as he checked the interior.

'It's clear,' he announced, strolling past her. 'Goodnight, *khamila*.'

His resolute farewell and pensive expression didn't leave room for further protest, and she crossed the threshold.

Their eyes locked as she sidled in and stayed that way even as the door slid shut.

She stood there, motionless, wondering whether to call out after him.

All she could feel was her chest rising and falling, and her breath catching in the weighted space between them.

After a few moments, she heard his impossibly light foot-steps trail down the corridor and away from her.

Only then did she run through the suite and fling herself onto the sumptuous bed.

She burrowed under the covers and curled into a ball.

Then, shutting her eyes, she placed a trembling hand over her pounding heart.

Who was she kidding?

After the evening she'd had, sleep would be an unimagin-able effort.

6

A Glimmer In The Fabric Of His Dark

KAINAN

The tall Edenite strode away from The Sable Group's guest suites, gritting his teeth.

It took all his meta power not to snap around, kick down her door, and wrap Selene in his arms.

Fokk, she was beautiful.

That hair, those eyes, that mouth. That mind.

From the moment he'd spotted her on the landing pad on Dunia, he'd felt an incredible pull towards her.

Although he'd seen her before in surveillance footage and on holo media reports, these glimpses paled into insignificance when compared to the real woman.

She'd been such a vision against the deep emerald backdrop of the wild forests surrounding Zulu One that he'd faltered mid-step, almost stumbling down his craft's air bridge on the orbital platform.

He'd been with many women, but he couldn't remember when he'd ever reacted to any of them so viscerally in his entire life.

It took all he had, every moment in her presence, to fight the urge to lean in, take a sip of her sweet mouth, and get lost in the vortex of her dark, flashing eyes.

To sink his hands into her overflowing curls and mold her voluptuous curves to his.

To drive his body into hers and lose himself in her lushness.

He sensed she also felt the intense attraction between them, and his lips twitched with amusement at how much she tried to resist it, even this evening.

She was brave, vibrant, spirited, and dynamic.

Her determination to fight for her people was admirable, and her fearlessness in asking for what she needed from him and his brothers was brassy as all *fokk*.

She was a vision of rare beauty and intelligence that tore through his every fiber.

He hadn't expected her to be so self-assured, and her strength, humor, and seductive energy washed waves of heated lust racing over his body culminating in his cock.

She didn't hold back her feelings or thoughts either.

Instead, they danced across her expressive face in a kaleidoscope of emotion.

Yet, despite their unmistakable heat, nothing could come of it.

Selene Munene was an enticing tornado he couldn't let himself become twisted in.

Deep in his spirit, he felt that the moment he kissed her, it would unite their souls.

Even if all barriers and decorum were set aside, there was no hope for the electric storm brewing between them. His very nature forbade it.

His every filament dictated it.

The injustice of it all welled up inside him.

It ate at his soul, reminding him how much he'd always longed for true intimacy and a small family to call his own.

Though they'd tried their best, his carers at the orphanage had never been able to fulfill those needs.

He'd always been the outsider, adrift in a sea of strangers.

His loneliness had shifted slightly when he'd decided to make chums with a new group of boys, also orphans.

For the first time in a long time, Kainan had felt like he belonged. They became his closest allies, accepting him for who he was. Over time, they became each other's anchor and universe.

Those same friends followed him into the Eden Guards, where he'd grown confident and even become a battalion leader.

But still, his young heart had struggled to accept that he had no blood family, especially after he and his fellow brothers had their collective world upturned in the most appalling way possible.

So for several years, after escaping his worst nightmare after landing on Eden II, he'd lived in a fog of mental and emotional agony, his soul aflame with bitterness, stoked by pain.

Then came an older woman on the rock who'd taken him under her wing and cared for him like a mother. She was and continued to be the most loving, kindest woman he'd ever met.

J'Kuu Kabi had been patient while he worked through his anger, showing him love and empathy when he'd raged at her, the world, and his past.

She'd been a soothing, calming presence who'd eventually helped him get beyond his trauma when he realized how deep compassion and affection could restore one's soul.

He sensed that he was touching a similar lodestone of devotion and care with Selene.

Their connection, though nascent, was wild, and he wished he could explore the potential of her being his true life partner, someone he could build a future with.

Which was in contrast to how he'd viewed the women in his past.

The last few years had been about building and consolidating The Sable Group's collective strength. Romance had sat on the back burner.

Those he'd dated had never been long-term options.

He liked them. He even respected a majority of them, but he'd never committed to any, a trend nearly all of his brothers had followed.

The Riders weren't lads with zero life experience. On the contrary, they were mature men in their mid to late forties.

Which was young, given that the life span for most residents of Pegasi was 200 years. So they all believed they had time to settle down if they wished.

Meanwhile, they enjoyed their bachelor status.

Take Kage, who'd had a serious girlfriend a few years previously.

It hadn't worked out, so now he had discreet flings with a slew of beauties, always keeping it casual, dropping them within weeks.

Xion was the king of one-night stands.

Zane cycled through one beautiful model or nubile socialite each year, changing them at the 375-day mark.

Riv was the only one who'd remained single, refusing to mingle. Because twenty years ago, he'd lost the love of his life.

She'd disappeared just before their wedding day, seen getting on an unknown vessel that had vanished into hyperspace.

Since then, he'd never stopped looking for her. He'd even turned his ship, Glimmer, into a hi-tech surveillance craft.

He traveled the System, scouring all corners for his missing woman, moonlighting as a bounty hunter.

At the same time, his cameras captured millions of data points as he sifted through innumerable faces. Searching for her, only her.

Secretly, Kainan wanted his own family and, even more so, a woman like Selene.

However, there was a darkness within him that no one, not even she, could touch. And even if he were free of it, he had a lot on his plate right now. Maybe too much to even contemplate a future with anyone.

He had an incursion to plan, a brotherhood of men to lead, and a mission to complete. One that had consumed him for so many years, ever since he'd first landed on Eden II, broken and torn.

Yet now there was a chance - a glimmer in the fabric of his dark existence.

Selene Munene either held the answer he was looking for or was the distraction he didn't need.

He wasn't sure, but he felt her presence in his life was

somehow a catalyst for something new on the horizon.

Regardless, he had to harness all his power to control the intensity of his reaction to Selene in case it took him off mission.

He needed to be on his A-game to stay ahead of whatever the future entailed. Failure was not an option.

Kainan strode straight back to The Sable Group's boardroom.

He thrust himself into a chair and faced his brothers.

They watched his entrance in silence and then broke into grins and laughter, bouncing off each other's mirth.

'*Fokk* off all you!' Kainan snarled, irritated at seeing the four burly, mature men lose their shit.

'Damn, *khosi!* You sure can entertain. On the one hand, a woman who's got you by the balls,' Kage guffawed.

'On the other, one who'd kill to have them!' Xion crowed. 'Blast that Uba! Impersonating inner beauty is not her destiny.'

They fell apart once more, roaring with amusement.

Kainan didn't quite see the funny. He sucked his teeth. 'Why are you *fokkers* pretending like you've never seen me with a woman?'

'You're different this time with Selene,' Riv smirked. 'Like you want to burn her up.'

'You're an exceptional piece of shit,' Kainan ground out.

'See? You're on mad defense, *khosi*,' Kage added. 'She's got you for real.'

Their leader shook his head, exasperated. 'You *kinais* need prescriptions. Or better still, warning labels. Or bibs because you all are acting like *kitotos*. Can we focus on the issue at hand?'

He gave them a baleful stare, one so cold they snapped to attention, and the mood in the room sobered up.

'The Technocracy is unquestionably here,' Kainan said. 'In our backyard. Is this the chance, the moment we've been waiting for?'

'Could be,' Riv said. 'We can't ignore how much of an opportunity this presents. It's not their entire armada. It's a tiny presence. Which gives us the best opportunity to test our plans.'

'Are we ready?' Kainan said looking over at Kage.

'We'll never be set.'

'But you're a perfectionist, so we'll never get to your version of nirvana. So, in your estimation, what are our odds?'

'Better than good. I'd back ourselves,' the scar-faced Rider said with a grin.

Kainan nodded. 'So I need to know if we are happy with our decision to go ahead.'

'This is going to expose us,' Zane stated. 'We won't stay in the shadows after this.'

'*Naam.* No doubt,' Kainan agreed. 'Can we deal?' he probed.

'It's inevitable,' Zane continued, his strategic mind flexing. 'We've managed to expand, and that's reflected in our books. We've amalgamated and absorbed most of our competitors in the ship-building space. Our ice mining and manufacturing concerns are booming. But if we want to keep growing, we've no choice but to project further.'

Xion nodded in agreement. 'Our security is tight. Our tech outguns the rest. We have a high concentration of young people we lead who are hungry to win. So we can extend and welcome risk while still being resilient and flexible. Our continued population growth also facilitates and supports the personnel drain caused by our military expansion and mercenary efforts.'

Zane took over. 'More of note, we can afford to pay for a substantial labor force as the economy expands. We're killing it. We have the workforce and resources to give our plans a red hot go.'

Kainan lifted a long finger in caution. 'Can't let it get to our heads. Take Rhesus. They're in decline because they believed in their hype and didn't prepare for their future. So, while everything we've accomplished and can now do is heady and dynamic, we can't rest on our laurels. We need to examine our intent with Dunia. What are we in this for?'

'Aiding a planet to regain control of its government means we'll be perceived as more dominant,' Zane rumbled. 'Helping Dunia is, in essence, a war of accretion from a cerebral perspective. We're winning minds and hearts. A huge move for us, *khosi*. Whilst meeting our own goals.'

'The deal will also bring in xentium and acquire that sexy-sounding tech to sustain our shipyards,' Kage said. 'Big advantage.'

Kainan nodded in agreement. 'Agreed. If we balance the achievement with the risk, we should be OK. Rhesia is declining. Dunia, Falasia, and Alloria are ascending slower than we are. Galicia is ahead in terms of size and population. Iccythria is a wild card. That said, our supremacy is our ships and innovation – huge pluses in future confrontations against our rivals. But we must keep to a clear, strategic plan and execute well, brothers.'

Kainan sat back in his chair and nailed his kin with a long, contemplative gaze.

'We're doing this? *Naam*? Not just for us, but for those we give back to and protect.'

'Let's go for it, brother,' Kage rumbled.

'Besides, there's a beautiful and smart woman who'll slice your innards if all the seduction you two were serving each other tonight was for naught,' Riv added straight-faced.

Kainan's molten eyes blazed. 'I hope you all choke on the shit you talkin'. Selene wouldn't barter her planet for cheap thrills.'

Xion threw up his hands in surrender. 'Damn! Who ate your bowl of sunshine, thundercloud?'

Kage dug even further with a snigger. 'Sensitive much? It's only been a day in her presence. How will you last the entire campaign with her around, *khosi*?'

'You losers are the reason the middle finger exists!' Kainan growled, pushing his seat back with force, thrusting the said digit at his brothers as he stalked from the room, leaving behind an amused quartet.

After a beat, he pushed his head back into the room with a small smile playing on his lips. '0300 start. Everyone at training, no excuses. It'll be all *Kubai Kommando*. Get ready for no rest squats, drills, push-ups, and an eight-klick run in under an hour. Time to see if you *kinais* are as fit as you think.'

The room groaned as one.

Kainan smirked at his more than compelling payback and

strolled away.

MASSIMO

High above Dunia's stratosphere, on the oscillating bridge of a Technocracy capital cruiser, Massimo Makori shook.

On any given day, the statuesque man was a force to be reckoned with.

He'd long enjoyed the reputation of being a terrifying aggressor known for obliterating his opponents at will.

With either a charm offensive from smiling lips, a glare from his cold eyes, a blistering tirade of abuse, or a stamp of his massive foot.

He'd often thrown around his bulk to bully his enemies into submission. He'd terrified them all - from army commanders to his fellow Security Council members and even entire nations. Yet today, he twitched from head to toe.

His reaction was due to the freezing temperatures and raging drafts that whipped through the gigantic airship.

And to a greater degree, the unrelenting dread that gripped his well-fed form.

'You assured us of a quick victory, did you not?'

The voice emanated from the figure who dominated the immense screen across the bridge, their feed transmitting from somewhere in the next galaxy.

Massimo studied the crat being, fascinated by the part

machine, part *whatever-the-fokk-they-brewed* in the evolutionary stew of the Omegaverse.

The silhouette was humanoid-shaped with limbs and a head, but that was as close as it got to being human.

Its body was hardshell, with a striking golden pattern running through the middle of its see-through armored carapace.

The head was transparent too, ovular, broad, with the long end sitting on the shoulders.

The same gilded patterning formed its eyes and mobile mouth. It wore a gold cloak over its exoskeleton that billowed behind it.

Massimo braced himself, smiling with unease. 'Eminence 478Q1, if I had known -.'

'That Dunia would awake? Even after assuring us this would never be the case because the Prime was dead, and with it, his ability to summon the planet's consciousness?'

'I swear, I did not know. If I had, I would have -'.

Massimo's words cut off when his present company, a unit of guard crats on one of the blockade ships, swiveled their glassy skulls away from him and onto the expansive holo screens that wrapped most of the bulkhead.

'Let us review the damage we sustained so we can make an informed decision.'

The vision on-screen, captured days earlier when Dunia had risen from its slumber, was a hellish wonder.

The crat force, too massive to land at the foot of any biodome, had set down in the open valleys at the center of the Zaalalum forests, a few hours from the mega city of New Malindi.

Then, they'd marched through what Massimo had

promised was a dormant ecology.

He'd been confident, seeing as the One Dunia Coalition he led had enacted its power grab and unseated the Prime.

He'd shot the Prime after ambushing him in his office.

He'd even fired plenty of rounds to ensure Kei'Lano Munene III was well and truly dead and would no longer summon Dunia to life.

Until the impotent planet awoke and unleashed the fury of its forests, flora, and fauna with zero *fokks* to give.

On-screen, a clade of 100-meter-tall phytaphylia trees tore apart the remains of armed flyers; they targeted the enemy fighters and crats with their long gametangia sprouting along their trunks.

In the distance, elephantine Dracula bees picked off the limbs of the invading army. Rainforest brachyphia ferns rose in waves over the ground, wrapping their fifty-meter fronds around escaping crats, coating each one with a slimy viscera, and stuffing them head-first into their innards.

Above, the maelstrom raged on.

'Status?' the lucent admiral demanded, breaking the dead air.

'Due to the planetary attack, we suffered casualties in the 208456 battalion. Neither 209458 nor 3907626 are in communication, Eminence.

At this time, only two of our squadrons made it to New Malindi and one apiece to Paris Minor and Rambasa. We also lost Rambasa to the defenders.'

The crat's Eminence turned back towards the hyperventilating man and glared at him through the glowing orbs.

'Massimo Makori. The Technocracy only goes to battle if it has a reasonable chance of winning. We withdrew our armada because this invasion, while noble it may be, seems to be a hopeless cause. We left behind three capital ships, one of which you're now on, to patrol the planet and await the outcome of this meeting. So the question to you is, should we retreat?'

'I'm unworthy to make such an estimation. I'll leave it to your Eminence's insight to make the right choice,' Massimo replied, licking dry lips.

'Our wisdom, Massimo Makori, for The Technocracy is one.'

The mechanical voice somehow, against all odds, sounded weary. 'I will consult with the other Eminences. Your survival depends on what we decide.'

The air on the bridge chilled even further. Massimo waited for what seemed a long moment as unseen consultations took place.

He knew he'd made a deal with the devil a few standard years ago.

When The Proxima Leadership had sent a go-between to request Massimo for a small amount of xentium for research purposes, as he'd been reassured then.

The intermediary, Lahita Togas, was a Rhesian underworld figure and owner of a brothel Massimo frequented on the pleasure planet of Zanyria.

She'd been quite persuasive and assured him he'd be well paid for his troubles.

He'd agreed, but only because his comm tab was ringing off the hook with frantic calls from his lenders scattered throughout the Pegasi system.

Massimo was surprised by the generous payment of jewels and gold at the exchange a few weeks later.

They amounted to four times the value of the lump of xentium he'd provided. Lahita had reassured him that the significant price was a sign of his sponsor's deep gratitude.

It had been more than enough to pay off all his debts. He'd used the excess to celebrate, throwing a lavish banquet for his friends.

Lahita Togas had been the party's VIP guest. But she'd never shown.

However, she'd called weeks later. Weeping and pleading for her life.

Begging for the return of the overpayment of jewels and gold, and imploring him to meet with her now enraged backers to find a way to remedy the situation.

He'd hung up on her and ignored her frantic calls afterward. Blocked her and wished against all hope that she'd go away.

She hadn't. Instead, she'd appeared, her body stiff with rigor mortis, on the steps of Massimo's holiday home on the coast of Rambasa, with a comm tab resting on her battered chest that contained clear instructions on where to rendezvous with his new benevolent sponsors.

He'd hastened to the secret meeting in The Badlands, afraid for his life.

He'd docked his ship with a Technocracy cruiser in the shadow of a darkened moonlet.

Inside, he'd met with Eminence 478Q1, also known as the admiral, who'd demanded he facilitate untapped access to xentium.

To construct more extensive, more lethal, and long-range battleships that could traverse their galaxy and help them win the war against The Alpha Imperium, their bitter enemies in the Omegaverse.

They encouraged him to meet with his Prime to make their dealings seem legit. To offer him their cutting-edge technology and resources to build high-tech-based services on Dunia.

Everything from advanced hospitals, factories, roads, infrastructure, and even weapons for the planet.

Dreading the inevitable, Massimo had returned home and approached Kei'Lano with the proposal. Instead, the Prime had shut him down in seconds.

Kei'Lano had schooled Massimo on the true intentions of The Technocracy.

The Prime reminded his Defense Minister that The Technocracy's empire and warfare capabilities had been built off the back of treaties with poorer planets in The Omegaverse.

Twas the same rewards they were offering Dunia.

The Technocracy forced these worlds to integrate with them over millennia, becoming resource cows for their conflict with their greatest enemy.

Kei'Lano reiterated that he had no interest in Dunia being the crats' foothold colony in the Pegasi galaxy.

He also did not want his people or their resources conscripted for an unending war with the Alpha Imperium.

He'd dismissed Massimo, not knowing that his defense minister had already sold him and Dunia down the river. For he couldn't repay their excessive 'gift.'

Massimo devised the only plan he could to save himself and his kin.

He went back to his benevolent sponsors.

He persuaded the crats to finance a power takeover, promising them this action would secure control over the xentium they desired.

His arguments had worked. They backed him, handing over more jewels and gold stripped from the colony planets they controlled. It was enough for Massimo to fund the coup he so needed.

If this complete overthrow of Dunia now failed, The Technocracy would exact revenge on him, his wife, their children, and their extended family.

Minutes later, Eminence 478Q1 strode back to the Dunian man.

'Massimo Makori, our wisdom says we cannot fight an entire planet. Not one that can ravage us like this. We have agreed that we will cut our losses and leave this system. We will not sacrifice anything further for a lost cause.'

Massimo started on his feet. He paled, clenching his fists against the waves of panic.

'Eminence?'

'This is the one solution The Technocracy will accept. We also need to be reimbursed for our troubles,' the shrouded leader continued. 'We expect to be repaid in full. In the next standard day.'

Massimo winced. *There was not going to be any repayment*, he thought. *Not now, not even in the upcoming 24 hours.* What he hadn't used to pay back his loan sharks, he'd poured into planning the coup.

And now his dynasty could be doomed, a bitter pill to swallow given the machinations and manipulations he and his family had devised over the last few years.

Never mind the hoops they'd jumped through and promises they'd made to even their most detestable rival dynasties— all to assure themselves of victory.

And for what? It couldn't be for anything. He had to prevail.

Perhaps there was a way out. The Prime's unremarkable offspring and apparent heir to the seat of the Prime was the key.

It was a known fact that the Munene progeny inherited the ability to speak with the planet. Maybe the Prime's daughter could tap into the sentient world's power and, with some persuasion, stop the mayhem.

But first, he had to find Selene Munene - soon, given the urgent bounty he'd put on her. Followed by getting her to give up control of the planet's powers.

This would lead to unfettered access to Dunia's most precious resource, restoring his dynasty's coffers and honor.

Then he'd get rid of her for good, which had been his plan until she escaped the metropolis and disappeared.

Rationalization complete, he bowed. 'Eminence, may I be so bold as to suggest an alternative?'

Eminence 478Q1 lifted its carapace arm and waved it, giving Massimo permission to continue.

A promising sign, he thought.

'What if Dunia is not a lost cause?'

'What do you mean?' the Technocrat asked, leaning forward.

'I still control the capital and the second largest city, Paris Minor. I still have access to a cabal of military generals and militia loyal to my mission. What if I can marshal my people and find out who summoned the planet? Can we get them to appeal to Dunia's sentience and make it work in our favor? We could manipulate them to allow us to oversee the entire world, including its consciousness. Which would ensure the xentium ore fields are made available to you. If we prevail, will you still be interested in keeping to our agreed arrangement?'

The obscure figure cocked its head and nodded in soundless communion with compatriots unseen.

Minutes later, it swiveled to face Massimo. 'Your offer intrigues us, Massimo Makori. Xentium is, after all, The Technocracy's most well-regarded prize.'

Massimo assented, making sure not to look too eager. 'Then will you likewise consider leaving me with the blockade ships plus a few, shall we say, soldiers, tools, and aids to make things easier so I can triumph?'

There was a short pause, which appeared like an hour to the ex-Defense Minister.

Then, his sponsor spoke up. 'We will grant you one last chance, Massimo Makori, to prove yourself. We will also give you the required aid and leave the three capital cruisers in rotation, but failure is not an option this time. But, should you prevail, send word, and we will return.'

Massimo was hit with a wave of weak-kneed relief.

Bowing and scraping, he thanked his accomplices.

Hours later, he crawled off a Technocracy rattler and dragged himself to one of New Malindi's smaller wall gates.

The rattler took off and went back to the cruiser in orbit.

Massimo banged on the gate's thermoplastic surface, yelling for someone to let him in. The startled Guardian of the Gate heard the outraged cries and came running.

Hiding his disdain at the newcomer's identity, he permitted the churlish self-appointed New Prime into the walls of New Malindi.

While Massimo stewed further, the Guardian of the Gate summoned a flyer to transport the interim Prime back to his palace and seat of power.

At long last, a vehicle from the House of Makori arrived,

engines screeching to a stop before the two men.

'Is the capital still mine?' Massimo demanded of his pilot as the Guardian helped him into the small aircraft.

'It is, sire. The loyalists' plans to take back the city have not succeeded.'

Massimo sank back into the paneled cushions with a smile of relief.

'Onward,' he commanded, missing the flash of disgust the Guardian shot at him as the doors hissed shut and the flyer ascended into the citadel's secure airspace.

SELENE

She fell into an uneasy sleep that was soon filled with a dream.

One where she saw Dunia's twin suns shrouded by the blue velvet darkness.

She saw herself walking down a cobblestone path through a forest where copious trails of tiny, glowing creatures rose from the earth.

'Pearls of heaven,' Selene whispered in her vision as she waded through the flitting bioluminescent patterns.

She stepped down a flight of stairs as the shimmering lightning bugs trailed after her, brushing her skin with their beating wings.

She ducked under an overhanging rock where vines tumbled down a stonewall enclosing a deep azure pool dotted with lily pads and blooming lotus flowers.

Water burbled out of the mouths of carved stone figurines shaped like Dunia's legendary oversized bees and winged moths.

A long and low seat hovered above the water, bookended with lamps.

Selene ventured forward into the tree-lined dell.

With an intense breath, sweet air flooded her lungs, mixed in with the fragrance of lotus blossoms and the heady perfume of lei'oia vine blooms.

She stared at the mirror-like surface, and her reflection danced back at her.

She saw a woman with dark curls, honey skin, brown eyes, a pert nose, and lush lips looking back at her.

She wasn't plain, but she didn't consider herself a knockout either.

She shifted in sleep, her worn appearance reminding her of the battle being fought for her planet.

She reached down into the water and splashed its coolness onto her face.

The liquid trailed off her skin and fell in luminescent drops back into the small pool, causing the mirrored reflection to dance.

She then felt tears seep from her eyes as the water's facade transformed to show reflections of faces. Of her long-gone mother, her father, and her sister, a medic on a relief ship in the far sector of the galaxy.

She'd let them all down by taking her eye off the ball.

Worst still, her dearest father was dead, and she'd done nothing to stop it.

She felt a wave of sorrow hit her, and she slumped on the

rocky seat under the waterline, defeated in grief, loss, and the weight of responsibility.

'*Why me?*' she whispered through slow tears.

They fell into the grotto's waters, which stirred into tiny waves that flowed and pulsed over, encircling her body.

Then came a whisper that echoed and resounded in the grotto. '*She who asks questions cannot avoid the answers.*'

Selene sat up, looking around, heart pounding. '*Who's there?*'

With a start, she remembered that Dunia was sentient.

It had a complex psionic mycorrhizal web controlled by a single intelligent mind made of mycelium strands that connected the whole planet's biosphere.

While this network distributed water, nitrogen, carbon, and minerals across the planet, it also merged over time to live in symbiosis with the entire ecosystem.

It even wielded power to direct the ecosystem to protect itself from its enemies using the sheer might of its leviathan-sized plants, trees, and animals.

The waters around her stirred. '*Be a mountain or lean on one.*'

Selene ventured with a whisper. '*Dunia?*'

There was no reply. Then she felt a wave of energy and a sudden rush of wind.

It slammed into her and whirled, agitating the deep pool of water in the cave.

She saw the swirling liquid rise into a high fountain.

It then plunged away into the reservoir, leaving behind waves of pure luminescence.

'*You are the answer.*'

Silence fell in the enclosed grotto.

Selene blinked, staring at the now still waters. It seemed that the planet had chosen to speak to her.

Heart thumping, she tossed around the words she'd heard in her mind.

Until she accepted their inevitable truth.

She was the answer.

Not because she was full of her hubris.

But because her father's passing had handed the baton to her and only her. There was no one else for the job.

She woke with a start and sat up in bed, unsure whether she'd been dreaming or whether the experience had been real because it had felt like it.

As her heart pounding calmed, she lay back, deep in thought.

She had to take on the responsibility of seeking a way forward for the people and planet of Dunia.

Her thoughts jumped to the man who was the key to finding a solution for Dunia. Kainan Sable seemed to have what it took to help her with her cause.

The problem was her attraction to him, which threatened to overwhelm her.

She needed to piece herself back together and level with her soul.

After endless debating, she told herself that there was no way on Dunia anything would happen between her and Kainan.

The timing was off, plus her father had taught her that being a good diplomat meant keeping a professional distance from your allies.

Anything beyond that was improper and unbecoming.

So she spent precious moments building up the walls in her

heart, brick by brick.

Until she felt she was armed enough against the tide of flames that was the man himself.

Hours later, having barely closed an eyelid all night, Selene abandoned any pretense of trying to rest.

Instead, she took a long bath, fueled herself with two cups of thick, dark *kahawa*, and managed a quick breakfast in the apartment suite.

Priming her body, mind, and soul before Kainan knocked on her door.

7

A Defiant Yearning

SELENE

When Kainan called the next day, she answered the soft chime at the door with a bright smile, her belongings clutched close like armor.

It slid open to reveal an enigmatic, quiet, and brooding version of the Rider, his thick forearms crossed over his broad chest as he stared down at Selene.

'Good morning,' she said, eager to forget the intensity of the night before and set the mood for the long day ahead.

He nodded at her cheery greeting.

'Ready?' he rasped, his gravel-laden voice sending jolts through her.

'Always,' she replied.

He strode off without warning, and she hurried after him,

almost catching her bag in the door auto-closing behind her.

He turned his profile towards her when she caught up with his lengthy strides. 'We're making a detour preceding our session today. I'm taking you to meet the Kugwe, J'Kuu Kabi. The leader of Eden II's Chamber of Elders.'

'Why's that?' Selene asked.

'As a courtesy, but also because I'll ask a lot from the people of Eden II over the next few weeks and months. I need the support of all key players if we're to be successful. It's an Edenite tradition to get the blessing of the Seniors before proceeding with any alliance of this magnitude.'

They'd reached a new entrance to the expansive concourse, and Kainan ushered Selene into a sleek, closed flyer hovering outside the doors.

'Welcome, Selene,' a voice intoned.

She scanned around the craft in delight, recognizing the utterance from the bank of monitors at the controls.

'Mirage?'

'*Naam*, Selene, I'm here. I've taken over one of Kainan's flyers to pilot you safely across the metro.'

'What if we walked?' Selene asked.

'*Nada*,' Kainan muttered. 'Too far. Besides, we're taking as many security precautions as possible.'

'Of course, thank you,' the Dunian woman said.

'Mirage, please take us to the Elders HQ,' Kainan murmured.

The flyer rose a few more feet to hover over the passing crowds, then took off without a hitch.

Selene steeled herself for the meeting ahead. 'Kainan, kindly tell me more about the Elders. How do you work together?'

Kainan leaned back in the cushioned seat, hands and eyes fixed on his comm tab as he spoke. 'The Elders deal more with our judicial matters and the rule of law, while The Sable Group makes most internal and external political and security decisions. However, the face of both branches is The Kugwe, J'Kuu Kabi. *J'Kuu* is an honorific title that also means respected aunt.'

'I see,' Selene said. 'Does the J'Kuu make the final call on missions such as what we're about to embark on?'

He gazed up, his golden eyes narrowed, penetrating. '*Nada.* All security and military determinations end with me and the other Riders.'

'How did The Sable Group get -?'

'Appointed? We were invited. The rock needed a stable approach to security. The Elder Council, comprised of members from all key communities on Eden II, thought we'd proven ourselves as part-time mercs and security experts. We'd also showed up with reasonable thinking on defense-related matters of Eden II. So they believed it was natural for us to take the role. We, on the other hand, were incapable of refusing. The Elders welcomed us here when we had nothing to our name. They invested in us, which paved the way to our current status. Being their security go-to was the least we could do.'

'I see,' Selene said, her curiosity sated.

He turned his focus back on the tab he held, his face and body closed off to her.

She sensed that he, too, seemed to have made some decisions overnight about how they were to interact.

A stab of disappointment hit, and she dampened it with a deep breath. Why that bothered her, she couldn't quite work out.

Instead, she concentrated her observation outside the thick plex windows.

At the columns and arcades of the concourse. At the dizzying heights of the living quarters that rushed by.

Further, at the invisible roofline of the massive vault above them. Her gaze followed the intersecting sky lanes that snaked under the dome.

Their internal and external lights winked in and out of sight, creating the effect of a diamond-like necklace encircling the moon city.

Soaring and dominating the entire view above the glass-paneled dome was a black firmament, dark and dotted with stars, even during the lunar day when the system's twin suns shone high in Eden II's atmosphere.

The moon's slower spin on its axis meant that one face caught the perpetual rotation of starlight and never-ending dawn.

Fractured soft radiance bounced off the shadowed moonlit ridges from the undulating cluster of stars and twin suns above.

The other face, where the metro dome had been built, was always aimed at Dunia, which hung in the same place in Eden II's sky as the sun and celestial bodies went through their monthly cycle around it.

It was a fascinating dichotomy of light and dark.

Before long, the flyer came to a smooth stop outside an impressive building that rivaled the most stunning architectural buildings in the System.

She stepped out of the vehicle onto an uncovered vaulted entrance, a sculptural statement of swirling structures and organic forms of three distinct branches.

She stared up and caught her breath.

'How magnificent. Where are we?'

Mirage answered from inside the confines of the flyer's holo nav. 'At the Edenite Civil Justice Center, within the triple wings, you'll find an amphitheater, exhibition halls, courtrooms, and last but not least, the council offices. The spacious, airy, glass spaces were designed to display the accessibility and transparency of our courts and judicial system.'

'*Sante*, Mirage,' Kainan rasped in a deep timbre. 'Wait here for us. We shouldn't be too long.'

He threw his hood over his head, cloaking his face from view, before leading Selene through the impressive building's transparent atrium.

They walked up a flight of stairs via an extended corridor of workspace, stopping in front of a solid, brass-covered door.

He waved his wrist comm over a security panel, and it pinged.

The door slid open, revealing a tastefully furnished and airy reception overlooking the concourse.

'*Khosi*,' a voice called out. 'J'Kuu is not here.'

They turned to see a young woman heading their way from an inner office. 'I'm Mariam, her assistant. She's at the New Eden center.'

Kainan nodded. 'Then we'll see her there. *Sante*,' he told the youthful woman, who gazed after him with longing as he stepped back into the corridor.

Selene hid a smile at his non-reaction to Mariam's admiration and let him lead her to a set of massive lift doors at the end of the building.

He punched the panel buttons, and the entrances soon revealed a private maglev elevator.

He ushered her in and air-typed their desired location.

Seconds later, the car lifted off, racing towards its destination across Eden II at high speeds.

Inside the lift, Kainan kept his gaze fixed outside, keeping conversation to a minimum. Selene ignored him, leaving him to his brooding thoughts.

In minutes, the high-speed train whispered to a stop, and the doors parted to reveal a corridor within another building.

A crystal-clear plex wall ran along one long hallway, looking out onto an open, busy square overflowing with people, stalls, and, at one end, a darkened avenue that seemed to dip under the moon's terrain.

At the heart of the square was a public maglev station from which bodies poured out, moving about their business across the massive lunar rock.

Judging by their clothes and manner, the people in the plaza were more ragged and desperate than the rest of Eden II's dwellers.

This was indeed the humbler extremity of the moon.

'Where are we?' Selene ventured.

'East Pikani,' was all Kainan told her.

They came to a juncture in the corridor. On the wall to the left was a small 'CYC' placard. The sign pointing right said 'NEC'.

'What is this place?' Selene asked.

Kainan paused mid-step for a moment to answer her. 'The CYC is a community-based organization offering education, care, and support to kids throughout the Pika neighborhoods. The Sable Group funds it and focuses on early interventions that empower young people and strengthen communities. The NEC – The New Eden Center – is a shelter for families and people off the streets that provides food for those in need. In addition, we provide housing and assistance for those who've hit hard times.

'I see,' Selene said, intrigued.

'We're headed to the NEC,' Kainan said, taking the right turn. They approached a set of brass swing doors. With a hand on her back, Kainan stepped her through them and into a reception area.

The space was airy, spacious, and packed with people.

Selene caught the sounds of laughter and the buzz of conversation.

A few volunteers in uniform waved at Kainan as they walked by.

She observed an assortment of people carrying boxes to and from a room beside the foyer. Also, a group of uniformed assistants divvied food into giveaway bags and parcels to give to those in need.

Some packages were whisked away behind another set of doors from where the enticing smell of cooking wafted.

Selene noticed more signs leading to more winding corridors. One pointed guests to a common area for socializing and relaxation, another to a communal dining space, and others to bathrooms, showers, and accessible laundry facilities.

There was even a door that announced the center's medical clinic and a legal aid and support services office next to it.

'Seems to be well run,' Selene remarked.

Kainan nodded. 'It has to provide the structure that the disadvantaged in these communities need. We've strict rules and regulations to ensure the safety and well-being of our guests—from a curfew to no alcohol and drug use—and we require everyone to follow the set behavior guidelines.'

'You seem quite knowledgeable and invested in it,' Selene noted with a smile.

Kainan, on the other hand, was solemn. 'It's been a long-term involvement for me. My first working gig on the rock was right here. Over the years, I've seen the NEC transform and develop the local community's capacity to provide equal education, healthcare, food, and shelter access. It's a 24/7 safe space that the Riders and I are proud to be a part of.'

Kainan paused at the sprawling reception desk. 'Looking for J'Kuu,' he told one of the volunteers helping at the front counter.

The volunteer queried the center's private network. 'She's in the kitchens.'

'*Sante*,' Kainan said with a dip of his chin.

He moved again, prowling towards the swinging doors from where intense smells were drifting.

He shoved them open, guiding Selene before him, his hand on her back.

They entered a central kitchen buzzing with life, spice, heat, and flames.

Inside, an older Edenite woman of generous proportions clad in a flowing rainbow-hued robe took center stage in the bustling cooking space.

As Kainan and Selene approached, she glanced up and clapped her hands in delight, the glyphs across her shoulders and arms dancing in an ancient tribal pattern.

She pushed the spoon she'd been using to stir the substantial pot of soup onto a holder and rounded the hot plates, reaching out to hug Kainan.

Selene tagged something she hadn't yet caught on his face before.

A wide smile.

It transformed his face from a plane of hard, chiseled, somber surfaces into a softer, carefree expression.

'Kipenzi!' the woman trilled, emotion pouring out her sparkling kohl-lined eyes. 'What a surprise. And who is this with you? Please introduce me to this beauty,' she invited.

'J'Kuu Kabi, I'd like you to meet Selene Munene, daughter of Kei'Lano Munene III and the soon-to-be new Prime of Dunia.'

J'Kuu swiveled her mighty presence toward Selene, folding her warm, soft hands over the younger woman's cooler ones.

'Of course,' J'Kuu said with a smile. 'I am sorry to hear what you've endured these last few days. Your father was a remarkable man, Dunia; rest his soul. May you defeat his enemies and honor his passing by taking back his seat,' she said with a fierce expression.

Tears prickled her eyes. 'Thank you. It's why I'm here. To seek justice. To get the help, we need to take back Dunia for his sake and the people on the planet.'

The woman sliced her eyes over to the tall Edenite and smiled. 'If Kainan is involved, you will get your equity!'

'I hope so,' Selene said.

J'Kuu turned to Kainan and pointed a finger at him. 'Where have you been all this time?'

Without a doubt, this was an overdue reunion.

'Here and there,' Kainan rasped with a loped smile.

'It's been too long, son. You were gone for weeks. So what did you find patrolling the system's outer reaches this time?'

'Enough to keep me busy, J'Kuu.'

The rotund woman swiveled to Selene and dropped her voice into a conspiratorial whisper. 'When Kainan isn't running the business affairs of our humble little station, he prowls the badlands and asteroids for pirates and privateers while rescuing the lost, the forgotten, and the wanderers in between.'

This was yet another revelation for Selene.

She twisted her neck to look at him. 'Is that right?'

J'Kuu nodded her head. 'He's our self-appointed knight in stealth armor. And we love him for that, especially when you understand how far he's come. He arrived here as a broken and young soldier. He fought his demons by serving on the streets and alleys of Eden II for years. He was working overtime here at the New Eden Center to feed the hordes of abandoned and refugee children he'd rescued from the drainage pipes and underbelly of a dark city. They loved him for it and followed him around in droves. They still do, to this day.'

Kainan gave a humorless laugh. 'Until you caught me stealing food for the kids and made me work in your kitchens to earn what I'd nicked from you.'

J'Kuu's fleshy neck shook with mirth. 'I owned a few warehouses back then, plus some eateries,' she explained to Selene. 'Kainan ended up working for me. And once he'd earned each schill back that he owed me, I promoted him to run operations. He brought along his Rider brothers and doubled my profits in a year. They used that to set up their various businesses. His every opportunity was a competition, and Kainan was always focused on winning.'

She turned to the hulking, silent man and spoke with almost a maternal pride. 'A strategy that worked well for you and the rest of Eden II. Look where we are today!'

He gave her a half smile, but Selene caught the deep affection in his eyes for the older woman. Selene sensed the bond between them was unshakable.

'Enough of the personal embarrassment,' Kainan deflected.

'Agreed. Although I'd love to dish out more, tell me why you've cornered me in my kitchens during our busiest day of the week?'

'We'll need a more private place to speak,' Kainan told her.

J'Kuu's eyes narrowed as she read the intense expression on his face. 'Come with me.'

She bustled them into an empty stock room and closed the door. 'Tell me everything,' she demanded, transforming into the Eden Council's stalwart and firm leader.

Kainan stepped in, explaining The Sable Group's offer to help Dunia. She listened without interruption.

After Kainan and Selene's detailed explanations, J'Kuu gave Selene a keen look. 'Have you thought about the expected impact of the war?'

'We have,' Selene replied. 'Apart from infrastructure difficulties and community displacement, we anticipate rising inflation and impaired economic growth, as well as more specific issues pertaining to the safety of our people on the ground and the Edenite soldiers deployed on the planet. We've got a working committee of trusted and loyal government and military leaders, plus Kainan's team engaged in ensuring the resilience of our supply chains and mitigating all aspects of the challenges we're about to face.'

Kainan nodded. 'We'll also contact the Eden Elder Council and yourself, J'Kuu, to aid and advise on the humanitarian and diplomatic front.'

Selene leaned in. 'We'd appreciate your participation in our discussions on re-prioritizing important resources. Similarly, can we tap into your knowledge and contacts to help build alliances and advocate for our cause among other planetary governments and philanthropic organizations?'

'It'd be my honor,' J'Kuu said. Then, she gave them her blessing. 'Kei'Lano would be proud of you both and The Sable Group. As long as the families of the guards, pilots, and troops you are involved in this counterattack are well informed and taken care of on our end, I approve of your chosen course of action.'

After a few more minutes of chatting and tasting J'Kuu's delicious soup, Kainan and Selene bade the Alderman farewell. Then, it was back to the maglev lift for a ride to The Sable Group's HQ.

Mid-flight, Selene slid a handful of furtive glances at the quiet, reticent man beside her. While he'd not quite struck her as talkative or ebullient, his energy today was downright reserved.

He wasn't ignoring her, but he was making it clear where the line between them stood.

She could scarcely say anything to him without appearing clingy and needy.

He'd made her no promises, and apart from the intense gazes and the occasional sparks of charm, he'd been an absolute gentleman.

He'd probably just been extending his brand of hospitality to her, and she'd read too much into it.

It was better this way, she rationalized yet again. Keeping it professional was the only way to keep her head screwed on tight while doing the job assigned to her.

Saving Dunia from Massimo Makori's greed was her priority.

So why did her heart yearn in defiance of her well-thought-out argument?

8

On The Cusp of A Thousand Worlds

SELENE

Selene, Mirage, and the five Edenite men dove deeper into negotiations and deal-making with Rina and the Council on Dunia.

Mirage had set up a series of direct, secure channels between the rebel leaders at various locations on Dunia and The Sable Riders HQ.

They discussed armaments, ships, AI, drones, troops, xentium, and strategy for hours until they brokered the final details of an arrangement that made sense to everyone.

'Are we all agreed?' Kainan asked both parties, those in the room and the Free Dunia Council on the planet.

There was a chorus of affirmative agreement, and the negotiations closed.

The assembly on Dunia said their goodbyes, and their secure feed's holo screen winked out.

Selene let her head fall to the back of her chair.

She was beyond exhausted.

She was ready to crawl into bed and sleep for weeks.

She'd zero energy for another night at The Osirian bar, decadent and thrilling though it promised to be. Instead, she was flat and drained; the last thing she needed was to pretend she was not.

Especially as she'd sat across from the man whose presence was still causing a kick to her core every time he spoke or moved in her peripheral vision.

She was about to ask Kainan for an escort back to the apartment suite when a loud warning klaxon rang through the conference room.

Her eyes flew open as her heart thudded against her chest.

In an instant, all five Sable Riders snapped to their feet, and their hands slid to the weapons on their hips.

'Mirage, report!' Kainan said, his face taut with wariness.

'There's been a breach of the building, *khosi*,' Mirage said, her tone faint. 'And of my systems too. We've been hacked. I've put up a wall so your neural nodes are secure. However, I can't stop the wave - it's weakening me. So I'm shutting down to -.'

The AI's voice trailed off, and Selene gazed in horror as the gyrfalcon, perched on her post, fell with a thud to the floor.

The lights in the room flickered, and the foundation they stood on rocked as an explosion roared through the building.

The primary doors of The Osirian Bar below them flew open, and Selene gasped as a group of dark, shadowed assailants poured into the space.

Klaxons kept blaring as the staff fled into the kitchens beyond a set of activated shield gates.

The attackers turned to face the security drones and guards who'd surged in behind them.

'What are we waiting for, *khosi*?' Kage grumbled, looking to Kainan, eager to counter the ambush.

Kainan placed the unconscious gyrfalcon form onto the table, then stalked to the glass view windows, his gaze fixed on the mayhem below. 'Let's see what they've got first, brothers, and what they're after. If our watchmen and quadcopters can't fend them off, we go in.'

Zane shook his head. 'Thank *fokk*, this happened before opening time, so the only people in the restaurant and bar beneath are our servers and bartenders.'

More blasts quaked through the air.

'Who the hell are these *fokkers*?' Riv ground out, balancing himself as the floor beneath their feet shuddered.

'They're not here for the good food and wine on offer, that's for sure,' Zane said between clenched teeth as he witnessed his establishment get blasted.

'Is this limited to just us?' Kainan asked the blue-eyed Rider. 'Can you check?'

'*Naam*, *khosi*,' Zane said. He closed his eyes and touched his right thumb and forefinger together, summoning a force from within.

Selene's eyes widened as Zane's own opened, revealing a wildness of blue energy arcs.

He tipped his head back, and the lightning-like arches reached into the air, scouring an unseen realm.

'What's he doing?' she whispered.

Kainan sliced his eyes towards her. 'Nothing to worry

about, *khamila*. He's tapping into his psionic sight. With Mirage out, his mind can travel between different dimensions and universes and cross over disparate planes of existence, spanning various forms of reality. In this case, he's searching the entire rock for other attacks.'

Selene shook her head in disbelief, watching as the blue force died down in Zane's eyes.

He closed his eyes again, and when he opened them, they were back to their meta-like glow.

He swayed from his recent effort. 'The attack is isolated. There's no other over the metro or the moon planet.'

'*Sante*,' Kainan clipped.

The sound of more explosions in the bar atrium below them dragged away Selene's attention—weapons discharged, shooting bolts of energy throughout the space.

The assailants prowled the room, blasting their lasers at any moving thing, including the security drones and defenders who poured into the area.

The newcomers fought with callous precision, making Selene's blood run cold.

'Bastards!' Kage ground out as one of The Osirian's protection personnel dropped.

'Not just bastards,' Kainan said. 'I've spotted something. Zoom in on their faces or rather lack of any.'

The Sable Riders went still as their irises contracted and their neuro nodes processed the data. They all shared a long look and an even longer neuro-linked conversation.

'What is it?' Who are they?' Selene called out, unable to stand the suspense anymore.

'Crats,' Kainan growled. 'The Technocracy.'

Selene's heart fell. 'Which means they're here for me.'

Kainan gave her a wry nod. 'Maybe so. Now that we know what we're up against, we need to get down there,' he said. 'Kage, you take the lead. I'll be right behind you.'

'Hell yeah!' Kage said, thundering towards the shelved walls. 'We'll require heavier firepower than handguns to counter the crats' weapons.'

He touched a hidden panel to the left, placing his eye on the camera above it for a biometric reading.

The wall detached and swung inward to reveal a second inner room, an arsenal hold.

Its partitions seemed secured with reinforced panels able to withstand bladed and blunt weapon attacks.

Selene noted that the higher levels of the weapon room's versatile display setup displayed a sequence of heirlooms and antique firearms inside clear fire-resistant containers.

Below, on the neo-steel modular gun rack system, hung a series of modern pulse rifles, multi-function weapons capable of firing low-velocity pellets and ballistic projectiles, laser guns, and handguns.

Stacked sword firearms were also accessible on a high-density vertical storage unit for quick and easy reach.

Kage, Zane, and Xion each reached for a sleek rifle and dashed toward the glass elevator. On his way past Kainan, Kage tossed one of the lethal firearms to his *khosi*, who caught it with ease.

Selene scrambled for her bag, trying to keep calm.

Another series of detonations shook the building, and she stumbled, falling back into a solid embrace.

'I've got you,' Kainan rumbled, holding onto her as she regained balance. He turned her around to face him. 'We designed this room with high-security, pulse-resistant ballistic panels that withstand small arms and bladed weapon attacks. They can't come in, but you can't leave until this firefight ends. 'Til then, you wait here.'

She gave him a steady look. 'You all go. I can take care of myself.'

'*Nada*,' he pushed back. 'You stay with one of us, always!'

'Riv, you're with Selene, brother,' Kainan commanded.

The man nodded, his magnificent sheath of dead straight silver hair shimmering about his pale face. Satisfied, Kainan jerked his chin at Selene before streaking after his friends.

Riv turned his white, irised eyes towards Selene.

'Want to see the show?' he whispered with a small smile. Despite his nonchalance, she sensed he was the most dangerous of the five Sable Riders.

He strolled to the glass wall, and she followed, albeit skeptical about the violence taking place below being termed a production.

The mayhem was something to behold.

The balance of power shifted when the Sable Riders landed on the ground floor.

The four men disappeared into a blur, their feet kicking, their arms landing heavy blows, and their laser rifles pulsing rhythmically as they moved through the room so fast Selene couldn't get a fix on them.

Moments later, the attackers fell back, unable to withstand the relentless punishment of the fleet-footed team.

The Sable Riders seemed to flit in and out of sight, and she thought she witnessed Kainan's body blur into a cloud of shimmering gold energy, almost like he'd de-materialized.

She shook her head. *Impossible*, she thought. It must have been a detonation of some kind, clouding her view.

As the fight intensified, furniture and banquettes exploded, chairs flew, and Jarok's bar rose in flames.

'Zane will be weeping now,' Riv murmured. 'He spent a year searching for the right color of Ebuli onyx for that counter.'

The enemy sent another wave of crats hurtling into the room, and they, too, were hammered.

With a pull and click, the four Sable Riders' weapons turned into energy swords, cutting like butter through the crats' metal limbs and torsos.

Riv grunted in approval. 'Seems the high price we paid for those Ccyth sword pulse rifles was worth it.'

He was a cool customer, Selene thought, flicking him a glance.

Her eyes strayed back to the restaurant floor as the fighting slowed.

At long last, it seemed all the attackers were down.

The Sable Riders appeared unharmed as they stalked around the room, checking the fallen enemy bodies for weapons.

Selene observed Kainan shout out, and staff ran into the devastated room to tend to the injured sec team members.

Then, the four Sable Riders did something unexpected.

They each found a crat and reached into their severed and broken craniums. They pulled something from the inner reaches of the bionic skulls and focused on the prizes in their hands.

'What are they doing?' Selene asked.

Riv lifted a hand to let her know he was waiting to learn more, cocking his head as his neuro node fired up.

In moments, he turned to her. 'We've all just linked with

the crats' nodes. We can confirm that they were sent here for you. We also think they slipped into the metro dome disguised as Falasian merchants. Our location was given to them by an accomplice resembling a staff member of one of Rhesus' well-known families.'

'What does a Rhesian House have to do with me?' Selene asked.

Kainan caught her words as he strode back into the conference room towards the pair standing by the glass windows.

'That Rhesian Dynasty, which incidentally is Uba Villan's family, is linked to the Makoris,' Kainan filled them in. 'She's most likely our leak after our previous night encounter.'

Selene's brow furrowed in disbelief. 'That was only 24 hours ago? How would this have happened so fast?'

'It's simple,' Kainan said. 'She, or someone associated with her, sent a message to Massimo last night that bounced to one of the Technocracy ships blocking Dunia, which is not too far from a capital ship. It wouldn't have taken long to organize a small infiltration horde, intercept a Falasian ship, and here we are.'

'Which proves hell hath no fury than a woman scorned, in this case, one woman,' Riv said as Zane, Xion, and Kage walked back in.

Selene couldn't help but touch Kainan's forearm with concern. 'Are you all right?'

He gazed down at her hand, which lay still on his arm, then back into her eyes.

She flushed with embarrassment and pulled away. Yet another sign from him that he wanted to keep a clear distance between them.

'I'm fine. We all are,' Kainan clipped. 'Only three of our

security team were injured, none seriously. The one person wounded in this clash was Mirage.'

They turned to look at the inert gyrfalcon, alone and vulnerable on the conference table.

Selene stared at it with worry. 'She'll come back to us, won't she?'

'She must, and she will,' Kainan said, walking over to the expansive desk where the silvery creature lay.

Just then, the sound of a crackle and hum filled the room. The holo screen buzzed, winked, and lit up, and the feathers on the gyrfalcon fluttered. The chrome raptor then stood upright.

'*Khosi? Khosi?*' came a far-off tinny voice.

'Mirage?' Kainan called, peering with concern at his close companion. 'Are you OK?'

'I'm fine, *khosi*. First, I shut down before they did much damage. Then, I managed to circumvent the breach and launch a counterhack. But it feels like I'll need some serious repair work shortly.'

Selene sighed under her breath while Kainan breathed out in relief. He reached a hand to stroke the gyrfalcon's feathers as Riv nodded in approval.

'I'll get you back to full working order soon enough,' Kage ground out.

'The hack revealed a few things,' Mirage said.

'What did you find out?' Zane asked.

'It's The Technocracy,' the AI said.

'We're across that already, Mirage,' Kainan said. 'We interfaced with their nodes and found who betrayed Selene's location. What else can you add?'

'The ship they used to get onto Eden II, a refitted rattler

fashioned into a Falasian cruiser, flew out of port several minutes ago, but I can't be sure of its trajectory yet in the system.'

'Get a satellite drone on it,' Kainan commanded.

'*Naam, khosi.* We have lost precious time, though, and they've probably disappeared into hyperspace. But I cannot confirm if you've terminated all the crats on Eden II's metro dome. There might be more of them hiding in the city. I won't know unless I've swept the whole place. Until then, I recommend that Her Excellency Selene be removed from the city and situated in new and secure accommodation.'

'Does that mean I can't return to Dunia?' Selene ventured.

'*Nada*,' came Kainan's curt reply.

'You're afraid The Technocracy may still be prowling the System,' she deduced.

'*Naam.* We're not quite ready to face them. We also don't want to risk crossing the blockade. Given we're not yet ramped up for the battle to knock them out to get you home, if they detect us,' Kainan said. 'We have to keep you on Eden II until we can be sure it's safe to return.'

'Then where shall I go?'

The Sable Riders fell hush, their eyes locked together in a silent discussion.

Kainan gave Selene a decisive look. 'J'Urg Mihòr.'

'Where's that?' Selene asked Kainan.

Riv answered her instead. 'The dark side of the moon. Where it feels like you're on the cusp of a thousand worlds.'

As soon as Kainan declared Selene's new destination, things began to move rapidly.

A Sable Group assistant was dispatched to gather Selene's duffle bag from the apartment suite and load it onto Kainan's Corvette.

Meanwhile, Selene made a secure comm call to Rina to update her on the recent attack. Her best friend was concerned, but Selene reassured her she was safe.

Mirage prepped her ship for departure, and The Sable Riders confabbed subvocally among themselves.

After a few minutes, Kainan lifted a hand, and Selene turned off her comm tab. 'For your sake, I'll run through the current sitrep,' he told her. 'Kage, you're in charge of prepping the armada. Xion, you'll recruit the crews, troops, and fighters while working with our sec teams to maintain peace in all domes. Riv, you'll make sure we're all well armed for the inevitable battle, and Zane -.'

'- He'll be crying over his destroyed onyx table,' Riv mocked, ducking as his slighted brother leaned over to slap the back of his silver-haired head.

The Riders, bar Zane, smirked.

Kainan continued with a slight smile on his face. 'Zane, you're on supplies, moving schills around, and assisting Xion and Kage to sniff out any more crats and security leaks we may have missed. I'll liaise with Mirage and Selene to secure the flight paths, find the best route for fighting the crats, storming their blockade, and slipping an entire armada unseen and undetected into Dunia's airspace. We'll also collaborate on a plan to launch simultaneous attacks on key facilities, coordinating with the Free Dunia Council on the planet.'

He turned his wildfire eyes towards Selene. 'You're with me.'

She nodded, wrapping her arms around herself in a futile effort to ward off the sudden panic inside her. *What would be the outcome of all these rapid-fire decisions? Would they work?*

Likewise, it didn't help that her anxiety was interlaced with the nervousness of being alone with Kainan again.

The pair said their farewells, and then Kainan led her to the elevator, which sank a few levels and opened onto a bland corridor.

'We're now in the underground passages of the metro dome,' he told her. 'It's safer than exposing ourselves on the surface to get to the spaceport.'

They walked through the dimly lit maze of passageways that trailed off to other ingresses unknown.

The tunnels were spacious, sleek, and modern. But they overlapped, and Kainan took sudden turns and corners she couldn't quite grasp herself. Had she been alone, Selene was sure she'd have been lost in the confusing network of conduits and arteries.

After what seemed like an age, they stopped outside a portal. A bank of polished helmets rested on a rack against the wall.

Below them, a series of exo space suits, jackets, and anti-grav boots.

'Wear this,' Kainan instructed, thrusting a clear plex helmet into her hands. 'It's a short dash to Mirage on the exterior that airlock,' he murmured. 'We won't need a full meta suit.'

She fumbled with the helmet's straps until he stepped forward and took it from her.

A jolt surged through her, aware of his massive frame looming. She shivered as his unmistakable heat and intoxicating scent rolled off him in waves.

Their eyes clashed, and the wildfire flecks of his glowing irises made her want to squeeze shut her own, but she was powerless even to move a single muscle.

Then he bent his head and halted, his lips hovering just above hers.

She stopped breathing.

'Only a fool tests the depth of a watercourse with both feet,' he rasped. 'And your river, *khamila*, is so wild it would pull me in body and soul. Then it would extinguish my fire and drown me.'

He ran a hot finger down one edge of her face and then pressed his mouth to the border of her mouth. Her heart was hammering so fast in her chest that she heard it drumming inside her ears.

The vortex between them broke off when he pulled back and placed the headgear over her head, cutting off their connection.

Her visor snapped shut.

Kainan toggled the controls to the tiny oxygen pack at the back of the helmet. She heard a hiss of air and static and then observed him tugging on his visor over his dark-haired crown.

'Can you hear me?' he asked as if he just hadn't flung another of his sudden chimeric storms in her direction.

She nodded.

He handed her a voluminous space jacket, which she shrugged over her jumpsuit and coat.

'Mirage is a few klicks outside this chamber. Hold on to your gear, and I'll grasp on to you.'

They proceeded into the airlock, which whooshed shut behind them. Then, using his wrist comm, Kainan activated the sensors on the other side. It slid open, and they proceeded through.

Into a deep black, expansive sky dotted with jewels of stars and Dunia's emerald profile. She sensed the weightlessness at once, and her feet just touched the fine, silvery talcum powder blanketing the surface.

With Kainan's strong arm banded around her waist, they moved through Eden II's bleak, barren beauty while the metro dome receded from view behind them.

She surveyed the breathtaking scenery. The moon's terrain was rocky, with craters and mountains stretching as far as the eye could see.

She spotted Dunia in the distance, an aquamarine marble hanging in the blackness of space.

She took in the magnificence of the spectacle and leaned into the potent man striding by her side. It was a perfect moment, one she wished she could capture forever.

He pulled her closer, and she strung a hand over his chest for purchase. Her heart leaped, and her core clenched with desire, so strong was her attraction to him.

His steady breathing sounded against her cheek, and she wondered for a beat what it would be like to wake to those breaths every morning.

Would she lean over him and steal a kiss? Would he open his sapphire gold eyes and embrace her? Perhaps nuzzle her neck, stroke her arms, and dot fiery kisses down her body? Would he –

She shook her head free of the fantasy as Mirage's sleek form materialized before them.

Hell. *What was she thinking?*

Despite her internal, unseen battle, she reacted to him as he kept his steely hold on her up the air stairs, into the waiting ship and its secure airlock.

Returning to Mirage meant reverting to gravity. Selene's feet settled on the ship's floor, not just because of the change in environment but also because of the inevitable loss of Kainan's physicality.

He stalked ahead, and she followed through the preflight sequence with Mirage's voice and Kainan's timbre in the far background.

She fought to tamp down her uncontrolled reaction to his presence and the surging awareness of being alone with him for a significant time over the next few days or weeks.

As the ship lifted off into the dark skies above Eden II, Selene wrestled her feelings back into control. Overthinking the unknown would be counterproductive, and stopping the fantasies once and for all would be prudent.

She called out to the ship's AI, hoping for a distraction. 'Mirage, please tell me more about where we're headed.'

The intelligence, confined to the ship while its gyrfalcon form was in repairs, answered. 'J'Urg Mihòr is an extensive mountain ridge – one of the loneliest points on our moon,' the AI told Selene. 'It's found on the other end of the biggest lunar plain, and the journey there, without a fast craft, is not for the fainthearted. The approach can only be achieved from the south. Even with a smaller flyer, all the routes are long and arduous, which has made it a favorite destination for long-range moonwalkers who take a slower three-night hike. Likewise, for the competitive types drawn to the appeal of a brutal one-day assault to the foot of the mountains in jacked-up racers or pleasure yachts.'

Mirage paused for a moment and then continued, 'It's also the starting point for the famous Eden II Endurance race.'

Selene was intrigued. 'The Endurance Race?'

'*Naam*, Selene. The biggest racing challenge in the Pegasi system. It's a trial test where the best pinnace navigators seek to break records for the one-million-mile race around Eden II's wider orbit. Entrants don't need any previous piloting experience. Divided into 21 legs, it features between 10 and 20 solo races. Pilots can choose to complete the full circumnavigation or select individual legs.'

'And who's behind the challenge?' Selene asked.

'It's organized by a committee that includes Xion and Zane. The panel raises the sponsor fees to supply a fleet of support yachts, each with a qualified pilot, first aid, food, and even a med bay to assist the racers.'

'Interesting. I'd love to watch it one day,' Selene responded, looking out of the holo screen onto a silver, cold wilderness featuring dead volcanoes, impact craters, and dried-up lava flows from eons gone by.

'It's quite the spectacle, I can assure you. You should know that Kainan and Kage won the grand prize title three years ago with a yacht Kainan designed himself.'

'Is that right?' Selene murmured, intrigued.

'Enough, Mirage,' Kainan warned.

The AI obeyed, falling mute. Selene, too, read the room and the tense set of the Edenite's shoulders.

The ship skimmed the landscape's surface, coasting over

the crusted rocky crust covered with regolith, molten rock plains, and lunar mares. The light dipped until only the jewels of stars and celestial bodies were visible in the cloaked skies above.

'Does anyone live out here?' Selene asked.

Kainan remained silent, lost in thought.

Mirage piped up instead. '*Naam.* A handful of brave residents and those who can afford the costs of setting up their biomes. There are also a few moonwalk replenishment stations for stop-overs at convenient locations throughout the flatlands.'

'What about this J'Urg Mihòr place? Is it inhabited?'

Kainan stirred and replied, not looking at her. 'Only by the owners of the mountain ridge. It's all private. It runs along the mountain's apex, reached by a flyer or craft like this one. A minimal number of ships are permitted access.'

Selene took in the shared information, mulling over it for a handful of minutes until her mind began to shut down, so she let her head fall back to the chair rest.

Kainan's gold-flecked eyes sliced over to her. He gave a long look and then commanded. 'Sleep. I'll wake you when we arrive.'

She had just enough energy to nod, and soon, her eyes closed, and the world around her fell away.

II

You are only truly alive when you
live among the stars

9

A Lair in Eden

SELENE

The sky was immense, dark, dotted with fireballs, meteors, and falling stars that whirled past so fast she became light-headed.

Selene stood before the vast expanse, transfixed and spellbound by the sheer magnitude of the scenery.

Only thick sheeted glass separated her from the uninhabited realm beyond. Yet still, she was small, a tiny creature, placed in the center of a wild, unadulterated, starlit megacosm.

She cast her eyes over the shadowy, black mountain ridge and then below her to the oceans of silver-laced sand that rolled almost in waves against the base of the soaring crags.

The fine, powdered sand had a potency of its own.

It whipped and danced in powerful energy surges as if magnetized and rippling to the tune of a fearsome, invisible force beneath the moon's surface.

The same overwhelming storm ratcheted her heart rate and pulse through her veins.

She held a hand to her chest and gave in to the moonscape's thundering power.

Moments later, she was distracted by a slight sound.

She shifted to see Kainan bring in the last load from his ship, parked in the shuttle bay built into the mountainside.

A few minutes ago, they landed on a pad that stretched out from a mountainous ridge face.

A magnetized walkway had enticed Selene into an ample cavernous space dominated by a soaring transparent force field.

The view had since bewitched her.

Kainan reached her side and glanced down at her, their eyes clashing.

He broke the shared gaze and turned his head back to the scenery.

'Welcome to my home,' he murmured.

'It's beautiful,' she breathed. '*Sante* for taking me in.'

He inclined his head. 'Anything to keep you safe.'

'Do you live on this ridge alone?' Selene asked, her eyes pulled back to the magnificence outside.

Kainan shook his head and jerked his chin to point towards the crags beyond that had formed over millennia into a pinnacled semi-circle.

'Each Sable Rider owns their crest, and we have our lairs within. You can't pick them with the naked eye because, like my own, they all have camouflaged screens that protect the interiors on the edge of the summit range.'

He then turned away from her and strode deeper into the space, which was just as sublime as the view outside. She swiveled around, her eyes tracking him. She followed, drawing a deep breath as the interior unveiled itself.

It was quite the revelation of the man himself, she thought.

The large room, a machine-hewn cave carved into the barefaced rock of the mountain ridge, was divided into generous sections.

An expansive fireplace forged of blackened metal separated the open-plan living and dining spaces.

The cave's milky white marble walls were exact forms of right angles and precise vertical columns. The surfaces alternated between smooth planes with stunning engravings etched into the rock in stratified waves that created a sense of motion.

At the center of the cave was a lounge space that featured a sunken custom-made sectional sofa that was the widest and deepest she'd ever seen. The couch was adorned with throw pillows and flanked by charming cocktail tables. A rug of sea green ping tai moss accented the polished stone floor.

To the far left, she spotted an exquisite sculpture of a space nymph, a cloud-shaped mirror, brass armchairs upholstered in a luxurious fabric, two antique leather fauteuils, and a vintage coiled Falasian tribal stool.

Large mixed-media artworks that captured the skies above Eden II hung on stone walls throughout the space.

She could tell that most were by the same artist, including an oversized canvas over the fireplace that depicted the silvery orb of Eden II hanging amid a sea of swirling stars.

Also displayed was a series of delicate art drawings in

smaller frames

Ranging from aeronautical designs to spaceship blueprints and patent schematics by the same artisan, going by the similar-looking scrawled signature on each exquisite piece.

The set-up was not just old furniture but a curated selection of clean-lined furnishings and masterpieces warmed up with ever-so-subtle touches, luxurious upholstery, and well-worn loved details.

A rare white wood table and carved bronze-like chairs took pride of place in the eating area.

Beyond the living and dining area, and to the front of the cavernous space, was an undercover infinity pool.

It fell away into the nothingness of the force field view and invited her to step in and indulge in its warm and lit waters.

Her eyes fell on a terrace and sports court far beyond a set of glass doors that spanned high up into the expansive ceiling.

She took in a long corridor that wound its way next to the elongated force field that ran the front length of the home.

It gave the dwelling a sense of openness and fluidity, as if the space was one with the sky.

It was clear this was Kainan's hideaway, where he could express his tastes and experiment with bold ideas while displaying the art and antiques he treasured the most.

She scanned it all, swiveling her head from side to side, sauntering from piece to piece, savoring them with her eyes.

Kainan stood at the massive kitchen bench, an ankle crossed over the other and arms banded across his chest.

His eyes tracked her as she wandered through his space with a hooded gaze.

After a beat, Selene turned to face her host.

'It's magnificent,' she told him.

He dipped his head, and his shoulders seemed to relax.

Her opinion held some weight with him, she thought, and somehow, her spirits lifted for knowing this.

Maybe he, too, was feeling something, like she and her estimation of him mattered, even if they were doing their best not to act on those feelings.

'I'll show you to our room,' he said, breaking into her thoughts. 'This way.'

He pushed off the bench and crossed the room.

He lifted her bag from the floor of the entrance hall where he'd placed it when they'd first arrived and took panther-like strides toward the corridor.

She followed behind him, still mesmerized by the view outside the force field and the awe-inspiring artwork inside.

She slowed at the sight of one canvas depicting the transcendent landscape of a far-off galaxy planet lit by a dying star.

The colors were a mix of bright golds, autumn oranges, and ethereal fuchsias. The painting was awash with movement, color, and passion, and she lost her breath at its intensity.

Kainan looked over his shoulder and backtracked to where Selene stood, her torso leaning into the exquisite gloss textile in flux.

'Dusk in Death,' she said, reading the tag on the painting.

'It's captivating,' she whispered, her eyes sweeping over the starry surface that shifted and glowed in the strange reflective light of Eden II.

'What makes it look so alive?' she asked.

'Metanoids and moon dust infused paint. It adds motion and life to the artwork.'

'Fascinating. Who's the artist?' she asked, glancing up at

Kainan.

He closed his molten eyes, and she sensed an uncomfortable shift.

'You don't have to tell me if you don't want to,' she called out.

He pushed a hand through his long locks, his eyes not quite meeting hers.

Why would this giant, colossal warrior be shy? she wondered.

A thought occurred to her, and she raised a brow. 'It's you, isn't it?'

He huffed under his breath. 'Let's get you settled,' he clipped, turning as if to walk away.

She caught the sleeve of his jumpsuit, and he shied away from her, staring down at their shared connection.

She lifted her hand off him.

'You're not embarrassed, are you?' she continued, refusing to be perturbed.

He hunched his massive shoulders.

'There's no need to be,' she said. 'They're amazing.'

He stared at her for a moment. 'You think so?' he murmured.

She nodded, studying his face.

'You've never shown them to anyone else, have you?' she probed.

He shrugged again, and she smiled.

'You've nothing to worry about,' she said, sweeping a hand toward the wall where other similar artworks were suspended. 'These would sell like hot Sinoni cakes at the best and most established galleries on Dunia and Rhesus.'

'I don't paint or draw for money,' he grumbled, his molten eyes flashing.

She studied him for a moment.

'I get that,' she accepted. 'But please don't hide these beauties away. Millions would travel thousands of light years to see them hung up and displayed. That's how incredible they are.'

'That remains to be seen,' he murmured, walking away and down the corridor.

She followed him at a pace, pausing at every canvas while shaking her head at the stunning artistry captured in each one.

'When do you get the time to paint and draw these, let alone run an entire metro dome and moon?' she called after him.

'There's always time to burn when you're hovering in space waiting for the next privateer or raider to rattle past.'

He'd stopped and leaned against a doorway that opened into a large bed chamber.

He jerked his chin, signaling that she step through.

She slipped past him, keeping a safe distance between them before looking around at the new space.

The room featured a coral-stone wall, against which was set a luxurious, wide bed upholstered in dark gold fabric.

A vintage Rhesian chandelier was mounted over the bed. It was grouped with side tables from the south of Dunia, inset lamps, and an antique bench at its foot.

A smart plex window also flicked from opaque to transparent at the touch of a button to let in or shut out the soaring lunar view.

'Nice,' she said with a smile. 'Is this my crash pad, or am I kicking you out of your room?'

'My room is two doors away,' he confirmed. 'This is one of three guest rooms. Your bath chamber is also attached.'

He pointed to a set of antique wooden entryways to the far right of the room. They soared to the stone ceiling and were carved with twisting vines, flowers, and ancient emblems.

Selene had noticed similar portals throughout the cave structure and recognized them as Paladian antiques, salvaged from the historical cities that had dotted the lost empire's planet.

They were rare and valuable, and the ones in Kainan's home were warped and leaning from centuries of load-bearing, splintered, cracked, and granular. Yet they shone and gleamed with polish, evidence of the care their owner placed on them.

Her host tossed her bag onto the end of the bed.

'I'll let you settle in,' he told her. 'Take your time, even a nap, if necessary.'

She was heading towards her bag when he half-turned to leave. 'Can I get you anything else?'

'*Nada*, please,' she said with a slight wave of her hand. 'I'll be fine.'

He gave her a careful once-over. 'Your room is more than comfortable. Inside, you'll find everything you need. Drink some water, too, and maybe have something to eat. There are some snacks on the credenza. I have several more things to finalize, but I'll be done soon and make us a meal in a few hours.'

She nodded, a tad overwhelmed.

He stalked out of the room in his typical soundless fashion, and the door slid shut.

Selene shook her head. *Message sent and received.*

It was clear Kainan was in no mood for chatter or pleas-antries.

No matter, for she, too, was barely holding on to civility.

There was only so much she could take of his presence without embarrassing herself.

She found a water cooler and exquisite crystal glasses on a carved sideboard.

She drank her fill and then sighed as it cooled her insides.

Beside it was a bowl of tempting fruits and snacks.

She couldn't be bothered to eat now.

All she needed was to bathe, lie down, rest her mind, and reorganize her wild thoughts.

She exhaled and stretched her hands over her head, weariness leaking through her system.

The nap during their flight from Eden II's citadel hadn't been long enough, and the thought of an extended bath and an even longer siesta seemed like a great idea.

It didn't take her too much time to unpack her meager bag and slip out of her stale clothes and boots.

Sliding into a robe, she stepped towards the wooden doors, caressing the breathtaking carved handles before flinging them open.

She gasped in delight. The bath chamber was more than just any old wash closet.

Mirrors covered the walls from floor to ceiling.

Against one wall was a shelf with towels and robes. The other featured a stunning washbasin with brass tapware and all the washing accouterments one needed.

That all faded into the background when Selene took in the oversized sunken bath in the middle of the room that glimmered with low underwater lights.

It could fit four or five people.

She grinned, shedding her robe and stepping into the

lowered pool with adjustable air and water jets. She sank into the warm water with a sigh.

She took a long bath, and her body sank lower with each minute spent soaking.

Much later, she dragged herself out of the water with a groan.

Then, she walked naked into the bedchamber and fell onto the enveloping duvet.

She let her head roll back on the sculpted pillow and closed her eyes.

In moments, she was fast asleep.

Selene woke with a start. She sat up in the vast bed and rubbed her eyes.

How long had she been out?

Glancing around her new chamber, she couldn't spot any chrono or timepiece and sighed. Then her tummy rumbled, and she was overwhelmed with ravenous hunger.

She dressed in a loose lounge suit and slid her feet into the old, comfortable leather slippers she always carried with her on her travels.

Then, she slipped out of the impressive room and meandered into the expansive living area.

It was empty, but she spied a covered platter on the kitchen counter.

Food, glorious food.

She rushed to the marbled edifice and lifted the cover.

It revealed a delicious array of olives, cheese, bread, pickled vegetables, sliced meats, and tiny sausages. She danced with delight at the enticing sight.

Starved, she used her fingers to stuff her mouth.

While she ate, she glanced outside, but the darkened view beyond the large windows gave little indication of time. Instead, she concentrated on filling her growling stomach.

'You like my chow then?'

Selene whirled around to tag Kainan, who was lounging against the far wall of the kitchen. She coughed, her mouth full of cheese and bread.

Then she choked.

He moved, opening a doorway to a cool room from which he retrieved a decanter.

Nabbing a tumbler, he prowled towards her and set the two pieces on the counter, pouring water and handing the carafe to her.

She scrambled for the glass and slugged the liquid down, spluttering as it spilled between her lips.

She bent over to regain her composure, coughing until the spasm in her throat passed.

Moments later, she righted herself to meet the twinkling gaze of the amused Edenite.

'Bastard! You surprised me!'

He lifted an eyebrow. 'Is that how you address your knight on a Corvette charger?'

Selene scoffed, charmed, as well as flummoxed. 'Knight, my ass. You shocked me.'

'You allowed yourself to be surprised, *khamila.* I thought

by now you'd have learned to practice situational awareness everywhere you go.'

'*Fokk* you!' she flung at him with a smile, raising a middle finger in his face.

His eyes heated, and then he seemed to shake off a deep, unspoken emotion with a grin.

'Kahawa?' he proffered. 'I'll make you one as a peace offering.'

'It'd better be the best damn *kahawa* this side of Pegasi for me to forgive you.'

She tracked him as he moved about his kitchen with ease, pulling a bag from the larder, filling the grinder, and tamping down the spiced beans for a rich, buttery brew.

'What time is it?' she asked.

'1000 Standard. You slept through the equivalent of a night, planet-side,' he replied.

'No wonder I'm so hungry,' Selene inhaled, still picking at the delicious cheese and olives.

She looked up to find him watching her with a loaded look. A delicious heat burned between them, and she glanced back at her snack plate.

'Do you want more? I can always make us a full breakfast if you wish.'

She took stock of her hunger status and nodded.

'I like that. A woman of healthy appetites,' Kainan said, placing a steaming cup of dark kahawa before her.

'Wouldn't you like to know?' she teased, then blushed at his low, rumbling laugh.

He seemed more open and relaxed this morning, and she welcomed the chimeric change.

She thought he must have slept well, too, preferring this

version of the Rider to his otherwise brooding self.

The undeniable truth was that she got a kick from talking to him when he opened up as he had on the evening they'd spent at The Osirian.

She'd relished his company that night.

He was a great conversationalist who, when he wasn't giving off recluse vibes, made her mind whirl with new ideas and concepts.

Since meeting him, she'd never needed to dumb down her words or adjust her attitude for him.

Most Dunian men had agreed with her because she was the Prime's daughter.

They rarely spoke with her; if they did, it was with condescension or flattery.

Many still avoided romantic overtures because they feared offending the Prime himself.

Kainan was different.

He seemed to enjoy the sincerity of their dialogue.

While he respected her, he didn't seem to care about kowtowing to her or, on the other extreme, mansplaining.

More so, she was attracted to him, and her heart raced whenever he was around her.

She had no idea what she would do if he touched her again, but her body longed for the feel of his lean fingers with their light dusting of deep caramel hair across the top.

Fingers, she studied as he prepared golden eggs, toasted pan bread, and a selection of fresh fruits to accompany the decadent meal.

She was a bit flustered by her reaction to him.

No matter how much she told herself that he needed to be put into the '*business only*' box, she was conscious that she desired him with an unfathomable potency that terrified her.

He intrigued, challenged, annoyed, and made her feel more alive than ever.

But now was not the time to explore her feelings further.

So, with a sigh, she tucked into the delectable repast he'd set in front of her. At the same time, she was willing her mind to focus on what had brought her to Eden II.

Selene walked into Kainan's study, a room lined with books, some ancient, some collectibles.

He stood before a bank of holo screens flickering with data, telemetry, news feeds, and winking maps. He turned and jerked his chin at her in greeting.

'Hey,' she called out. 'May I please send a tight beam to Rhesia?'

Kainan whirled around to face her, his eyes narrowed. 'A tight beam?'

'It's the one thing I must do before our meetings today,' she warned. 'I must contact the Rhesian King and tell him our plans.'

'Why?'

'As part of the pact Dunia signed with Rhesia many years ago, I have to inform them, as our allies, of any military or defensive-related programs we undertake. Especially if they have to do with a third foreign or alien government that could upset the balance of power in the System.'

'Do they have to know about us?'

Selene sighed. 'I can try and keep The Sable Group out of my update with them, but I'm sure they'll figure it out somehow.'

'What will they say about you working with us instead of reaching out to them?' Kainan countered.

'I don't think they can do much to help us even if I insist on it,' Selene told him. 'It's not a well-kept secret that Rhesia, for all its champagne and baubles, is in economic strife.'

'What do you know?' the Rider probed.

'For centuries, the Rhesians relied on mining orhial, their fuel source similar to Earth's coal. It's been depleted in most mines for a few years now, which is why they came to us for the supply of xentium a couple of months ago. We agreed to send it to them, but not enough for their entire planet's needs.'

Kainan raised an eyebrow. 'I can tell you're apprised of their situation.'

'You're not surprised to hear what I just said, so you know they're in trouble.'

He shrugged.

'That said,' Selene continued, 'They've left their negoti-ations too late and are on the cusp of an energy meltdown. Why? Because they've always been reluctant to ask for help from the other planets in this Universe. The Rhesians have always been too proud to beg for what they need, arrogant in their image as the founders of the System. They've allowed much of their world to get run down and kept the extent of it secret. They wanted to maintain the semblance of sophisticated wealth when, in fact, they've been struggling for years. Because of their precarious economic position, I don't think they have the funds and resources to help us arm against The Technocracy.'

'Would they have any say in how you conduct the incursion?'

'In one word, no.'

'But you still need to comm them,' Kainan stated dryly.

'It's courtesy and part of my duty. Is it possible to reach them?' she insisted.

He gave her a wry smile. 'Anything's feasible, Selene. Anything for you.'

Kainan touched his wrist comm and turned to the large screens. 'Mirage, can you initiate a two-way tight beam comm to Rhesia? Using a random pattern encrypted with a spread spectrum? And patch it to King Auban's office?'

'*Khosi*,' the AI said. 'That's no problem. Who will be making the call, may I ask?'

'Selene.'

'And you want to hide our location and any markers?'

'Scrub the link for all Sable Group involvement. Place her in the middle of a forest on Dunia. Somewhere near the Enclave, I picked her up from.'

'*De nada.* Not a problem at all.'

Kainan raised a hand and gestured to Selene.

She walked over to him.

'Stand here,' he instructed, indicating the space in front of his screens. 'Speak straight to the camera. You'll appear as if you're on the planet at Zulu One, and your location will show the same. Do you know what you'll say, or do you need time to think it through?'

Selene closed her eyes for a moment. 'I'll be fine. Let's do it.'

The Rider stepped away and slipped into the shadows of the study. 'Go for it.'

One of the screens flickered, showing Selene standing in a clearing between a lush green meadow of trees. She recognized the scenery from Zulu One. Kainan's speakers emitted the sounds of nature, and she saw birds wheeling above her head. A rush of air fanned around her face, and a breeze ruffled her hair on-screen.

A second screen flashed to indicate that the secure beam connection was successful.

A discombobulated woman looked into the display from the Rhesian end. 'You've reached King Auban's private office. Who may I say is calling?'

'Selene Munene, from the office of the Prime of Dunia. I'm reaching out about an urgent matter. I need to speak with King Auban now, please.'

The woman gave Selene a tight smile. 'One moment.'

The screen blanked out for a beat.

Selene glanced over to the dark recesses of the study, to where Kainan stood.

She tagged his silhouette, hands crossed over his chest.

However, his molten gold eyes shone through the darkness, and a shiver ran through her.

She turned to the monitor just in time as it glimmered to reveal King Auban's face.

He was still as handsome as she remembered, yet there were a few more deep lines on his forehead, and his golden hair seemed streaked with more silver.

The Rhesian royal looked puzzled. 'Selene Munene. You're Kei'Lano's daughter. I remember you from my brother's party.'

A minor expression flitted across his brow, and Selene caught the pain and a flicker of bitterness in his eyes.

Nevertheless, he continued. 'What's so urgent that you had to reach my private line? And who gave its auth to you?'

Selene smiled to appease the man and disarm him. 'I know you've many questions, Your Highness, and I apologize for springing this on you. But I was insistent you had to hear it from me first. My father, the Prime of Dunia and your good friend, was assassinated a few days ago.'

The King drew a sharp breath, all concern for his privacy swept away. 'I wondered why all traffic to and from Dunia had been shut down. I can't believe Kei'Lano is dead. Murdered? By whom?'

'By his defense minister, Massimo Makori. Who went on to lead a coup against the government.'

The royal's face blanched. 'My dear child. I'm so very sorry for you. My deepest condolences.'

A stab of sorrow hit Selene, yet she managed to nod in acceptance. 'Thank you. Massimo had help. From The Technocracy.'

King Auban's eyes widened further still. 'The crats are in play on Dunia?'

'Yes. We believe they're after our xentium ore. I was asked to command an alliance to resist the coup. The Free Dunia Movement is now my focus. We'll marshal our troops to defend against the crats, the coup organizers, and their militia.'

'Do you have the military on your side?'

'A good part of the army, navy, and air force is still loyal to Dunia, so yes.'

The King shook his head, great worry written over his face. 'But the Technocrats, Selene. They're evil. Unstoppable.'

'Evil, yes? Unstoppable? That's yet to be seen.'

The King sat back in his chair, still concerned. 'I'll chat with my Prime Minister, Feldman Terion, and discuss how we can help. It won't be much. But I promise to try my best. Because what's to say if they prevail, that they won't come for us too?'

'Indeed, Your Highness. If you can send help, we'll take it. But for now, we'll have to act quickly. My people are dying, and we can't wait.'

'You seem very sure you can handle the crats.'

'I'm not sure of the outcome. But, I'm passionate about saving my planet - of that, I'm confident.'

King Auban considered her for a long moment. 'Go well, Selene. Fight for Dunia. Please keep me apprised of developments, and I'll liaise with you regarding our support.'

'I may be the one to reach out to you, Your Highness. Sadly, we're under a crats' blockade here, and they've shut down most of our comms.'

'So, how are you reaching me?'

'We still have some tight beam access. However, it's constrained.'

'I see. I'll wait for you to reach out.'

'Your Highness.'

The secure comm link winked out.

Selene's screen blackened, then flashed on again to show her standing once more in Kainan's study.

Selene pushed her hair back with a huge sigh. 'That was intense.'

Kainan eased off the wall he'd been leaning on and moved

towards her. 'Indeed. He wasn't alone, you know.'

'He wasn't?'

'*Nada*. I detected a shadow to his left. Perhaps an advisor. No matter; he now knows. I'm not sure what that means for you.'

'Not much,' Selene sighed. 'By the time the King organizes anything, we'll be well into executing our plans.'

'I still don't understand why the Rhesians need to know about your sovereign actions,' Kainan said low and quiet.

'My father signed a pact with them. He would have loathed it if I had ignored it. Plus, every planet in this System, except for Eden II, owes Rhesia. They were the first humans to colonize the region. They helped each new generation ship and population settle on the different planets. They gave us the technology and resources to kickstart our habitats. They made peace and cooperation pacts and honored them through the years. But, of more importance, King Auban and his father, King Bastian, were great friends of my father. The honor code between them was robust.'

'If you say so.'

'Why do you say that?'

The Edenite pursed his lips. 'I happen to think the Rhesians can be ruthless. And underhanded. Rumor has it that they funded the civil war in Alloria, providing endless assets to Rhesia to prop up its economy. I like Auban, but he seems a tad naive. While he might have had nothing to do with Alloria, he's let control slip away. His extended Royal house is in some disarray, with a series of dangerous power moves being made against him that he doesn't seem to be a step ahead of. The fact that members of his own family have it in for him is a major concern. So I'm not convinced of the

Rhesians' honorable nature.'

Selene cocked an eyebrow at Kainan. 'Sounds like you've got intel that I don't.'

'Maybe so. But it won't affect our plans. So let's focus on those for now and leave Rhesia's sob stories for another day.'

'Agreed.'

KING AUBAN - ENIA, CITY, RHESUS

Back on Rhesus, the head of the System's oldest empire rose to his feet and paced the Ghuxian fur-lined floor of his ornate office. Despite the heat of summer outside, he was cold to his bones.

'You caught what she said?'

The man he spoke to nodded. 'Very concerning indeed.'

'Can you reach out to Prime Minister Terion to find out what we can spare to help the Dunians, please?'

'I'll get to it now.'

The man exited the luxurious royal offices and walked fast through the palace. Until he got to a workspace on the opposite end of the great building, rushed inside, past a secretary's desk, and entered an inner office. He slammed the door and sank onto a couch.

He tapped a command into a comm tab and spoke with urgency.

'The Dunians have reached out. But, they're not surrendering as we'd hoped, damn them! Instead, they intend to fight the crats.'

A laugh emanated through the comm tab's speakers. 'Like they'll ever have a chance of winning!'

'I don't know about that. The Prime's daughter seemed very confident. Also, she contacted us via Auban's direct line, which I am sure no one on Dunia had.'

'Maybe Auban gave it to her father; may he rest in peace.'

'I doubt it. Somehow, her confidence, the tight beam, and access to Auban make me think she has some assistance.'

'Who from?'

'The Galicians? The Iccythrians? Who knows. Look into it. While I flap around and work with our holier-than-thou, sanctimonious, and self-righteous fool, Prime Minister Terion, to try to find anything to appease Auban's request to help them. We're thinly spread as it is, which will limit us even more.'

'Which is why we have to stay focused. We need this to be a success. For the sake of Rhesia and our hapless King.'

'The Technocracy? Will they come through for us?'

'They're the most powerful force in and out of this galaxy. So we have to believe they will.'

'To the Triumv.'

'True and sure.'

10

The Winged Horse, Pegasus

SELENE

After the tight beam call to Rhesus, Selene and Kainan huddled before a wall of holo screens that took center stage in Kainan's study.

Each screen was linked to feeds from the other Sable Riders as they patched in with their updates.

First was Kage and his preparations with the armada - getting the fleet ship shape, ready, and fueled for the coming skirmish.

He was working with Zane and Xion to manage the supplies' logistics, moving schills around to purchase what they needed.

To pull off a successful feint against the Technocracy's blockade, they'd decided to have the armada hide in the asteroid shadows just beyond Planet Alloria's rings.

Xion gave his update. He'd recruited 1000 crew members, troops, and fighters from The Sable Group's network of mercenaries on Eden II, plus a few Galician, Falasian, and Rhesian ex-soldiers and warriors.

'Are they up to the task?' Selene asked at one point.

'You can rest assured we recruit the best,' Xion told her. 'Don't forget we've hired out our services for many years, which means we have a long list of people on our books to help make this happen. To be listed as a freelance merc for Sable Riders Inc., you must maintain your tactical fitness, be certified in the latest weapons and explosive devices, and be an excellent shot.'

'Plus, be an engineering and first aid all-rounder and have the required medical checks, inoculations, and mental health training to take on our jobs,' Kage added.

'We've everyone on our books, from sensor operators to surveillance, search, and rescue teams, plus experts in surface warfare and airborne countermeasures,' Xion added.

Selene nodded in approval. 'Sounds like The Sable Riders are always on alert.'

'We have to be. Our livelihood depends on it.'

Riv reported no further signs of the crats on Eden II since the attack on The Osirian.

'We'll still need to be vigilant,' Kainan told his friends. 'They have the tech to wage a terrible war, just like we do. And if they've shared any of their tech with Massimo, we might be in bigger trouble than we thought.'

After a long day of discussions, Selene and Kainan worked with Rina and Mirage to map a safe route for the Edenite armada to slip unseen and undetected into Dunia's airspace.

'As well as our stealth tech, our corvettes and flyers are covered with a fractal coating that absorbs most radiation that hits it and scatters the rest,' Mirage announced. 'Sweep it with a sensor scan, and nothing comes back directly. So from the view of any known sensor array, we won't exist.'

They also strategized on plans to launch simultaneous attacks on critical facilities on the planet, working with Rina to digitally identify and map out each key infrastructure location the crats now controlled, with the crucial goal of improving the armada's targeting.

After hours of hard graft and with everyone on the same page, Selene sank into her seat while Kainan refilled their kahawa cups.

'I think we need a break from screens and meetings,' the hulking Edenite declared.

'I can't think straight anymore,' Selene said. 'What do you suggest?'

'I think we need to get the hell out of here,' Kainan said. 'And escape to the wide-open skies.'

Into the nether of Pegasi, they flew.

Past a swathe of satellite dwarf galaxies twinkling with a trillion stars. They streaked by colorful nebulas.

Far below them, Eden II and Dunia seemed like jewels hanging on a string of pearly stars surrounded by a spherical halo of illuminated gas embedded in an even larger circle of invisible dark matter.

Selene imagined the dark mass at Pegasi's center, remembering what she'd learned from her school days. She knew everything in this galaxy revolved around this powerful gateway to nothingness.

In its immediate surroundings was a close-packed region of dust, gas, and stars known as Pegasi's bulge. Sprinkled within the bulge were globular clusters, collections of ancient stars, and forty dwarf galaxies orbiting or colliding within the spread-out galaxy.

She sucked in air at the sight of the System's brightest star and twin sun, which formed one corner of the Square of Pegasus, once with a constellation designated δ-Peg.

'Due to Eden II's rotation, we're closer to Alphetraz, perhaps as close as you'll ever get,' Kainan said, his deep voice cutting through her reverie. 'Mirage, please come to a stop.'

The AI obeyed, and the Corvette hovered in position, hanging in space.

Kainan rose from the pilot's chair. His eyes lit with energy and, to Selene's amazement, an almost wide-eyed excitement as he gazed out of the plexiglass at the bright mass.

He joined her by the expansive view, and they stared at the whirling mass of light.

'Stunning. Even though I know it's a twin star, it looks like one gigantic sun,' Selene said.

'Tis,' Kainan told her. 'Although it appears to the naked eye as a single entity, it's a binary system composed of two stars in close orbit.'

Mirage piped up. 'The chemical composition of the brighter of the two stars is unusual as its atmosphere contains high levels of mercury, manganese, and other elements, including gallium and xenon. This makes it the brightest mercury-manganese star ever known.'

Kainan leaned into the view, his face lit up by starlight. 'Alphetraz is also called Sirrah, as well as surrat al-faras, which means the navel of the mare horse and corresponds to the winged horse, Pegasus. It's also known as one of the "Three Guides" that mark the prime meridian of the heavens, the other two being Beta Cassiopeia and Gamma Pegasi. It was believed to bless those born under its influence or those drawn close to its light with the promise of long life, love, honor, and riches.'

'We should be so lucky,' Selene murmured.

They shared a long look.

'We may yet still be, *khamila*.'

Kainan's words were heavy with promise, and Selene shivered, glancing up at the vast pulsing star.

'How about a drop of Galician whiskey to seal that promise?' he murmured.

'Sounds like a good idea.'

Kainan strode to a hidden storage unit on the command deck. He pushed a few buttons, and the door revealed a well-stocked spirits bar and fridge.

Minutes later, she was swirling a glass of golden bliss.

'To finding rare stars in orbit,' he said, saluting her with his glass, his sapphire gold eyes flashing with deep meaning.

'To stars that make you believe in the impossible,' she added, her words too laden with significance.

He gave her another of his rare smiles and tossed back his drink, exposing his muscled, glyphed neck.

She did the same and felt her eyes water as the alcohol

heated her insides.

She wanted to lie down and then lie there forever, staring at the beauty of the paired stars.

'I can pull out a couch for you here,' Kainan said, cutting through her thoughts. 'I have one in that panel that's king-sized. It fits under the view screen.'

It was as if he'd read her mind.

Selene nodded. 'That sounds good,' she said, although what she knew she needed to do was get away from the man causing her drowning need. 'It's been a long day.'

Kainan's brow furrowed in concern. 'Then let me.'

'*Sante*,' Selene said with some relief.

Moments later, she'd eased herself onto the spacious day bed he'd pulled out, leaning against the chaise's velvet backrest.

He kept a polite distance, seated back in his pilot's chair, his whiskey glass in his large hand. He aimed his molten eyes at Selene. 'Kick back, Prime. Enjoy the show. Forget the troubles of today. Tomorrow will take care of itself.'

Curling up on the bed, she sipped her whiskey and stared into the wild skies above. The glowing gaseous landscape was illuminated and carved by high-energy reactions and strong stellar winds. It was awe-inspiring, as was this moment, here with this man.

She breathed in Kainan's windswept scent emanating from the cushions behind her. Longing flooded her every atom.

Then she remembered her father's wise words, derived from an ancient, long-forgotten canon. '*However long the night, Selene, the dawn will always break.*'

She felt an uneasy peace come over her. Whatever happened in Eden II or between her and her enigmatic host, whether dark or light, would pass, and balance would return just as life would go on.

Worrying over what might be would only distract her from her cause.

With that wisdom repeating in her mind, the ache between her breastbone and thighs eased somewhat.

The quiet hum of the Corvette's air vents stilled her racing mind.

Until a burning heat danced over her skin.

She looked up and into molten desire.

Kainan's eyes were fixed on her, almost aflame with the raw need.

She couldn't pull her eyes away from his swirling depths of sapphire gold.

They stared at each other for a long moment. Selene's lips parted, her skin flushed with heat, her heart thudding and drumming with need.

'*Khamila*,' he rasped. 'You're so beautiful.'

Her breath stopped.

He leaned forward, placing his elbows on his knees. 'How long will we keep playing this game, Selene?' he whispered.

Holy Dunia, she thought.

Selene dragged air into her lungs. 'What game?'

He closed his eyes briefly, then opened them with a wry smile. 'This push and pull between us.'

Her heart hammered in her chest.

'We both want each other. Admit it,' he challenged with a husky voice, leaning forward in his chair, his voice rough and laced with desire.

Every fiber of her body screamed with a longing she fought hard against. She took a long moment to reply while he stared at her, raking her face with his heated gaze.

She spoke, weighing her words. 'I admit there may be some attraction.'

He scoffed. 'Some attraction, *khamila*? We're scorching the air between us.'

She blushed, and he cocked an eyebrow. 'See?' he said.

'I see,' she admitted, ducking her eyes away from his. 'But we can't –?'

'But we can, Selene. We both want this. It's inescapable.'

He rose to his feet, and she watched as he stalked towards her. First, one knee hit the edge of the couch. Then the other.

'Mirage, standby mode,' he commanded as he fell onto all fours, stalking her on the couch.

A soft tone sounded as the AI complied and regressed into the nether of the Corvette's controls.

Neither Kainan nor Selene noticed.

Selene was transfixed.

She scrambled to sit up.

But still, she didn't stop him, staring at his beautiful, heady masculinity heading towards her.

Then those thick thighs straddled her, and he loomed over her aching, throbbing body, his long hair falling into a curtain she longed to slip her fingers into.

He stared at her for a long moment, and she felt herself yield. Her reservations fell away, liquefied by the molten desire in his eyes.

Kainan groaned in a deep rumble that thundered between them.

'*Khamila*,' he whispered. 'I can't take this anymore –.'

His head lowered, and she closed her eyes to the unexpected storm of emotion between them.

First, she felt lips against her hair, then a large hand wrapped around her side before trailing to her lower side, under her back, to pull her up and into him.

'Selene,' the rugged Edenite murmured, dotting the lightest of kisses and nips to her forehead, her eyebrow, her cheek, and trailing lower to her jaw and into the crux of her neck where he inhaled her essence. 'Stop me, for I cannot stop myself -.'

Selene's thoughts skittered just as her heart thudded. *Was this happening?*

She reached out to feel the taut chest muscles of the man embracing her and gave in to the wave of longing, surrendering to the inevitable after days of holding back.

'Kainan,' Selene breathed, moving her hands to clutch the back of his head, knitting her fingers into his thick hair.

She reached forward and kissed him along his broad brow and hairline. 'Maybe I don't want you to stop,' she muttered.

He looked up and met her wide gaze, his sapphire gold eyes flashing with energy and lust.

'Then I won't until you're mine.'

His lips fell onto hers, heated, firm, and so enticing.

She gasped into them as he set about nipping, sucking, his tongue bending and twisting with Selene's, in ravenous feeling.

She pushed into his chest, breathing in the intoxicating scent of the man holding her firmly in his arms.

She felt him run his hands to the back of her thighs, powerfully pulling her up until he'd wrapped her legs around his slim, taut hips.

He continued to devour her mouth, groaning with intensity.

Then he pulled away and ripped aside her silken shirt and

matching pants.

Pearl buttons flew into the air as Selene's clothes fell away until she was left bare before him.

'Stunning. Better than I'd ever imagined.'

He worshiped her with his wildfire gaze that burned downward, past her generous breasts, over her tummy mound, before pausing between her shapely thighs.

'So you've been imagining me?' she teased out.

'Every moment I'm around you, my entire being goes wild for you, woman. My mind even more so,' he ground out.

He stood over her for a moment before resting one knee beside her.

His beautiful fingers roamed over her skin before slipping to the prize between her thighs.

She arched her back and widened her legs, and his long fingers stroked her wetness.

She could hardly take the heat from his fingers, and she moaned when he added more fervor with his mouth closing over her right nipple.

He used his tongue to tease and stroke her nerve-laced mound, taking turns between sucking and lashing the engorged tip before switching to her left breast.

Selene thrust her hands into his long, lush hair, grabbing his scalp to push him closer to her needy flesh. He reared his head back and met her heated gaze.

'*Nada khamila*, you don't get to run this show,' he warned with a growl. 'Not on our first time.'

She tried to buck her nipple back into his mouth, but he grinned and entered her wet center with a curl of a forefinger.

He used a thumb to flick her clit, and she moaned.

His middle finger thrust even deeper, joining the first,

while the thumb worked her engorged bud, sending ecstasy through her body.

Kainan looked down at her panting mouth and undulating hips as they lifted off the bed, trying to find the release her core sorely needed.

'You're so wet, *khamila*, so wet for me. So beautiful.'

'Kainan, I can't –.'

He stopped Selene's protest with a deep kiss.

His tongue thrust into her mouth, and she sucked on it with all abandon.

She reached for him, slipping under his soft shirt to caress his heated chest, his nipples, his lower stomach, moaning when she found what she was after—the thick, pulsing steel rod between his thighs.

She stroked, then gripped the swollen, ridged appendage through the material of his pants, stroking her hands to a sensual rhythm, her hips thrusting to the same dance.

She wanted to see the powerful cock her hands could barely grip, so she reared back and away from his erotic lips.

'I need you, Kainan,' she declared, twisting his pants downward and slipping her hand into the space between them.

She sighed as her fingers wrapped around the base of his pulsing and scorching hot thickness.

She squeezed, and he groaned again against her hair.

She stroked him from base to tip and back down again, gazing reverently at his weeping, ridged, gloriousness.

His fingers paused their heated dance inside her slit, and his head fell back, the black locks shot with silver, sapphire, and gold in a waterfall over his shoulders.

She shifted on the bed, moving to kneel beside him.

She bent forward and licked the heated member crowned with seeping moisture. He jerked as her lips closed over the tumescent tip and sucked it with reverence.

She ran her tongue along the throbbing vein on his underside, and he bucked his hips in a sweet response.

'*Fokk khamila*,' the groan dragged out of Kainan's thickened throat. 'You'll be the undoing of me.'

She squeezed his heated, hard length harder, and it wept in submission.

Then Kainan surged to his feet, and she lost purchase.

He dragged off his shirt and reached for his pants, whipping them off before standing before her in all his glory.

His hair fell over his broad shoulders and massive chest.

The sapphire and gold tattoos on his skin and muscled neck, arms, and back moved sinuously.

His stomach was a washboard of rippling power above a thick, hard, dark, and oh-so-beautiful cock, pulsing and bobbing with raw need.

She fell back and widened her legs, reaching out to him. 'Come, *khaji* -' she implored.

His eyes melted at her Edenite endearment.

'I need you,' she whispered, weak with need.

'Only if you're sure,' he ground out, his heated gaze ensnared by the juncture of legs, where her wet lushness was erotically displayed.

'I am,' Selene whispered.

'I'm also clean,' he rasped. 'And my contra-plant is up to date.'

'So is mine,' Selene nodded, confirming that she had the female version of his injectible contraception implanted under her skin.

Kainan placed a knee between Selene's thighs, nudging them further apart before settling between her legs.

A rough palm slipped under her knee, pulling her legs up and onto his shoulders while he bent down to look between them.

He used his hand to drag his cock head over her clit, and she almost lost it.

Then his engorged tip was nudging her clit, sliding through the wetness into her slit.

'Look at us, *khamila*,' he groaned, and Selene did as he commanded.

She gazed as their bodies merged into one, a slow inch at a time.

She tried to rear up with impatience, but Kainan stilled her with a low whisper.

'Mouth,' he demanded, and she offered her lips to his.

He took them with a vengeance, his tongue sliding in cadence to his cock below. Selene's body hummed, her nipples raked across his broad, muscled chest, and she moaned against her lover's mouth as he slid to the hilt.

Where it seemed he'd always belonged.

Their kiss was deep, long, and filled with searing heat.

He teased her, nibbling, stroking, sucking, and dirty talking in between, whispering Kwavi and Edenite words she couldn't quite comprehend.

She blushed, her body responding to their sensual meaning.

'Holy Dunia,' she whispered when he lifted his lips to lock them on her throbbing nipple.

He pulled his hips back, and she cried out, her hands clutching at his firm behind to haul him back in.

He laughed again, low and slow, stilling his hips. 'I'm still running this show, *khamila*. Just sit back and enjoy the ride.'

'Please,' she begged, grinding her hips against him to entice him back into action.

He hovered over her for the most extended moment before acting in mercy, thrusting with molten savagery, pumping into her with abandon.

Then he stroked his hips over and over again, faster and faster, harder and harder.

Their bodies came together in heated bliss, sticking to-gether and apart, as sweat dripped off them onto the velvety couch.

They groaned against each other, their kisses molten and unceasing. She became impossibly wetter, and he incredibly harder.

Their lovemaking became an alchemy of heart, body, and mind.

She felt the wave of an orgasm rush towards her.

'Kainan! I'm coming,' she breathed.

The declaration served to make him work harder.

He surged to his knees and pumped with a passion and strength she'd never thought possible. On and on, he slammed into her with powerful strokes until she fell apart.

She exploded with feeling between her legs, stomach, breasts, and soul, clamping his thickness as she came harder than she'd ever done in her entire life.

With a cry, she sank into darkness and fell back to the satiny couch, convulsing with passion while he continued his passionate thrusts.

He fell over her, and she pushed her face against his heated neck, one hand thrust into his hair, the other urging his hips onward.

'*Khamila*, you are everything,' he breathed.

Kainan's head fell back, and he thundered as he convulsed inside Selene, his cock pulsing with heat as he came deep inside her, flooding and overflowing to her womb.

He gave a few more wild thrusts before collapsing against her slick, spent, and sated body.

Selene took his weight, her clit still exploding with minor aftershocks, her body still connected to his.

She ran her hands over his glyphed back, over his heated body, pressing her lips into his neck while she watched the metanoid-infused patterns shift and dance over his skin.

Kainan kissed her. 'That was everything I dreamed of and more, *khamila*.'

He brushed his long, lean fingers over her brow, pushing away the damp hair.

Then he bent his magnificent head and kissed Selene long, slow, and sensuously until she felt the stirrings of more arousal.

'You feel that?' he murmured against her lips.

'I do,' she said, squeezing her muscles around his lengthening cock.

'We can't get enough of each other,' he said with a low laugh, twitching inside her. 'But I'm no superhero; I need my rest in between.'

He rose away from her, running a hand over her cheek when she moaned, protesting their parting.

He moved toward the head in the cabin, selecting a washcloth he used to clean himself before returning to the couch to do the same for her.

With a kiss on her shoulder, he lay beside her, curling his magnificent body around her own.

He moved his lips to hers in a heart-stopping kiss until she ducked her head under his neck, and they silently held each other close until exhaustion pulled them into a deep slumber.

A few hours later, they woke and repeated their sensual lovemaking.

Two hours later, they did it again.

And on return to Kainan's lair, they made love several more times.

Insatiably, ravenously, unquenchably.

11

Alphetraz's Silver-Paired Stars

SELENE

The next few days were a blur for Selene.

Hours and minutes flew past, and she lost the ability to tell night from day.

It didn't help that the view from Kainan's windows shifted between starlight and never-ending dawn.

Where fractured light bounced off J'Urg Mihòr's shadowed ridges from the undulating cluster of stars and twin suns above.

After making love for hours at night, most mornings, they would rise and eat in a nook Kainan had built that overhung the cliffs outside his home.

Three of the nook's walls were cast of the same material as his vast windows - magnesium aluminate, which was more robust and harder than glass.

It gave her the sensation of floating over J'Urg Mihòr while lost within the spectacular star-studded sky.

Kainan made her lie on the transparent floor a few times while he sketched her.

He used luminescent pencils with graphite lead mined from the rocks of ancient asteroids.

The resulting sketches were studies of her face and body, with shadows, tones, contrasts, and strokes that captured her mood so well they seemed to leap from the paper.

He gave her one and kept the rest, claiming they weren't perfect.

She hid the one he'd gifted her between the pages of her notebook, intending to frame it as soon as she returned to Dunia. And display it alongside the first sketch he'd drawn of her and her father.

One morning, she woke alone and wandered his lair, searching for him, with two cups of *kahawa* in her hand.

Only to find him beyond the inner pool, down a staircase, and past a gym. In a generous room on a level that extended under the living space.

The space overflowed with canvases of every size—some fresh, some complete, and a few somewhere between.

She spotted tables where paints, brushes, and oils lay scattered over every available surface.

Kainan stood in loose pants before a large black canvas and an expansive easel. On the table beside him were sets of paints, pans, and brushes, which he worked with studied ease.

He glanced up to where she stood at the doorway.

His eyes lit up into a soft flame. 'Come in, *khamila*.'

She welcomed the invitation, wandering into the space.

She handed him his cup, and he took it, placing it on his paint table. Then he lowered his mouth to kiss her, slipping a hand into her silk robe to caress a hardening nipple.

Her eyes closed with pleasure, and she felt his arousal pressed into her.

His eyes softened. 'Soon. Just a few more moments,' he promised.

'Sit,' he stated, pointing to a couch nearby.

She pulled away from his touch with a sigh and curled herself on the daybed.

Taking a sip of *kahawa*, she watched the man whose head was bent again over the canvas, mixing a dance of silver and gold hues onto its surface.

Her brow lifted as she recognized the scene.

It was Alphetraz, the pair of binary stars.

Somehow, he'd captured them as intertwining, weaving together, and with movement. She shook her head in amazement.

He then lifted a vial of swirling blue liquid from a holder on the table and squeezed a drop into the paint pots he was working from.

The reaction emitted a bright light, and she gasped. 'What was that?'

'An infusion of my metanoids,' he answered. 'They give movement to my work.'

Surprised, Selene stepped back, watching with awe as he continued to paint the essence of the magnificent star outside with elegance and finesse for a man of his bulk.

'When did you start painting?' she ventured.

Kainan worked for a few long, hushed minutes before replying. 'I've always sketched, even as a child, especially when my orphanage handlers left me alone for hours. Later, when I was conscripted into the Eden Guards, I found drawing helped me make sense of my reality. So much of our deployment involved long patrols and longer waiting periods between missions. Painting became a cure-all for boredom, pain, and anger. After a battle or conflict, it became an outlet for my frustration, helping me work through it. I soon became very good at it. I even thought of leaving the Guards to pursue it full-time. But it was not meant to be. After we arrived on Eden II, I needed to feed myself and my brothers, the Riders. I also cared for some orphans and street kids on Eden II. So, painting fell by the wayside. It's only after we'd established the Group, and I was on patrol once more across the stars and badlands, that I rediscovered my brushes.'

She dug deeper, infused with a longing to know this man to the utter center of his core. 'What does it do for you?'

'It gives me clarity, *khamila*,' Kainan murmured. 'It's where I can capture nature's fokkin' great beauty while washing out any darkness within by pouring it onto a bare, clean, untouched canvas. Painting is where I give myself over to lucidity.'

He looked at her and gave her a rare smile, his sapphire gold gaze piercing her soul. Then his expression fell as he considered her.

'Forgive me, *khamila*, this is taking longer than expected. You must be hungry.'

'I'm fine,' she said with a small smile. 'You do your thing. I'm happy to watch.'

Kainan returned to his painting, his hands moving with poetic beauty across the canvas.

This man.
Strength.
Artistry.
Passion.
A lover who challenged and entranced her.
How much more could she handle?

After watching him paint for a few minutes longer, Selene could not tamp down the growing ache in her chest. Overwhelmed with emotion, the need to either embrace or escape him washed over her.

She must have made a sound because he looked up.

Their eyes clashed, and he shot her a seductive smirk.

She felt it to the core, clenching her thighs together.

His eyes fell there, and then he moved.

Throwing his brush to the table, he stalked toward her.

She barely had time to place her cup on the floor when he crashed his lips on hers.

Moments later, he was on a hot trajectory towards her molten center. His lips dove between her sensual ones, his tongue attacking her clit, his supple fingers dipping into her slippery folds.

Selene moaned as she rode his face, pulling at his long strands of hair.

She crested and broke with a cry muffled by the return of his searching, hungry mouth. His large palms widened her thighs and entered her, his thick cock burning to her center.

She wrapped her thighs around him and rode his storm until they both crashed in a maelstrom of passion and fever.

They couldn't get enough of each other.

They snuck in making love and losing themselves in each other, around their work hours, planning the incursion and defensive attack on the One Dunia Coalition.

They caught up with The Sable Riders, their lieutenants, Rina, and the Free Dunia Council to organize their tactical strategy.

They aimed to retake the cities lost to Massimo's militia and the cydroid army while minimizing casualties and improving efficiency.

They planned to ensure the Sable/Edenite and Free Dunia Alliance had enough armored and configured infantry formations backed by significant air power to support a successful ground incursion.

Seven days later, after an afternoon spent confirming the alliance's readiness, Kainan turned off the screens.

'D-day tomorrow,' he said, turning with a smile towards Selene, curled up on the couch beside him.

'Do you think we're ready?'

He shrugged. 'As we'll ever be. We've done our best to prep in a very short time. The rest of it is up to the weather, the leadership on the day, and the discipline of our people.'

'Then all we can do is hold onto that,' she said.

They fell into silence, and Selene looked away through the soaring windows to the beauty of the night sky and winking stars beyond. She thought of her people suffering in Dunia.

Her heart twisted, and she felt a pang of guilt. Making plans to take back a planet typically didn't involve copious amounts of sensuality.

Yet, in her case, this was the truth. Since their flight back from Alphetraz, she and Kainan had only left his bed to eat, shower, and take calls from the planet and the Riders. Their lovemaking was heated, unceasing, and fervent, for the Edenite was a masterful lover.

She'd never felt revered, adulated, or worshiped in all of her life. And the bliss of their lovemaking amid the crisis unfolding below in Dunia was almost too much to bear.

She glanced back towards Kainan and found him watching her with an expression she couldn't quite fathom.

'What?' she asked.

'Come here, *khamila*,' his voice was low and loaded. 'It seems I need to do something to get rid of that sad face –.'

'What are you proposing, *khaji*?' she asked, her breath hitching in anticipation.

'Come and find out,' he invited, reaching out to her with a muscled, glyph-encircled arm.

She unfurled her feet and crossed the small space between them.

Kainan pulled her head down to his and kissed her long and deep. One hand pulled her shawl away from her shoulders and pushed aside the straps of her dress to reveal her aching nipples. He rubbed and pinched her right one while his other searching hand slipped between her legs to her bare wetness.

He'd ripped apart most of her other underwear, and she'd given up wearing them around him. So now she was at his mercy every moment they made love.

She moaned as his finger slipped up and down her slit, shamelessly rubbing herself against him.

Then he rose, lifting Selene into his arms and carrying her through his vast living area, down the art-lined hallway, and into his expansive bedroom.

He pushed her onto the bed, his mouth covering her own with an urgent, hungry passion.

Selene squirmed under his thick thighs and heavy body, trying to reach between them to grasp the hard length throbbing against her tummy.

He wasn't having any of it and wrenched his lips from hers, dragging them down towards her drenched core.

'*Khaji*,' Selene groaned as his lips took purchase of her heated center, licking, nipping, and teasing until she shook as pure white hot ecstasy rushed through her body.

Kainan kept lapping at her until her second orgasm hit.

Then only did he lift himself to rip his shirt and pants off before sinking and sliding into her with a powerful thrust.

He teased her, moving sensually. The base of his hot cock rubbed against her clit, sending lightning-fast stabs of pure pleasure through her core.

She grew impatient with his pace.

'Faster, Kainan!' she urged him, chasing her third orgasm.

He obeyed with a smirk, his lean muscled body arching above her, his hips slamming into her own, and his cock deeper into her core.

Selene could hardly hold on with her hands, so she wrapped her thighs around his center, just able to keep up with his brutal, bucking strength.

He pulled back his head and stared down at her, and she felt her head spin, drawn into the sapphire and gold galaxy of his gaze that cut straight through to her heart.

'Harder,' she urged him, pushing up and closing her eyes against the swirling storm, losing herself to the thrust of his hips.

She felt her orgasm build higher and higher, and then it thundered over and inside her.

Kainan shook above her as his body gave in to the churning sensation.

Just like they did every time, their lips found each other, and they nipped and sucked at each other while Kainan slicked in and out of her until they came down off their sensual high.

Spent, he rested his brow against hers.

She wrapped her hands around him and rubbed her lips against his shoulders. He reciprocated with small, soft kisses of his own.

Blissed out, she turned towards the view outside of nebulas streaking past Eden II and felt an avalanche of emotion.

'I love this,' she whispered. 'Lying here with you, looking over the ridge to a sky streaked with stars. I could stay here with you, in this place, forever.'

Suddenly, Kainan stilled. His muscles locked.

She felt a rush of cool air as his body left hers. He rolled onto the bed beside her, his chest heaving.

She slow-blinked, puzzled.

Since their first time together, they'd always spent long moments after their lovemaking in each other's arms, reluctant to part.

This sudden withdrawal was new and unlike him.

With an abrupt twist, he knifed himself upright and strode out of his chamber into his large bathroom.

Then, the doorway between the two rooms slid shut behind

him.

Selene sat there, stunned.

Moments went by before she scrambled for one of Kainan's robes at the end of the bed, wrapping it around herself.

She heard the head turn on moments later and the splash of falling water.

She racked her brain, trying to understand his sudden departure.

Her heartfelt confession at the end! *Had that spooked him? But hadn't he, too, been saying sweet nothings all week?*

Confused, she rose and traversed the space into the bathroom. The door slid open.

There he was, in all his physical magnificence, the shower jets cascading over the gigantic planes of his body in a silken waterfall.

One powerful arm was stretched out and leaning against the shower wall—the other hung by his side.

This wasn't the confident lover who'd just given her so much pleasure.

Instead, the supple flow of his large, muscled body seemed somewhat slumped, in some form of defeat.

His body jerked at the sound of her entry, but he didn't look up. His long hair fell like a dark curtain over the side of his face, hiding his features.

She approached him and touched him. Only then did he push the hair from his eyes and look up to meet her gaze.

'You OK?' she asked, running her fingers along his arm.

He nodded, pulling away from her touch, and she froze.

He didn't say anything for a long moment.

At last, he turned over the head, and the shower stopped.

Leaving the sound of water dripping on the tiles.

He took a deep breath, his graveled murmur slow and laden with unexplained emotion. 'The thing is, Selene, I don't do *forever*. It's not what this is.'

A maglev train hit her right in the center of her solar plexus.

She stared at him long enough that he looked away.

A fit of irrational anger rose from deep within her and poured out.

Moments later, she turned, missing the glance he shot her and the flash of momentary sadness that followed.

Heart thumping, Selene took a step away, then another, until she found herself walking out of his chamber and moving with care towards her guest room.

Once inside, she locked the door and leaned against it. Then she sank to the floor, her back against the ancient wood.

How could she have been so stupid?

Selene recalled the bitter expression on Uba, the woman at the bar on Eden II.

Was this how she'd felt? Had she, too, read much more into the situation as Selene had?

'*Fokk!*'

Selene mentally kicked herself, slapping her hand on the carpeted floor.

She'd made a schoolgirl error and assumed his affection level matched hers.

Granted, Kainan had not made her any promises of any future relationship, let alone forever.

She'd blurted out her feelings.

Yet it seemed that he was only after a physical connection.

She'd allowed his wicked tongue, beautiful body, and sweet words to lull her into a sense of security, into a fantasy where their passion meant more than a temporary sensual fix.

A lone tear streaked down her face, which she dashed away with a growl.

The truth was she'd let herself get sidetracked from her mission. But no more.

She owed it to her father's memory to get her shit together and forget trying to juggle saving a planet with chasing fanciful illusions of forever.

She stumbled to her feet and threw Kainan's robe to the floor. She wanted nothing more to do with his scent, touch, or lovemaking.

Not now. Not ever.

KAINAN

Forever.

The one word that sent him into a tailspin. One that thrust him into a whirlpool of memories.

Of a quiet, still voice that had tortuously whispered the horror of what 'forever' meant into his bleeding, wounded ears.

For weeks, days, and hours on end.

Until it was seared into his soul and psyche.

Memories of his past agony consumed his mind.

The recollections were always the same. He would see that face, hear its voice, and feel overwhelming anger and fury at his helplessness.

Kainan tried to push the memories away, to focus on something else.

But they were always there, lurking in his mind, waiting to resurface.

For years, he'd distracted himself with work, hunting raiders, art, and anything that could take his mind off the pain.

But no matter what he did, the past always found a way to creep back in.

He'd been in pain for as long as he could remember, and no matter how hard he tried, Kainan couldn't escape it.

He knew he needed help, but didn't know where to turn.

He felt alone and didn't know how to escape the pain. He slumped against his bathroom wall, lost in his despair.

Would he ever find a way to heal?

The familiar, heated, flaming darkness welled up in him, threatening to overflow, and he gritted his teeth to quell it rather than inflict his tortured pain on Selene.

Although she'd lifted him from deep darkness for a moment, he had to protect her from himself in the long term.

He'd seen the pain in those beautiful hazel-gold eyes at his asshole words. He'd felt it like a stab straight through his heart.

He loathed the look of pure rage she'd thrown his way as she'd left.

He wanted to replace it again with the softness he'd become accustomed to after their lovemaking, with the half-lidded passion that blazed from her very core and the abundant joy that burst out of her during their heartfelt conversations.

But it was not meant to be. He had no right to want any of it.

Not when he couldn't give her what she deserved.
Forever.

SELENE

Hours later, Selene ventured out of the guest room.

The lair was quiet and peaceful, the only sound of a strong wind howling between the ridges outside.

She headed for the kitchen, where she rummaged for something to eat.

Pulling leftovers from the cool room, she dove into a plate of delicious sliced meats and Falasian fried rice.

Then she noticed thumping, a steady beat from beyond the indoor pool.

Curious, she wandered through the crystal doors towards the source. The thuds were closer in resonance now, and she pinpointed them to the wide staircase at the far end of the lap pool. Peering over the railing, she found her quarry.

Kainan.

He stood in his expansive gym on the floor below, in front of a swinging boxing bag that hung from the ceiling above.

His hands were gloveless, but he still drove them into the bag with a savagery she'd never seen before.

He alternated the punches with rapid-fire side, front, and roundhouse kicks.

Sweat was pouring off his body, and she noticed, with concern, silver-dark blood leaking from between his fingers from the broken skin on his knuckles.

Why was he torturing himself?

She must have made a sound because he looked up, and their eyes met. She snapped her body away and dashed back to the kitchen.

She was in no mood to deal with him, with them.

Suddenly thirsty, she turned to the tap and nabbed a glass, taking a long drink of water.

'For whatever it's worth, I'm sorry.'

Selene whirled around at Kainan's voice.

'Holy Dunia! You scared me,' she snapped, trying to control herself.

He'd approached in his silent panther style.

Now, he stood in nothing but a pair of dark-colored training shorts, winding a white bandage around his bloodied knuckles.

Her traitorous heart leaped as she flicked her eyes over him. While her even more mutinous pussy clenched.

Damn! All it took was seeing the man who'd given it, and her so much pleasure this past week.

The swift pull toward him was followed by a slash of pain and the shame of rejection, and she winced at the unexpected emotion.

Silence bloomed between them as they warily eyed each other.

'What did you say? I missed it,' Selene ground out.

Kainan's expression was cool, cagey. 'I said I'm sorry.'

Selene drew a ragged breath as she battled to suppress the pent-up rage leaking from her pores. 'Sorry for what? You made me no promises, and I accept that. It was a fling, which was fun while it lasted.'

He caught the bitter edge in her voice and flinched. 'Selene, it doesn't have to be this way.'

'What way would you prefer it to be, Kainan?' she clipped. 'You want me to be hysterical? Crying? Begging for you to give me something you're not ready for? Or perhaps you want me to scream at you and call you a playboy who runs hot and cold, seducing women and discarding them when he pleases?'

His face tightened, and his eyes flared, almost as if with flames.

He blinked as if she'd delivered one of the front kicks he'd just been practicing to his center. Selene stepped back, unsure of what would happen next.

After a few angst-ridden moments, he spoke, the words dragging out of him. 'Do you think that poorly of me?'

'I don't know what to believe. And I don't think I have the right to ask why you said what you did. The fact is, you don't want this, us, whatever it was. And I'm a big enough girl to live with it.'

Kainan interjected. 'It's not that I –.'

However, Selene had had enough. She couldn't take the pain or humiliation any longer. She lifted a hand to ward him off. 'You know what? Let it go. I want to try to forget this happened and focus on the mission.'

She watched as Kainan's firm nostrils flared and his face coalesced into stone, the shutters into his soul flying up. Even the glow of his sapphire gold eyes turned to a frozen icy blue flame.

He gave her an icy glance. 'If that's what you want, *Excellency*.'

She grimaced at the taunt.

He stared at her coldly for a few long seconds before stalking away.

He paused at the hallway entrance, his face averted away from her. 'Kage sent word while you were in your room. We'll rendezvous tomorrow with the rest of the alliance's armada at 0600 standard. I'll start packing the ship now. I'll appreciate it if you can place your bags at your door tonight so I can stow them on Mirage.'

Every razor edge of his icy, glacial words cut into her soul.

Unable to deal with the tattered heartbreak, she dragged her eyes away from his stiff silhouette to look sightlessly out of the extensive glassed-in views.

'What can I do to help?' she whispered.

There was no answer. Turning her head, she found she'd been speaking to empty air. She sighed as a frisson of frost rushed all over her body.

It felt like even outside, Alphetraz's silver-paired stars had lost their warm sparkle and were now twinkling cruelly at her.

12

A Whole Fleet Of Badassness

SELENE

'Excellency! Welcome to Phantasm's Command Deck.'

'Mirage! It's so good to hear your voice.'

'Indeed, it is good to hear yours too, Excellency,' The Sable Group AI responded. 'It's been a few days since we've seen you.'

'And for a good reason,' Selene said, stepping through a sliding doorway into a smart, gleaming master control center. 'I didn't want to get in anyone's way.'

Or in the path of one particular Edenite.

The bridge she'd entered was a hub of low-humming organization and precision. Inside, smartly dressed crew members in The Sable Group's fleet uniform manned a series of control stations featuring large screens arranged in three tiers.

She spotted science, weapons, and life-support functions alongside the curved wall. While at the center of the room, she saw a series of swivel chairs and more officers behind the nav monitors controlling the cruiser's flight and propulsion.

'But enough with calling me Excellency,' she whispered. 'Mirage, you now know me well enough. Call me Selene.'

'When on mission, we encourage the use of our official designations and call names, *Excellency*.'

The dry, cold remark came from the long-haired, handsome man seated at the helm of the bustling, well-oiled operation.

Her heart slammed in her chest, anticipating the worst from their first encounter in days.

But Kainan didn't even bother looking up from the screen he was consulting beside his captain's chair.

Selene flushed, mortified by his public chastisement and blatant dismissal.

Fokk you, she thought. *Two can play this game.*

She chose to hold her tongue. Then, ignoring Kainan's taunt and dragging her eyes away, she moved as far as she could from his chair. She sidled along the back wall, trying to be unobtrusive, hauling the large duffle bag that she needed to keep with her on the ready.

Mirage, however, didn't get the memo. 'Excellency,' she called out for all on the bridge to hear. 'We've assigned a station for you on the command deck.'

Selene looked around, panicked. She did not need to be anywhere close to him.

'I don't want to be in any officer's way. Can't I sit at the back?' she said, pointing to the shadowy corners of the bridge.

'How about the upper deck where you can see everything, *Excellency*? Where you can focus *only* on the mission?' Kainan rasped, sarcasm dripping from his lips.

While still not giving her a single glance.

'Good idea,' Selene mumbled, her face hot and flushed. She hurried away, moving as he'd suggested to the upper galley of the command deck to sit behind an empty station where her credentials had popped up.

Selene sighed in relief. Here, she could lurk in peace while taking in her new surroundings and, at the same time, being as far away as possible from *His Saltiness*.

All evidence indicated that he was still butt-hurt about their most recent confrontation. *Why, when he'd been the one who'd walked away from whatever-the-fokk they'd been?*

She shook him out of her head and looked at her new surroundings. She had a bird's view of the bridge. There was no doubt about it; the Phantasm was a stunning vessel— a sleek, neo-steel plated behemoth designed with the same faceted streamlined sleekness as Kainan's corvette.

Yet the battle cruiser was a significant upgrade, with all the teeth, bells, and whistles required to act as a planetary bomber and raider. Moreover, its lasers and cannons were state-of-the-art in all things lethal.

Phantasm was, from what she'd learned from her comm tab, a general-purpose warship and a command vessel for extended campaigns.

It ran on a mix of nuclear energy and antimatter that powered its warp hyperdrive and gravity accelerators, allowing it to achieve FTL travel.

In addition, it had a secondary, short-range warp drive

to reduce wear and tear on the main one and operate in atmospheric conditions, using sophisticated anti-grav tech.

Its black skin and stealth tech allowed it to slip unseen in and out of systems.

The ship boasted a weapons system unlike anything she'd ever seen.

An enormous cargo bay fit up to ten full-size corvettes and multiple small fighter crafts.

It also sported a large, extendable flight deck and hangar for multiple drone-piloted air systems equipped with weapons that could target the enemy without harming the crew.

Also appearing on its manifest were defensive hypersonic missile tubes and directed energy weapons with the power to stop any small enemy craft.

In addition, on the outrigger hulls were mounted torpedo tubes to fire super-cavitation torpedoes capable of super-sonic speeds.

The fast-moving neo-steel city housed over eight hundred crew and troops and came complete with a well-equipped medbay and a brig.

She'd already attempted to tour the gargantuan ship's cantinas, rec rooms, and bars, trying to wrap her head around its size.

Its interior was modern, with every surface gleaming white, gray, and silver and kept squeaky clean by an army of bots. Cabins were spacious and roomy, packed with all the mod cons a Dunia girl would want—from a small kitchen to holo screens, a generous head, and even a tiny library.

Her respect for The Sable Group's operations had grown just by being on board this behemoth. Their enterprise had to be raking in gazillions of schills to afford the sophistication of its fleet.

Especially its battleships – for the Phantasm was a behemoth of a battlecruiser, escorted by the Sable Group's two frigates that the Riders had brought to the mission.

A whole fleet of badassness, with Kainan as its linchpin.

Speaking of.

She and he were still avoiding each other, which had been somewhat awkward during the 10-hour flight on Mirage to rendezvous with the rest of the Sable/Edenite and Free Dunia Alliance fleet.

They'd hardly exchanged a word, each taking great pains to avoid the other except at mealtimes and when liaising with the incursion's planning team.

Selene remembered her relief when the Corvette had docked beside the Phantasm.

She'd walked onboard behind the hulking Edenite, then slipped away at the first chance, fleeing to her new quarters aided by Mirage's precise directions on her comm tab.

And there she'd remained until her comm alert had trilled and Mirage had announced a general stand-up meeting on the Command Deck.

A meeting that was now coming to order.

The screens on the bridge and at the station Selene sat on buzzed with feeds from all the key players. Most were on vessels that made up the armada assembled within the asteroid shadows of Rhesus' rings.

'Excellency, I'll turn on your camera at this station,' Mirage told Selene.

'Thank you,' Selene said, shaking her head, impressed by the AI's efficiency.

A holo screen projected the armada's formation in 3D in

front of Kainan's chair.

It displayed his gunship hovering next to the Phantasm, its bridge in Mirage's complete remote control. Also included in the projection were the two other frigates supporting a fleet of corvettes captained by various members of the broader Alliance.

Selene spotted Kage and Riv on the incoming feeds, each captaining their stealth corvettes and in the lead position to infiltrate the planet.

Xion was in his corvette, hovering in stealth mode closer to Dunia's orbit, dodging The Technocracy's sensor arrays.

Zane patched in from Eden II, where he monitored the operations' logistics and worked with The Sable Riders' patrol boats to keep wanderers out of affected space lanes until the operation was over.

The last feed was from the planet's surface, where Rina and the Free Dunia Council assembled in the Zulu One boardroom.

Kainan rose from his chair and approached the main screen that took over one wall of the massive bridge. He opened the meeting, cutting to the chase.

'This is the Phantasm. We're the command ship for this op, which we've dubbed the Ghost Incursion. You'll understand why very soon.'

Kainan prowled the bridge, so full of barely controlled power that the highlights in his hair flared as if lit with an invisible flame.

Selene could sense the waves of pure, palpable energy flow from him, throbbing through the bridge as he spoke.

'We're one system jump point away from Dunia,' he said, in complete command of the room. 'But we'll not just be jumping into theater. Instead, we'll be coming in quiet, cold and in stealth mode, which means we're four hours away from the start of our attack. The countdown starts now. Commander Xion - call name Phoenix - has been testing the scanning sensors of The Technocracy for the past few days to determine whether they can be interdicted. Our stealth tech has held up to its reputation. None of Phoenix's attempts to slip in and around the crats' blockade have been detected. To The Technocracy, all our fleet ships are wisps of smoke. Ghosts. Invisible to any sensor scanning. Our mission is to slip past the Technocracy's three capital ships and, from what we can tell, up to fifty fighters. We have seven corvettes that will act as blockade runners, their small size and speed making them ideal for ghosting through at seven ordinal points. We also have a proven and mapped route for the corvettes to infiltrate the System. None of the corvettes can deviate from their course once set; otherwise, the sensors will pick them up.'

He pointed to the screen to orient everyone to the plan. 'Our two frigates, Notus I and Notus II, captained by our friends, Majors Ira and Azriel from our tri-alliance corps, will act as bait. They'll approach and fire on the capital ships while cloaked. The crats will go after them, and instead, they'll eat our cannons, giving our corvettes an even better chance to slip into Dunia's atmosphere. The second the frigates or the Phantasm maneuver away from our designated course, it'll light them up to everyone by exposing our heat emissions and exhaust plume. The Technocracy will be able to see us by tracking the burn. We must steer as fast as possible to not give them time to calculate new orbital trajectories. We'll also concentrate on blasting them from existence. Notus I will act as our backup for an attack if the blockade is a feint.

Notus II will provide turret cover for all corvettes, then head in after them to protect the inner System should the other battlecruisers fail in our mission.'

Rina leaned into her screen. 'What if the enemy's patrol ships send for help from their main fleet?'

Behind her, the rest of the Free Dunia Council shared worried looks.

Kainan was quick to address their concern. 'The Technocracy's main fleet was last seen in the Omega IAZL System, returning to HD 638974 b. It'll take them at least five or more days to return to Pegasi, even at full burn through hyperspace. By then, we hope we'll have taken back Dunia and given them nothing to come back for. Does that answer your question?'

'To some extent,' Rina said. 'The Technocracy, however, is known to be relentless, unyielding.'

Kainan nodded. 'We know, which is why we're working on how to get rid of them for good. To end their terror for all time.'

This was news to Selene, who sat up in her station, surprised. Neither Kainan nor The Sable Riders had ever discussed ending the crats. She gave Rina a loaded look via the holo feed. Seconds later, a message pinged on her wrist comm, and she checked it. It was a message from her friend.

What's spooking you about what he just said?

Selene typed out a quick reply.

Don't worry about it. I'll follow up with Kainan later.

She hoped that would deter her friend from probing Kainan further during the meeting. Yet tendrils of nascent doubt began to niggle at her. *Why hadn't he mentioned this 'End to The Technocracy plan' earlier? Were they being played? Was Dunia a pawn in a much bigger plot?*

She made a mental note to quiz him herself as soon as the briefing was over.

Meanwhile, Kainan's reassurances had worked, and the Free Dunia Council members relaxed. He continued the briefing.

'Once we have control of the airspace in and around Dunia, we'll keep Notus I and II on patrol. Two Sable corvettes, led by Commanders Kage and Riv, call names Shadow and Wraith, respectively, will take out all the enemy-controlled surface-to-orbit weapon platforms and gain control of the spaceport. Phantasm will remain in orbit on patrol while I go down to the surface with Mirage and set down at Zulu One. Behind us will come landers and transport helos to deliver the troops and equipment necessary to help the Free Dunia Council take control of the capital. Until we've set down on Dunia, no ships in this alliance fleet should transmit to each other. Unless and only if necessary, you can comm the base on Zulu One, which has adequate orbital comms and a tracking network to bounce the signal to the ship you want to reach. The downside is that ship-to-ship messages will take longer. Please be advised that any inadvertent comms between ships could be the single point of failure that could affect the op.'

Kainan paused for a moment to let the battle plan sink in. 'Are we all clear? Any questions?'

Those he addressed shook their heads, confirming they had no doubts.

'No questions,' Selene spoke up for everyone. 'All clear.'

Except for that one niggling issue which she'd tackle in private.

With no other matters raised, Kainan closed the meeting, and the screens winked out.

'Phantasm and the Free Dunia fleet, please prep for stealth flight,' Kainan announced, stalking back to his captain's seat.

The engines, which had been warming up, rumbled in readiness.

He swiveled his chair and looked about the room, giving each bridge crew member a nod, a chin up, and a dip of his head in encouragement.

His eyes sliced over Selene on the bridge's upper deck, and she felt the freeze before his chair swiveled forward.

'Ghosts away,' he snarled, and with his words, the armada leaped forward into the void of space as one.

SELENE

Once the fleet was well underway to Dunia, Selene stepped down the stairs towards the command deck floor.

She wondered at the steadying power of Phantasm's inertial dampers, for it felt like they were sliding like silk through space.

Not a tremor or vibration marred their progress.

So why did her feet wobble and her hands shake as she approached the captain's ready room?

The door to the private office slid open, and she stood there watching the man before a series of screens.

His hands flew over a holo pad; his head cocked like he did when speaking non-verbally with the other members of The Sable Riders, some of whose faces she could see on the feeds.

She stood at the entrance, waiting for him to notice her.

She knew the moment he'd tagged her in the room and felt the unspoken roar of attraction and connection between them.

His jaw clenched, but he ignored her.

Eventually, he lifted his head and leaned back in his chair. '*Excellency*,' he rasped, not quite looking at her face but at a point beyond it. 'What can I do for you?'

She ignored the jolt of desire that jettisoned through her body at the sound of his voice. Instead, she stepped forward, and the door slid to a close behind her.

'We need to talk,' she said.

He raised an eyebrow.

'About your plans for The Technocracy,' she clarified.

'This is not the time or the place, *Excellency*,' he murmured, his deep voice laced with steely resolve.

Selene's face tightened. 'When is the right time and place? I need to know.'

'Perhaps after we've helped to liberate your planet from your enemies?'

He paused, and she saw his nose flare with deep, hidden emotion. 'How about then?'

'Now,' she insisted, striding closer to his desk. 'Before my people get caught up in something I can't explain. Like your stated plan to end the Technocracy. What is it?'

Kainan rose to his feet and rounded his desk.

He rested one hip against the desk and crossed his arms over his muscled chest. 'The thing is, *Excellency*, it's none of your business, and I don't need to explain what doesn't concern you to you. Once Dunia is free, once you're free, you won't need to know.'

'The thing is, *khosi*, without understanding your full plan, I don't know whether to trust you,' she snapped.

He leaned forward, and she caught her breath at the flare of wildfire in his eyes.

'It's too late now, *khamila*, isn't it?' he whispered, bending lower so his face was close to hers. He was taut with emotion, unconsciously slipping into his endearment for her. 'Too late to distrust me, to distrust us –.'

Selene felt his cold disdain and the force of his derisive words reflected in the flames of his eyes.

Her face grew hot at his bitterness.

'Fine!' she conceded, pulling away from him. 'Keep your secrets. Tell me one thing. Are you using us? Are you using Dunia in any way for some other play we're not privy to?'

Kainan snorted. 'Remember, *Excellency, you* came to us, not the other way around. We didn't need you,' he ground out, his double-edged words cutting her like blades. 'But this incursion forces us to accelerate some of our other plans. The moment our plans cross over with yours, you will be advised. But not a moment before then.'

They glared at each other, their stubborn hearts clashing.

The hum of the ship's ventilators and the quiet rumble of its engines faded into the ether around them.

Selene cut through the silence. 'Rina said you were honorable. And we've cut a deal that you have to come through on. So, I will choose to believe that we're not mere puppets. And that you'll keep to the terms of our agreement well before you unleash whatever other mad plans you're making. But know this, *khosi*, we've had enough pain to deal with recently. Please don't add to our – my people's – misery.'

With those hard words, Selene whirled around and stalked

away through the open sliding doors.

KAINAN

His lips twisted as he watched Selene leave.

The heat from her anger rolled back toward him and seared his soul.

'*Fokk*,' he ground out, stalking around his desk, letting his body fall back into the seat. He closed his eyes in defeat.

'Damn! That was rough,' said Riv, looking up at Kainan via his feed.

'You heard that?' Kainan snapped his eyes open, swiveling his chair back to face his display.

'Heard? *Nada*, I felt it. Every heart-wrenching emotion between you two.'

Kainan groaned. 'Brother -!'

'You left your sound on, *khosi*. Sorry, not sorry,' Riv shot back with a sloppy grin.

He sobered at the anguished look on his friend's face. 'You told her why you're freezing her out?'

Kainan bit his upper lip. '*Nada*,' he admitted.

'Why?'

'She doesn't need to know, see, or hear about it. All it means is I can't give her what she needs.'

'You haven't told her the truth, and you've not given her the benefit of the doubt for when she hears it. You're cutting her out because you're assuming the worst of her. As a result, you're suffering, brother.'

Kainan scrubbed his face in frustration. 'It can't be helped!'

Riv studied his friend's face. 'What can we do to help?'

Kainan shook his head. '*Nada*. No one can help. You know this.'

Riv gave Kainan a long look. 'The Sable brothers are one. So when one part suffers, the whole suffers with it.'

'Riv, *fokk* off with your poetry,' Kainan said with gruff affection.

'It's not just poetry,' Riv said, gesturing to make his point. 'It's the truth. We need to fix this. For you, for her, for us.'

'She's not in this equation!' Kainan snapped with a strangled sigh, running a hand over his hair.

Riv laughed. 'The *fokk* she's not. I see how she looks at you and how it affects you. From all accounts, she's a good woman, and the last I checked, you're a great *kinai*. You're good for each other, and you need each other. But you both won't get there without redemption. You both need redemption. And obstinacy does not redeem anyone.'

Kainan looked up through the open doorway towards the command entrance, where Selene had paused to speak with a crew member. Their eyes met, clashed with heat, and he jerked his head away, back to his screen.

'Let's focus on this incursion, brother,' Kainan groaned. 'There's only as much as I can take. Then maybe after, we can explore my options.'

SELENE

She swigged her glass around in one hand. She set it down with a thump, using a spoon to squish the savory pancake on her plate into the patterns below.

Her appetite was trashed, reduced to ashes.

The encounter with Kainan in his ready room had jarred her so much that she'd fled the bridge. After asking directions, she found the nearest open bar, hoping to drown her sorrow with good food and a strong drink.

It hadn't worked.

Hours later, all she was doing was brooding.

About the man her heart and body longed for, but her head was starting to loathe.

His bitter words kept washing over her.

We didn't need you, he'd said.

That had been the kicker. Nothing he'd said before had made her feel so unwanted. Yet she probably deserved to hear it, for it was the truth.

Any way you sliced it, she'd been the one in need. She'd been the one who'd begged for The Sable Riders' help. She'd been the one who offered Dunia's money as payment. She'd been the one to prostrate herself to him.

He'd even asked her to call a stop to their lovemaking on their first time.

But she hadn't been able to.

She'd been the desperate one.

Realizing the fact made her skin crawl. Selene had always been a strong woman, in charge, in control.

This new feeling of helplessness and dependence on The Sable Group for Dunia's freedom and on Kainan for his attention was unnerving.

Except now she was one hundred percent sure she did NOT need him any longer. Nope!

'Yes!'

She looked up from her messed-up plate at the sound of delight.

A young recruit seated at a nearby table was grinning and pumping his fist as he stared at his comm tab screen.

His friends crowded around him as he shared his happy news.

'The Sable Group just OK'd my scholarship to flight training!' he crowed.

His friends thumped his back and whooped with congratulations.

'So badass!' one girl said. 'I've been asked to be an apprentice to Shadow for the Eden II Endurance race.'

'Ay! They take care of *kienyeji* for real,' chimed in another young recruit, this time one with blue tattoos across his skin, similar to those of The Sable Riders. 'Even paid for my mother's clinic treatment when I asked for leave to visit her in Eden City last month -'

Selene sighed, staring at her drink, which was now a watery mess of gloopy syrup and melted ice.

She faced more reminders of Kainan everywhere she turned, evidence of his exemplary leadership and the deep respect felt by all under The Sable Group's command.

It sounded like the Sable Riders were the second coming of

Pegasi's long-gone Paladian gods.

She couldn't get rid of the feeling that she was the delusional one, that she'd been so wrong for believing he would have ever been interested in her. Why would a not-so-mortal god be interested in her? He had too much to do, too much to accomplish, and too many people to care for.

Damn! She was doing the one thing she'd promised herself years ago never to do: belittling herself while placing a man on a pedestal.

Just then, the ambient light in the bar dimmed, and a pulse of blue and red heliograph flashed throughout the space.

It was the sign to get to their stations, maintain radio silence, and avoid communication unless it was essential.

A quiet hush fell throughout the Phantasm.

It was GO time.

With a shake of her head, Selene collected herself and rose to her feet.

She tapped her wrist comm and swiped a payment and tip to the solemn-looking barman behind the counter.

His till pinged, and he dipped his chin in appreciation. He saluted her with a fist-to-shoulder gesture that she returned.

Selene joined the wave of disciplined recruits and officers as they exited the bar.

She wended her way back to the bridge, sliding through the blast doors unseen by Kainan, back to her assigned station on the upper deck.

She stored her bulky duffle bag in a locker above the station and strapped herself in case of sudden ship maneuvers.

The screen looming over the bridge showed a cluster of Technocracy ships huddled together in close orbit over Dunia - two massive capital ships and a couple of fighters.

The third capital ship was on patrol on the shadowed side of Dunia. There was no indication they'd spotted any signs of infiltration.

This was because the Ghost fleet was approaching along a geodesic between Alphetraz and Dunia, hiding their approach within the System's brightest and noisiest astronomic phenomenon.

Braking was made possible using a solar sail with the highest possible absorbance and adequate thrust of a maximum reflectance sail.

The Phantasm cruised at a higher elevation to the capital ships and the armada's frigates, extending its sail cover over the fleet and giving it a panoramic view of the coming action.

Kainan's gunship, connected to Mirage's AI controls on The Phantasm, flew next to the giant battleship, matching its every movement.

Selene watched as Kainan and his flight officers tweaked the thrust, braking, and propulsion controls.

Their gazes switched between the holographic display that showed the six stealth corvettes slipping past the blockade and the screens in front of them.

There was a palpable tension in the air when the six ships barely rippled through the sensor array.

'Party time, Voids,' Kainan whispered. He'd crossed his arms over his large chest with a hand gripping his chin and forefinger, tapping the side of his nostril in concentration as Notus I and II bore down on the capital vessels. 'Show us what you've got.'

Selene knew from their battle plans that they needed to get as close as possible to the capital ships before firing and before the crats could bring their point defense cannons online to intercept the rounds.

However, the Sable Riders had estimated that because the capital ships were so massive, dodging or turning from the first rail gun volley would not be an option for the enemy.

The timer on the screen ticked down to the last few seconds in silence.

It slipped to zero.

Simultaneously, both frigates, now five seconds away from The Technocracy, let their guns rip.

Thousands of projectiles poured out like a stream, and in milliseconds, they hit pay dirt.

Selene gripped the arms of her seat as explosions bloomed from both capital ships.

Notus I and II leapt away while the Technocracy's crafts scrambled to respond, swarming after the frigates.

The frigates responded with more rail gun volleys, blasting the first wave of crat flyers into oblivion.

The capital ships fired again after the exhaust plumes of their unseen enemy. But the frigates were moving too fast and with great agility.

They dodged much of what the crats tried to fire at them.

'Don't back down,' Kainan instructed Notus I and II's pilots, speaking at normal volume now that there was no need for radio silence. 'Your stealth kit and hulls are heavy enough that it'll take numerous anti-fighter missiles to down you.'

After they'd hammered the crat flyers for a few more minutes, Kainan called out to them.

'Step back, Voids. Now it's my turn to play.'

The frigates turned and accelerated as fast as they could in real space towards the Phantasm.

Which flung packed missiles and beam cannons towards

the crats. Each volley was heavy enough to cut through the capital ships, which tried to turn around, their turrets swiveling drunkenly in search of their attackers.

'I thought The Technocracy was way more efficient than that,' the Phantasm's pilot, a pretty young Falasian called Cilia, observed.

'They usually are. But we didn't just hit them with any old ordinance.'

'We didn't?' Selene asked from the galley, surprised by yet another new revelation.

Kainan acknowledged her with a stiff nod. '*Excellency*, we laced them with a little of their own medicine.'

'More secrets, *khosi*?' Selene clipped, her irritation showing in her raised eyebrows and narrowed eyes.

Kainan looked away, his eyes flashing with a warning.

The pilot, Cilia, piped up, saving Kainan from a reply. 'With what, *khosi*?'

Mirage entered the conversation. 'The barrels of our rail guns and handguns have been tipped with an inactive metanoid disassembler device. All our bullets and weapons, supplied by the Sable team, are coated with metanoids. When these bullets leave the weapon, the metanoids inside them reanimate and awaken. By the time they reach their targets, the 'noids are ravenous. They're not just smashing through their hull plating. They're chewing through reinforced armor and their crats like soft candy.'

'Where did all this tech come from?' Selene asked, keen to know more.

Kainan shrugged, keen to move the conversation on. 'It's just some new toys Mirage and Shadow have been working on. Let's keep focused –.' He paused with a smirk. '– On the mission. To make this a job well done, let's blitz the enemy. Bombs away.'

The Phantasm dropped a series of laser missiles towards the lower and faster orbit of The Technocracy fleet. Selene almost whooped as the projectiles smacked into their ships at a frightening velocity, shredding the two capital ships.

One exploded in a fiery mass while the other's bridge was annihilated, leaving it a husk of molten steel tumbling through space.

The bridge officers pumped their fists at the victorious strike.

Kainan issued more orders. 'Notus I and II stay in theater to pick off the few fighters left. Mirage, update?'

'Reports are coming in that the corvettes are well on their way to their targets. Wraith also reports he's downed the crats' sensor array.'

An alarm blared throughout the command deck.

According to the 3D holo projection, the third capital ship was rushing to defend its fleet within range of the planetary defense system.

'Zulu One,' Kainan said, speaking to Rina and her team on the planet's surface. 'You now have a clear shot at The Technocracy's third patrol boat.'

Within seconds, Rina sent fire, and they watched on-screen as the incoming warhead crashed into the remaining capital ship. In seconds, it was torn apart by the crushing force of its orbital velocity, meeting the missile and the resulting explosion.

Discarding all need for stealth and radio silence, the air-waves between the incursion fleet lit up as the alliance fleet cheered.

Selene could hardly believe it. *But, thank Dunia, their plan looked like it was working.* The swarm of Edenite stealth ships had become The Technocracy's worst nightmare.

The Phantasm's bridge crew celebrated. Selene spontaneously hugged the science officer whose station was next to hers.

She felt an arc of energy from across the room.

Her eyes were pulled to the deck below when she extracted herself from the male science officer's innocent embrace.

Her heart jumped when her gaze clashed with the hooded, heated one of Phantasm's captain.

Kainan jerked his head and looked away, but not before she noticed the micro expression that had flashed across his chiseled face.

Jealousy? Her traitorous heart pounded for a moment until her logic took over.

No. Just NO.

She couldn't take the heartache once more of hoping against all hope.

Kainan's commanding voice cut through her thoughts. 'Stage One of the incursion is complete—great work, crew, officers, and team. The next stage is the more protracted one. Landers and shuttles on the ready. Corvettes protect those helos and troops on their way down. Cilia, you have the chair.'

The young pilot beamed, hopping up to salute her captain. 'I'll keep an eye on all event ETAs up on the net and holo and keep you across anything extraordinary.'

Kainan nodded. '*Sante.*'

He flicked his eyes over the command deck and the reports scrolling on the screens and the ship's net, and, conceding

223

that nothing urgent needed his attention, he rose from his chair.

Kainan gathered his comm tab and great coat, which he slipped over his vast shoulders.

'Selene, Mirage, with me,' he said in a terse command.

He strode towards the sliding doors at the bridge's entrance. Selene nabbed her comm tab, reached for her duffle bag and jacket, and ran out of the command center after the disappearing man.

His long legs ate up the miles of the deck, and she found herself breathing hard to keep up.

Yet she kept a small distance between them, taking the coward's decision to stay as far away as she could from him.

He paid her no attention, keeping his eyes forward and chin hardened.

He nodded to the few recruits and officers they passed. They saluted as he swept by, their eyes worshipful.

Some even gave whoops of joy when he saluted back, their yells of elation like those given to a rock star.

What else could he seem like to them besides a hulking, chiseled superhuman hero? Who led an elite army of badass warriors to obliterate The Technocracy? Selene thought.

Soon, they rounded a corner into a corridor leading to one of the Phantasm's airlocks. It led to an air bridge that slotted into Kainan's gunship airlock.

Kainan lifted a hand, waving his wrist comm. The airlock slid open, and he strode forward while Selene trailed in after him, storing her bag away in Mirage's storage lockers.

They went through the familiar preflight sequence in silence.

Selene strapped in while Kainan patched into his screens,

speaking with Mirage.

'Phantasm, we're detaching now.'

Selene felt the grapples fall away as Mirage and Kainan maneuvered the sleek gunship away from the vast cruiser.

When they were at a safe distance, their engines rumbled up, and they pulled away from the fleet.

'We're going in, people,' Kainan said, warning the fleet of Mirage's descent to Dunia's surface.

Selene tightened her seat straps in anticipation of the bumpy ride down.

'I can report that our corvettes have also succeeded,' Mirage announced. 'Most of the One Dunia Coalition's surface defenses have been hammered into submission from a stand-off range without being intercepted and destroyed. The spaceport is also ours. Another victory.'

The AI followed the victorious report with a sober reminder. 'However, we've lost one corvette, and we can't get a hold of it - too much atmospheric interference.'

'Who's at the helm?' Kainan asked sharply.

'Major Levine, from the Galician corps division,' Mirage informed.

'Do what you can to get him back online, and if we don't hear from him in the next half hour, send Shadow, Phoenix, or Wraith after him. What other casualties do we have?'

'Twelve of our soldiers were wounded on Notus II when one of the Technocracy's missiles hit Deck 9. They're in the med bay and in the care of the medics. Other than that, the fleet is mostly intact.'

'Good. Shadow, report.'

Kage's face swum up on-screen. 'We're parked at an altitude above New Malindi, keeping an eye out for the landers and helos for a safe set down and waiting for you before we launch our targeted assault on all the critical strategic locations on our list. Phoenix is holding down the spaceport.'

'We're right behind you, Shadow,' Kainan announced.

'Wraith, all good in your neck of the woods?'

Riv jerked his chin on camera. 'Couldn't be any better. All's quiet over Rambasa. If the crats venture out of the dome, we've got the heavy guns ready to hold ground.'

'See you soon, Wraith,' Kainan rasped.

''Long as you don't burn up in the atmosphere, get crushed on impact, or break apart on landing, *khosi*,' Riv said dryly with a smirk. 'Or still, get murdered for no reason other than you chose not to seek redemption.'

The Rider comm'd off with a sly look on his face.

'Ignore that,' Kainan ground out at no one in particular. 'Wraith seems to think he's got jokes. He doesn't realize that one day, he could get killed for it.'

His sculpted, handsome face was livid, and Selene wisely kept her mouth shut.

13

Good Stalking

SELENE

The descent to Dunia was bumpy as Mirage dove around pockets of compressed air and wind as it burned through the atmosphere.

Mirage's thrusters had to work hard to deliver multi-g deceleration that would ensure a smooth landing.

The gunship's interior warmed up, but due to its super-efficient shields, it escaped most of the massive heat generated outside.

Selene felt her body tighten in anticipation of what was to come.

This was the final push.

The most critical step was gaining control of Dunia's military command centers, seats of government, infrastructure hubs, landing zones, and ports. They had to succeed; there was no other option.

Mirage broke through the atmosphere, and below them unfurled the Arumba continent, home to millions of people, including the inhabitants of New Malindi.

Kainan, still taciturn and stoic, guided Mirage towards Zaalalum.

The jungle rushed towards Selene's holo screen, and she took a deep breath, leaning forward until she noticed a dark mass over the sprawling forest.

A storm front.

They hit it with such impact that Mirage shuddered against the powerful external forces of nature.

Selene gulped as large plate-sized salvos of water flung from drenched skies slammed down to the planet's surface. Lightning flared; moments later, thunder crashes rocked the gunship.

'Dammit!' Kainan snapped as Mirage struggled against the planet's fury. 'Mirage, revert more power to your dampeners. We're getting slammed out there!'

'Something's happening, *khosi*.' Kage's voice thundered, radioing in from his Corvette. 'We're seeing massive storms picking up all over the continent.'

'Here too,' Xion said on-screen, his calm face screwed up in concern. 'The trees above Rambasa are going wild, moving against the wind, kicking up leaves and hail. Visibility is shit.'

By then, Mirage was close to the tree line above Zaalalum's altiphyte valley, now a seething mass of movement. On the view screen, soaring phytaphylia trees whipped themselves from side to side.

Mirage managed to duck a long-reaching thorny

gametangium that unfurled from its trunk.

Selene watched in shock as brachyphia ferns rose in waves above ground, crashing against themselves in a fury, aided by the extreme forces of vertical and horizontal wind shear.

'It's the planet!' Selene whispered.

Kainan whipped around to face her. 'Did you say the planet? Selene, what-in-the-actual is going on? Because this storm is not natural at all. It's not letting us through.'

Selene stared back at him wide-eyed. 'I think I know what's going on. I believe Dunia is resisting.'

'*Dafokk?*' Kainan ground out, his brow furrowed.

'The planet is semi-sentient,' she told him. 'It's fighting us. It probably thinks we will harm it and the people of Dunia because our corvettes attacked the spaceport and the other locations. So it now thinks that we're the enemy.'

Kainan's eyes narrowed at her words. Then he shook his head and whipped his chair back to the controls.

'Mirage, pull back up to a safe altitude, out of reach of the tree line. Please do the same for the Sable Team and all corvettes in space above the planet. And stay safe above the storm in a holding pattern until Her Excellency and I sort this out.'

His hands flew over the controls before he whirled around to face Selene.

'You're not *fokkin'* around about this sentient business, are you?' he demanded.

She shook her head.

Kainan gave a mirthless laugh. 'I'd heard about it but didn't think it was this psychotic. I thought it was meditation pools and spiritual mumbo jumbo.'

Selene took a deep breath. *Dunia, help me with this man,* she thought.

Forcing herself to sound polite, she spoke up. 'Please don't insult what you don't understand. I'll let your ignorance slide because you're under the pump, Kainan. '

His nose flared, and he curled his lip, looking away. 'Won't happen again,' he groused.

All she could do was shake her head in disbelief.

His eyes sliced back to meet hers. 'So what do we do to ensure we can land?'

She sighed, relieved that he'd calmed down somewhat. She paused, her head tipped back as she thought.

'We don't have all day, Selene,' Kainan growled. 'I've got an entire fleet in limbo circling the planet.'

'I know!' she said, giving him a cool look. 'A moment, please. I need to think.'

He crossed his arms over his massive chest and glared at her.

She ignored him for a long moment.

At long last, she spoke, choosing her words with care. 'I think I can try to speak to the planet, to appeal to it. To convince it that we're trying to help. However, to do that, I need to get down to the Enclave, to the grotto.'

'*Fokk* me!' Kainan cursed. 'How do we even get you down there? Safely?'

'I have no idea.'

He glanced out of the windows, eyes fixed on the horizon where the storm still raged, lost in deep thought.

'We need a small, maneuverable yet powerful form of insertion,' he hypothesized, speaking low and deep, almost to himself.

His wildfire eyes darted around the bridge and to the

storage lockers below Mirage's deck.

'The meta suits,' he concluded.

'I was going to suggest the same, *khosi*,' Mirage piped up.

'Now you speak up!' Kainan huffed, shaking his head, still frustrated and irritated.

Selene sensed it was due to more than just the storm raging outside.

'How about you find a way to hover above this crack-ass storm,' he railed at the AI. 'While Selene and I battle these massive storms and try to land with a powered shell casing to protect us from the madness outside?'

'*Khosi! Naam, khosi!*' the AI shot back with a sarcastic edge. 'You'll still need my help navigating through that squall in your suits.'

Kainan grimaced at the thinly veiled taunt, then rose to his feet, gesturing at Selene to do the same.

He moved fast, sliding down the command staircase and again to the cargo and storage bay. She ran behind him and down the stairs into the bay.

Kainan strode to one side of the spacious storage area, opening a series of neo-steel lockers.

Each locker revealed rows of armored gear, above which a few helmets hung.

The suits looked unremarkable to her.

The headgear, however, was familiar, the same design as the one she'd worn on their flight to J'Urg Mihòr.

'You'll need to strip,' Kainan murmured.

She ogled her eyes, and he raised an eyebrow. 'Nothing I haven't seen before.'

They shared a heated glance before he looked away. 'Hurry, Selene, time is not on our side.'

She let her inhibitions go and shed her cotton jumpsuit, stepping out naked before him.

Eyes hooded over, he handed her a soft-looking, almost silken garment.

'It's a smart meta under-suit,' he said. 'It can handle any concussive forces with sensors built into key points to provide biofeedback to the powered joints and musculature. It also helps with load support and comfort, and keeps track of your body functions.'

She stepped into it, and it slid on, instantly contouring her curves.

She smoothed her hands over the material, astonished by how luxurious it felt and the incredible sensation of sensors melding to her skin.

'Next is the hard frame, which is a meta-flow material. It can resist any ballistic weapons and laser beams. Its meta features include full stealth mode that extends to any weapons in your hands.'

Selene took the outer armor from him and stepped into it. It also seemed to come alive, sliding over her body, the overlapping flexible plates snapping into place.

The metanoids formed into anti-grav boots, rugged neo-steel outer soles appearing under the incredible velvet-like insole.

'The external frame houses a small, fast-charging nano nuclear RTG,' Kainan added.

'RTG?' she asked.

'A radioisotope thermoelectric generator,' Kainan replied. 'A nuclear battery that uses an array of thermocouples that provides the suit with a compact and dense power source. The suit is lightning-proof and has heavy-duty shielding to protect you from inner and outer radiation. The metanoids embedded into the plates will counteract any dents or impacts and intuitively 'heal' the suit. It can withstand most kinetic forces and resist heat up to 1500 degrees Celsius. Plus, it houses a respirator that can stay powered for up to 25 hours. It also has inbuilt force amplification, which means you can jump up to six feet high and punch through light walls if needed. It won't go through reinforced or thick walls, so don't get too brassy.'

After his short spiel, he handed her the helmet. 'You remember this?'

She nodded as she slid it over her head, the clear plex helmet fitting to the meta suit below it with a soft hiss.

Sound and air equalized in nanoseconds, and Selene watched as the 360-degree HUD lit up, showing a full charge and scrolling telemetry.

'I didn't give you a briefing on it then because I didn't think it was needed, but please listen up now - for your safety,' he continued. 'The helmet's integrated computer can maintain the atmosphere inside the armor. It regulates all armor integrity and has motion-sensing radar, thermal, and heartbeat sensors. The inbuilt cameras and HUD patches with Mirage, and she'll guide us using our cam feeds down onto the surface.'

She looked up at him, her visor still open. 'What if I need to go?'

His brow wrinkled for a moment until his brain caught up. He sighed. 'Selene, do you need to go?'

'*Nada*,' she said with a wry smile. 'But what if I need to?'

His lips quirked. 'Then the suit will whisk away any waste before you even know you must go. Don't worry. Your every need will be taken care of.'

Selene felt the familiar desire and pull between them as their gazes clashed.

Then came the loss of their connection when Kainan turned away and began to strip himself.

Her mouth watered as she darkened her helmet's visor with a thought.

This allowed her to stare, unobserved, at his magnificent body, the beautiful sapphire and gold glyphs that slid over his smooth skin, and the muscles that pulsed with heated energy.

She turned away.

For he had never been hers, to begin with.

'Ready?'

Kainan's timbre reverberated through her helmet.

She turned back to find a menacing, towering silhouette standing there.

She shivered at the sight of his looming badassness.

Complete with a lethal-looking steel gray rifle strapped to his back and two laser handguns in a belt at his hips.

'Why don't I have one of those?' she asked, pointing to his hip. 'I can handle most weapons if needed.'

'Because I doubt you've been trained on our laser meta tech. Also, because weapons invite fire, you should know that. The last thing I need is you attracting any rogue crat sniper.'

'I appreciate the care and concern,' she clipped.

'Anytime. Let's go.'

They stepped into the rapidly closing airlock above the throbbing drive core of Mirage's reactor.

Kainan tapped a small power button on her suit and did the same to him.

She felt a lift from her maglev boots just as Mirage's outer door slid open, and Dunia's rage lashed out at them.

Kainan's thick forearm hooked into her own, and then he flung them out of the gunship's airlock into thin air.

They twisted mid-air and sped forward toward the angry jungle below. Rain was sheeting down over their helmets, but inside, the external camera's feed gave her a panoramic view of their re-entry, free of rain and static.

Branches and debris flew towards them, and Selene drew in her breath, ducking her head and bracing herself for impact.

'Excellency, relax,' Mirage said into her ear. 'I'm in control.'

There was no impact.

Mirage worked the suits' sensitive full-body force-feedback interface, making fast maneuvers that dodged the waving ganglia, the vast slabs of rock, and the wild debris coming their way.

Selene turned her head to glance at Kainan's hulking armor.

He'd since let go of her arm, yet he remained close to her side, almost touching her as they flew in tandem.

She could hear his steady breathing in her HUD speakers, calming her heart.

They dove and weaved past a furious clade of trees, escaping a giant boulder flying through the air. Then, they dove through a swarm of livid giant bees that screeched past them, attacking with enormous proboscis and extended claws.

However, they couldn't escape the hail.

It battered their suits, and Selene looked on in awe as the outer plates absorbed the damage and reknit themselves without her feeling anything.

Mirage's piloting, however, ensured they dodged the more

significant obstacles the planet was sending their way, and soon enough, Selene relaxed into the flight.

With Kainan beside her, it seemed that they were dancing through the skies, and Selene felt the contradictory beauty of the moment.

Then, they were past the tree line, coasting towards the gates of Zulu One. The Enclave was sheltered by the large trees that had just attacked it.

They bent their wide branches around the perimeter of the garrison, stopping the barrage of nature from getting through.

The worst storm surge and the blast of strong wind, hail, and lightning were behind them.

Selene felt the suit decelerate, using its nano thrusters to slow down until she and Kainan landed with a gentle bump of compressed air.

'*Sante*, Mirage,' Selene muttered in relief, even as the sound of the driving hail and rain clattered against her helmet.

They'd landed just outside the gates to Zulu One, which were now sliding open to reveal the anxious faces of the Free Dunia Council, led by Rina.

Mirage had comm'd ahead, and they now all stood awaiting the new arrivals under the broad awning of the gate, safe from the pouring rain.

Selene was overwhelmed with sudden emotion and whipped off her helmet, running towards her best friend.

'You made it!' Rina breathed, folding Selene and her armored suit into a hug.

'So good to be here,' Selene whispered into her friend's ear.

'That bad?' Rina asked with a raised eyebrow.

'Tell you later,' Selene replied, jerking when Kainan's

hulking physique appeared beside her.

Rina tagged Selene's narrow-eyed expression, keenly looking at the giant warrior beside her best friend. She raised her eyebrows even further, and Selene shook her head.

'OK, let's get to business,' Rina said, snapping to attention.

'Your Excellency, good to have you back.' The speaker was Ines Motho, the Dunian Education Minister, a short, stout, dark-skinned woman with pretty features and a sharp mind.

'It's good to be back,' Selene said, pointing to the hulking man beside her, shaking his long hair free of his helmet. 'You remember Kainan Sable.'

'Of course,' Ines simpered, a slight blush appearing on her plump cheeks as she stared at the towering Edenite as he removed his headgear.

Then she snapped back to professionalism. 'We thank The Sable Group for their immense help in our time of need. We just got the word you were arriving, but we've had no context yet. Maybe you can tell us why the ground assault hasn't begun.'

'Apologies, Minister, we've had no time to brief you,' Selene replied. 'The thing is, our corvettes can't land. The planet is fighting them.'

The Council members shared glances.

'We feared this would be the case. So what can be done?' L'Ogano Rai, the sallow-faced, tall, and thin Minister of the Interior, fielded the question.

'I've got an idea, but I'll need to move fast.'

'Do what you need to,' urged the Commerce Minister, Genevieve Ravi.

She bowed, as did the rest of the Free Dunia Council members. They parted so Selene could move past them while

Kainan prowled behind her.

Selene grabbed Rina's arm as she strode forward. 'I need to get to the grotto. Now.'

Rina's face fell, confused. 'Why?'

'I'm going to speak with the planet's spirit, its sentience.'

Rina's eyes widened. 'You *now* think you can talk to the planet?'

They hurried past the gates and into the well-armed facility.

'But I thought you didn't have the gift?' Rina continued.

'Something happened one night when I was on Eden II.'

'Go on,' Rina encouraged.

'I had a dream that suggested I might be able to speak to Dunia's spirit,' Selene said.

Rina arched an eyebrow. 'Really?'

'Call me crazy, but Dunia's presence was with me. It spoke to me. Maybe I can reach out to it now, and it'll listen.'

'I think you're mad, but if you believe this can work, get your ass out there!' Rina said, pushing Selene forward. 'As Her Honor said, do what you need to.'

Selene nodded to her friend and the Council members hovering in the background. Then she took off at a jog. She heard footsteps, and in seconds, Kainan was beside her.

The meta suits made their run effortless, and before long, they were striding over the jungle behind the Enclave, helmets held in their hands. Despite the storm, waves of tiny, glowing creatures rose from the forest floor, creating bioluminescent patterns around their feet.

Selene caught Kainan's awestruck expression as he brushed off the shimmering lightning bugs fluttering around his face.

She found the flight of stairs leading to the grotto's cobblestone path.

She ducked under the overhanging entrance while Kainan contended with the vines tumbling down the cave's natural awning, reaching out to ensnare him.

He pushed them away, allowing him to step beside the stone wall enclosing the deep blue pool of water dotted with lily pads and blooming lotus flowers.

He studied all around him in wonder at the carved rock figurines, the flickering lamps, and the draped lotus blossoms.

Selene watched him and felt a pang of longing, wishing she'd brought him here under different circumstances.

But she had no time to waste.

'I've got to get in the water.' She set her headgear down on the edge of the stone wall and shed her meta suit and boots, leaving only the soft, smart undersuit.

She stepped barefoot into the water under Kainan's watchful gaze, gasping at the cooler temperature against her hot body.

The pool's mirrored veneer stirred around her hips, and she ran her hands under the surface, lifting them out and watching droplets fall away.

She studied the surface of the water for a moment.

'Well, Dunia,' she muttered. 'Where do I start? I've no idea what exactly to say, but here goes. First, I realize it's not easy to distinguish attacks from space or mid-air as being friendly or enemy fire. The armada circling the skies above Dunia is on our side. They are an alliance between our people and those of Eden II. Together, we're an incursion fleet, here to fight off The Technocracy's army and a coalition of traitors who killed the Prime and tried to take over the planet. They're here to help me take back control. So please let them land as they're not the enemy.'

She paused for a moment. 'Secondly, the sooner you let them land, the quicker they'll be able to liberate the cities and help keep more of our people alive.'

Her voice fell away, leaving just the sound of the lapping water and the distant call of birds outside.

Selene waited for a minute or two. Nothing happened.

She shook her head, turning to face Kainan in desperation. 'Do you think it heard me?'

He shrugged.

Silence fell once more in the cave.

Selene was about to speak again when a whisper echoed through the hallowed space. '*The wise speak. Dunia listens. And blessings follow.*'

Selene took a big breath at the sound of the voice. 'It spoke. You heard it, right?'

Kainan had a small, bemused smile on his face. 'I did.'

They watched wonder-struck as the cave's waters stirred into tiny waves that flowed over and around Selene, pulsing.

Then, the same column of water she'd seen before rose out of the swirling liquid, and then it fell away into the pool, leaving behind waves of pure luminescence.

'Oh my,' she whispered.

Kainan held up a finger and cocked his head, listening to his neural node.

After a few long minutes, he nodded, looking nonplussed. He gave a low whistle of disbelief. 'Seems to have worked. Mirage and the Sable Riders report that the storm is calming down. The forests have stopped attacking, and the planet is letting through our corvettes and landers, for all intents and purposes.'

'Thank Dunia,' Selene said, relieved.

She sunk into the warm waters and ducked her head under the surface, letting the planet wash away all the frustration and pent-up tension she'd felt over the last few days.

When she emerged, she noticed Kainan crouched against the stonewall. His hands were clasped together, hooded eyes on her.

She ignored him, pushing away the curls plastered to her scalp and shaking them out.

'The power to summon a planet, huh?' he murmured.

She shrugged, pulling herself out of the water to sit on the flagstones by the pool that pulsed with luminescent light.

Her upper body remained in the water, and she played with it, pushing it to and fro with her arms. 'This is all new to me, as it is to you,' she told him. 'It was the Prime's - my father's - thing.'

Kainan gave her a long look.

'Your thing too, it would seem, *khamila*,' he said, his endearment charging the air between them.

The pool stirred as if also sensing the shifting mood between the pair.

'It's incredible,' he went on, rising to his feet and walking towards her.

'You're incredible,' he rasped, looming over her before crouching beside her.

She tried to turn away, but he reached his large wrists to clutch her upper arms.

He pulled her body toward his, lifting her further up the flagstones, leaving her feet on the edge of the lapping pool.

'What do you want from me?' she said with a ragged whisper, eyes fixated on his hands and their heated connection.

The sudden whiplash in his demeanor was messing with her heart and mind. 'I can't handle how hot and cold you are,' she shared.

Kainan slid one heated palm up and down her arm in reassurance.

She could tell he was searching for what to say next.

After a beat, he looked up at her. 'I'm sure of what I want. But I'm unsure whether what I can give you is what you want. So, I'm not certain what this could be. But no matter what we are or will be, I'll never hurt you, Selene. Please believe me.'

'The one thing I know beyond doubt is that I was the one who made a mistake,' she stated, her hurt naked across her face.

'A mistake?'

'The mistake of thinking this was anything more than just a fling,' she added, her face wooden.

His lips twitched, and he leaned forward.

He kissed her on her chin and neck, dragging his firm, warm lips along her sensitive skin.

She shivered, and her body gave a jolt at his sensual caresses.

'It wasn't a fling, though, was it?'

His voice was a deep drawl against the underside of her neck.

'Neither for you nor me,' he insisted, moving to brush her ears, then their tips, with his mouth.

His hands on her arms had stilled, but his thumbs reached out to gently stroke the tips of her hard nipples, pushing out against her soft undersuit.

This sent bolts of desire through her, and she jerked again.

'You feel this connection between us, *khamila*, don't you?'

he said, running his hot tongue within the folds of her ear. 'Because this connection is what I'm sure of.'

She couldn't take any more. She pushed Kainan back. 'You also said you're unsure what this could be.'

He gave her a rueful smile with genuine remorse. 'All it means is that I can't predict what happens tomorrow. Why can't we live day-by-day and enjoy what we have now, in the present?'

Selene was unconvinced. 'Because day-by-day is temporary as all *fokk*. I want to be with someone in this to the finish line.'

His hands fell away from her arms, but he remained close. The heat radiating off his large body warmed her skin.

His shoulders dropped, and his weariness crept into his voice. 'You don't know just how much I understand about the finish line.'

'Don't!' she warned him, giving him a pleading look.

'Don't what, *khamila*?'

'Don't call me *khamila*, and don't start what you don't want to finish.'

He paused, his wildfire eyes glowing with a strange light. 'What if I do want to finish it? But I can't?'

She threw up her hands in frustration. 'I don't even know what that means. What are you talking about?'

A flash of pain crossed his face.

He sucked in air, his deep breaths filling the cavern.

His eyes stared at her, hardening.

Yet she sensed a hidden longing and sorrow within him.

'You won't tell me, will you?' she asked, her voice low and quiet.

He closed his eyes and shook his head.

243

She sighed. 'As I told you before, Kainan, keep your secrets, but please don't play with me. It just underscores how little you think of me.'

He shuttered, the warmth in his eyes fading as if the walls in his heart were slamming up again. His hands pulled back, and he seemed to lean away from her.

She looked away, unable to handle *him, it, them*.

There was a long, tense silence between them.

'What happens now? With the incursion?' she sighed, changing the subject while keeping her eyes fixed on the swirling water below.

Kainan rose to his feet, crossing his arms over his chest. He seemed like a colossal giant silhouetted against the sky, darkening over the planet.

He looked to the side, listening in to his neural node.

When he finally spoke, all previous affection had disappeared from his voice.

Instead, he was pure business: cool, calm, and back in control. 'Our troops have managed to land from their drop crafts in all key locations. Shadow, Phoenix, and Wraith have also touched down and are leading the planned assaults.'

'That's good progress then,' Selene said, gazing at the waters below.

'Shadow - Kage - is about to storm New Malindi,' Kainan added. 'I think it's best if I go in to support him.'

His announcement sent a frisson of fear through her core. Fear for him.

She hadn't thought much about where he would go after landing.

Kainan hadn't shared details of his plans, of how and where he'd be during the incursion.

She'd assumed he'd stay at Zulu One.

'Now?'

'Now.'

'Don't you need to be at the command post here? Running the show?'

'Rina's in charge of the ground operations. She's more than competent.'

Selene kept her eyes lowered, her heart still smarting from their conversation.

'I should come with you,' she offered, cringing as the words left her lips.

'*Nada*,' he growled.

Her eyes shot up to his, flashing. 'Why? Because you can't afford to be slowed down by me?' she blurted out.

'Something like that.'

'I have military training, Kainan,' she protested. 'I can keep up with the best.'

'That may well be. However, tis not what's required now. We need you safe at Zulu One, liaising with the Council, addressing your citizens, keeping our people informed, and boosting general morale. That's where you're best utilized.'

She couldn't argue with his fair assessment, Selene thought to herself.

However, it flew against all her instincts to remain by his side, no matter what.

'Fine,' she clipped, rising to her feet.

Water dripped from her body, but the smart suit wicked away the wetness.

In seconds, she was dry again, and she reached for her meta suit and pulled it on, trying to block out the man working triple time to remain aloof in her presence.

'I'll offload your bags myself from Mirage and bring them to the command center,' he offered.

She gave him a stiff nod of thanks. 'I guess this is goodbye then,' she muttered when she was all suited up.

Kainan frowned. 'You ought to say 'Good stalking' instead. To wish me well because I will return.'

'Good stalking then, Kainan,' she shared, her eyes averted as she brushed past him to climb the stairs out of the cavern.

KAINAN

His stoic facade collapsed the moment Selene said goodbye at the grotto.

When she'd walked past him, her enticing scent had filled his nostrils and stoked the now ever-present ache deep in his chest.

'Look at me, *khamila*, when you wish me well,' he'd muttered, breaking his detachment and grasping her upper arm as she climbed the steps, needing more from her that she wouldn't give him.

Selene served him a sad smile, her eyes not quite meeting his.

She shook his hand off, walking away.

'You won't even look at me?' Kainan had called out after her, his voice bitter.

This time, it was he who was left speaking to empty air.

He sucked his teeth, as his large frame slumped against the vine-lined wall.

The cave's lianas reached out to him, and he let them trail over his weary body this time.

Then the cavern's pool began to stir, with little waves that lapped at the stone edge.

They began to form into tiny fingers, and he imagined for a moment they were beckoning at him, inviting him into the warm waters.

He stepped towards the edge, and the waves lapped up even higher as if welcoming his approach.

He shed his meta suit, just like Selene had, and eased into the mirrored water to wade into the center of the deep pool.

The sensation was almost euphoric.

He lost all thoughts of the battle raging on the planet beyond and the responsibilities on his shoulders.

All he wanted to do was sink under the surface and wash all his sorrow away.

He ducked his head under the surface, swam onto his back, and closed his eyes, letting go.

His log-like arms, muscled body, and thick thighs felt weightless as he was enveloped in the cave's warmth, as time slipped away.

A wind blew, and suddenly he heard a whisper.

'*Your inner flame is fading, Kainan,*' came a small, still voice.

He panicked at the sudden words, flailing in the water while struggling to open his eyes.

'*Rest Edenite, rest,*' the voice repeated.

'Who are you?' he called out, trying to rise out of the pool.

Yet a powerful energy seemed to hold him back, gently yet firmly.

He felt an intense desire to close his eyes and sleep forever.

There was a long silence before the whisper returned. *'We are those who conceal ourselves from the mind of man but reveal ourselves to his heart.'*

The waves lapped against his body, lulling him to pure relaxation and stillness.

'You need healing,' the voice continued.

'Where will I find healing?' Kainan groaned.

'Dunia not only vanquishes its enemies, but its forests and waters are full of the remedy you need.'

'You can't heal what I have,' Kainan slurred. 'It's unfathomable.'

'When there is no enemy within, the enemies outside cannot hurt you. So return to us when you're ready to believe,' the quiet voice said.

Silence fell once more in the grotto, and Kainan lost all track of time.

After some time, he felt a slight bump from a wave, and the waters slowed the rocking massage of his body.

After a few long minutes, he sensed a release of energy and shifted his body, swimming to the edge to pull himself out.

He sat on the flagstones for a moment, feeling refreshed.

That's when he looked down at his wrist. To where an old scar had once snaked its way across his hand. His eyes rose at the sight of the baby smooth skin.

He thought for a moment, then shook his head.

'Impossible,' he whispered.

He gazed at the water and wondered how it had lured him earlier.

Or had he been that exhausted? From sleepless nights spent thinking about one enticing woman on the one hand and the battle ahead of them on the other.

All of that, plus the growing dread of his diminishing existence.

With his present cares rushing back into his mind, Kainan did what was second nature to him.

He blocked out all apprehension and focused on the task at hand.

'Mirage?' he called out, shrugging back into his armored suit and strapping his wrist comm back on. 'You still in orbit?'

'*Naam, khosi,*' came the prompt response.

'Please fetch me. I'll be waiting on the orbital landing pad at Zulu One.'

'Copy. On my way,' the AI confirmed.

He dragged his helmet on and jogged out of the stunning grotto.

'Where is Her Excellency?' he asked the AI.

'She's at the Enclave's command center.'

'*Sante.* Please keep tabs on her and report any changes to her status at once.'

'*Khosi.* Will do. Do you want an updated report on your status?'

Kainan shook his head with some impatience as he ate up the distance between himself and the orbital launch pad. 'What do you mean?'

'While your chimera cells are still in flux, I'm seeing an increase in the levels of healthy blood cells, positive cardiac biomarkers, a higher oxygen count, and a lower overall body temp.'

At Mirage's words, Kainan slowed his run to a walk. 'Is that right?'

'*Naam* and I'm also seeing -.'

'Enough,' Kainan said, cutting off the AI. 'I don't have the time or headspace for this. Just get me the hell out of here. We've got a battle to fight and a war to win.'

14

Big Energy

SELENE

I t took three days to take partial control of the beleaguered city of Paris Minor and the capital, New Malindi.

Street by street, they fell to the Alliance's elite troops and were handed over to Free Dunia's control.

Twas a relentless incursion: no pauses, rest breaks, or respite.

Selene followed every battle, every skirmish, and every report she could get her hands on.

She was driven, but soon her weariness caught up to her.

On the morning of the fourth day after the landings, she yawned over her fifth cup of *kahawa*, trying to take in the latest update on the battle on her comm tab's screen.

She was ever grateful for the Sable-led Edenite troops. Indeed, they were skilled soldiers trained to operate for days without external support.

Phantasm's landers had delivered them onto Dunia's surface along with high-tech, all-terrain troop vehicles and support weapons.

They set down on a planet quite unlike their own.

However, the Edenites' extensive experience in aggressive high-mobility assaults and tactical flexibility meant they could adapt to the unexpected, including Dunia's unique ecology.

Once they reached the cities, the Edenites blasted in, using giant lasers to cut through the dome's defense walls like butter.

The Technocracy's fabled military and defensive superiority were tested by the defenders' nano-laced bullets that weakened their circuitry.

Causing their fighters to crash and malfunction by altering their perceptions and signals.

This made them easy pickings for snipers and gunners.

However, they were still a lethal force that adapted quickly.

But the Edenites adapted even faster.

Under the leadership of the Sable Riders, the troops on the ground held ground, consolidated gains, and followed up initial assaults.

They also provided heavy support, flank protection, and security alongside the planet's army, which was still loyal to the Free Dunia Council.

Zane was supporting the incursion from Eden II.

He'd been working overtime to send nano-laced weaponry and astromech droids to the Edenite troops.

He was a clever operator, moving schills, troops, and equipment efficiently and in bulk.

In addition, he'd masterminded a streamlined supply system between the Notus I and II frigates and landers while the Phantasm patrolled the planet from orbit.

With the new leading-edge weaponry and machinery, the Alliance proved victorious over key battlegrounds and reduced most of One Dunia's militia and the invading crat army into rubble.

Casualties on the One Dunia Coalition side had racked up to over 470 soldiers and over 3,000 Technocracy crats, all lost.

On the other hand, the Free Dunia Alliance's losses were low.

They'd lost thirty soldiers.

They also mourned the loss of Major Levine, the Galician corps pilot of the single corvette that The Technocracy had downed over Paris Minor.

The major had been found shot to death in a remote forest location after he'd ejected from the downed ship.

The Corvette, call name Aura, had disappeared with no trace.

The Sable Group was still searching for it and, at best, hoped that Dunia had swallowed it into itself.

At worst, its tech was now in the hands of unknown persons.

Nothing, however, could be confirmed either way.

Thankfully, Rambasa and the Neo Valley, the sources of Dunia's rich deposits of xentium, were still secure.

So was Axuma. Where Harlow, Selene's friend, had her lab and home.

However, after a worrying report that Massimo Makori

had sent a shadowy group of assailants to track her down and capture her and the critical research she was developing, Selene had asked the Riders to find a way to get her out of the lakeside city.

Zane had taken her comm request since Kainan was focused on the ground incursion. Plus, Selene had been chicken to ask Kainan herself.

Zane had recruited Kage to do the honors.

The Edenite had moved fast, taking his Corvette to find her in Axuma.

He'd found her blissfully unaware that she was in danger.

After some initial resistance, Harlow had seen sense and allowed Kage to airlift her away from danger and deposit her at Zulu One a day later.

News also came that the One Dunia Coalition had tried to invade Wadi and the archipelago off the western coast of Usmina.

But they'd been rebuffed by a platoon of Edenites led by Kage, Riv, and a few more of The Sable Riders' best mercenaries.

As his influence and short grab for power dwindled, Massimo, the now self-proclaimed Prime Minister, continued to bombard the news holos with bloated assertions of control.

In addition, he assailed the airwaves with baseless accusations of terrorism and contrived grievances about the unfair treatment of his loyal followers, who were now regretting their life choices as they faced treason charges.

The Free Dunia Council fought back with proof of his shady deals and corrupt payments to the governor of the Wadi province in exchange for mining rights.

He blustered against the Justice Minister, who wanted to

take him to court for signing fraudulent contracts with a shady mining conglomerate that was a front for The Technocracy.

When Massimo tried to deny the charges against him, he tasted the bitterness of betrayal.

A few leading lights of the One Dunia Coalition, now captured, attempted to negotiate lighter sentences by swearing that they'd witnessed Massimo offering to sell xentium to The Technocracy.

However, the most damning evidence against the man proving his betrayal was a viral video showing him storming Parliament before Prime Kei'Lano's untimely death.

The riots in New Malindi had gone into overdrive with this latest development, and the local hospitals and clinics were overwhelmed with casualties.

Under Kainan's leadership, the Alliance troops swarmed into the capital's streets and quelled further infighting.

Holo bulletins urged residents to shelter in their homes as the elite troops were on patrol, breaking up brawls and hunting down the crats.

Ultimately, the Free Dunia Council declared a curfew, and relative peace returned to the streets.

Yet pockets of resistance remained.

The few remaining Technocrats and One Dunia militia had resorted to guerrilla attacks and cowardly bombings of civilian locations to drum up fear and terror.

Their attempts were feeble, and their positions obliterated, for the Alliance troops were well supplied and protected with the Sable Rider's closed air support and superiority.

Selene and Rina monitored the entire ground incursion from the command center at Zulu One.

The four Sable Riders in theater - Kainan, Riv, Kage, and Xion - were now in charge of large swathes of territory, taking strategic and tactical direction from Rina.

She was coordinating the ground operations - from logistics to troop movements. Her military prowess and leadership were on show for all to see as she worked in tandem with the Riders.

They, in turn, gave her the respect she deserved to run the operation, which impressed Selene with their lack of ego.

Given their military prowess, they could have run roughshod over Rina. But instead, they treated her like one of their own, giving her no mercy and razing her for any awkward calls she made, which were for her, fortunately, far and few between.

Even though she'd given him the cold shoulder when they parted ways at the grotto, Selene looked out for every sign of Kainan's movements.

She knew he was patrolling New Malindi and was secretly watching him via his location tracker, which pulsed off a hidden page on her comm tab.

Her nerves were beyond ragged by the fourth day of imagining him dodging snipers and running into surprise militia attacks.

She wasn't sleeping and was spending her days glued to a series of small and large screens.

She was obsessing over the displays, switching from one battle zone live feed and map to another, when she heard Mirage's voice over the comms.

'Command, we need more troops or air cover over in the east zone of New Malindi. The *khosi* is taking heavy fire.'

Selene sat up in her seat, worry and dread flooding her.

She set her *kahawa* cup down in haste.

'Rina!' she cried out, signaling to her friend standing over their logistics holo, scrutinizing troop movements with a colleague.

Rina looked up, noted the panic on her friend's face, and jogged straight over.

'What's up?' she asked, sliding into a chair before the command screens.

'You need to talk to Mirage. She's got news on Kainan.'

Rina noted Selene's wide, panicked eyes and slid her gaze back on-screen.

'Mirage, I can hear you,' Rina said, swiping across her comm pad and screens to zero in on Mirage's location that pulsed on the holo map. 'What seems to be the matter?'

'The *khosi* and I were on patrol, and we stumbled on a pocket of crats hiding in an abandoned storage depot. Unfortunately, I'm in gyrfalcon form, so I can't give him air cover. I could summon his gunship remotely, but I'd have to get past too many skirmishes and snipers and may not reach him in time.'

'Has Kainan been harmed?' Selene found herself asking.

The crackle of radio static filled the comm waves.

Then came the familiar deep voice.

It sent shivers down Selene's back that coalesced in her fast-drumming heart.

'I'm fine, *Excellency*, not a scratch. That said, I'm running out of ammo.'

Selene sat back in her chair. Rina shot her a sharp look, which dropped to the visible tremble of her best friend's arms.

She reached out a hand to calm Selene before continuing to monitor the situation until she breathed out in relief. 'Echo

257

One is close to your location. How many bogeys are you up against, Kainan?' she asked.

'Nine. Five down,' he replied, his deep voice tight with tension. 'Their circuitry is breaking up on a few of them, and their reactions are erratic. Nonetheless, I need support. They've got more ammo than I have, and I can't hold this position much longer.'

'Two minutes away,' Rina reassured him.

'Send me their comm trackers, please,' Mirage added. 'Kainan's too focused on taking them out. In turn, I'll paint the bogeys with my signal so you know where they are at all times.'

'Copy,' Rina said, swiping her comm tab to send over the links of the required signals.

'Thank you, Colonel. Mirage out,' the AI added.

Silence fell between the two friends at Zulu One as Rina focused on guiding the Echo One battalion to Kainan's position.

Selene switched from the Enclave's oversized monitors to her comm tab, where a lone red dot pulsed on the map.

The two minutes Rina had promised seemed to drag out for an eternity as the fifteen red dots of Echo One approached the single pulse.

Then, the two friends watched as the sixteen dots joined together, and the bogeys' signals flickered off one by one.

'Thank *fokk*!' Rina said when it was all over, closing her eyes. 'That was insane.'

She opened them to Selene's wooden face.

'Sel, you can breathe now.'

Selene inhaled before giving her friend a mirthless smirk.

'Why do I care so much?' she whispered after a beat. 'Why does he get to me like this?'

Rina cocked her head, studying Selene for a moment.

'Come, let's walk it out,' she suggested, grabbing Selene's hand to pull her up from her chair.

Rina handed over command of the center to her junior, a pleasant young lieutenant.

Then she led her reluctant friend out of the Enclave's Command Center and into the late afternoon sunshine.

They walked past the mess, where Rina darted in and nabbed a flask and two tin cups before leading her exhausted friend to a bench in the small courtyard overlooking Za-alalum's soaring emerald forest.

The dell and valley below teemed with birds, bushbucks, and squirrels playing in the dying sunlight.

Rina pushed Selene onto the bench and poured a clear liquid from the flask she'd appropriated into the two cups.

She handed one cup to Selene, then sank beside her best friend with the other in her hand.

'Drink, woman. You need to drown your sorrows and sleep for the next 48 hours. But first, we talk.'

Selene took a sip of the drink in her hand and almost choked. 'What the hell is this?'

'Only the very best *wake-Selene-the-fokk-up* neat gin. It's the secret to longevity and healing strokes, insomnia, and even broken hearts,' Rina quipped.

Selene gave her friend a cold glare, then tossed back the drink, spluttering after she swallowed.

She wiped her mouth with the back of her hand and grimaced. 'The hell?'

Rina gave her a narrowed look. 'Seriously, now Sel, what's going on with you and him?'

'Him who?' Selene said, feigning ignorance.

'You know who. The sexual tension between you and that gorgeous mountain of a man was off the charts even way back in Eden II. And it seems that's shifted between trying to ignore his existence and acting like you'll pass out whenever you spot him in battle. Don't think I haven't noticed you're stalking him on your comm.'

Selene glared at her friend before looking down into her empty cup for a long moment.

Rina took the opportunity to fill the vessel once more. 'Talk to me, Sel. Your reactions to this man are wild.'

'Fine,' Selene sighed, taking a sip. 'I haven't said anything because I'm still trying to figure it out. The short of it is that - he's everything I never knew I wanted. He's beyond my dreams. He's magnificent. But he doesn't want me.'

'So you made love to the man? Like I suggested?'

'Hmm,' Selene muttered, her face heating up. 'When we were hiding out on J'Urg Mihòr.'

'I figured as much,' Rina huffed. 'How was it?' she added.

Selene blushed under her honey skin and rubbed her flaming cheeks.

Rina pealed with laughter. 'That good, huh?'

'I couldn't - we couldn't - get enough -,' Selene confessed.

'Then what?'

'Then he made a vague statement about how forever was not in his wheelhouse and that he only wanted a day-by-day arrangement. After that, I couldn't cut it. So I may have shut him down after that.'

Rina scrubbed a hand against her frustrated face. '*Fokk* Selene, you've never been able to have a fling, have you? Remember Javier? The Senator from Rhesus, whom you had a thing with years ago?'

Selene groaned. 'How could I not? I had such a major crush. I embarrassed myself with him.'

'Selene, you asked him to marry you. I've never seen a man run that fast into a shuttlecraft and hoof it off the planet as he did.'

The two friends laughed until tears of joy fell.

'Am I that tragic?' Selene asked her friend with a sad smile when they'd calmed down and wiped their delirium away.

'You're just a believer in true love. There's nothing wrong with that. You're a forever kind of girl. Our hopeless romantic.'

Selene shrugged. 'I can't help it. It's the way I'm built. I've tried to forget him, forget what we had, but something keeps pulling me back in. Or maybe he infused some of his metanoids into me because I can't seem to get rid of him here,' she said, pointing to her chest.

'So what now, Sel?' Rina asked, compassion wrinkling her forehead.

Selene looked off into the distance, where tiny fur balls dared to frolic, unaware of the storm within her. 'I have to find a way to forget him somehow,' she sighed. 'I know I'm acting all stalkerish, so I'll stop monitoring his movements - it's not helping me.'

Rina nodded. 'Agreed. I'll stalk him for you. It's part of my duty, after all. Do you want to know if anything does happen to him?' she asked.

'Of course,' Selene sighed. 'I can't turn off the fact that I care for him.'

'Do you think he cares about you?'

'I can't tell,' Selene said, her gaze trailing off to the peak of the forest beyond. 'He speaks to me as if he does, but we met during a time of great tension and emotion. I don't know whether he sees me as just another wartime hookup or, worse still, a Sable Rider groupie at hand to help him release the tension of battle.'

Rina contemplated Selene's words for a moment, then shook her head. 'Don't think so. Everything I've seen about Kainan tells me he's a very considered individual. He's strategic and puts a lot of thinking behind everything he does.'

'That may be so. But Kainan also seems to have all manner of beauties across the System lusting after him.'

'That doesn't mean he's slept with them or is a playboy,' Rina countered.

'Well, about that - I did meet one of his ex-lovers, groupies, whatever -.'

'*Nada!*' Rina scoffed.

'Yes, ma'am,' Selene said with a small laugh. 'So much drama. She passed on my Eden II location to Massimo when he sent the crats after me. In revenge for seeing me with Kainan.'

Rina shook her head. 'Wow, just wow!' She took a drink from her cup and continued. 'But I'll lean on what I've seen and heard so far from him. I see that he's honorable and a great leader. He's also a healthy man who probably had no desire for commitment until he met you. But you shouldn't underestimate yourself, Selene. You're the Prime-in-Waiting of an entire planet. You're beautiful, kind, caring, intelligent, strong, and badass. He'd be stupid not to see that; we know he's not dumb. He must have a valid reason for making you focus on what you have now. It sounds like he hasn't closed the blast doors on your connection. He's just slowed the trajectory down. So, if I were you, I'd wait this out. See what happens and allow him to work out how to win your heart. If he chooses to pass, it's the universe saying there's a better man for you.'

'Woah! You need to quit the army and start a motivational holo business, woman,' Selene teased, raising a brow at her friend. 'Seriously, though, what you've said makes sense. If he chooses to be with me, so be it. If he doesn't, I'll survive it, somehow. For now, I need to concentrate on regaining control of this planet.'

'That old chestnut - and teeny weeny task on your list,' Rina grinned.

Selene leaned over and gave Rina a spontaneous hug. 'Thank you for listening and for being such a good friend.'

'Anytime, boo bear, anytime.'

Victory!
  Free Dunia Day!
  Dozens of militia and treasonous leaders arrested!
  Rumors of Massimo's capture!
  Massimo's treason means death!
  No slackening until Massimo is behind bars for life!
  The One Dunia Coalition is ousted!
  New Malindi is in complete control of the Free Dunia Council!
  The True Prime to take back her seat!

The holo news headlines were fervent and high-pitched with excitement. They reiterated victory news and proclaimed the date of Massimo's capture as the official freedom day.

Exultant crowds poured into streets across Dunia's cities to celebrate the news.

People had taken to dancing in public, blasting 'freedom' music from speakers, and throwing spontaneous outdoor parties. Which often involved any bemused Alliance infantry soldiers and troops still patrolling the cities.

The celebrations had ramped up even more after Selene had announced the release of the thousands of supporters arrested and detained illegally by Massimo.

Including the five hundred councilors and administrators loyal to the true Prime.

Selene looked out the window of her flyer, wending its way over the flower-lined avenues of New Malindi.

As if sensing the excitement and joyous victory of the majority population who'd supported the Free Dunia Council, the planet's trees, bushes, and plants had unleashed an unexpected explosion of colorful blooms.

The stunning clash of violet, primrose, honeysuckle white, pink, and deep red hues was made even more lively by swarms of the rainbow-streaked Palisades butterfly, one of the rarest butterflies in Dunia.

The birds, too, added to the celebratory sounds with lilting calls and distinctive whoops in large swarms that took to flight.

'It's incredible,' Rina commented, seated beside Selene.

'Which makes what's about to happen even harder,' her friend said. 'We should be out there dancing with our people instead of heading to Massimo's mansion to arrest the man.'

'So you'd prefer someone else did it?'

'Hell no,' Selene demurred. 'I can't wait to look him in the eye and read the treason charges. First, I want to see him squirm. Then I want to see him put away for the rest of his miserable life and even more. Still, I'd rather be celebrating.'

'You'll be recommending the death penalty then?'

'He committed high treason. If the now-established security council and the high court make that determination, I won't deter it. Heck, I might even volunteer to be his executioner.'

'Give me your gun,' Rina insisted, pointing to the weapon strapped to Selene's meta suit.

'Why?'

'In case you're so enraged when you see him, you lose your damn mind and blast him away before he gets the justice he deserves. He needs to face a judge and jury so we can get the court-mandated answers we need.'

Selene's eyes narrowed, but she handed the laser weapon to her friend without another word.

They left the city center and flew over the beachside suburbs where New Malindi's rich and even more wealthy gathered.

They flitted between golden beaches across the coastal haven and their modern and art deco homes with gorgeous views over New Malindi's harbor and golden peninsula, where the median house price was a whopping 25 million schills.

Selene didn't envy the wealth. She knew well enough that corruption, greed, and exploitation had acquired most of the waterfront homes.

Something her father had fought against, and a battle which she, too, was keen to pick up as soon as Massimo's arrest was done and dusted.

In the far distance, high above the sea and the skies, was the arched dome that had remained intact over the seaside capital.

Selene thought she saw a Corvette high in the sky above them, so she peered out of the flyer's upper hatch window.

Unfortunately, the clouds and reflection from the dome hid any sign of a drive plume, and she leaned back in her chair, disappointed.

Rina glanced at her friend. 'Still keeping an eye out for him?'

'You won't tell me where he is,' Selene accused.

'He's well - and he's been running a special op for the last few days. That's all you need to know.'

Selene pursed her lips, her heart still lost in a deep longing.

'You'll see him soon, I promise,' Rina said. 'He hasn't abandoned you to the stars, that you can be sure of.'

Rina's words sparked a memory, and Selene lost herself, remembering how she'd lain on a glass floor looking up at a bright duo star wrapped in the arms of a particular man. It was enough to get her heart racing.

'Heads up, Prime, Colonel,' the flyer's pilot announced, breaking through her thoughts. 'We're one minute away.'

Rina jerked her chin at her friend and slid on her HUD headset. Selene also donned the headset attachment to her helmet and meta-suit, the last remaining connection to Kainan.

She wondered if he'd send word to take it back, but not even one message had come. Instead, every communication in recent days with The Sable Group and Riders had been formal and official, mostly from Zane, who was still running the Alliance's Sable-related ops from Eden II.

She got the distinct feeling Kainan was avoiding her and doing a mighty damn fine job at it too.

They flew low over a tree-lined avenue and a line of boutique shops and elegant cafes, where surprised patrons pointed at the sight of the sleek military flyer so close to the ground.

Then they headed towards an ostentatious gate and extensive driveway leading past an incredible garden and a gleaming white house at its apex—the Makori mansion.

The flyer set down in the garden in front of the house, its engines charring a large circle onto the delicate grass.

Not that Selene cared. *Fokk Massimo's grass. Fokk his entire existence*, she thought.

The doors slid open, and Selene dismounted and paused mid-step on the stairs.

Because theirs was not the only vessel parked in and among the flower beds of the rolling garden.

With a shimmer, Mirage appeared, uncloaking itself from stealth mode. They watched as the Corvette's air bridge extended itself.

Kainan's familiar hulk descended the gunship, and Selene felt the same breath-stealing kick to her chest as when she'd first met him.

'Told you you'd see him again,' Rina said from behind Selene, smugly.

It had been two weeks since their last encounter, but he was still taller than any man in Dunia.

Still more muscled than most. Still with the intense energy.

267

Still sporting those large, powerful, ropey, thick thighs that she'd trailed her hands along.

Still devastating and attractive in his matte black power suit.

Still enticing with light, lustrous caramel skin covered by stunning nebula gold and sapphire glyphs.

Still with those rippling dark locks shot with silver at the temple.

Still, those full lips, high cheekbones, and most devastating, still those pools of molten gold, flecked with flashes of electric sapphire.

Which now searched her face. Before he flicked his glance away and towards Rina.

'Excellency, Colonel,' he said, greeting both women, his face set in stone.

His chimera call name was perfect for him, Selene thought crabbily. She'd never met a man so adept at the hot and cold gambit.

'What are you doing here?' she murmured, masking her annoyance.

'I tracked down Massimo and placed him under house arrest,' Kainan stated. 'I've been here ever since.'

Her eyes narrowed. 'You didn't need to stay. I'm sure you've got more important things to do on Eden II.'

His eyes flicked to her as if sensing her freeze-out.

'I made a promise to you, Excellency,' Kainan replied quietly. 'I told you I'd be here every step of the way. So here I am.'

Selene nodded at him, unable to say more. So she looked away and worked on keeping calm and collected around him.

The tension in the air ratcheted up a notch.

Rina saved the day. '*Khosi*, we're here to take Massimo off your hands. The Security Council and the new government await his arrival at Parliament House.'

Kainan nodded. 'He's inside, stashed in his study, along with his wife, also complicit in the coup. I also found his two sidekicks, the Minister of Strategic Planning and the Undersecretary of Defense, with him. They're all here. I'll show you through,' he offered.

'Thank you,' Selene said. Then, she took off towards the house while Rina and Kainan trailed behind her.

'Where are you planning to hold him?' Kainan asked as the trio headed towards the grand entrance.

'We're flying him straight to the prison planetoid of Gineliv III. The maximum prison allied to Rhesia, Galicia, and Dunia,' Rina said. 'In the isolation cells, deep underground, where no one can reach him. We'll conduct the court case from there as well via holo feeds. The people of Dunia don't want him here, not even for another day.'

Kainan nodded his approval. 'It's what he deserves.'

At the patio, an Edenite sentry saluted the trio and opened the door to the mansion.

They entered a lurid entrance littered with gold furniture, glittering lights, and a flashy ceiling.

The high-ceiling walls dripped with gold leaf, carved stone, and rare marble.

Selene sighed at the gaudy fixtures, striding past a marble-topped living and dining room with a tiled fireplace containing niches fitted with prominent sculpted figures.

Sculpted roses climbed the fireplace and windows, Paladian rugs covered the floors, oil paintings hung on the walls, and ceiling murals and chandeliers lit up the rooms.

It was all so over the top. Ludicrous and wildly expensive.

This was where Massimo had sunk the vast chunks of his stolen money, Selene thought, rolling her eyes.

They were ushered into the study by yet another guard.

It was decked out in mahogany wood walls and floors, with baroque-style dining chairs and a large gold-dipped desk. Behind it, a large, defiant man sat, glaring at her entry.

Selene shook her head, returning the glower with a cool death stare. After weeks of waiting, she was face to face with the man who'd terrorized their planet and killed her dear father.

She felt bitter loss and pain twist in her guts as she stared at the towering figure before her.

She raked her eyes over the thick chains of diamonds and gold adorning his plump neck and wrists and the silken, gold-threaded robes that enveloped his rotundness.

How dare he, she thought. *How dare he dress like he's going to a banquet? What he deserved was to be in sackcloth or prison stripes!*

A tired-looking woman also inhabited the large room. She was slumped on a silk couch, and two other men sat at a large side table, their heads hung in shame.

Five hulking Edenite guards stood in the room while Selene saw more soldiers patrolling the grounds outside the picture windows.

'If it isn't the True Prime?' taunted the large man she'd once considered charming and funny.

'Well, if it isn't the treasonous ex-Minister of Defense, soon to be known as Prisoner X,' Selene clipped.

Massimo's swarthy face paled at her words.

She ignored the naked fear that snaked across his face.

Crossing the gaudy room, Selene stopped before the large desk.

Rina stepped behind her, flanking Selene to the right, while Kainan paused beside her to the left. She welcomed their collective support, which strengthened her cool and calm demeanor.

Selene handed her headset to Rina, keen to be free of any obstruction to her view. This way, she could see the emotion in Massimo's eyes when she nailed him for his indiscretions and crimes.

'Massimo Makori, on your feet. Would your co-conspirators also rise?'

The man stood before her and bent over his table, his hands spread on the surface. He met her gaze with a defiant one of his own.

While his three other guilty-looking companions kept their eyes on the floor.

'Why you?' Massimo's face twisted as he spoke through dry lips.

Selene gave him a cold smile. 'I asked the Council if I could be the one who read these charges against you in person, as an officer of the high court and the daughter of the man you murdered. They all agreed.'

Massimo's lips pursed with displeasure.

Selene was undaunted. 'Massimo Makori, the government and people of Dunia have found your actions in the last month constitute acts of high treason against our planet state,' she announced. 'You conspired to cause harm or death to the one true Prime. You were also involved in assassinating the Prime, resulting in the death of the Prime. You mobilized a war against the government and people of Dunia. You instigated non-Dunia citizens to carry out an armed invasion of the planet and the territory belonging to the people of Dunia. You are, therefore, charged with treason. As such, the crime of treason attracts the penalty of life imprisonment. Or if otherwise determined by the courts, the death penalty.'

Selene then turned to the three individuals. The woman swayed, and the two other men scrambled to support her. Selene ignored the histrionics.

'Teresa Makori, legal partner of Massimo Makori, you have also been found complicit in the coup and treason. The pair of you, Emil M'Isov, former Minister of Strategic Planning and Mining, and Marko M'Crolla, former undersecretary of Defense, have also been found to be co-conspirators in the coup and are also charged with treason. Your treasonous actions include assisting Massimo Makori in his bid to escape punishment for their crime. You are also charged with failure to give information to the Security Council regarding Massimo Makori, whom you knew intended to commit the crime of treason. As well as conspiring to assassinate the Prime and assisting in the mobilized war and armed invasion of the planet and the territory belonging to the people of Dunia.'

Selene fell silent. The room, too, as the severity of the charges hit home with the accused.

Massimo piped up, his familiar, ebullient voice just above a ragged whisper.

'We were acting for the good of Dunia,' he said, throwing his hands out before him in a plea. 'We sought the wider export of xentium, which would enrich the planet, the armies, the entire population, even the Council.'

'You could have advocated for all that without murder,

assassinations, and an invasion,' Selene coldly said.

Massimo smiled in an attempt to charm her. 'What if I pay for the harm caused? I'm not a rich man, but I can access funds and resources to help with any damages I've caused to any victim, such as yourself.'

He suddenly reached under his desk. Kainan surged forward, sliding Selene behind him. A lethal laser rifle he'd unsheathed from his side was now trained on the ex-Minister.

Massimo threw one palm up. 'Peace, Edenite, I mean well.'

He used his other hand to withdraw a suitcase, which he threw on the large desk.

It flipped open to reveal its contents.

Selene peered over Kainan's shoulder and sighed. The briefcase held thick stacks of high-denomination schill notes and clear plastic bags of diamonds, rubies, and xentium pearls.

'Not rich? I would beg to differ,' Selene scoffed.

Massimo continued undeterred, desperate to plead his case. 'This is just a portion of what I can offer you. It amounts to over 100 million schill, which can be divvied as damages among yourselves and maybe the greater Security Council. But, Selene, allow my -' he stumbled, then started again. 'Allow me to find safe passage out of Dunia, and we'll never darken your shores again.'

Selene was beyond ropable. She pushed past Kainan to confront her worst enemy. 'You think I'm as corruptible as you are? You've lost your mind. Serving Dunia is the only honor I seek. My name, service, and sacrifice will always be better than wealth. So fokk off with your bribes! All you deserve right now is a lifetime in jail and, if I've anything to do with it, a death sentence!'

Massimo dragged his beady eyes over her face, and sensing her unrelenting commitment to his downfall, he changed tack. 'This will be the end of you,' he hissed. 'I'll kill you myself if I have to, just like I did your father. I didn't even have to think about it. I just plowed the man down where he sat. He couldn't believe it. He never saw it coming,' the man cackled.

Selene sucked in oxygen. Her neck flamed with rage. She felt Kainan's hand against her back and pulled from his energy to calm herself down.

'There he is,' she drawled. 'The true Massimo. You've dropped the 'poor me' act and unleashed your true dark self. You're just another honor-free murderer!'

The man before her dissolved into a sniggered laugh, his jowls wobbling. 'Oh, Selene, your heartfelt passion for Dunia and your naïveté have never ceased to amaze me. It closes your eyes to the truth, so you always underestimate your opponents. That was why I killed Kei'Lano. He was weak. The nebulous concepts of honor and virtue swayed him. So, too, were you. You both stood in the way of progress, industry, and strength! All your honor will do for this planet is impoverish it. Thank the gods I won't be here to see it.'

Selene noticed with a slight panic that as the man spoke, he'd inched backward towards the back wall of the grotesque room.

'Stay where you are,' Kainan snapped, stepping forward and extending his rifle.

'Or what?' Massimo taunted. Then he moved fast for his wide girth. He withdrew a small handgun from his voluminous robes. Then, pointing it at Selene, he fired.

Kainan reacted in milliseconds, pushing her out of the way,

so the bullet crashed against his meta suit. With a clink, it fell to the floor.

Teresa screamed, and the other guards in the room rushed towards the other co-conspirators and overpowered them.

Kainan reached out to Selene, who'd fallen to the floor, and helped her up.

'You OK?' he rasped.

'I'm fine.'

Massimo tittered at the confusion he'd wrought, then launched against the wall behind him and pressed his hand into a shelf.

The edge of a hidden vertical cantilevered doorway appeared and swung open. Kainan and Rina opened fire, and Selene saw Massimo stumble into a dark corridor beyond.

The hulking Sable Rider leaped over the desk and rushed to the door. But he was too late. The heavy, cantilevered door swung shut with a thud.

Kainan threw his armored shoulder against the surface, but there was no give. He canted his body back and fired a series of rounds on the edges of the door, but the rounds bounced off, and everyone standing behind him ducked to escape the ricochet.

'It's impenetrable,' Kainan growled. 'Where the *fokk* does that corridor lead to?'

He whirled around and pointed his rifle at Teresa. She cowered against the silk couch, screaming.

'She's no use,' Rina ground out.

Kainan swung the weapon barrel towards the two ex-civil servants.

Emil shook his head, looking at Kainan with a helpless expression. 'I don't know. He wouldn't say.'

Marko blanched at the hulking soldier. He lifted a trembling hand and pointed outside, towards the southern end of the property.

'You're sure?' Kainan thundered.

'Yes! He told me as much. He wanted me to go with him.'

'What about me?' screeched Teresa. 'I'm his wife. You were only his lover!' she sobbed.

Kainan ran past the cringing trio and their petty drama.

The Sable Rider burst through the floor-to-ceiling glass windows of the study, vaulted over the marble balcony, and loped due south over the immaculate grass and pristine garden.

Rina and Selene were close behind him, and they made it to the southern boundary, to a wall overlooking the Makoris' neighbor.

'Nothing!' Kainan grunted. 'There's not one external building or exit I can see.'

'Look harder,' Selene urged. 'Maybe the exit is built into the ground.'

The trio started a sweep of the grass lawn and garden when they felt a rumble shake the ground, followed by a loud whine.

Kainan whirled around in a circle, trying to determine the source of the sound.

An almighty explosion came, followed by a massive crash and the rumble of a spacecraft lifting into the atmosphere.

Debris flew all around them. Selene fell to her knees and covered her helmet-free head.

Rocks crashed around her, and she cried out when one large boulder fell against her thigh. Her suit took most of the impact's brunt, but she still felt the thump of pain and air knocked out of her chest.

Moments later, she was enveloped by a larger body.

Kainan.

Protecting her yet again.

After some time, the shower of rubble died down.

Selene coughed at the still-swirling dust while Kainan lifted himself from her. She staggered to her feet with his help.

A large crater was before them, where the neighbor's palatial home had stood minutes ago.

'Rina?' Selene called out, looking for her friend through the dust-filled air.

'Here,' came a reply. 'I'm OK.'

Rina emerged from the gritty atmosphere, covered in fine soil.

She joined Kainan and Selene, who stood over the gaping crater. Grass, mud, stone bricks, and what looked like supporting beams kept crashing into the gaping hole in intervals.

Behind them, the security guards who'd rushed to help also gawked at the large fissure.

Rina brushed residue from her suit. 'Fokk! Was that what I thought it was?'

Kainan whipped off his helmet, coated in dust. '*Naam.* That was a spacecraft.'

Selene couldn't quite believe what she was seeing. 'Hidden in what looks like an underground hangar under the neighbor's house.'

'Mirage, can you track where that bogey went?' Kainan said.

The AI responded, her dulcet tones drifting from his wrist comm. 'I had eyes on the property when the spaceship crashed through and flew off. I caught it on-screen and tracked it as far as I could. *Khosi*, it was a Technocracy rattler. An augmented one because it moved fast. Quicker than normal. I suspect it has an xentium core. That, mixed with crat tech, means it could be swift.'

Kainan groaned. 'Where is it now?'

'It went into FTL the moment it touched orbit. A mere 18.5 seconds after it launched. I don't have eyes on it now.'

'Fokk!' Kainan roared, flinging his helmet to the ground. 'I missed it! I searched Massimo's home but didn't consider the entire neighborhood. I should have brought him straight to the central slammer -.'

Rina interjected, shaking her head. 'That wouldn't have been a good idea, given we're still trying to weed out the One Dunia's loyalists. They've infiltrated every government sector, and I bet you there are some rotten eggs in the local prison system.'

'Still,' said Kainan. 'I should have done better.

Selene interrupted his furious jag. 'Don't be hard on yourself. Massimo's been working on his subterfuge for years. That doorway materialized before us with the help of The Technocracy's mechanization. Maybe that's the same reason why you couldn't penetrate it. The corridor seemed well shielded, and the hangar had been here since he built the house and was well hidden. You wouldn't have known.'

'I should have known,' he raged. 'I didn't think.'

Kainan's sapphire gold eyes met hers, glowering in anger.

Selene glanced back at the mansion, where Massimo's trio of betrayers stood on the mangled balcony.

A guard stood over each of them, holding the prisoners' shackled chains.

'The best thing we can do right now is to ensure those three get to Gineliv III. They'll be interrogated to find out if they know where Massimo is going. Marko comes to mind as being the best bet for probing for more intel.'

'I'll get onto it,' Rina promised.

'But first, we have to tell the Council about Massimo's escape,' Selene said. 'I believe that after all we've gone through, they'll be more forgiving than we think.'

Kainan snorted. 'You think so? We just lost the most important asset of this war.'

'I beg to differ,' Rina said with a twinkle in her eye. 'I know we did not because she's beside you.'

Kainan paused, giving Selene a long look. 'That she is.'

15

Day And Night

MASSIMO

The rotund man felt every shudder and jitter deep in his fat, cushioned bones as the rattler he was in hurled itself through space at 1g.

It felt like he was perched on the edge of a hot gas giant, and he felt the scald of the engine below burn through his skin.

He groaned and squirmed in his seat, where he sat, half-naked in his socks and slippers. The rattler, on autopilot, shuddered once more, almost as if it were snickering at him.

The craft had a tiny holo screen, but when Massimo peered out, all he was met with was darkness and occasional streaks of light.

He sighed.

What he'd give to be on his spanking new pleasure yacht moored at Dunia's spaceport. He'd had it delivered just three months ago, ironically from the best space yacht builders in the System—The Sable Group.

His Sable Sloop TX was a state-of-the-art craft with soft carpeting, raised waterbeds, wrap-around sofas, a luxurious onboard gym, and a grand spiral staircase that connected each level.

It was capped off with a bar overlooking an expansive space viewing lounge, providing views of the passing stars and nebulae.

In contrast, the Rattler was made for a single-crat pilot with no need to stretch its cybernetic legs.

There was also a tiny pillion for a second individual behind the main seat. The cockpit was tiny, and the walls were covered in technocracy-labeled hieroglyphic controls, which he couldn't fathom.

There was no mess, no san, and no luxuries whatsoever.

All Massimo had was a small survival pack with him that Marko had stored in the rattler over 28 months ago.

Which was when the craft had been sneaked into Dunia - at the height of Massimo's planning and strategizing. It was evident Marko had never had to prep for a long-haul flight on a bare-bones craft.

He'd packed a survival knife, a tube of antiseptic, gauze, cotton balls, a few bulbs of water, and four packs of self-heating army ration noodles.

He'd included a change of clothes sealed in a large zip lock bag, but it seemed the dolt had packed his size, and nothing fit Massimo's larger bulkier form.

The pack also revealed a flashlight, a compass, and a wrist

comm that had stopped working when it was out of range from Dunia.

Massimo had gulped down the noodles, then realized he had nowhere for his waste to go.

The inevitable had happened, and the resulting stench in the small rattler had relieved him of any appetite.

Along with the hunger pangs was the painful throbbing of the injury on his side. One of the Edenite warrior's bullets had nicked his fleshy side handle. While the round had gone straight through, it had left a small mess.

Massimo had used the little medical knowledge he'd retained from his days in the army to wash out the wound using up one of the precious bulbs of water.

He then slathered on antiseptic cream and ripped his voluminous robe into strips, wrapping them around his generous middle.

His escape via rattler had not been the plan at all.

His lover, the ridiculous Marko, had suggested it as a worst-case scenario. Massimo had never considered he'd need a plan B, let alone this option, plan F.

Flush with cash a few years ago, he'd handed over to The Technocracy a few thousand xentium gems pilfered from the mines in Rambasa for the craft.

They'd used some gems to fashion a fast engine for him, experimenting with a new xentium and nuclear fission design.

After bullying the family into conceding to his demands, he bought his neighbor's property for well under market value. He'd commissioned the hangar, but only at night to avoid curious eyes, and stored the rattler inside once it was complete.

Despite the inadvertent bullet to his side, the strategy had somewhat gone to plan.

He'd run hell for leather along the expensive plasma-shielded tunnel to the waiting crat ship.

He'd hit the large red button on the console, just like he'd been instructed.

The engine had turned on, a small missile had blown apart the house above him, the autopilot controls had kicked in, and the rattler had blasted through the underground shuttle bay into space, flitting into FTL before anyone down on Dunia had a clue what had happened.

His deal with The Technocracy had also included an extraction.

And so he'd waited for a few hours, again as instructed, until the radio on the ship crackled to life. Signaling that he was in the range of one of The Technocracy's dreadnoughts.

A tinny voice confirmed his identity and informed him that he had a few standard days of travel left before they could intercept him.

This left copious amounts of time on Massimo's hands.

Time, which he now put into planning his next step.

He'd learned some interesting news via a drone in One Dunia's control. It had been flying covertly over Enclave Zulu One. It captured footage of Her Excellency Selene Munene entering a hidden grotto within the Enclave.

Presumably, to speak with whatever power controlled the planet because Dunia had ceased its attacks on the Alliance ships soon after.

This was intel he could use as a bargaining chip for his life and a way to finagle his way back to Dunia. The next problem to solve was how to get to Selene Munene.

He needed to exploit all her weak points.

He thought for a few long minutes until he caught onto the tendril of an idea.

Massimo smirked despite the heat burning his nether regions, the hunger twisting his insides, and the pain slashing his sides.

SOMEWHERE ON RHESIA

Far removed from Massimo's misery, a man settled into the soft mycelium leather seats of his droid-chauffeured Sable flyer as it cruised the capital city of Rhesia. He stared at the bright, neon-strobed strips of shops, buildings, casinos, and leveled dwellings shining with sparkling lights.

Little did the people strolling under them realize that it took over three million klicks of neon lights to illuminate Enia, giving it its distinctive characteristic of being visible from space.

In addition to the glow that flooded the streets, there were also lights galore inside the hotels, casinos, bars, and dance halls, illuminated to prevent patrons from perceiving the difference between day and night.

This ensured they stayed all night, all week, and in many cases for months, spending big in the bauble of the System.

For millennia, the energy needs of Enia had been met by mining orhial, which powered the lights of the giant metropolis.

In recent eras, however, the depletion of orhial from Rhesian mines, the exponential demographic growth of the capital, and the development of larger and more brightly lit establishments made it essential to find new energy sources to feed the needs of this city and the planet itself.

They were running out of time. Orhial deposits had slowed to a trickle. They had a few million terratons of it left in storage.

If Rhesus—the throne and the government—didn't act soon, they would be five years away from turning off all lights.

A soft trill broke through the man's dark thoughts. He glanced at the screen on his flyer's dash. It showed a hidden contact trying to get through. No one he knew had an anonymous ID, yet he sensed he'd need to take this call.

He flicked his wrist comm with a twist to his lips, unamused at his after-hours ride being interrupted.

'Who is this?' he barked.

'You sound displeased. And here we thought you'd be delighted to hear from us,' a mechanical voice said.

The man grimaced. 'I had no idea it would be you. You cloaked the call.'

'How else would we comm you? By announcing it to the entire System? Are you that naive about the art of being clandestine?'

The man bristled at the put-down. 'Speaking of clandestine, what happened on Dunia, Eminence? The fact that the lowly citizens of the planet drove your not-so-clandestine operation out of there is not a fact I'm naive or uninformed about!' the man snapped. 'We also discussed keeping your nose out of the affair and letting Massimo be the face of the operation. All you were meant to do was fund his coup, not lend your rattlers and weapons to him. How did it all fall apart?'

'We suffered a small setback.'

'A small setback?' The man hissed. 'You lost a war. Against a tiny force that's barely organized. Let alone armored well enough.'

'I'd not go so far as to say that. Like you, we underestimated their strength and ability to purchase mercenary help. But we have a plan, thanks to Massimo.'

'And what might that be? I need to know now so I've something positive to tell my people. So we can enact our plans.'

The tinny laugh echoed through the line. 'Patience, my friend. The less you know, the better. Remember what I just taught you about the art of being clandestine? This is another similar lesson. We'll be in touch.'

The line dropped. The Rhesian man sneered at the darkened screen of his flyer's comm. The holo screen lit up once more. This time, the caller's name was displayed.

'*Fokk* me!' the Rhesian hissed. 'When it storms, it floods!'

He reluctantly tapped his wrist comm to take the call.

'This is The Klatsch calling,' a voice informed him. 'Will you take the call from your handler?'

The man sighed. 'Of course. One never refuses The Klatsch.'

'Brace yourself. They have many questions about the recent mess on Dunia.'

'I bet they do.'

'To the Triumv.'

'True and sure.'

The man sat back in the flyer and resigned himself to his

fate.

III

If the full moon loves you, why
worry about the stars?

16

Souls In The Sky

SELENE

While they regretted it, the Council forgave Kainan, Rina, and Selene for the escape of the coup's leader, Massimo Makori.

They were more than pleased that the three of them had worked so hard to free the planet from the control of the One Dunia Coalition.

They reassured Kainan that the planet saw him and the Edenites as heroes who'd worked tirelessly for their freedom. They'd then insisted on celebrating the victory in style.

Regardless of their support, Kainan had seemed unconvinced about the praise and accolades they'd given him when the trio had reported to the Council on the same day of Makori's escape.

Selene knew he was smarting about the fiasco. So she'd shut her mouth and let him come to peace about it.

It seems everyone else had. The Council, her ministers, and even Rina were focused on celebrating the True Prime's return to power.

Her return to power.

This thought alone terrified her somewhat.

Yet she took on the mantle with some grace despite the grief and swirl of emotions that still rocked her every night when she closed her eyes.

Never-ending thoughts about her father. Kainan. Dunia.

They all consumed her until she fell into a restless sleep and haunted her waking hours.

'The first official government banquet to celebrate Free Dunia Month is tomorrow evening,' Commerce Minister Genevieve Ravi's announcement cut into Selene's thoughts at the first Security Council meeting held since the coup.

'It's '*month*' now, is it?' Selene asked with a smile.

'At this rate, it's going to be '*year*' very soon,' Rina quipped from across the expansive Cabinet room as yet another loud cheer emanated from the streets below.

It was three weeks after the victory, yet the people were still celebrating. Spontaneous dancing still stopped traffic.

Thousands of civilians catered up a storm each night for the infantry still patrolling the streets.

The cookouts and barbecues turned into all-night parties. Singing bands played non-stop outside the Parliament while crowds gathered each evening for the rendition of the planet's anthem.

Wineries and distilleries created signature batches honoring the victory. Fashion labels designed one-off 'Free Dunia' collections for hundreds of balls and parties all over Dunia.

There was even a new trending pastry, the 'freedom' bun, which sold like hot cakes in all local bakeries.

The circular buttery delight featured local whiskey-soaked dried fruit with a big dollop of cream decorated with strips of colored marzipan in the planet's flag colors of gold, white, and purple.

Though short and contracted, the fierce battle for Dunia's control had impacted its people, the victory launching them into feverish displays of loyalty and love for their planet.

'Who are we expecting tomorrow?' Selene asked Paloma Mware, the event's foreign minister and official organizer.

'Almost the entire system will have representatives, Excellency,' Paloma said, consulting her comm tab for confirmation. 'We have RSVPs from King Auban VI and Queen Sanjana of Rhesus, King Judahk and Queen Nevaeh of Galicia, Emperor Micinus and Empress Noanus of Iccythria, Prime Minister and Sheikh Bagua of Sirius III. The Economic Alliance Commissioner, President Cora Yuzeria, will also be among the dignitaries. The Kugwe of the Ruling Elders of Eden II, J'Kuu Kabi, and her elder Council will also attend. As will the Sable Riders, all of whom have RSVP'd.'

Selene's heart knocked in her chest at the mention of the Edenites.

'The Sable Group has also kindly volunteered some of their elite guards to help augment security at the banquet,' Rina added, giving Selene a quick but loaded glance.

'That's very kind of them,' Selene murmured, ignoring the sudden kick in her heart.

'Our local dignitaries have all RSVP'd,' Paloma continued. 'All senators and key representatives, mayors from the major cities across the planet that remained loyal to Free Dunia. The navy and army, of course, including General McKenzie, now the General of all Armies and the Special Ops Command Force stationed at Rambasa -.'

Selene tuned out the minister's voice, letting her mind wander.

She'd last seen Kainan twenty days ago, on the fateful day when Massimo had escaped the planet. After reporting to the Security Council, he'd left on Mirage, claiming he had work to return to on Eden II. She hadn't heard a word from him since then.

She'd tried to put him out of her mind. She was filling her days with work. First, with the arduous task of replacing the entire Ministry of Defense department.

She'd been in endless interviews with candidates across the spectrum for the position of its head but still hadn't found anyone she could trust well enough with the role.

She'd asked Rina, but her best friend seemed battle-worn and had begged off the function, claiming it was too much to handle and that she wasn't cut out for it yet.

Selene instead proposed that Rina help in a temporary capacity, overseeing the ongoing security of Dunia.

Rina had agreed and was liaising with General McKenzie.

Who needed time to rebuild his armies, focus targeted investment in tanks and personnel, and enforce a new doctrine around the planet's security readiness moving forward.

The one thing Selene agreed with Massimo on was that her father, Kei'Lano, had been too much of a pacifist in the years before the coup. This had led to Dunia's military suffering from years of fiscal neglect.

The coup had illustrated its shortcomings.

The armed forces had barely been capable of staging a feasible planet-wide defense and had yet to fulfill their constitutional mandate.

Selene had been forced to step in to augment their forces by appealing to a foreign power. She had no intention of keeping Dunia in such a poor bargaining and strategic position ever again.

However, she needed a competent Defense Head to take full responsibility to enact everything she wanted.

Someone who could work with General McKenzie. To assess and clarify the internal and external defense capability required to build a credible deterrence alongside the quantity and quality of personnel necessary to meet this capability.

Selene also dealt with the effective governance of all government portfolios, with a long-term focus while balancing any partisan planet-wide responsibilities and system-wide diplomatic relations.

She felt overwhelmed.

She also wished, with some futility, that Kainan was close by her.

To give her his level-headed opinion and lend her his incredible knowledge of armies, defenses, and political machinations.

'Will you be making a speech, Excellency?'

Selene shook her head to clear her daydream, realizing that Ines Motho, the Education Minister, had been addressing her.

'I'll say a few words,' Selene said, her words coming out in a rush. 'But I would much prefer to thank the friends who helped us win this victory and award their medals of valor.'

'Just like we planned,' said L'Ogano Rai, the sallow-faced,

tall, and thin head of the Interior Ministry.

'Indeed. I also want all cabinet members on the dais with me when we do the presentations.'

'Of course, Excellency,' Ines agreed.

'Is that all we need to discuss?' Selene asked.

'We just need to ensure you're all at the security briefing here, at 1800 standard, where you'll all be assigned your personal guards,' Rina reminded the assembled Council.

Selene adjourned the meeting and rose to her feet, checking her comm tab for her next appointment.

'A couture dress fitting with House of M'Armin?' she groaned.

'Did you do this, Ri'?' she hissed as her best friend sidled past the Council members, filing out of the room and towards her.

Rina grinned at her. 'You've not gone shopping in years, Selene. No more recycling the same tired gowns you've worn to every ball and dinner party over the last ten years. Tomorrow, you're the Prime. You need to shine. You can't let Dunia down with a drab dress from a Rhesian catalog circa ten years ago.'

'Fine,' Selene conceded. 'For planet and people, hey? But you're coming with me.'

She crowed at the look of horror on Rina's face. 'And picking a gown for yourself as well. Enough with the military jumpsuit look, woman!'

Selene sat sipping a glass of prosecco in the salon of House of M'Armin, one of Dunia's most elegant dress shops. She looked out the grand salon's windows at the stunning view.

It had a prime position on a hilltop overlooking Lamina Bay, one of the picturesque mini harbors along New Malindi's coastline.

The mid-afternoon sun playing on the waves made the boats and yachts on the water sparkle.

The sand, too, where young children frolicked, their laughter wafting back towards her.

No one looking at the scene without knowing what had transpired over the last few weeks would believe the city had been under siege recently.

Life had soon returned to normal here, and for that, Selene was thankful.

Lamina Bay was special to her.

She'd often come with her father and sister for breakfast in one of the waterfront cafes.

Sheba's favorite pick on the menu had always been avocado and feta cheese on toast; for Selene, pancakes and bacon. Kei'Lano had always chosen eggs florentine.

Together, they'd eat, catch up on all their news, and laugh. They'd also toast Astrea, the girls' mother, and Kei'Lano's first love.

She'd passed over two decades ago. Over the years, their memories of her had softened and faded at the edges.

Selene remembered a warm, smiling woman with the softest touch and kindest words. And now her father had joined her wherever souls went to dance in the great expansive skies of Pegasi.

Selene sucked in air to control the emotion that threatened

to overwhelm her.

She'd cry for her parents when she had her sister beside her. Until then, Selene was determined to tamp down the waves of sorrow that threatened to drown her.

She couldn't break down, not here, not now. So, instead, she lifted her glass to her father, mother, and Sheba and took a long, much-needed sip.

Moments later, a House of M'Armin attendant bustled into the room. 'Not long now, Prime.'

'That's fine,' Selene said. She was waiting for her ball gown to be adjusted. Something about tightening the waist.

She'd been tempted to leave and ask the design house to courier the dress to her. But for some reason, she'd chosen to stay and wait for the tailors to finish their alterations. Perhaps it was the view.

More likely, the memories and reminders of visiting the bay with her family, when life had been so joyous, simple, and good.

Just then, her comm tab trilled.

It was a code she didn't recognize.

Her gut told her to pick up, so she swiped the call screen and waited.

'Selene Munene?' came an unknown voice in an abrasive tenor.

'*Naam*,' she confirmed with some uncertainty.

'This is Prince Emian. From the Royal House of Rhesia.'

'Ah, I remember you,' Selene said.

How could she forget the King's dour-looking brother? *And the trivial disdain he'd had for her dress on the evening of his brother's birthday party*, Selene thought peevishly.

'And to what do I owe the honor?' she continued.

'My older brother informs me that you're now the Prime of Dunia. And I'd like to discuss something vital with you.'

'Yes?' she encouraged.

'I'll cut to the chase. We know that your celebration ball will bring together many of the System's leaders and politicians, and now that the coup is behind us, they'll be keen to discuss their access to xentium. We want to pre-empt any of their discussions. We request that you guarantee our access to xentium and increase our stake. To 40% of your exports. Up 10% from our current arrangement.'

'Guarantee?'

'Yes, we'll be willing to pay well for a higher percentage of xentium sales than we agreed upon back on Enia months before the coup. We're thinking of a small, separate, generous donation to secure what we need.'

Selene knew the Rhesians had struggled to send just one Corvette to Dunia's aid. *But, now, they had a generous fund to pay her off? Impossible.* Unless, of course, there were other cashed-up parties involved.

'And who are *we*? The Rhesian government?' she probed.

'A group of invested individuals supported by the Royal family.'

'Is your Prime Minister or the King across this?'

'We don't worry those two with such trivial matters until they're finalized, Prime.'

Selene scoffed at the low-key put-down.

'No doubt. And how much is your vested consortium willing to part with for your generous gifts?'

The Prince paused for a beat.

Most likely to consult someone else in the room with him. 'They're open to numbers in the region of 25 million schills,' he eventually said.

'Payable to whom?'

'To you, of course, Prime.'

Selene bristled and decided to pull the plug on the awkward charade. 'Are you aware that this offer you've just made constitutes paying for preferential access? Which could lead to multiple counts of bribery, penalties, and censure from my government?'

The Prince bristled. 'I wasn't suggesting that *you* receive this money. We can spread it among all key officials and even donate to Dunia's charitable causes. Perhaps a fund to help all the families affected by the coup?'

The gall of the man. To call her out of the blue and try to twist her arm. With a piss-poor bribe couched as philanthropy.

He probably thought she was an immature, inexperienced leader who could be manipulated.

This was Rhesia's perpetual weakness these days – being so removed and out of touch with the reality of its people and allies.

Let alone being unaware of the System's changing balance of power and its emerging leaders' low tolerance for bull spit.

The problem extended to its governance.

Once, Rhesia had been an energy titan due to its orhial mines.

However, a lack of planning, over-mining, poor management, and corruption had since undermined its dominance.

Their manufacturing companies were struggling for energy resources, and their desperate need for xentium was a play to claw back some of the clout Rhesia had lost in the last few years.

The Rhesians thought Dunia was the same, a monopoly

sitting atop immense wealth, inefficient, politically driven, and corrupt, with officials allowed to siphon off cash for their greedy goals.

Selene was keen to disabuse the Prince of this notion.

'Prince, Dunia has never been for sale. Besides, we have stringent agreements with Galicia, Eden II, Alloria, and even Iccythria that we can't just toss out to accommodate your sudden and increased need for xentium. So I'm sorry, but the answer is no.'

An awkward silence ensued as Selene took another blissful sip from her glass.

'You've no idea what this means,' the Prince snarled.

'You'll find that I do know what it means.' *A fokk you to your entitlement,* she crabbed to herself.

'You'll live to regret this, young lady!'

'Don't young lady me, Prince, and don't threaten me. I won't budge. I also won't stand to be bullied. Dunia just kicked down what was supposed to be the System's greatest threat. So don't think we can't protect ourselves if we have to,' she said.

She paused for a beat, struggling to keep her angry breathing from flaming the airwaves between them. 'Now, was there something else I could help you with?'

'*Nada!*' came the curt, clipped reply.

The line dropped with no warning.

'Well, someone's not happy,' Selene whispered to herself. 'Must have been something I said.'

'What's that?' Rina asked, strolling back into the room.

She'd been trying a few gowns in the next room.

'Prince Emian of Rhesia. He just tried to bribe me for preferential access and an increased stake in xentium.'

Rina rolled her eyes. '*Fokk* xentium. It's starting to trigger me every time I hear the word,' she said. 'I know Rhesia is having energy problems, but damn, Emian sounds desperate. I don't know if his brother knows he made that call. It doesn't sound like a move King Auban would make.'

Selene sighed. 'Kainan said something about the Rhesians sometime back. He said he thought they were ruthless. I didn't buy his theory then, but now I'm unsure. He may have been right.'

'The Sable Group would know if anyone on Rhesia is being two-faced. They have the best surveillance setup in the System. So maybe get them to look into it.'

'I might just do that.'

The problem was reaching out to Kainan. But he'd disappeared just when she needed his strategic mind, advice, and insight.

Damn, she missed him. But she had no idea how to bridge the gaping chasm between them.

KAINAN

On Eden II, the dark half of the lunar month had long since enshrouded the moonscape. The sky above was cast in inky black velvetiness.

Against it, the neon lamps of Eden II glittered and gleamed throughout the moonscape, lighting up the architectural columns of a multi-story building and flashing over the slew of flyers that whisked past its darkened doorway.

The low-lit entrance led into The Osirian, which lay deserted and devoid of life.

The sign on its street entrance stated it was closed and soon to reopen after refurbishments were complete, which took a while.

This was partly due to the slow order time for the replacement onyx and marble bar destroyed during the crats' attack and the coup that had occupied the Sable Riders these last few weeks.

The fridges still worked and were well stocked.

Cold refreshments were still available for the Riders, their merc teams, and the fleet crew.

The latter chose to flit in and out daily to replenish themselves.

They'd been thirsty after their successful incursion on Dunia for some reason.

However, the few who'd come by that day had since left.

It was pretty late in the hour. Most of Eden II was asleep in their apartments, dens, and tunnel shacks.

Except for one man.

He sat at the far end of the bar's still-cracked onyx surface, his face pulled into a scowl. Back leaning into the chair, feet up on the shattered bar top.

Earlier, he'd nabbed a glass of the Galician whiskey brand he loved and was now sipping it morosely, staring at the darkened far wall.

The air on his neck bristled at the faint sound of an almost silent approach.

Followed by a second set of light footsteps.

He mumbled under his breath.

Kage materialized on one side of him while Riv slumped onto a bar chair.

The pair nailed him with concerned looks.

'What do you two want?' Kainan shot at the pair after a long moment.

'It speaks!' Kage murmured.

'Could you just leave me the *fokk* alone?'

'We ain't going nowhere,' Riv insisted. 'We're also over-joyed, brother, that you're stringing words into sentences now.'

Kainan took another sip of his drink and ignored the pair.

They shared a glance and decided on a different tack.

'You going to this shindig on Dunia?' Kage probed.

'Maybe. Maybe not,' came the clipped reply.

'Why '*maybe not*'?' Riv insisted, leaping over the counter to get himself a drink.

Kainan didn't reply, choosing instead to glower into his glass.

'You don't want to see *her*,' Kage guessed. 'But you're dying to see *her*!'

'Brother –' Kainan protested with a low rumble.

''Tis true,' Riv went further. 'Life with you these past weeks has been as miserable as those first weeks after the crats captured us over twenty-five years ago. You've become the most flamin', growling, angry, prickle-assed son of a bitch we've ever lived with.'

'And all because you won't admit that you can't live without her,' Kage added.

'*Fokk* off, you two. I *can* live without her,' Kainan ground. 'I've been through the worst shit. This is nothing!'

'So why are you acting like your world is ending?' Riv kept

on. 'Vastly different, Kai, to the smiling cat calling us every day when you two were alone at J'Urg Mihòr. Looking like he'd tasted the sweetest nectar in all of Pegasi.'

Kainan half rose in his chair and eyed Riv across the split bar, a heated rage washing over his face. 'Watch your *fokkin* words, brother,' he warned with a growl. 'Give her some damn respect!'

'See!' Riv said, triumphant. 'She turns you into an over-protective Simian bear. You need her. From what I've seen and heard, she needs you too.'

Kainan slumped back into his seat and glowered for a long moment. 'Riv, I can't. You know I can't tell her what I am.'

The words dragged out of him.

'Give her the benefit of the doubt. Let her make a choice,' the silver-haired man shot back.

'Look at it this way, brother,' Kage proffered. 'If the tables were turned and she was suffering from something out of her control, what would you want her to do?'

Silence fell in the expansive bar.

After a while, Kainan stirred. 'I'd want her to tell me so I could *fokkin*' turn over the moon and stars to make it better for her.'

Kainan's friends exchanged a look. The trio fell silent.

By and by, he huffed under his breath. 'Nice. Color me reversed with your pop psychology.'

'So you're coming?' Riv murmured with a grin.

Kainan shook his head at his two friends, exasperated. 'Damn it all to Iccythria and back. I'll be there — I need to straighten out a few things with her. So I s'pose tis the best time as any. What does one wear to these kinds of shindigs anyway?'

Riv shot his friend a grin. 'Between Zane and me, we've got your evening dress needs covered from top to toe.'

'*Fokk* me,' Kainan groaned. 'You're going to truss me up like a peacock!'

'All's fair after the wounded Ccyth dragon act you've been pulling all week,' Kage said, ending the discussion with a grin and a whiskey pour into three glasses.

SELENE

The biggest night in the history of Dunia!

Selene looked up at the flashing neon holographic sign floating above. In line to deposit her onto the red carpet, her flyer inched towards the iconic front steps of Parliament House.

Crowds lined the streets leading to the event.

Large LED lights lit up the night with prismatic and shard-like beams. Drones flitted mid-air, some capturing video, projecting Dunia's happy faces and overjoyed souls into the dark sky.

Others looped and danced in sprawling aerial displays and illuminated, synchronized formations over New Malindi's city and bay.

'Didn't think Dunia had it in us,' Selene commented. 'We're rivaling Enia with all these lights and colors.' She smoothed her dress and fiddled with an earring.

'We'll probably never see this kind of spectacle again in this lifetime,' Rina said.

'Yet it feels so wrong, celebrating before we say farewell to my father,' Selene added. 'But as he said, the people of Dunia and our service to them come first, before our personal troubles and grief.'

'You also wanted to wait for Sheba's return,' Rina said, giving her friend a compassionate look.

'I did. It'd be sacrilegious to have Father's funeral without her. Any word yet?' Selene asked.

Rina shook her head. 'The relief boat must be far away, past the reaches of our comms. We've left buoys in various parts of the System. They're broadcasting the same message to her. I'm hoping her ship will pick it up soon.'

'What does it say?'

'I kept it simple. I said she needs to contact you or me and make plans to return to Dunia.'

'She doesn't even know Father has passed,' Selene said softly. Tears threatened to spill over her lids, and she blinked them back. She inhaled, trying to push down the grief threatening to overcome her.

She fumbled with her purse and took out a small mirror to check that her eye makeup was still intact.

She didn't recognize the woman staring back at her: a sophisticated, stylish, graceful beauty with soft, sublime, understated makeup and an elegant chignon that tamed back wild, riotous curls.

Her neck was adorned with a chain of rare Galician gold pearls, old-mine cut diamonds, and xentium gems crafted into a choker.

In addition, it featured a three-in-one ruby pendant that

was almost 200 standard years old—a priceless piece on loan from Dunia's Planetary Museum of Jewels.

'You look more than fine,' Rina drawled from the opposite seat, sprawled in a Galician-styled unisex trouser suit, tabbing through her comm screen. 'Darian and the House of M'Armin outdid themselves. From makeup to gown.'

'You wriggled out of a gown tonight,' Selene said, putting her compact away while running an envious eye over her friend's more casual style. 'Unfair. I hate you.'

'I know,' Rina smirked.

'Didn't you get the memo? Genevieve insisted that the official dress code for the Ball is white and gold glam. I thought you'd already picked out the white dress that looked killer on you during our fittings.'

'Yeah, yeah,' Rina mocked. 'All attendees need to embody the grandeur of Dunia's Paladian Age,' she added, parroting words from the Council's extravagant invitation cards. 'AKA prosperity, power, and progressive development. Bring on the gold!'

'So why are you in all black?' Selene challenged.

Rina glanced up at her from the screen. 'Next to army green, black is my happy color.'

'You're so full of it,' Selene snapped back, picking at the jewels sewn into her dress.

'Not at all, woman. On the contrary, I need to blend in. After all, I'm your personal security guard for the evening.'

Selene snorted and looked away to a view of a city ablaze with light and excitement.

Screens in every street broadcast the event with the entire planet glued to their holos so they wouldn't miss out on any of the A-List arrivals.

For days now, holo stars, magazine editors, journalists, fashion designers, and all manner of glitterati had been hammering the government's hotline to score an invitation.

However, because of security concerns, only a few civilians had the coveted tickets to the Ball.

The organizers gave the rest two choices. Either sitting in bleachers in a nearby park to watch the evening's events on a sizable holo screen or lining the red carpet to cheer the dignitaries as they arrived.

Which happened when Selene's flyer slid into position at the start of the red carpet.

'Calm now,' Rina urged, stepping out first. She stood beside the door while Selene stepped out, trying her best not to lurch face forward onto the glimmering red path.

Given the wave of jubilation thundering from the crowds behind her and the red carpet, she must have managed it with aplomb.

She lifted a gold-gloved hand and walked forward, smiling, waving, and mouthing her thanks to the crowds and the media drones that hovered like giant flies above the melee.

Rina hovered close behind her, keeping a close watch on the crowds.

Selene noticed a series of tall, threatening guards standing at intervals along the promenade, and she felt a rush of gratitude. The Edenites had gone above and beyond in their generosity.

Even refusing payment for the deployment of the extra patrols they'd left on the planet after Freedom Day, who were now on duty protecting the ball's attendees.

Selene caught sight of Paloma Mware, the foreign minister and official organizer of the evening, rushing down the red carpet toward her.

'Excellency, you look divine,' gushed the dark-haired woman, her face wreathed in smiles.

'As do you, Minister,' Selene replied with a smile. 'How are we looking?'

Paloma fell into step with her leader, flapping her hands about. 'Everyone is here. Kings, queens, senators, generals, mayors, dignitaries across Pegasi – it's beyond exciting that they've all made it.'

'I guess the planets needed an excuse to celebrate,' Selene said, smiling. She reached out her hands to greet a few individuals she'd recognized standing beside the barriers.

Paloma waited until she was done to continue. 'Don't underestimate the appreciation they have towards you, Prime. You helped get rid of our worst enemies from the System, and for that, they'll be eternally grateful.'

Selene considered her words. She wasn't as confident that The Technocracy was done with Dunia or Pegasi.

Just then, a drone floated above her, and a fluid display unfurled to reveal the ravishing digital visage of the AI known as Yilia—one of Pegasi's most famed fashion journalists.

'Excellency, you look scrumptious in gold. That extravagant, cascading train is to die for,' the AI simpered. 'What are you wearing?'

Selene smiled, aware that the AI was broadcasting live to hundreds of millions across Pegasi who followed her every post.

'The House of M'Armin was gracious enough to lend me a gown from their latest couture collection. New Malindi's intricate architecture inspires the sculptural bustier and pays homage to this venue, Parliament House, and its soaring

Paladian-inspired columns. The train features stars from the constellations above Dunia. Last but not least, the three-in-one purple ruby pendant symbolizes the three major continents of Dunia and its people, most of whom fought so bravely for our freedom.'

The crowd roared in approval at her response, and Selene curtsied before hurrying forward.

To her relief, the red carpet soon ended as Paloma ushered her into the grand entrance of Parliament House.

The interior echoed the ornate elegance of ancient Paladian temples.

From the soaring tempered glass vaulted roof, the jeweled rafters, the walls covered in ancient art, and the sculpted columns that stood like giant sentries in the lofty, airy chamber.

Floral fabrics created by the great Dunia design house M'Artelli hung from the roof, and the ancient artworks and tapestries added to the grandeur.

An honor guard of Dunia's finest soldiers stood at attention, forming a corridor. As Selene approached to walk between them, the Principal Orchestra of The New Malindi Philharmonic struck up a triumphant tune.

'Here comes your grand entrance,' Rina whispered from behind, a smile in her voice.

Selene held her head up and sailed past the honor guard to the entrance of the vast, curved grand staircase.

The music welled up, filling the cavernous space with a soaring symphony composed by one of Dunia's own Elene M'Unzel, a violinist and composer of at least 21 of the planet's most loved concertantes.

She glanced below at the spectacular and impressive ballroom, unmatched in history, elegance, and grandeur, and featured high ceilings, bespoke light fittings, and original chandeliers.

To where a glittering bevy of guests from all corners of Pegasi waited, looking up at her.

There were hushed gasps as the guests took in her flowing dress and the train. She smiled, taking great care to broadcast it across the entire room.

For a moment, she thought she spied a tall, hulking man at the back of the room.

With an inhale, she looked away, knowing that if she indulged herself, she'd end up tripping down the grand stairs.

She took her time on the descent, giving her utmost to the moment and battling to tamp down the emotion swelling inside her.

When she stepped onto the ballroom floor, the orchestra ended the symphony with a flourish, replaced by the loud hand claps of the gathered assembly.

She stepped forward to greet the dignitaries.

First in line, ironically, were King Auban VI and Queen Sanjana of Rhesus.

The handsome royal bowed, and Selene sank to the floor per tradition. 'Looks like you triumphed after our last conversation. Congratulations to you.'

'Thank you, Your Highness,' Selene said with a smile.

He held on to her hand; his face clouded with a severe expression. 'I may soon be the one calling you for assistance, Prime. Just promise me that when I do call, you will answer.'

Selene looked into his eyes and noted the open honesty and a touch of worry. She squeezed his hand. 'Of course, Your Highness. I'll send you my private comm code so you can reach me. Anytime.'

The relief on his face was palpable.

All was not well with Rhesia, Selene thought.

She nodded to Rina, who was standing behind her.

Rina handed Selene her comm tab, who worked it quickly, and the trio soon heard the low sound of a vibration emitted by a slim device tucked into the royal's jacket pocket.

He smiled in gracious acknowledgment.

Selene turned to face his wife.

'Good to see you again, Prime,' said the elegant woman in an incredible white and gold lace gown. 'Last time you curtsied to me, and now I curtsy to you. Let's hope you catch me if I fall.'

They exchanged a laugh before Selene was whisked away to the next waiting dignitary.

The next hour was a whirlwind as Selene shook hands with the royalty in the room, conversed with prime ministers and emperors, and paused to listen to renowned singers from across Dunia entertain the guests.

Selene felt heated eyes on her throughout the hour, watching her with intense heat, but she ignored their delicious pull, focusing instead on her diplomacy.

The cocktail hour atmosphere was spectacular.

Servers danced around the room, handing glasses of rare champagne donated by none other than the royal court of Rhesus.

Trays of delicious nibbles circulated among the festive soirée.

On the high-gloss hardwood dance floor, couples and groups whirled to music that vacillated between symphonic harmonies and the latest pop hits from New Malindi's streets.

When she was speaking to the Chancellor of New Malindi's University, the crowd parted for a moment, and she caught sight of the man she'd not seen in weeks.

Her heart slammed in her chest.

She'd never seen Kainan in anything but an armored meta suit, casual jumpsuits, or nothing at all. Now, there he was in all of his suited magnificence.

Oh my!

He'd been poured into a white custom-fit tuxedo, accentuating his powerful musculature.

His dark locks flowed over a sapphire and gold-stitched high collar in an intricate Edenite pattern.

The same gold stitching snaked along the long line of the angled coattail jacket that cut off at his powerful thighs, the tails designed to fall to one side.

He wore dark navy pants that sculpted his long legs and dress boots so polished they reflected light from the chandelier crystals above their heads.

His wildfire eyes met hers, and she almost swayed. She reached for the Chancellor's arm to steady herself.

Still, Kainan held her gaze, and she returned it.

She was drawn in by his energy, by their crazy polarity. Her eyes were fixed on him, pulled to him.

Selene couldn't quite read his expression, but knew if he turned away from her, it might break her heart for an eternity.

Murmuring her apologies to the Chancellor, she pulled away and walked towards Kainan, her heart beating a wild rhythm in her chest.

He watched her approach, his eyes low and hooded, and she felt their heat burn the air between them. Then, a few lurching heartbeats later, she reached his side.

'Kainan,' she whispered. It was all she could manage.

'Excellency,' he uttered with a catch in his deep voice, turning to face her while raking his eyes over her face and dress. 'You look beautiful. You are the sun and stars in one, lighting up the room tonight.'

'*Sante*. You, too, are magnificent,' she said, then gave him a teasing look. 'When you choose to be.'

His lips quirked. 'Kage, Zane, and Riv pushed me. I had no choice but to follow the evening's dress code, Excellency.'

'Please,' she said, reaching out to touch his arm. 'Let's not be so formal tonight.'

He tracked her hand with his eyes, and she recognized the wariness lurking there.

He conceded with a slight nod. 'Selene, then.'

She felt a small stab of disappointment, for she'd hoped for another name.

One he'd often lapsed into calling her when the connection between them blazed.

She pulled back her hand, tucking it under her other wrist at her waist, resisting the desire to run her hand along his jaw, missing their previous, private intimacy.

She gathered herself and gave him a somewhat strained smile. 'Thank you for coming and lending your guards to us tonight to bolster our security.'

'*De nada*. It's the least I could do. Given my recent failure,' he ground out, tipping back the contents of the glass in his hand down his throat.

Selene shook her head at him. 'I thought we cleared this up, Kainan. You were not at fault.'

He gave a soft huff. 'The security council let me know how they felt, Selene, but I still have no idea how *you* feel about it.'

Selene studied the man for a long moment. 'You think I'm angry at you.'

His eyes shuttered. 'I don't know what to think except that I let you down.'

They stared at each other for a moment before Kainan looked away.

'*Khaji*,' she said, leaning in with a fierce whisper. 'You did nothing of the sort. On the contrary, you were my rock, my defender, and, without being sappy, my hero. I wouldn't have done any of this without you.'

His molten eyes whipped back to find her own. 'You think so?'

His voice was ragged and rough, filled with longing.

She felt her body react to his need. 'I know so. I so appreciate your help. And let's not forget that you saved my life at Massimo's mansion.'

Kainan's eyes flared with deep emotion. 'You're welcome, *khamila*. Anytime.'

She smiled at the tender word she'd been waiting for. 'I also need to apologize.'

His brow furrowed. 'For what?'

'For expecting more from you than you're ready to give.'

His mouth softened, and he reached out a hand to touch her own.

'Excellency!'

A voice cut into the moment, and Kainan withdrew.

Selene almost jumped, whirling around, eyes drawn downward to see Sheikh Bagua of Sirius III and an entourage of about five men gazing up at her.

'We need to talk xentium!' the Sheikh beamed at her, his

green eyes twinkling up from his short frame.

'A moment, gentlemen,' she said, nonplussed.

She turned back to Kainan. 'I have to –.'

'Go, Excellency,' he urged. 'You have your formal duties to carry out.'

He gave her a short, formal bow and turned as if to walk away, pausing when she called out after him. 'I won't be long. Please wait for me so that we can finish –.'

'I'll wait for you as long as you need,' he said quietly.

Then he bowed once more and walked away, leaving her to the mercy of the Sheikh and his gaggle of ministers.

Minutes later, the dinner announcement saved Selene from the Sheikh's rapid-fire demands.

The party filed next door to the banquet hall, where long candlelit tables were lined with centerpieces of gold and white lily bouquets, the blooms flown in from a famous valley where rare blossoms grew in Central Arumba.

Celebrated chef Mark M'Osia had prepared an exclusive multiple-course menu for the main event.

First, they feasted on generous portions of caviar from the bay of Rambasa, followed by oversized lobsters cooked with butter, spices, lemon, and capers.

Next, stuffed rock oysters, truffle crepinettes, and spatch-cock roasted in citrus, fennel, and caper brown butter were received with gasps of delight.

So, too, the fresh platinum salmon grilled with organic capers and seasoned wagyu steak from the windswept cattle ranches of Wadi.

Each exquisite course was served on white-and-gold Free Dunia marbled glass flatware designed by the House of M'Osian for the special event.

Champagne, wines, and whiskey flowed while more celebrated singers crooned for the assembled guests between each course, making the special evening nothing short of memorable for eons to come.

While they dined, from her raised table, Selene found herself pulled towards where Kainan sat.

Their eyes met, and she felt her breath catch each time. She'd look away when their shared gaze bordered on inappropriate or when Rina dug an elbow into her side. But when she did, she felt his hot eyes linger on her face.

A tendril of hope rose inside her.

Then she felt another short jab to her side from the woman seated beside her.

'Stop mooning at the Edenite and give your speech,' Rina hissed in her ear.

'I'm not -.'

'You so are. Any more stares between you two, flames will burst across the room.'

Selene served her friend a narrow-eyed, dirty look and a fake smile.

'Before the dessert course, please, and before Paloma has an apoplectic heart attack!' Rina urged.

Selene clicked her teeth at her friend while keeping the smile on her face, ever the consummate diplomat. She rose to her feet and clinked her dessert fork on her glass, and the room hushed.

She inclined her head with appreciation at their attention and launched into her short speech.

She thanked everyone for joining them at the auspicious event and, more so, all the enlisted soldiers, volunteer forces, and heroes who'd fought so hard for Dunia.

She praised them for their bravery and selflessness and underlined that Dunia's gratitude would never be enough.

She then moved to the dais, where the entire cabinet lined up for the awards presentation. One by one, the award recipients filed to the front of the room, receiving a generous bouquet and their medals.

Selene greeted them with a smile, placed the sculpted laurels on their chest, and thanked them. 'I'm grateful for all you've given in the service of Dunia,' she told each one.

The Sable Riders—Kage, Xion, Riv, and Zane—too stepped forward, their hulking heights looming over most guests in the room.

They received a Medal of Bravery for their courage and risk of life above and beyond the call of duty.

Even their AI received a Medal of Honorable Mention from Selene.

Kage accepted it on her behalf.

He leaned in and whispered to Selene. 'Mirage says *sante*. It means so much to her when someone appreciates her. Now she includes you in our little family.'

Selene smiled and squeezed his arm before he stalked away.

Last was Kainan, whom the Council had designated to receive the highest honor for a non-citizen.

Selene trembled as she presented him with the gold-plated, purple ruby Medal of Valor and pinned it on his broad shoulders.

She thanked him, her voice breaking with emotion as she spoke. 'We cannot quantify how many lives you saved with your aid to us. We will forever be grateful for the commitment of The Sable Riders, your leadership, your alliance, and the support of the entire citizenry of Eden II.'

Kainan blinked, he too fighting the great emotion of the moment.

Selene squeezed his hand tightly before letting go.

'Thank you, everyone,' she said through the thunderous clapping reverberating across the room.

With Kainan's hand helping her down, she readied to step off the dais when L'Ogano Rai stepped forward. The former head of the Interior Ministry and the man she'd now named as Deputy Prime judicially blocked her descent.

'Back to the dais, Excellency,' the older man insisted.

Surprised, she obeyed. She returned to where L'Ogano beckoned, still clutching onto Kainan's arm.

'There are two more awards to give,' L'Ogano announced to the room.

Selene blinked, unsure of what was happening.

L'Ogano continued, undeterred. 'We would like to honor our former Prime, His Excellency Kei'Lano Munene III, and our True Prime, Her Excellency Selene Munene, for their selfless service to this planet.'

Selene's knees gave way. She felt Kainan step forward to take hold of her waist. She leaned against him, seeking his support.

The Deputy Prime took an intricate medal hanging on a velvet cord from a box held by Ines and draped it around Selene's neck.

'This is for you. The Dunia Medal of Honor, for distinguishing yourself with gallantry in bravery, sacrifice, and action during the recent insurrection.'

Selene's tears flowed, and she placed a hand on her chest to calm herself.

He then opened a purple box. Inside was the highest medal

in Dunia—the Purple Bravestone.

'And this is for your father,' L'Ogano intoned. 'Today, his memory lives on in the lives he served. In the legend of his sacrifice and the hearts of his family that he left behind. We know that no award could ever make up for the loss of your father and for not having him here today. Still, I hope today you take some pride and comfort in knowing his bravery, sacrifice, and service are receiving the full recognition they deserve.'

Tears fell from Selene's eyes as she accepted the award, clutching it in her hand.

She barely heard the thunderous applause from the assembled guests and hardly acknowledged the standing ovation or the roar of the crowds outside.

All she heard was her father's voice whispering to her from the skies, from where he looked down at her.

'Job well done.'

17

An Unfathomable Anomaly

SELENE

She stepped off the dais at the banquet hall of Parliament House and into a swarm of people congratulating her.

She felt Kainan's hand slip away from hers until their connection broke off, pulled apart by the crowd around her.

She instantly missed his presence, smiling through moisture-laden eyes as the guests' adulation swamped her.

When the rush abated, she looked around for him, but no matter how much she searched the vast room, it was clear he wasn't in it.

He was gone.

Rina further confirmed her suspicions as Selene approached her with a question on her face. 'The Sable Riders left soon after the awards ceremony,' she told her friend, watching her keenly.

'Are they still on Dunia?'

Rina shrugged. 'I don't have eyes on them, but my sec team tells me they saw their corvettes launch and head for orbit minutes ago.'

Selene's heart fell. 'He said he'd wait,' she whispered.

Rina touched her friend's sleeve. 'Oh, honey.'

Selene took a sharp breath. 'That's fine. He has more important things to do.'

Rina gave her friend a sad smile. 'You OK?'

Selene plastered a smile on her face. 'I'll be fine. I always am.'

Despite the deep disappointment, Selene continued with the evening.

She had no choice.

Her role as Prime meant she had to sacrifice her personal needs for the good of her people.

After the dessert course, the glittering crowd decamped back to the ballroom for more cocktails and dancing, a fitting end to one of the most glamorous celebrations in Dunia's history.

Selene tried to enjoy herself. But between the harrowing awards ceremony and the ache in her heart, she found her energy and resolve flagging.

'I need to leave,' she whispered to Rina during President Cora Yuzeria's opinionated monologue on the economic outlook and growth projections for the Pegasi System.

'About time,' her friend whispered back.

Using the excuse of needing to secure her father's medal

in a safe place, Selene bade her guests goodnight. Leaving them in the capable hands of Paloma, her Foreign Minister, who was twisting and shaking her hips to the sound of Polaris Nebuli, one of the most popular and enduring bands in all of Pegasi.

Selene fled up the grand staircase, out of the large, soaring doors to Parliament House, and into her flyer, its door held open by her official driver. Rina scrambled in after her.

'Home?' Rina asked.

'Home.'

They flew past the still-heaving streets full of victory-drunk citizens towards the East of New Malindi, where the Prime's residence sat by a private bay.

Rina darted a few concerned looks at her friend's stony face, but she bit her tongue.

The flyer slipped past the electronic gates where two soldiers stood guard and whispered its way to the courtyard of the sprawling residence.

The pair exited the vehicle, and Rina walked Selene to the front door.

'Do you need me to stay?' Rina murmured.

Selene shook her head. '*Nada*, I just need to be alone for a while.'

'Call me please,' Rina pleaded, watching her friend walk wearily through the black onyx entrance.

The door closed behind Selene with a soft thud.

She kicked off her shoes and slid her bag onto the floor.

She'd cradled both medals she'd received in her hands since leaving the ballroom, and she headed with them into the study that was once her father's and now was her own.

Walking behind the beautiful ebony wood desk, she knelt

before a panel in the wall and waved her wrist comm in front of it.

A small door swung open with a click to reveal a secure safe inside.

She slid open a shelf and placed both boxes on it.

She then locked the safe and rose to her feet. Her head throbbed at the movement, and she groaned.

Suddenly, she felt constricted and in desperate need of fresh air.

Her skirts swished behind her as she hurried through the house towards the lounge overlooking the large garden outside.

Her arms swept open the sliding doors, and she stepped out, sucking in the fresh, sea salt-tinged air.

She welcomed the sight of the residential garden sloping off towards a generous beachhead where the water lapped against the sand. The beachhead reflected the city's lights beyond the bay across from where the house stood.

The Prime's residence belonged to the people of Dunia and had been constructed hundreds of years ago to house the first Prime, Silas Munene.

The parcel of land is sat on, and the beach beyond was generous enough to ensure the utmost privacy.

She'd often taken walks on the sands with her father as they hammered out strategies and discussed policy.

She now gazed out to the beach, feeling the intense loneliness of the moment.

Who would she share the anecdotes from an evening such as this one? With whom would she discuss the future of government?

Who would she debate the pros and cons of taxing the uber-

wealthy to help eradicate poverty in a changing system?

Who would listen to her views on migration, sustainability, and mining?

Who would indulge her, challenge her, cherish her?

She looked up at the skies above where Eden II hung like a silver bauble in an inky black sky.

She imagined Kainan flying back to the moonscape without her, having forgotten her.

A pang of agony ripped through her, and she turned, wanting to run inside to her bed, where she could dive under the covers and remain lost for days in her grief and loss.

Just then, she thought she saw something ripple in the air along the beach.

Her heart lurched, first in fear and then in wild hope.

The empty air above the sands shimmered and flickered, revealing a dark, sleek corvette that had been set down on the sand for a while.

Her pulse hammered, her eyes transfixed on the beach.

The corvette's door materialized against the matte radar-absorbing skin. Light spilled from the interior of the ship as its air bridge unfolded.

She clutched the railing on the balcony as a figure stepped down and then sat on a step halfway to the ground.

She couldn't see his features from this far away, but she could see his profile looking straight at her through the dancing shadows and low silver light bouncing off Eden II, high in the night sky above.

Kainan.

He'd waited. For her.

They stared at each other for the longest time across the expanse of the garden and the sands beyond.

Then Selene moved.

She strode from the balcony, forcing herself to breathe and move calmly. She grabbed a shawl from the hallway cupboard and ran down the stairs to the back door.

Moments later, she was outside.

Where her resolve and calm demeanor crumbled.

Bare feet flew across cobblestones, grass, and then sand.

Moments later, she came to the foot of the air bridge and glanced up to where Kainan was waiting, seated on a step, his hands resting on his knees.

With a bottle of Galician whiskey in one hand and two glasses on the step above him. His sapphire gold eyes glinted in the dark, and his mouth quirked as he gazed at her.

'You waited,' she stated, almost accusatory, as she pulled her shawl closer around her shoulders.

'I said I'd wait.' His voice was deep, low. 'Did you doubt me, *khamila*?'

'I thought you'd left. For Eden II.'

He shook his beautiful, dark head for a moment. 'We'd unfinished business, remember? A conversation we needed to have?'

She nodded. 'True. But what if I hadn't come out of my residence tonight?'

'I'd have broken down the doors and come for you.'

'You'd have caused a diplomatic incident.'

'*Nada*. I'd have silenced your guards long before they'd call for help.'

'Ruthless,' she commented with a half smile.

His lips twitched once more. 'Always, when it comes to you.'

He twisted his upper body and reached for one of the glasses on the step behind him. Then he poured out a snifter of whiskey. He handed the glass to her.

She mounted the air bridge steps to reach for it.

Their fingers touched as she wrapped her hands around it, and she felt a jolt of pure electricity between them.

She found herself settling her body next to his.

They drank from their glasses for a long moment.

Then she sliced her eyes to his and found him looking at her with such longing that her core clenched.

He leaned in, his molten eyes searching her face, asking her a silent question she dared not answer.

Until their lips met.

This was not a gentle, exploratory kiss.

Instead, Kainan took her mouth with sensuous forceful-ness, licking, sucking, nipping.

His tongue thrust itself inside, and he drank of her nectar.

She moaned and kissed him back with all the pent-up passion she'd held back these last few weeks.

He shifted to throw his snifter onto the sand.

She did the same and then twisted to hike her thigh over his own. He groaned, his thick fingers pushing her couture-made bustier down past her chest to her waist, which gave him clear access to her breasts.

He stared at them with lust-soaked molten eyes and dove in, lashing the peaked nipples with his tongue, sucking and soaking her with his desire.

His fingers pulled and pinched, and Selene found herself grinding her hips against the thick length she felt under his elegant trousers.

Then his hand slipped further south, pulling up her long couture skirts, growling when it took longer than he wanted.

With some quick flicks, he found purchase, his fingers roughly pulling aside her underwear and sinking into her wetness.

She gave a little scream as he worked his thick fingers into her wet, weeping slit, his thumb whipping across her clit.

She leaned forward, trying to get past his lips, still assaulting her nipples, until she found what she was after.

She wriggled until she could stroke his thick, hot length, still hidden in his trousers. She squeezed it with fervor, and he snarled, pushing her hand away, capturing it to hold it across her back.

He used the powerful arm to hold her still, which had the effect of pushing her nipples even deeper inside his mouth.

He laughed in triumph, his hands driving her to the brink of madness.

Then, the ripples of ecstasy began in her core. She bucked against the fingers so deep inside her that they dripped with her juices.

She lashed her head back, trying to harness the bay's cool, soft wind to cool her heated skin—to no avail.

Kainan himself was giving off such a burning heat that she could not escape it. It lit her from inside, and she'd never felt so glorious.

Then she came. The waves of a forceful orgasm hit her with the force of exploding nebulae.

She screamed into her hand, biting her flesh to stop her from crying out and summoning the entire battalion of guards stationed in front of her home.

He pulled her hand away from her mouth, and his lips took over for a drawn-out, luscious, tantalizing, and weakening kiss that had her hanging onto the back of his head.

Kainan kept his thumb on her clit, gently thumbing it as the aftershocks of her orgasm shuddered through her body.

After a long, drawn-out moment, their lips tore apart, and she fell forward, her arms around his muscled chest, her ear to his heart, listening as it thudded away.

Then she noticed the bulge still tenting his trousers.

She reached for him, but he pulled her hand away.

'Not fair,' she grumbled.

'Later, *khamila*, I can wait,' he told her thickly as she cuddled against him.

She leaned back and pulled down his beautiful, dark head to kiss him.

'I don't want you to wait, Kainan. I want you to let go, to let me give you the same pleasure. I want you to stay,' she moaned against his lips.

He went still, and she felt a stab of fear race up her spine.

She pulled back and looked at him, her hands framing his face.

'Did I just do it again?'

'Do what?' he said, rubbing his nose along her own.

'The Kainan magic trick. Where I say something, and you disappear for weeks?'

He huffed with laughter against her mouth.

They fell into a long hush, their foreheads resting against each other.

'We need to talk,' he murmured.

'Then talk, *khaji*,' she told him.

He breathed in hard, then pulled her off him.

She straightened her dress and tucked her shawl around her shoulders.

He then ran a hand through his luxurious dark hair.

The silver at his temple had extended in the past few weeks.

She leaned over, stroking the strands along his forehead and brow.

'I promise to listen and respect whatever you tell me,' she whispered.

'Will you still want to know me when I reveal my true self to you?' he asked, so quiet, so low she could hardly hear him.

'I will,' Selene said. 'Nothing you can ever say will change the fact that the man I've come to know these last few weeks is everything and more than I could have ever imagined.'

'Ah, *khamila*,' he groaned. 'But you don't know me, not this way.'

'What way is that?' she urged, fear creeping into her voice.

He stared at her for a long moment. 'What I'm about to show you, what you're about to see, remains between us. Also, no one else can see us because I instructed Mirage to hack into your security and recycle earlier footage of the beach and garden. So all your guards can see right now is the same old view they're used to. After you arrived, she extended the ship's stealth tech to the beach and garden beyond. No eyes can penetrate that shield.'

Selene's imagination ran wild, but she kept her expression calm. 'I can keep a secret,' she reassured him.

He rose to his feet and strode down the air bridge steps. They rocked with the weight of him. He cut across the sand and stood a few meters away.

'Stay there,' he said, pointing to the steps. 'It's the safest for you. I can control myself so you don't get hurt, but I don't want to chance it in case something goes wrong.'

He gazed at her with eyes so forlorn that it sheared away at her soul.

'This is what I am, *khamila*.'

He stood there and extended his arms out.

She saw tendrils of white, red, gold, sapphire, and silver coalesce inside his body and under his skin. It was like watching a piece of coal burn from within. First, the white-hot, red, and sapphire heat spread across his body, leaching onto his hair, fingers, and toes.

She gasped as his clothes burned up and fell off his body in ashes.

His molten eyes blazed with flames, and then his entire body combusted.

She recoiled, falling back against the step she was seated on.

It was HIM?

This was the same being she'd seen on Enia at Prince Occaro's birthday party. On the night, the Rhesian royal had gone up in flames.

She gaped as a whirlwind began to form under and around the resulting flame columns and blazing tongues of energy.

Intense rising heat scorched her skin, so she scrambled backward up the highest step of the air bridge.

A turbulent wind kicked up, forming whirling eddies of air.

That turned into a tornado-like vortex that sucked in sand and air from the vicinity.

She began to choke, and that's when the whirling force of the blaze slowed.

Kainan's body reformed, and the vortex ceased.

Selene forced herself to watch as his body reappeared.

The tendrils of fire retracted, cooling, curling back under his skin.

He slumped onto the sand on one knee, naked.

She felt conflicted. Torn.

Yet she refused to judge him until she knew the whole story.

She made up her mind. She flung herself down the stairs and across the sand.

He watched her come to him, his eyes wide with confusion.

'But I'm this anomaly,' he whispered.

Selene ignored him, kneeling before him, gingerly touching his body. It was hot, but nothing she couldn't handle.

She leaned forward, wrapping her hands around him.

'*Khamila*?' he groaned.

'You're not an anomaly. But you will need to explain that trick to me in detail.'

'*Fokk*,' he rasped. 'That little trick took over five years of pain and agony to come up with. Doesn't it scare you?'

She sat back on her heels and took one of his hands. 'A tad bit. But it's not new to me. I've seen it. I've seen you in this form before.'

He pulled back from her arms, nailing her with a narrowed look. 'Selene, what are you talking about?'

'Have you used this power before?'

'*Naam*,' he stated. 'But purely in defense and to mete justice, *khamila*,' Kainan said. 'The first time was when slavers tried to steal a couple of orphans from Eden II. The kids were friends of mine. I had to do something. It's where the whispers and rumors of my chimera abilities started. Some orphans saw me transform when I confronted their captors in a tunnel underneath the city. The next time was when a horde of pirates decided they wanted to take over Eden II and make it their home. I obliterated all their ships. They've also been a few wayward royalty scums and a crime lord or two I've had to deal with. Plus the crats when they attacked The Osirian. Only those who've crossed The Sable Group and refused to take no for an answer.'

'Like Prince Occaro? Of Rhesia?' she exclaimed.

Kainan's eyes sliced to her own. '*Naam*,' he rasped. 'How do you know about him?'

'Because I was there that night. I was outside the door of the Prince's office. I saw you in there, in this form you just showed me.'

Kainan's eyes shut in deep distress. '*Fokkin*' hell, you saw that?'

'I did. Don't you remember?'

Kainan cocked his head, trying to recall. 'You were the woman outside in the corridor,' he said, searching for words as his memory of the night came back to him. 'When I'm in my chimeric form, I tend to focus on the task because it takes so much energy from me. Other details can be hazy. But I've never harmed an innocent person. It goes against my nature, which is why you were safe that night. You'll always be safe with me.'

She searched his eyes until she was satisfied with his response.

'I believe you. However, why did you do it?' she probed. 'I received some high-level intel afterward on him, but no confirmation of who got rid of him or why.'

'He crossed the wrong people, love. The King of Rhesia, for one. Whose son the Prince tried to murder.'

'Did the King hire you?'

'He approached me, *naam*.'

'His own brother?'

'There was no love lost there for many years,' Kainan confirmed. 'I know they were at each other's throats since childhood. But I didn't do it for Auban or his son. Neither did I take any payment for it. I did it for the innocent families slaughtered on that space liner. Over 3,000 people lost their lives. They were just refugees looking for a safe home. We'd offered it to them on Eden II. They died needlessly because of one man's greed. Justice had to be served.'

Selene's eyes were as wide as they could get. 'You know Rina called you and the Riders vigilante badasses, but this is on another level.'

'Does it make you want to run?'

'Does it look like I'm running?' she shot back.

He studied her for a long moment. 'Nevertheless, will you want to stay? I won't be here for long, my love. This power isn't doing my body any favors. Unfortunately, my life is in peril, and the end might be gruesome.'

Selene blinked as she considered his words and then reached for him. 'Kainan, you're my man. You'll need to do way more than this to frighten me off ever again.'

She saw and felt something break inside him.

Then he wrapped his arms around her as his body was wracked with soundless, heart-wrenching sobs.

'I am the true embodiment of the word *chimera*.'

Kainan spoke quietly, his gaze fixed on the expansive ship's window that opened to the night sky above New Malindi.

The moonlight had waned somewhat with Eden II's gradual shift in the night sky. And the stars above were plumper, closer.

After Kainan's confession, they'd knelt in the sands for what seemed like hours.

Until he'd recovered and gathered his cool.

Then he'd lifted Selene into his arms.

They'd escaped the cooling temperature outside and retreated inside the gunship.

He'd slipped into his quarters, where he found a fresh pair of pants, pulling them on before leading her by hand to the command deck.

Now, Kainan's arms wrapped around Selene, who lay with her head on his chest.

The time on the gunship's chrono showed it was inching towards 0300 Standard. They were inside Mirage, sprawled on the familiar king-sized couch that Kainan had pulled out of the panel on the gunship's command deck.

He ran his hands over her skin, and she shivered, not from the cold but from his heated touch. She snuggled in closer to him, traced her lips along his jaw, moving lower to place a kiss on his chest.

'I'm a quantum biological mess,' Kainan continued. 'My metanoids exist alongside my atoms and cells, giving them the ability to carry extraordinary energy. I can release them at will to cause an insane reaction. When I transmute into a flame vortex, it can spread out over great gulfs of space before returning to my form. My mind spreads over the area my atoms cover and the 'noids to control each element down to single molecules. It's a powerful but exhausting transformation that takes everything from me.'

'Were you always this way?'

Kainan gave a mirthless laugh. '*Nada.* I'm the result of hundreds of experiments. It was no fast process; the complete mutation into becoming a chimera took years. The time needed for my body to grow and build new structures and components. My height and size are due to my appetite and body being tampered with, too, so I could ramp up my energy stores to aid the mutation process. Which was pure torture as my body warped over the years. The chimera cells infused in me comprise two DNA strands forcibly linked with my meta-human one. So I'm a mix of a meta-human, a flame creature from an unknown planet, and a sentient high-energy radioactive organism, which I suspect was harvested from a hydrogen-rich nebula.'

Selene half sat up, looking at him while shaking her head in horror.

Kainan stroked her cheek to calm her distress. 'The problem, *khamila*, is that I'm dying. The different DNA strands inside me are too distinct from each other. I rarely use my chimera powers because each vortex transformation kills my metanoids. It burns them off. Day to day, the foreign strands are using too much energy to remain compatible with my DNA, so they're breaking down. They can't regenerate fast enough, and those that remain are dying, leading to thousands of incompatible and simultaneous impacts on my body. Nothing that the so-called architects of these experiments could have known or anticipated.'

Selene pushed herself and sat up, tucking her legs underneath her.

'Who did this to you?' she asked, her face contorted with outrage. 'Who are these monsters?'

Kainan flicked his eyes to the stars.

'The Technocracy,' he muttered.

'*Fokk*,' she hissed. 'How? When?'

'Years ago. Remember I told you when we first met on Eden II that we were Kubai warriors, the Kwavi's most elite soldiers? Eden City needed to expand. We were getting overpopulated due to taking in so many refugees from Planet Earth. We had to find a new satellite home for our people and secure passage. So we were sent out to scan for security weaknesses before our science ships and generation arks could launch.'

'We?'

'The Riders as you know them. We were all under twenty-five with different years of experience, most of it together. Most of us were orphans. As I shared before, I was one too. My mother died in childbirth on the streets of Eden II. I was born premature, drug dependent, and underweight. The Kwavi Elders had an orphanage. They nursed me to health, took me in, and put me through school, where I first met Kage, Riv, Zane, and later Xion, Ki'Remi, Kisan, and Sax. The Elders enrolled us all in their military academy when we were seven. We were in the same warrior training class in Eden City. We did the hard yards and became the best of the Eden Guards. Which is why they entrusted us with the mission.'

Kainan paused, gathering his thoughts and memories with a sigh.

'Our small platoon of eight was sent from Eden City to Pegasi on patrol. In a small corvette, conducting re-con in this system. I was a pilot and first lieutenant, leading the platoon. I was assisted by Kage, acting as a platoon sergeant and tech specialist. Riv was our sniper and marksman.

Ki'Remi, whom you've yet to meet, was our medic. Xion, our gunner; Zane, our logistics officer, and deputy squad leader. We also had Kisan, our alien languages interpreter, and Sax, our science officer.'

'Fifty days after we left Eden City and a few days past the galaxy borders, we were caught in a massive asteroid storm. It hit our patrol boat real bad. We lost engines, and our shielding was toast. Kisan was seriously wounded when he fell from his crash couch during the turbulence. He broke his back, and our med bay was destroyed, so we couldn't help him. We drifted for days, off course.'

'We were isolated, so we had no other option but to broadcast for help. Unfortunately for us, The Technocracy had planted surveillance satellites throughout the galaxy. One of them picked up our signal. We were quick to capture because we didn't have it in us to offer any resistance. They had, at the time, more lethal weapons, more crazy tech, more superior crat soldiers.'

'They took us to one of their dreadnoughts, called The Posteriori, meaning what comes before and after. It was a giant floating experiment lab.'

'They were elated that they now had meta-human test subjects to work with. But, so far, their efforts to breach the Milky Way and Earth were thwarted by the Iccythrians living on the farthest edge of Pegasi, where the three galaxies meet.'

'The ship itself was massive—over 30 decks. Our deck and the med lab had enough room for ten subjects, 45 guards, and 20 crat medical staff. There were food storage, testing, and workshops. The food supply came from raiding uninhabited planets across Pegasi. The crats were able to recycle and purify water, and after experimenting with a few options for synthesizing long-life food, they could generate 1 ton for each of us every year. There was an operating and observation room to gather tissue samples and expose us to whatever hell they imagined for us.'

'Because they were also keen to understand how we lived as metahumans, they kept us together. We slept in one open dormitory. The rest of the ship held the command deck, propulsion systems, fuel and water desalination, and a water recycling plant. It was a ship design we'd never seen before.'

'The ship prowled the edge of Pegasi close to the border with the Omega IAZL System. Using large lasers, it would fly into nebulas, scooping up gases and elements. They'd then run it through a fusion reaction to make heavier elements, providing power and thrust. This allowed them to stay out there for years, unseen. During which, we suffered years of torture and experimentation.'

'First, they took our blood, spliced our DNA, and played around with our metanoids.'

'They also played with our physiology. They reinforced our bones with carbon metanoids and infused our skin and body cell walls with a latticework of liquid noids to withstand punches, blows, ballistics, and zero-g space flight better than most. Our pain receptors were also tweaked to auto-compensate in the event of injury. Also, they hard-wired a neural computer chip with metalloid latticed protection into our brains. Next, they linked all our nodes so we could interact neurally. Then, they downloaded into them a wealth of information and knowledge bases from all over the known universe.'

'They wanted to observe how we interacted with the new

data. And also how we took it in through the nodes' distributed network that algorithmically updates itself when our hard-wired knowledge is outdated or when something new is learned.'

'They used ankle bracelets with tech that prevented our metanoids from activating without their auth. When we refused to wear them, they beat us with no holds barred. Our science officer, Sax, was vocal in questioning their treatment of us, so they took him away. We never saw him again. Due to his earlier injuries, Kisan didn't survive the experiments. He died three years into captivity.'

Selene ran a hand over Kainan's face. 'How tragic. I'm so sorry, *khaji*.'

Kainan continued, his voice low and quiet. 'We weren't even able to mourn him. They took his body away for more experiments, most likely.'

He was subdued, his eyes bleak and focused far into the past. He sucked in air before continuing. 'Over time, their security became lax. So we began to plan our escape. Kage put his tech skills to work. He managed to get hold of one of their drones and hack it. It helped us to get to their ship's AI, determine where the mind control had its epicenter, and manipulate it. Their AI, curious about us and longing for a connection with carbon-based lifeforms, became our friend.'

'Mirage?' Selene guessed.

Kainan gave a slight nod. 'Mirage. We built a relationship with her; she learned what it meant to care for others, and we emulated it back to her because that's how AI understands the human condition - by experience. We then persuaded her to use deep machine learning to recognize and distinguish the crats from ourselves. We also asked her to take over the ship's

AI-controlled drones and, when we were ready, unleash a precise ship-wide attack.'

'Our escape came five years after being captured, almost to the day. Mirage first deactivated our ankle and nodal controls, releasing a virus hack attack. It knocked out most of the base crats. Mirage also locked out the higher-functioning command crats in the higher decks. The ship's power fluctuated, leading to certain decks shutting down, which aided our escape. We reached the hangar when I used my chimera metanoids to burn through the emergency blast doors. We all managed to get into one of their gunships. Kage transferred Mirage's hard drive onto our escape ship, and I got my men out.'

Selene sucked her teeth in commiseration. 'How did you get to Eden II?'

'Mirage, again. She was our saving grace. She used her Technocracy maps to get us to Pegasi's safer, more populated regions. She cruised straight into Eden II's bare-bones refueling station, which was all it was then. We traded the few supplies on the gunship for safe harbor, and there we stayed. That was over twenty-five years ago.'

Selene shook her head, still caught in disbelief. 'Holy Dunia! What did freedom feel like?'

Kainan's eyes tracked a shooting star across New Malindi's sky before he turned his molten gaze on her.

'Sweet. Like the heavenliest honey found only in Eden City's gardens. But we all were so weakened by the experiments that we were walking skeletons. We were ravaged— body, mind, and soul. I was worse than the others because I was the one who was experimented on the most. It took years to recover, both physically and mentally.'

Selene's hands crossed her chest, feeling his pain to her core. Tears slipped between her eyelids, and Kainan reached out a finger to wipe them away.

His face softened at her compassion. 'Don't cry, *khamila*. I stopped grieving many years ago. But the harsh reality remains. I have three different DNA strands in me, and that combination is killing me.'

'What about the other Riders?' Selene asked softly.

'My other Sable brothers only have two each. Kage can cloak himself with the same stealth 'noids as on our ships; Riv has shape-shifting abilities; he can change into any form he desires. Xion has super speed and reflexes. Zane is a psionic mastermind at syllogizing, computing, and mathematizing. And, Ki'Remi, whom you haven't met yet, has heightened senses such as exceptional vision, touch, and hearing, and the ability to manipulate matter, making him a great medic.'

'But they don't have the same regeneration problem I do. As I said, my metanoids are dying from DNA incompatibility, which means I have only four, max five years left to live.'

He paused for a moment, then spoke, his voice dipping lower. 'Which is why I can't give you forever.'

Selene slanted and shook her head. 'That's what you've been trying to tell me all along,' she murmured.

'Yes, *khamila*. I want to be with you so much. I adore you. But I can't give you a long life together.'

'You can give me today,' Selene countered. 'I don't care who you are. I care what you are to me - and what we can share while we have each other,' Selene said.

Kainan turned his head and gave her a long look.

Then, he reached for her, and their lips met, melting into a deep kiss.

343

'Is there no cure whatsoever?' Selene asked with a sad smile a few minutes later.

Kainan closed his eyes for a moment and shook his head. 'A few years after we'd escaped the crats, when we'd begun to find our equilibrium here on Eden II once more, Ki'Remi, our medic, began to test all of us. To see how we'd been affected. He found the metanoid DNA anomalies and regeneration issues in my body, which worsened immediately after using my chimeric vortex. He tried everything he knew. Nothing worked.'

'I'll search high and low to find a cure,' she said fiercely.

'You think you'll do better than Ki'Remi? He searched the entire system for a cure. We traveled most of Pegasi - from Galicia, Rhesus, and even as far as Iccythria. We found nothing.'

Selene shook her head. 'He didn't look hard enough.'

'He did, I did.'

Selene swatted his shoulder. 'I can't believe how calm you are. Aren't you angry about all of this?'

'Six stages of grief, my love. I've been through it all. Now I'm at acceptance. I've been here a long time and resigned to fate. I've cheated death many times and am lucky to have survived this long. I now live in the present. In the now. Trying to enjoy what I have for the little time I have left. It's still agony, but agony that I now have tools to deal with.'

'Ki'Remi took a different tack,' Kainan went on. 'The failure to find a cure for me hit him pretty hard. He couldn't face losing me, not after he'd lost Kisan. So he left Eden II on a cruiser we outfitted for him as a medical clinic, ironically with the same self-reliant fuel and food systems as The Posteriori. He now cruises Pegasi's far reaches, searching for other victims of The Technocracy's experiments. He'd heard there were others out there. So he finds them and offers them free medical care before sending them on their way.'

Selene shut her eyes for a moment. *It was almost too hard to bear.*

She thought of him, living with this burden for years. And she got over herself.

She opened one eye. 'Can nothing be done whatsoever?'

'Nothing, as far as I know,' he gave her a wry smile that told her he needed a break from the heavy emotion of their discussion. 'And that's all I can say about it, *khamila*. Are we done now?'

Selene gazed at the man she loved. For loved him, she did.

Leaning over him, she stroked her lips over his. 'We'll never be done. I won't give up on you or on looking for a cure. But for now, let's live in the moment, *khaji*. I meant it when I said I'll take two years by your side versus a lifetime of never loving you.'

'*Khamila*,' he groaned, reaching for her.

Kainan kissed her neck and nibbled on her ear, stroking his tongue along her skin to her earlobe, which he suckled. Every lick and touch stoked up hot flames along her nerve endings.

He undressed them, slipping off her couture gown and the undergarment that gave the dress its body. Stepping out of his pants, he pushed her back onto the couch.

He stared at her, trailing his hand over her body until he slipped it between her thighs.

'You are so beautiful, Selene,' he said thickly. 'Your hair - so rich, so dark, so full of life. Your eyes give me life. Your skin looks and tastes like the rarest honey from Issakar. Your heart and mind are pure, kind, wise, and giving. You're the embodiment of a goddess, my love. And here you are, so wet, so tight for me. I could never have imagined being so lucky.'

He stroked his length with his other hand as he spoke, his hot sapphire gold eyes running over her lush curves.

He squeezed his thick, hard cock as he stroked her sensitive core.

He closed his eyes, reveling in the moment's pleasure, and groaned, his hands moving faster on his cock.

Selene blushed at his seductive words; her eyes fixated on what he was doing to himself.

'Do you trust me, *khamila*?' he asked, opening his eyes to look down at her with molten need.

'With my life,' she whispered, her eyes flicking back to his.

He smiled and then leaned his entire body back on his knees.

Her eyes widened as a wisp of blue and red energy curled up from deep within his glyphed chest to the surface of his skin.

She fought for breath as the surface under his chest, arms, torso, and lower body transformed into waves of colored heat that ranged from violet to white, orange, sapphire, indigo, and gold.

The effect was a glowing halo of fast-changing hues under his skin, from deep blues and reds that coalesced into purple, which emitted a high heat, to cooler reds and yellow and white hot flashes.

She reached out a hand in wonder, and he took it, pressing it onto the heated skin over his racing heart.

'I won't hurt you, *khamila*,' he promised. 'But I'll make love to you as only a chimera can.'

'This won't hurt you?' she asked, remembering what he'd shared.

'*Nada*, love. My metanoids regulate the reactions, keeping my body from flaming, which is when my control becomes untenable.'

'Amazing,' she breathed as he leaned down, propping his glowing body above her. The colorful energy under his skin moved and danced, sometimes imperceptible, then suddenly grew vivid.

Then he lifted the back of her knees and pulled her feet over his giant shoulders.

He took her arms and held them still above her head with one hand.

Before sliding his heated cock into her slickness.

She felt the thick, hot rod fire her up. She arched her body, trying to move from the restraint of his hand to reach for him.

His muscled chest lowered, grazing her nipples. The heated contact was the most arousing she'd ever had.

Steamy, searing, incandescent.

She felt hot, cold, and everything in between, charged by the waves of energy coming from his body.

His wired ardor rubbed off on her, inflaming her as she'd never felt like she was receiving zaps of pure electric pleasure from head to toe.

He was in complete control of his chimeric energy as he

moved, stroking in and out of her, using the fast-moving energy bands to inflict pleasure at an atomic level.

Then he shifted, slipping out of her to flip her onto her stomach.

He pulled her up from the waist, and she shivered, lifting her backside to him. He found her wetness again and then, leaning over her, sank again into her depths.

She bucked up against his thrusts as he stroked her full tits, pulled at her hard nipples, and nibbled at her neck and shoulders.

Then he whispered into her ear.

'I love you, Selene. I love you so much,' he groaned, lips searching for hers.

She twisted her head to the side, kissing him back. 'And I love you, Kainan, entirely, overwhelmingly,' she breathed against his hot mouth.

He groaned at the pleasure heating up between them.

He used a glowing hand to band across her chest, pulling her back as his thrusts became more frantic, more frenetic.

His other hand reached the apex of her body, where they joined together. He thrust a finger into a creaming slit, tugging on her swollen heated clit.

She screamed, unable to hold her passion in any longer.

She fell forward, jerking and thrusting into his impossible heat as she felt her orgasm crash over her in scalding waves of ecstasy.

He growled and grabbed her hips, slamming even faster into her.

Until he snarled even louder, she felt his fervid cock jerk inside, spilling a paroxysm of scorching hot seed into her depths.

He collapsed against her spine. Then they slid to lie down, panting. Selene couldn't speak for a few long minutes, so overwhelmed by their lovemaking.

'Let's keep looking for that cure, *khaji*,' she gasped. 'But please! Let's hold on to that particular power. I can't go back to normal lovemaking after this.'

She pulled up to her knees and gazed at the man lying there, who looked so seductive, with an arm flung over his eyes and a broad smile on his face.

He dropped his arm as she crawled over his body to kiss him again.

'Promise?' she pleaded.

He grinned, pulling her closer. 'Promise.'

18

When Love Is Deep, You Won't Fear The Storms

SELENE

There was nothing like waking to the warmth of New Malindi's twin suns on her face.

Selene smiled, feeling languorous and liquid, a sensation she hadn't enjoyed for years. She tried to shift.

That's when she felt the heavy hand draped across her waist, followed by the warm wall of pure muscle.

That stretched behind her, the length of her body, and beyond.

She turned, and her smile widened.

Kainan, in sleep, was a vision.

He looked so carefree, so relaxed.

Even the tiny creases by his eyelids had disappeared in

slumber.

He seemed all innocent, but she blushed, recalling the husky, racy, and steamy words he'd whispered as he'd heated her core for hours.

She'd come so much she'd become delirious, begging for release from the intense need that he'd inflamed inside her over and over again.

In between their lovemaking, he'd flown Mirage to a small deserted island off New Malindi's coast to prevent any possible detection.

Then he'd turned around and scorched her again with his sultry kisses and blazing hot strokes.

She'd spent hours imagining this moment with him, but for all of her wild fantasies, the reality was far sweeter and more poignant than she could have ever hoped.

Yet his confession of the challenges he faced had put a dampener on her joy.

Nevertheless, she knew she was now linked to this stunning being and was committed to being by his side until they found a way out of his present predicament.

He was so beautiful, she thought, her eyes trailing over his features.

She was about to reach a hand to stroke his face when she noticed the time on the command deck chrono.

Fokk! Was it 1600 hours already?

She scrambled for her wrist comm but couldn't find it.

Then she spied it on the crash couch in the distance, where Kainan had discarded it in the heat of their lovemaking.

She wriggled as gently as she could from under her man's embrace. He protested in his sleep, reaching out a muscled arm to try and pull her back.

'*Khamila*,' she heard him murmur, twisting to try and find her on the expansive couch, revealing more of his magnificent glyphed nakedness.

She felt her insides clench with desire, and she bit her lip, wanting to run back into his arms.

Damn, wasn't four times in one night enough? she scolded herself under her breath.

Obviously not, because she only wanted to race back to the couch and revisit the night.

But first, duty called.

She hoped against all hope that no one had needed her in an official capacity these past few hours.

Kainan rolled and settled into sleep again as she walked to the couch.

Her body ached, still unused to the pleasurable punishment it had received most of the night.

She gathered her shawl from the floor, wrapping it around her as she flipped over her wrist comm and swiped.

She blinked at the sight of six missed calls, all from Rina.

Curious and concerned, she returned to the king-size couch where her lover lay and tapped the screen to return the last call.

Its visuals flickered on.

To reveal the face of an enraged woman.

'Selene! Where the hell are you? We've been trying to reach you for the past six hours.'

Selene's eyes widened at the ferociousness of her friend's opening salvo.

'You're not in your residence,' Rina yelled at her friend. 'We've searched the grounds, but you're nowhere to be found. I was about to raise the alarm and get Dunia's Security Forces mobilized for a major search. Reason for the op? The Prime is missing after a night spent celebrating the planet's victory over a coup where she was persona numero uno on a system-wide hit list!'

Selene winced, wracked with guilt. 'I was - kinda - busy?' she flinched.

Rina paused her outrage. 'Busy with what?'

Her eyes suddenly widened at the sight of the sleep-dazed man who appeared behind Selene, rubbing a hand over his drowsy eyes, face, and beard.

'What's going on?' Kainan yawned, running a muscled hand down Selene's arm.

'Dammit, Selene!' Rina groaned with aggravation, taking in the sight of her friend's lover. 'You were booed up? Couldn't you have sent me a message to tell me where you were?'

Selene lifted her eyebrow, giving her friend a loaded look.

Rina rolled her eyes in response. 'So you were too busy kicking it or *whatchamacallit* to comm me?'

'Something like that,' Kainan called out with a snigger from over Selene's shoulder. 'You Dunians have some strange vocabulary,' he added, knifing himself out of bed in all his naked glory.

Rina squealed and covered her eyes. 'Too much people, too much.'

'Need a shower,' Kainan smirked, touching his mouth to Selene's. Then he muttered, 'I adore you, *khamila*.'

With that, he grinned and strode down Mirage's command deck stairs to the cabin deck, out of earshot and away from Rina's sight.

'Holy Dunia,' Selene said, staring after him. 'I'm sorry,'

she added, returning to her friend.

'*Nada*! You're not!' Rina scoffed.

Selene gave her friend a smug look. 'You're right. So not sorry!'

Rina scowled. 'At least someone's in a much better mood than I am.'

She then broke into a tired smile. 'If whatever happened last night means you've both pulled your fokkin' heads in and decided you're better off together, then I'm delighted for you.'

Selene beamed. 'Thank you, Ri. This time, it feels like he's ready to explore something meaningful.' Her face fell for a moment, and she lowered her voice. 'We're taking it day-by-day, though, for reasons I'll tell you at the right time when I have his permission.'

Rina nodded. 'I understand—secrets between lovers and all that shit. You look happy, Sel, and that's what matters.' She paused for a moment. 'Which is why it sucks that I have some not-so-happy news for you.'

Selene sighed. 'What now? I don't think I can take any more bad news.'

'Then I apologize in advance,' Rina sighed. 'Because there's no way to say this other than to cut to the chase. Earlier today, we received a distress signal. Well, it's more like we intercepted a radio signal from a seemingly impossible origin. It was patchy, to say the least, but our comms team managed to splice it together -'

'And what?' Selene urged, leaning closer to the screen.

'We think it came from Sheba. Our techs managed to match the voice to our Dunian key personnel database. We keep voice data records of all our government civil servants and their families.'

Selene felt her stomach sink. 'Are you sure?'

'There's no doubt.'

'What did it say?'

'The exact words?' Rina looked down at a display on her end of the call for reference. 'It said, *'This is Sheba Munene of the Haven Mercy Ship. This message needs to be relayed to the Prime of Dunia. Tell him that I – and the ship I was on, The Haven Mercy – have been captured by The Technocracy at the attached coordinates. Please come and get us; we need help to escape.'*

Rina swallowed as she studied Selene's face. 'The message also includes a location in the far reaches of Pegasi.'

'No, not Sheba,' Selene whispered.

Just then, Kainan thundered towards the command deck from his quarters, taking the stairs two at a time. He'd pulled on a Sable Group fleet jumpsuit and held his comm tab in his hand. 'Selene,' he growled. '*Sheba*. That's your sister's name?'

She whirled around, her heart racing. 'Yes! What have you heard?'

'A distress signal was sent on wide-band and to The Sable Group's comm nodes. I'd turned off mine since last night, so I missed it. Kage also sent me a few messages that I also missed. The call came directly to our nodes. Which means a Rider is involved.'

Selene rose to her feet. 'That's what Rina was just briefing me about. Her techs also got wind of it. So what do we do?'

'Let's call the rest of the Riders,' Kainan commanded.

He strode to the pilot controls and flicked on Mirage's wake switch.

'Mirage, raise Kage and whoever else in the core Sable Group you can find. Get them on screen for a con call now, please. Add Colonel Rina to the call as well.'

'On it, *khosi*,' the AI said.

'I need to get dressed,' Selene muttered.

'Go,' Rina said. 'See you in a few.' She disconnected the call.

'*Khaji*, normal clothes, please?' Selene said, calling out to Kainan, lifting her crushed ball gown.

He glanced at her. 'My quarters. I've got a few jumpsuits in the cupboard there. They're nanotech, so they'll adjust to your size, *khamila*.'

'Thank you.'

She rushed downstairs, appearing minutes later in a jumpsuit similar to his own.

Kage was speaking on-screen as she walked up to the command deck. His holo was flagged by feeds from the other Sable Riders who appeared alongside Rina. 'How did the message get to our nodes?' he asked. 'That shit is locked down tight.'

'There's only one explanation,' Kainan clipped. 'Which also explains the 'us' in her message.'

The Riders slid into their neural network, speaking among themselves.

'Hellooo?' Rina interjected after a moment. 'Selene and I would love to be part of this conversation too.'

'Apologies, force of habit,' Kainan said. 'We were just saying that the only possible option is that Ki'Remi, our sixth Rider, somehow recorded Sheba's message and broadcast it from his node.'

Kage nodded. 'He must have used a random pattern, one

less likely to attract attention. But he knew that if every day techs missed, his fellow Riders wouldn't. He also laced it with white noise, making it much harder to detect. The signal also contains encrypted data in a tiny fixed packet structure that proves his identity and provides his current coordinates. He then used a spread spectrum signal sent to our nodes. That only we six have access to. It's him.'

'So they're together?' Selene hypothesized.

'Most likely,' Kage stated.

Kainan nodded. 'Agreed. She's a medic too, right?'

'Correct,' Selene confirmed. 'She was on The Haven Mercy, a large medical relief cruiser the size of a battleship. A charitable alliance of Rhesian, Dunian, and Galician medics runs it. So what's Ki'Remi's ship called?'

'The Umbra,' Kainan replied. 'Mirage, check to see if we have any data about those two ships meeting at any time in the last few months.'

'*Khosi.*' Seconds later, she piped up. 'I've found something. A shuttle from The Haven Mercy docked on Theia 171's refueling station at the same time as The Umbra. Three months ago.'

'Makes sense,' Kage said. 'The Haven Mercy, being a large interplanetary craft, won't have wanted to descend into the moon's gravity well. So instead, they sent a shuttlecraft to the station to refuel and exchange personnel or cargo.'

'That's not a coincidence we can ignore,' Kainan murmured. 'It's also likely that the Haven Mercy's crew somehow crossed paths with Ki'Remi and maybe even recruited him to join their mission. I can see him doing that. That would explain why he'd have been on the same ship as Sheba when she was captured.'

'Damn,' Selene said.

'How do we tackle this?' Rina asked the group.

'Simple. We rescue her,' Xion said, leaning back in his chair.

'It's a big rescue job,' Zane called out. 'Who's going to pony up the schills?'

Kainan crossed his hands over his chest. 'We are. The Sable Group.'

Zane scowled. 'Brother, not advisable. We've got the coffers but also have a strict budget.'

'We have to. Ki'Remi is out there too, remember?' said his leader. 'We've also got a valid reason to get deep on this one.'

The Riders again fell into their sub-vocal conversation while Selene and Rina exchanged worried looks.

After a time, Kainan spoke out loud. 'Have we agreed it's our best chance?'

'Tis the time,' a silver-haired Riv added, his eyes lit with a rare white glow.

'What time?' Selene interjected. 'What are you talking about?'

'The moment the Riders have been waiting for,' Riv told her. 'A strike back at The Technocracy.'

Selene's head whipped so fast around to face Kainan that her curls bounced. 'You're saying you want to use my sister's rescue to exact your revenge?'

He raised his hands in surrender. 'Hear me out, Selene. We can't get your sister out of the crats' clutches without bringing in the big guns. Otherwise, no one will come out of this alive. We also can't leave The Technocracy standing. They'll just keep coming back. And we've been planning a hit on the crats for years. It just so happens that we're at a juncture where we're ready, and they're accessible. We have the teeth now to bite and inflict as much damage as possible. So why not combine our two goals for the good of us all?'

Selene took a deep breath. She tilted her head back and closed her eyes, taking a moment to think, then opened them after a beat to look at the faces of the gathered group. 'Fine. I don't want to be unreasonable. If this is the best way that the biggest badasses of this System think they can get my sister back and meet their goals, then so be it.'

Rina still needed clarification. 'Look, Riders, Selene, and I appreciate everything you're offering to do, but I still don't understand what you're proposing.'

Kainan shot her a glance. 'I'll save you the misery. Please light up the coordinates from the radio message, Mirage.'

The screens flickered to show an interstellar map of the Pegasi System. In addition, a red location beacon appeared on screen.

Kainan pointed out the Riders' plan on the map.

'Phantasm's hyperspace engine will get us to the radio coordinates in less than a day. We'll ensure their position by sending a drone ahead of us. We'll jump out of hyperspace as close to the crats' ship as possible. Then we'll use our cannons to bombast the sucker with a metanoid cloud. The metanoids will paint themselves on their ship's hull – and then the fun begins.'

'Fun?' Selene asked, arching an eyebrow.

'The metanoids are our true weapon, our payload. One we've been developing for years. Kage, please take over, as this is your baby.'

The gruff, bearded man nodded. 'With pleasure, *khosi*. The metanoids are laced with a lethal kill code and designed just for the crats. It'll take milliseconds for the metanoids to find their way into the ship, through every available nook, cranny, port, hole, chink in the armor, and even via their external cameras. We're taking advantage of the fact that The Technocracy's machines, bots, grids, and even their AI all have high-speed, subconscious encoders built into their visual sensors. That allows them to decode and encode data within their physical and neural network. After our time with The Technocracy, we tapped into Mirage's knowledge, searching for a vulnerability in the crats' decoding software. We found an arbitrary code that could unleash a convoluted attack that would exploit the auto-execution functions of these droids' encoders. This will direct each droid, AI, or bot on that ship to download a malicious file embedded in the metanoids. Once in the network, this file will spread like wildfire, instructing the machines to brand themselves with the malicious code or paste it onto their other systems. The virus should self-propagate at a terrifying speed. Each infected element of the Technocracy will act as an evolutionary catalyst to the virus and cause an infinite number of mutations, which would cause them to fail or commit self-termination.'

'What about The Technocracy's defenses? Their fighters and rattlers?' Rina interjected.

'We'll repeat what we did with the incursion,' Kainan said. 'My gunship will provide point defense. We'll use a combo of the inactive metanoid disassembler devices and metanoid bullets. We'll fire these from our rail gun and practically chow down on their ships, rattlers, and armor.'

'Will this harm Sheba and whoever else she's with?' Selene asked.

'It shouldn't, as we're hoping she'll be on the main ship,'

Kage said, shaking his head. 'Once we're in hailing vicinity of The Technocracy's ship, we'll contact Ki'Remi. Our neural node network is more robust at a closer range and less vulnerable to detection. We'll ensure he gets the same nano virus instructions to begin moving to safety, place her in protection, and get her out of there as fast as possible.'

'That should keep your sister safe,' Kainan told Selene.

'The plan sounds good on paper, but have you tested it?' she asked the Riders.

Kainan turned to his brothers. 'Kage, Mirage, how did the most recent analysis go?'

Kage gave him a chin-up. 'The captured test subjects responded to the virus with great results.'

'The captured who?' Rina asked, flabbergasted.

'During the coup, we caught a few crats we didn't think anyone would miss,' Xion filled her in.

'Then we infected them with our nano-virus,' Mirage announced.

'You took prisoners of war and subjected them to experiments?' Rina choked.

'Nothing they didn't do to us. Besides, Colonel, have you read the Pegasi War Convention agreement?' Xion drawled from his screen. 'It states that we must treat human and meta prisoners with compassion. The convention does not cover non-sentient, droid base crats. Especially those committing acts of terrorism across the System.'

'I get that. It still doesn't feel right,' Rina grumbled.

'Oh, bless your bleeding heart,' Xion taunted.

Rina snarled at him, and he grinned, winking at her.

'We never said we were Mr Nice Guys, Colonel,' Xion added, his gaze on Rina intensifying. 'We're dangerous when crossed. Plus, we take a no-holds-barred approach to justice. So, if your ethics can't stand up to it, you're welcome to walk. But you won't because, under your straight-laced uniform, you're just as feral as we are.'

'You don't know the half of it!' Rina snapped, her characteristic serenity ruffled.

Xion leaned in, his eyes twinkling. 'Oh, but I'd like to know very much!'

'Enough foreplay, you two,' Kainan interjected. 'Now that we have the how, let's nail the who. I'll lead the mission.'

'I'll come with you,' Kage said.

'So will I,' Riv added. 'We won't let you go in alone, brother.'

'*Sante*,' Kainan muttered. 'Xion, Zane, please stay on Eden II to keep our ops running. No one needs to know where we're going or leaving at all.'

'I'm also coming, and no one will stop me,' Selene added.

Kainan's sapphire gold gaze lingered on her face for a moment. 'You're sure, Selene?'

She nodded. 'I can't let you go without me. I need to be there when you rescue Sheba.'

'*Khamila*,' Kainan protested. She could see the stubbornness on his face.

'This is more important than the incursion, Kainan,' Selene insisted. 'She's the last member of my family that I have left. I can't imagine not being there for her.'

Kainan's eyes softened. 'And your Prime duties?'

Selene swiveled to face her friend. 'Rina, would you please act on my behalf? First, I'll brief the Security Council and be clear with them about the mission. Given all the radio hams out there, they'll hear about Sheba anyway, sooner rather than later. Once they've been briefed, I'll hand Dunia over to you. For a little while, of course.'

'Of course,' Rina confirmed with a small smile. 'I miss Sheba, and I hope this works so she can come home.'

'I trust you to hold the fort, Ri,' Selene said. 'Thank you again, my dearest friend. I don't know what I'd do without you.'

She turned to the Riders. 'I sound like a broken record, but thank you, Sable Group. I don't know what more to say or do to show my appreciation for saving our butts every time these last few months.'

'Just keep Kainan loved up and happy,' Riv called out with a grin. 'That keeps him off our back.'

'And growling less,' Zane said, breaking out of his customary quiet nature. 'You'd have thought there was a giant, oxygen-sucking, semi-flaming beast let loose in our offices all last week.'

'Fokk you all,' Kainan grumped, sticking a rude finger at his Rider brothers. However, his eyes twinkled, and Selene noticed how much more relaxed he seemed despite the daunting task ahead.

'Let's do this, people,' Kainan added. 'Let's kick some Technocracy butt across this galaxy.'

It took two days to get their act together.

One day, Selene briefed the Council and arranged her affairs.

She shifted all the meetings and appointments she could. And reassigned the ones she couldn't wriggle out of to Rina.

It took another day to fly to Eden II's orbital station and load up the Phantasm and Mirage with all the needed gear.

The Sable Group's engineers and crew techs outfitted Phantasm's cannons with metanoid-laced missiles, extra weapons, food stocks, and medical supplies.

Kainan kept the rescue mission crew small, with just twenty other Sable crew members running the mess, engineering, and ops.

He tasked Cilia with piloting the battlecruiser while he led the rescue team.

Mirage transferred her sentience to the gyrfalcon form, which was back in operation after the attack on its systems on Eden II.

She flitted in and out of the parked battle cruiser at will, feeling as free as a bird.

Before they flew for the mission that night, Kainan invited Selene, Kage, Cilia, Riv, and Mirage for a dinner party in his quarters on the battlecruiser.

It was a mellow evening, and Kainan had gone extra with the food, aided by Kage, whom he'd told Selene was an excellent cook. The air was fragrant with the aroma of freshly grilled meats, crusty bread, rich sauces, and a spicy stew.

The table was set with flickering candles and a colorful array of dishes laid out.

As they enjoyed their meal, the conversation flowed, and there was a sense of camaraderie and connection among the group, made even warmer and inviting by their shared purpose.

After dinner, they moved to the living area, where they

lounged on comfy chairs and sipped glasses of wine.

Beyond the quarter's windows, the stars twinkled, and laughter and conversation filled the air.

The jokes, laughter, and constant bickering between the Riders left Selene and Cilia in stitches. For at least a few hours, they chose to enjoy the beauty of each other's company, which helped Selene forget the enormity of their forthcoming mission, which was a resounding success, at least for one evening.

Later, she watched Mirage race to the exit, laughing as the gyrfalcon slid between the door, shutting behind the last of the guests.

She began to put away dishes and straighten out the lounge area when Kainan called out to her.

'Come here, *khamila*,' he drawled. 'Leave the cleaning up for later.'

She spotted him through the open inner doorway. He was sprawled on a bed in the generous captain's quarters' inner chamber.

'This is amazing,' Selene said, wandering into the expansive room. 'However, all these different Sable Group quarters I've been in lately are all beginning to look the same.'

Kainan shot her a long, slow grin.

'Seriously,' she said, sitting on the edge of the bed to toe off her shoes and shimmy out of her dress. 'I've changed beds so many times in the last few weeks I feel like I'm on a never-ending trip away from my home on Dunia. But I don't mind if you're by my side.'

His gaze turned into liquid gold as he watched her undress.

'Do you mind changing beds often yourself?' she asked, sliding off her earrings.

He shook his head, shifting the dark locks of his flowing hair. '*Khamila*, I've slept in the worst places, from underground bunkers to desert dunes. But I don't care where I sleep, and I am comfortable moving around. I often bed down on my ship when I'm away working, which is about ten months of the eleven months of the year. The rest of the time, I'm in my real bed, in my real home on J'Urg Mihòr.'

She looked out of the holo screen that displayed Eden II's silvery radiance and city dome in the distance.

Just a few clicks above the moon rock where the Phantasm was parked on Eden II's orbital space station.

For a moment, she wondered what life might look like when everything, and she hoped everything, had settled down. *Where would they live? Would they live apart, part of the time together, or do the long-distance dance between Eden II and Dunia?*

'You're leaping too far into the future, beautiful,' Kainan said, gazing at her.

She turned and gave him a soft smile. 'How do you read me so well?'

'Your face is Pegasi's most expressive, my love,' he told her. He crawled across the bed to envelop her in his hot, naked heat. 'You might as well be shouting out your thoughts.'

'Would I win at poker?' she teased, looking at his molten eyes.

'Depends on who's playing,' he growled, nibbling her shoulder and slipping a hand under one generous breast.

He blew on the nipple, watching as it hardened. 'You'd never win against me,' he said, leaning down to lick the hot, tight bud.

She moaned, sinking her hands into his long hair. 'That's

because you're a cheat. You use my passion for you to break down my barriers.'

'So true, *khamila*,' he murmured against her skin.

'I forget everything when I'm with you. Even the crazy rescue mission we're about to go on -.'

'More truth, my love,' he whispered before making her forget herself. 'As our elders say, when our love is deep, there is no need to fear the storms.'

Phantasm broke free from Eden II's orbital station six hours later and rumbled into space.

With a flick of Cilia's controls, they leaped into hyperspace.

The sleek battle cruiser hardly shuddered as it entered the jump.

Selene felt her stomach churn as the stars outside the window stretched and then winked out of view.

However, her tummy settled as the vessel thrust forward smoothly on its powerful hyperdrive engine.

'Seven standard hours to our destination,' Mirage called out.

Phantasm's cabin lights brightened, signaling that walking around after the jump was safe. Selene didn't hesitate to strip off her chair straps and head for the lower deck.

She passed by Kainan, Riv and Kage. They were hunched over a screen, deep in an unspoken discussion.

There was no point in disturbing them, so she left the bridge and wandered towards the mess.

There, she ordered a hot *kahawa* from the smiling mess officer.

She had a chat with a few of the crew. She also checked her messages while she waited.

There was nothing of note from Rina except a long-winded whine about the extreme boredom she was experiencing attending Selene's appointments on her behalf.

She'd also attached cheeky notes and commentary on the people she met to her comm message.

Selene choked at her uncanny characterizations.

She then spent a few hours on her comm tab reviewing her extensive list of things to do, chugging down endless cups of *kahawa*, and snacking on a salad.

When she was done, she ordered another brew with her takeaway mug in hand, and she headed back to the bridge, still smiling at Rina's clever quips, which kept landing in her comm box.

Just as she was about to round the corner onto the bridge's main corridor, strong arms grabbed her from behind and pulled her into a dark storage hold hidden in the corridor wall.

She gasped, squirmed, and then relaxed, recognizing Kainan's scent and, at that moment, was overcome with longing.

She hadn't been alone with him for a moment since they'd left his quarters to begin prepping for the mission. Her soul danced at his touch after hours away from him.

He must have flicked a switch because a light turned on in the tiny space.

'Where did you go without me, *khamila*?' he griped, leaning down to nibble at her lips.

Since their reconciliation, he'd turned into an assertive, insistent lover. Who loathed to let her anywhere out of his sight.

She loved it.

She kissed him back for a moment, relishing the feel of his firm, sensual lips against hers. 'I needed to catch up on some work and recharge,' she said, rubbing her lips on his.

She thrust her mug between them to show him.

'*Fokk kahawa*,' he murmured. 'I'm the only recharge you need.'

He took the cup from her and shoved it on a shelf above him.

Then he turned his full attention to her. She shivered in anticipation.

His lips dove once more to claim his prize.

They nipped and sucked at each other until their passion was feverish.

'How can we be like this?' Selene breathed. 'Why are we not going over our rescue plan on the bridge?'

'We've gone over it several times, *khamila*,' he murmured, squeezing and pinching her taut nipples over her shirt and bra. 'We know it well. Now is the time to stop overthinking it. Let's concentrate instead on how we will use our free time until we exit hyperspace. And I, for one, do not plan to spend the next few hours analyzing -.'

Selene silenced him with a smoldering kiss. She'd become so much bolder with her affection recently.

She moaned against him, thrusting one hand under his long-sleeved tee to stroke his heated, muscled flesh.

The other slipped under his loose pants.

To capture his thick rod in her smaller, hot hands.

She stroked him and alternated her movements to pump his thickness tightly. His lips left hers as his head thrust back against the shelves.

'Are you going to finish this, *khamila*?' he groaned, looking down at her briefly, his sapphire gold eyes shining.

'Watch me.'

She slid down the band of his pants to slip him out into the cool air of the storage room.

She then lowered her mouth, ignoring the strangled protest from his parted lips.

Her lips and tongue went to work, sucking, licking, and wreaking havoc on his control. Overcome, he thrust into her mouth, and she took his length, kneading him in between licking and suckling.

Then, he lost all abandonment and began to power his hips, pushing his member into her waiting mouth.

She felt her knees tremble and a rush of wet desire between her legs. She took one hand away from his body and slipped it under her pants.

Then she stroked herself in rhythm to the lashing she was giving him.

'Selene!' he savaged between gritted teeth. 'Take me, take it all!'

She felt his cock throb then his seed gushed into her mouth, salty and so utterly sensual. His hips shuddered as he came.

She felt the ecstasy rise to her thighs and core, and then she, too, exploded, her fingers pulling at her clit.

She descended from her pleasure mountain, licking him until he was clean.

Then she used her hands to bunch his tee together so she could crawl up to collapse against his slumped body.

'You are incredible,' he breathed against her forehead, tugging her fingers into his hand and licking her essence off them. 'Did you –?'

'Yes, lover. Always with you,' Selene told him.

'I'm addicted to you, *khamila*,' he said after a while.

He dragged her curls away from her face, staring at her with his molten blue and sapphire eyes. 'I love you so much.'

'And I you, my love,' she said softly. 'I'm just as addicted, so make sure you return to me after this mission.'

A reminder of what they were facing came rushing back at them.

Kainan took a deep breath. 'Should anything happen to me and I don't come back –.'

'You'll come back!' Selene interjected, pulling at his tee.

He looked at her with somber eyes. 'What we're about to attempt is dangerous, love. But, if I have to use whatever I have in my power to keep my crew, your sister, and you protected, I will.'

Her eyes widened as she realized what he was suggesting. 'But you can't use your chimeric vortex. Please Kainan, don't.'

He gave her a long look. 'If I don't return or anything goes wrong out there, and I'm injured beyond saving, swear to me that you will take care of yourself first, *khamila*. Swear to me that you will not let the outcome of whatever may happen cause you to do something you regret.'

'I can't,' she refused, shaking her head. 'I can't make a promise I won't keep. I'll do whatever I can to ensure you return with us.'

371

He leaned his forehead back onto hers in surrender and huffed. 'Who knew a badass like me would get bested by a kick-ass woman like yourself?'

She kissed the side of his mouth. 'Get used to it, *khaji*. Remember what I told you when we first met?'

He gave her a quizzical glance.

'I told you I don't give up, and I don't hold back.'

'That you did. Was what happened earlier the no-hold-back portion?'

'You'd better believe it!'

'*Fokk*! Sexy, sensual, pushy, and smart. I think I won the Pegasi lottery of the century,' he said, bending his head to assault her lips again.

They emerged from the storage room many minutes later.

Only to be faced with two wide-eyed expressions belonging to Kage and Riv, each paused mid-journey, carrying empty trays of food back to the mess.

Selene and Kainan came to a standstill.

Riv's white irises lit up with amusement. 'Damn! I knew all that banging noise I heard earlier wasn't from engineering.'

'Don't think I've ever seen the *khosi* so red-faced in our four decades of knowing each other,' Kage rasped with a knowing grin.

'He's not red-faced. He's het up by love,' Riv sniggered. 'Hey Kai, you may need a scarf!'

Kainan gave his friend an irked and puzzled look.

'To cover that bright red love bite on your neck!'

The two Riders sauntered off, guffawing between themselves, leaving behind their flame-faced leader and his woman.

Kainan turned his magnificent dark head and nailed Selene

with a soft lover's glare. '*Khamila*, you're destroying my credibility.'

'Sorry, love,' Selene said, shrugging her shoulders. 'I couldn't help myself. I can lend you some of my makeup if you wish,' she offered with a cocked eyebrow and snigger.

Just then, the ship's lights dimmed, and a wave of warning lights flashed through the corridor. Kainan's countenance hardened.

'Battle stations, Selene,' he warned, sobering up in seconds.

He strode forward, and she sped up behind him, headed for the command deck.

'Report?' Kainan called out to Cilia and Mirage.

Selene ran up the command stairs and took her position, strapping in.

'The drone we sent to scout the coordinates just sent back confirmation,' Mirage confirmed. 'The Technocracy's ship is where the message said it would be. But it's hovering close to the Haven Mercy. Which seems to be damaged and dead in the water.'

'How are your calculations for the exit?' Kainan probed.

'Good,' the AI confirmed. 'I'm using detailed telemetry to fine-tune my calculations. But, making those complex calls takes a ton of processing power.'

'That almost sounded like a gripe,' Kainan teased. 'Get as precise as you can. Remember, we need to avoid the risk of the Phantasm materializing too close to the crats.'

Selene listened in on the conversation, amazed at the moxie of what the Riders were trying to pull.

'Mirage, you will also make sure you can get around between those two ships?' Kainan asked.

'Shouldn't be a problem, *khosi*. I can shift and change directions to make my way around.'

'*Fokk* yeah!' Kainan grunted.

At that moment, Riv and Kage jogged onto the bridge and slid into their chairs, strapping in.

'What have we missed?' Kage demanded, his commitment to the mission as fervent as Kainan's. And indeed, each of the Riders.

Mirage filled the Riders in while Selene watched from her station.

She smiled at herself. She'd not had to work hard to secure The Sable Group's support. Yes, they had their agenda to accomplish.

But in the light of everything, it was a cause she could get behind. However, they could have refused to help. They could have decided to go about their revenge on The Technocracy in a different way.

They'd come on board and were now all in. They were undoubtedly the most ballsy, assertive operators she'd met.

Yet, also the most generous and kind vigilantes in all of Pegasi. She felt a pang of profound gratefulness because she couldn't envision anyone else volunteering to face the crat army to rescue one woman: agenda or no agenda.

'Strap in, people,' Cilia said, cutting through Selene's thoughts. 'We're about to decelerate out of hyperspace.'

The screen before them started a countdown to the exit.

60 standard seconds.

Selene braced herself.

'Cannons ready?' Kainan asked.

'Ready, *khosi*,' Riv replied.

'Shields?'

'On it,' Kage said.

'Mirage, gunship ready to exit the cargo bay the second we're in normal space?'

'Absolutely.'

Kainan nodded, satisfied. 'Here we go, Riders.'

They all watched the countdown until it clicked over to zero. On cue, the Phantasm trembled as it thrust from the clutch of their hyperspace tunnel into an inky black universe shining with nebulae, gas giants, and stars.

They'd almost landed on top of the Technocracy's ship.

They roared towards their quarry, which loomed larger than Selene had ever imagined. It was enormous, covered in silver armor and bristling with massive electromagnetic rail guns.

'Paint it!' Kainan barked as the Edenite warship bore down on the capital ship.

Riv complied, his fingers dancing over his touchpad.

The Phantasm's guns roared, releasing its metanoid missiles.

They screeched out of the cruiser's state-of-the-art hypersonic missile tubes and mounted torpedo tubes at supersonic speeds.

Seconds later, Phantasm's bridge crew watched the displays in awe.

The missiles exploded into a roiling combustion of white-hot heat.

The metanoids exploded from the missiles and formed a cloud that coalesced onto the surface of the enemy ship.

'Looks like we have ourselves a metanoid storm!' Riv said with a grin.

The Phantasm thundered over the enemy's battleship and

away from it for a few thousand klicks.

Cilia guided the battle cruiser into a semicircle formation, turning so its bridge faced the crats again.

They saw the capital ship's dock area gape open to deploy rattlers.

They winged through the air in search of their attackers.

Instead, Mirage greeted them with a shower of rail gun projectiles and painted them with metanoid-laced bullets.

'Payload!' Kage reported. 'Now let's give these little suckers time to work their way into each ship. Their encoders are downloading my files as we speak. It'll take a few more seconds for the file to spread and cause the mutations, leading to eventual failure or self-termination. So watch out for the fireworks.'

Kage leaned in with eagerness, keen to see whether the tech he and Mirage had worked on for years would succeed. He wasn't disappointed.

Suddenly, the rattlers shrieking towards Mirage, and the Phantasm seemed to falter.

Seeing over fifty rattlers and interceptors lose thrust, and wheel through space was incredible.

The capital ship's rail guns that had taken a few potshots at Mirage and the Phantasm flailed about and collapsed on themselves.

Lights all over the battleship flashed off and on. Small explosions bloomed all over the surface of the ship.

'Status?' Kainan called out.

'I'm reading multiple system failures throughout the ship,' Mirage replied. 'Their shields are obliterated. Thrusters are gone, and station keeping is now inactive. As a result, they can't dodge any debris, nor can they maintain their orbit for much longer. A few hours at the most.'

'And that, people, is how you take out a dreadnought and an entire fleet,' Kage crowed.

The Phantasm's crew whooped in celebration.

Selene, however, had her mind elsewhere. 'What about Sheba?'

Kage whirled his chair to look up at her on the higher deck. 'Selene, remember the scout drone we sent ahead?'

She nodded.

'Well, we used it to bounce a stealth-cloaked neural node signal towards the ship. With a message interlaced in the signal band. Mirage, how's that going?'

The AI piped up. 'I just got confirmation the message was received. I can't tell by whom because the recipient has cloaked their signature. But that's probably just Ki'Remi's common-sense caution if he indeed sent the original message. He now has the same nano virus instructions. Here's hoping he's on it, securing Sheba and himself so they can leave the ship. We'll keep broadcasting to him so he knows where we're at.'

'He'll need to move fast. Before any CO_2 build-up chokes them because air is likely not circulating past the scrubbers,' Kage added. 'If systems have failed, then any breathable atmosphere in that ship is toast.'

Kainan nodded. 'Then we'd better leg it! Mirage, send the gunship back to our cargo bay. Boarding party, let's go.'

Kainan rose from his chair. Kage, Riv, and Selene followed. They moved swiftly to Phantasm's command deck lift.

Once inside, Selene moved to one corner, leaned against the railing, and bit her lip. Kainan proceeded to wrap Selene in his muscled arms.

He bent down to kiss her forehead.

'It's going to be alright, *khamila*. I'm here with you. So too are the Riders.'

'Thank you,' she whispered, lifting her face to his to press her mouth against his lips. 'For everything, *khaji*.'

Kainan's fellow Riders looked away while the couple shared what was to be their final kiss before the mission.

19

Auric Eyes

SELENE

The lift doors opened to Phantasm's expansive cargo bay.

It was a hubbub of activity as bots and a slim but efficient crew team swarmed over Mirage, moving fast, fixing any damage she'd sustained in her brief encounter with The Technocracy's guns.

The boarding party jogged into the Corvette, where the three Sable Riders slipped into their meta suits.

Accustomed to a quick change, they left the storage deck to give Selene some privacy.

She was soon done, and at her signal, the Riders filed back, checking weapons and suits in readiness for the fight ahead.

Shortly after, Mirage lifted from the cargo hold's grapples

and used thrusters to push toward the emptiness of space.

After weaving through the flotilla of the dead, floating, and rolling rattlers, the quick flight was soon over.

Mirage set the gunship a klick above the surface of the capital ship's dock area.

'Anything, Mirage?' Kainan said into everyone's earpiece.

'*Khosi*, not a crat is stirring. Not even a bot.'

'Everyone, on me. I'll take the lead,' Kainan stated. 'Selene, you're behind me. Riv, you follow, Mirage, you help us map the interior of that ship, and Kage, you know what to do.'

To Selene's amazement, Kage's body and suit flickered and disappeared.

'Did that just happen?' she asked in a small voice.

'I'm still here,' she heard Kage say in her helmet's speaker. 'I've just activated my metamaterials. My body's meta nanostructure can trap light in a fractal-shaped pattern, producing a very dark black. It also reflects light along a specific path. It interlocks with my suit's metanoids. Making me appear transparent when viewed from all angles, up or down.'

'You Riders never cease to amaze me,' she said in awe.

'You haven't seen the half of it,' Riv grinned. 'Our suits all have stealth features but chew too much battery, so we rarely use our cloaking tech. On the other hand, Kage has inbuilt bio-meta in his blood, so he uses that magic trick whenever he wants to; lucky bastard.'

'Enough banter, people,' Kainan cautioned the group. 'We're stepping out. Weapons ready. Stick to the shadows. Move with care. Avoid detection. Wait for Mirage or me to let you know if an area is clear of any crat elements before moving forward.'

Somehow, Selene knew he'd listed the parameters just for her. The rest of the Riders were consummate warriors who needed no instructions for an op that resembled hundreds of others they'd been on.

Kainan stepped out of the airlock with his helmet seated against his lethal-looking rifle.

Selene followed, gripping her handgun in both hands, her weapon at eye level with the sights.

Riv was at her six, his rifle held in a point-shoot stance. Kage flitted somewhere behind them, unseen.

Their suits activated and lowered them to the ship using their mini jet packs' micro thrusters and gentle maneuvers guided by Mirage.

They floated down, their anti-grav boots auto-powering as they touched the crats' deck floor in zero-g.

The hangar-like deck was devoid of movement. It was also dark and imposing.

Kainan used two fingers to beckon the group forward.

They raced to the edges of the open hangar door.

'Mirage, is it safe to go in?' Kainan asked.

'Should be *khosi*. All energy barriers and shields are down.'

Kainan gave another hand command, and the group slipped after him into the cavernous space.

Selene shivered. Even though her meta suit balanced her temperature, the bay they were in looked and felt cold, and her mind intuitively reacted.

The space was flat, lifeless, colorless, and drab.

She saw faint signs of ice forming on the surfaces of the walls and even on the floor.

'It's freezing,' she noted.

'It's what happens when you have an acute exposure to the

381

vacuum of space,' Kainan told her. 'The ship has lost shields, so the temps have dropped, especially in such a large open cargo bay. It's also suffered a complete loss of power. Most likely due to the loss of the heat producers, which we disabled as well.'

Most of the capital ships' rattlers and interceptors had been deployed to defend against the Sable Rider's sudden attack. Only a few sat at the far end of the deserted bay.

'Damaged or in repairs,' Riv said, jerking his helmeted head toward the large skeletal forms.

'This place is beyond huge,' Kainan said. 'I need a working route, Mirage. Any chance you can get into their systems?' he asked.

'I'm working on it. First, I must piggyback on my hack to find any operational systems. I'll also slice into their terminals and drives, retrieving any sensitive data I can find.'

'Aha!' she exclaimed. 'Looks like I still have access to legacy systems from my time here so long ago. I'm waking up internal sensors.'

The group crept along the hangar bay walls, looking for any signs of movement. Inside, it was strangely serene.

'Bogey, to the left,' Riv warned.

They all looked. And saw a crat slumped on the bay floor, legs jerking as the destructive code worked through its systems.

A few steps forward, they stumbled on more bots and crats. All of them were inactive or in the process of becoming so.

'Non-functioning,' Kainan observed.

'There's nothing to see here,' Riv complained. 'We must get to the captives if they're still a-.'

He stopped himself with a sharp hiss. 'Sorry, Excellency. I

didn't think.'

Selene dismissed his apology with a quick gesture. 'Riv, call me Selene. And please don't censor yourself on my behalf. I get it.'

'*Khosi!*' Mirage called out. She sounded excited. 'I've managed to access the CO_2 and heat sensors. And I've found a huge concentration of signatures on the third deck of the ship, where the bridge is, if I remember well. So all indications, with that level of heat and gas, are that we might have human activity in that section.'

'How do we get there?' Kainan rasped.

'I'll guide you. I think I have an old map of a similar ship that we can use as a guide. I'll also use the sensors as a guide.'

'Let's go,' Kainan urged.

'*Khosi*, it's going to be a long ass walk to the bridge at this rate,' Kage said from behind them. 'May I suggest an alternative?'

'Absolutely. Anything to make this mission move along faster.'

'Listen up,' Kage said. 'They must have some major ventilation. And on a ship this big, it'll be a huge sucker of a fokkin' shaft.'

'Brother!' Riv winced. 'There's a lady present.'

'What?' Kage snapped back. 'It's the only way I know how to express myself.'

'Gentlemen, I've heard worse,' Selene commented. 'Kage, please continue.'

'*Sante* milady,' the cloaked man said. 'Back to what I was saying. Despite The Technocracy being machines, et cetera, et cetera, they still need air to cool a large ship like this from the lower decks to the bridge. They'd need a *fokkton* of it to maintain optimal temperatures in the number of machines in this place. So what we're looking for is wide and long. It should be accessible by a panel somewhere in here. We should fit in it and, using our suits, fly up to the deck 3 equivalent exit, and voila!'

Kainan nodded. 'Mirage, can you help?'

'I'm searching.' There was a short pause. 'There, to your right. The wide man-sized ventilation panel. It opens right into the larger ship-wide shaft.'

Kainan jogged to the wall of the immense bay to a metallic panel, which he wrenched from the wall in a single move.

'There it is. The upward vent by which so many ships flame out,' Kage quipped.

Kainan gestured towards his general location. 'You go in first. Secure it.'

They paused as they imagined Kage jogging to the wall. There was a slight creak as he eased himself through the large panel.

Moments later, his voice came through their HUDs. 'All clear.'

Riv went in next, followed by Kainan, who reached a hand out to Selene.

He helped pull her through and touched a button on her chest to activate her suit thrusters.

She floated into the cavernous space and joined the rest of the Riders, catching a fleeting shimmer of light, which she guessed was Kage.

'Up and away,' Kainan said.

The cylindrical space was vast, and they moved up it fast.

Through the ventilator, they saw evidence of shield generators designed to stop invasions, but thanks to the Riders' machine-lethal metanoids, those were dead and inoperative.

'Almost there,' Mirage told the boarding party after they'd swept past several decks. 'You're coming out to the shaft exit on Deck 3.'

The group decelerated while Kainan led them to a similar-looking panel that led to the shaft like the one they'd entered below.

He pulled out the panel cover, and it floated away.

They exited the shaft and found themselves in a large open corridor.

'Where next, Mirage?' Kainan murmured.

'Those signatures I detected earlier are to your left. I'm sending you a rough map. The air is breathable, too. But I'd keep your helmets on for obvious reasons.'

'Of course,' Kage said.

'*Khosi*, I'm also picking up a small amount of power nearby.'

Kainan's voice dipped in surprise. 'I thought the metanoids deactivated the ship's power grid?'

'This isn't coming from the power grid. It's from a source that I can't work out. Also, *khosi*, this part of the ship, has somehow been shielded from our attack. It's in complete lockdown, except for the shaft, which our metanoids didn't get at. So watch out. There could be crats close by still alive and kicking.'

'Noted, Mirage. *Sante.*'

'You're welcome, *khosi*.'

The group crept forward, sweeping corridor after corridor, room after room.

'I'll repeat it. This place is a planet in itself,' Riv groused after more long minutes of careful advancing.

They rounded a corner where a large doorway led to a massive room beyond. They walked towards it and through the open blast doors. Lights flashed intermittently, illuminating instrument panels, loose wires, and yet more crats slumped over on the floor.

'The bridge?'

'One large holo screen, a captain's console, various stations, and multiple displays. *Naam*, this is it. Ugly as *fokk*, though,' Kainan observed. 'You'd think they'd have updated their interior designs since the last time we boarded one of these ships from hell.'

They walked down the top balcony of the deck, stepping onto the lower part of the bridge. It was just as colorless and drab as the rest of the crat boat.

'It's been designed as an armored capsule surrounded by the bulk of the spaceship's structure, and reaction mass tanks deliver a great deal of radiation protection without requiring large amounts of extra shielding,' Kage said, geeking out.

Suddenly, they heard a cough at the entrance to the bridge.

Followed by the spit of a weapon, a warning shot over their heads.

'Down people, we've got company,' Kainan hissed.

Selene fell to the floor as Kage and Riv sent a barrage of laser fire and bullets across the room.

'Hey!' they heard a new voice call out. 'Stop fire! Stop fire! Unless you want to kill the very people you came to save.'

Kainan raised a hand, and the firefight ended.

'It's safe, *khosi*,' Kage whispered to Kainan. 'I've now got eyes on them. And we were right about the ID of the message sender.'

At Kainan's signal, the boarding party rose to see three new people standing before them.

A woman with features very similar to Selene's.

A lean, tall, and muscled man stood beside her with a quiet, steady gaze.

And Massimo Makori, with a gun in one hand, dug into the side of the woman's cheek.

At the same time, he'd wrapped his other flabby appendage around her throat.

His tight clutch around her neck had been the cause of the earlier warning cough.

'Brother!' Kainan growled into the private channel of their HUD speakers.

'Sheba!' Selene whispered. She took a half step forward, but Kainan's wrist shot out, pulling her back.

Selene almost fought him, but logic won, and she eased back.

'The Sable Group, I presume,' Massimo said oilily.

'Damn!' Riv murmured into his HUD. 'I thought we got rid of this *fokker* for good.'

'He just took off like the loser he is, and this is where he fled to,' Selene snapped, rage flowing through her body as she ran her eyes over her sister.

Sheba had bags under her weary eyes, mussed hair, and a bloody scratch across her forehead.

Yet, judging by the narrowed set of her gaze, she stood defiant and unbeaten.

'Who speaks on your behalf?' Dunia's ex-Defense Minister said. 'I need to see their face, so I know who I'm negotiating with.'

Selene made another half movement, and Kainan shook his head imperceptibly. He muttered into his HUD. 'If he sees you, Selene, he'll do whatever it takes to get at you. You're his ultimate bounty. We can't risk that.'

'We can't risk my sister either,' she warned.

'Then leave it with me. I don't want to have to negotiate three prisoner handovers instead of two.'

'Makes sense,' she said after a beat. 'But please help her.'

'Of course, *khamila*. But whatever you do, don't reveal yourself to her until we're safely off this ship. Otherwise, she may ID you, and we lose our negotiating edge.'

The conversation, low, whispered, and masked by their helmets, was out of Massimo's earshot.

The large man grew impatient, and he gripped Sheba even tighter. 'Someone, please talk to me now. Otherwise, she dies!'

Kainan signaled that Selene stay back while he moved forward and tugged off his helmet.

He faced Massimo, nailing the treacherous man, somewhat diminished in size by his recent ordeals, with a cold glare.

Massimo responded by pressing his gun harder against Sheba's neck, and Selene saw her sister grit her teeth. Selene took a harsh breath while Ki'Remi, inert at Sheba's side, clenched his jaw and fists.

'Who are you?'

'I'm a nobody,' Kainan shot back. 'But we've already met. In your study. Before you legged it like a coward out of Dunia.'

Massimo flushed. 'I don't recall you. I also don't care where we met or who you are in The Sable Group's hierarchy. All I know is that you've spoiled my plans.'

Kainan quirked an eyebrow. 'Which were what exactly? From what I've seen, any plan you've tried to enact has turned into a *fokkton* of manure. Now let the woman go, Massimo.

Whatever game you're playing, The Technocracy is done. We've prevailed against them.'

'All I need is Selene Munene and her ability to speak to Dunia. I won't let this woman go until her sister shows up.'

'Why? What have you planned for her?'

Massimo sneered. 'The plan is to entice her here. So I get face-to-face to persuade her to communicate with Dunia's sentience. And pass on a critical message.'

The contempt fell off his face, replaced with a cold, calculating glare. 'After which I'll get rid of her -.'

'Just so we're clear, get rid of Selene? The Prime of Dunia?' Kainan said, his voice clipped with rage.

'Yes! Keep up, man! She's no use to me alive after she shares her planet's powers. Neither are any of the Dunians who supported the shit show we just experienced. All because the former Prime and his unremarkable daughter had no vision for the planet's best future. On that note, why are you here? I didn't send for you. I hadn't enacted my plan yet. I was waiting for the rest of The Technocracy fleet to get here so we could advance to Dunia and use my little prize as leverage.'

Kainan arched an eyebrow, and Massimo scrambled to fill in the silence. 'Maybe one of my dynasty members was loaned some schills and hired you to find me?' the desperate man said. 'It'd be incredible, given they've been lazy, ungrateful, and unintelligent mooches all their lives. Who loved untethered access to my accounts more than anything in the entire system.'

Kainan's jaw tightened. '*Fokk* all this talking, Massimo. It's not all about you. And we weren't hired by anyone to fetch you. We have separate business with The Technocracy.'

'Fokk you! Fokk the Sable Group,' Massimo ranted. 'You're all fokkin twats. Loyal to no one, bought by the highest bidder. And frankly, a piss poor set-up.'

'I'd be careful how I phrased that. The piss poor set-up you speak of kicked you off Dunia and quelled an uprising. With ease and great pleasure.'

'Pah! You were lucky,' Massimo blurted, spittle flying everywhere. 'You only had to deal with three of the crats' capital ships. You'll fail against fifty, which is why we've been holding out here in the back of nowhere for days. Waiting on the rest of The Technocracy's massive fleet. I convinced them to come, seeing how desperate they were to prevail. But we needed a few more days to ready ourselves for the entire crat fleet to rendezvous with us before we attacked Dunia en masse. But instead, you showed up to try and attempt to ruin our plans!'

'Like I just said, our pleasure.'

'Now that you've downed this ship and since you prostitute yourself for cash, can you either bring me Selene Munene or, if not, get me to safety? I've got a few million schills I can pay you. Either get me the bounty I need or get me off this sinking boat with a promise to drop me off in Zanyria, and I'll return these two to you unharmed. In addition, I'll throw in a few bags of jewels. You'll be well recompensed.'

'It's unlikely. We don't have space for your particular style of oversized baggage.'

Massimo grinned a mad, chaotic smile that slashed across his leering, desperate visage.

'Then I've no use for you. Maybe the next nobody passing by will be much more cooperative.'

Massimo lifted an arm, pointed the barrel of his gun at

Kainan, and fired.

But not before the man by Sheba's side moved so fast that he was a blur.

He grabbed her and whisked her across the room.

A second shot rang out, and Massimo's voluminous gown burst into a red cloud. Selene gasped as Massimo's body hit the deck floor, twitched, and fell still.

Kage's voice came over the headsets. 'Man down. His blathering was tiring, and he was begging for some lead.'

'Nice shot, brother,' Riv quipped. 'Good to see you can finally aim straight.'

'Everyone, stay where you are. Mirage, are we clear?' Kainan asked.

'Not entirely, *khosi*, the bridge is secure, but I can't confirm about the corridors outside. Those strange energy signatures are getting closer to your position. I need time to work out what they are before, I'm sure. Don't want you to walk into an ambush.'

'Copy. Team, we can move around here, but please don't venture outside.'

Selene nodded, relieved she now had permission to walk about. She nabbed Kainan's arm. 'You OK after that shot?'

'I'm fine, *khamila*; it missed me. See to your sister.'

Selene set off, sprinting through the drab, cavernous bridge to the top balcony of the strange, lonely deck until she dropped to her knees beside the couple on the floor.

Sheba lifted her hands instinctively to protect herself from the armored stranger she saw. Selene whipped off her helmet, releasing her curls.

'Sheba, it's me,' she whispered.

Her sister cried out in delight, throwing her arms around

391

Selene.

'Oh, Dunia, you've been here all along!'

'Honey, yes! I came for you. I had to.'

'Sel, I can't believe it!'

They held onto each other for a long moment. Selene buried her face in her sister's neck, relief and joy flooding her.

Just then, a pair of heavy boots stepped into view.

Selene pulled away from her sister and looked up into Kainan's smiling face.

She turned to her sister. 'Sheba, this is Kainan. He and his friends, the Sable Riders, are why I'm here. Why you're safe.'

Kainan bowed his head. 'A pleasure to meet you, Sheba.'

The man by Selene's sister's side unfolded himself to his full height. He shared a small smile with Kainan. Then they wrapped each other in a big hug. Riv joined the embrace, wrapping long, ropey arms around them from behind.

'They know each other?' Sheba said in wonder, rising to her feet.

'They do. They're part of the same brotherhood. The Sable Group. They helped me get to you.'

Sheba pulled Selene aside. 'If you guys are the reason I'm safe now, Ki'Remi is the reason I'm still alive for you to rescue me. He's been by my side through this entire ordeal.'

Selene glanced at the Riders, who were still catching up with Ki'Remi.

'Sounds like a good man.' She turned back to her sister, filled with curiosity. 'Sheba, how did you get free?'

'Long story. I think Massimo targeted The Haven Mercy, looking for me. To get to you.'

'Targeted?'

'Massimo knew I was your sister. He ID'd me by going

through the Haven Mercy's ship manifest. He and a few crats questioned me. They threw me about. They asked questions about you. When the crats left, they sent Ki'Remi to clean me up and tend to my wounds. He stayed by my side, and the next day, he just started speaking to me telepathically, which shocked me. I knew he was one of the relief doctors on board, but he'd never spoken to me verbally or aphonically. I didn't know I was telepathic myself. I'm still not sure how he did it. He came up with the plan to send the SOS message. First, he insisted I fake the extent of my injuries. Then he instructed me to tell the crats he had to come with me onto this ship from The Haven Mercy. So that he could keep administering medical aid to me because the med labs at The Haven Mercy had been destroyed. Once transferred here, he sent the message. When we got the reply and instructions for the metanoid-virus, he was able to use them to take over some systems and command the crat watching over us to open the door to our prison cell. Soon after, he fell to the floor, and Ki'Remi told me it was because of the metanoid attack you'd set off. We couldn't use his weapon because it was coded for crats only. But we managed to get out. We hid, not knowing where to go until Ki'Remi got the coordinates. Massimo ambushed us while we attempted to reach the rendezvous point that Ki'Remi had received in his neural node. And here we are.'

'But how did the Haven Mercy get captured?'

'How else does a dreadnought overcome a relief ship, Sel? They threatened to destroy us. We surrendered. As simple as that.'

'And everyone else on the Haven Mercy?'

'Still on board as far as I know. They were locked in the

brig. Hopefully, they're all still alive.'

Selene sucked in air, dreading what she was about to say. 'Speaking of alive, there is one thing you'll never forgive me for if I don't tell you about it now. It's about our Father. He's-.'

Sheba's face fell. 'I know. That demon Massimo told me. With great pleasure.'

The two sisters held hands, trying to wrap their heads around the terror of the last few weeks.

'Bastard,' Selene said, shuddering as she glanced at the prostrate traitor's body that had slid down a wall onto the floor. 'And good riddance. Can I say I'm somewhat OK with seeing him lying there in his own blood? He almost destroyed Du-.'

Selene was interrupted by the sound of grating, shrieking, and squealing. Two doors on the lower section of the battleship's bridge were sliding open.

Kainan gestured, and the boarding party whipped their helmets back on and got their weapons ready.

'Remember those signatures, *khosi*?' Mirage said into their headsets. 'They're now at your position.'

The Sable Riders, Selene and Sheba, stared as three dozen crats stalked into the strange bridge.

The six leading the group sported the gold cloaks of the high crats, while the rest were mid-level guard crats in silver cloaks, each brandishing raised weapons.

A voice rose from among them, metallic and uncomfortable.

'Our esteemed guests. Welcome. What a surprise. For you, I mean. You thought we were all gone and that your clever metanoids infiltrated and destroyed us all. You were wrong.'

'You're the Eminences of this ship,' Kainan ground out, his voice emanating through his helmet's speakers.

'A winning observation,' the metallic voice continued. 'We are high crats with maximum level shielding built into us. In addition, we and our guard crats have inbuilt antimatter batteries under our cloaks, each running at a near-100% efficiency. This means we can run individual shields that prevent any attack from reaching our forms.'

Kainan scoffed. 'Regardless, we've distributed our metanoids and hacks throughout your fleet. Which is why your full armada hasn't shown up yet.'

One of the high crats stepped forward. He then ripped off his head covering to reveal a pair of auric eyes floating within the strange transparent carapace face.

'Well, well,' it stated. 'I remember that voice. If it isn't my protege? Meeting you here is an even better outcome than we could have imagined. A reunion with my favorite experiment of all.'

There was a pause as the creature's words echoed in the tomb-like space.

Selene sensed the Riders bristle, their level of menace ratcheting up. Their reaction was personal, raw, and chilling to the core.

'*Fokk*,' Kainan stepped back, spitting his words between clenched teeth. 'If it isn't 478Q1.'

'The one and only. And it seems that my work on you had outstanding results. We've heard of your exploits in technology, armaments, and ship drives. Most impressive. Better still, your metanoid research is exceptional. We just experienced a little of what you are fully capable of. We believe there is more you can share with us. Your knowledge will be a great boon to The Technocracy in our war against The Imperium.'

Kainan chuckled, a laugh imbued with an edge of menace. 'You want more of what we have? Haven't your numbers been decimated enough?'

'You forget that all you've done is kill off the base crats—the most replaceable soldiers in our armies. Arriving in just a few moments is the might of The Technocracy. Fifty ships that are, contrary to what you believe, still operational. Albeit with fewer base crats. You see, us higher crats are immune to your metanoids. This means that the high crats on those ships were not affected by your metanoid storm. But the technology is intriguing. We will retrieve it and use it for ourselves. Maybe even use it to replicate stronger and more versatile base crats. You owe it to us.'

'Owe? The Sable Group never makes promises to the poor and never owes a debt,' Kainan drawled.

'You owe us. You stole our tech, our AI, and our ship. Unthinkable!'

Kainan scoffed, his voice calm and controlled yet laced with a wild rage. 'You forget that you stole our lives. Unforgivable!'

The room fell silent as Kainan and Eminence 478Q1 glared at each other.

The Sable Rider was now trembling with rage in his meta suit, and Selene felt the roiling heat flow off him in waves.

'Who is he?' Selene hissed into her headset.

'A monster,' Kage rasped, loathing coating his words. 'Specifically, the monster who conducted experiments on us many years ago.'

'There's one punishment for you,' the Eminence stated.

'We'll wait for other ships to arrive to outwork your fate.'

He and his fellow eminences swept from the room, leaving behind the silver-cloaked guard crats, who trained their guns on the Riders and three humans.

Just then, Mirage's voice cut through their headsets.

'*Khosi*, there's a problem. I'm detecting 50 or so crat ships converging at this point on FTL speed. My calculations tell me they'll be here in less than 10 minutes. So what do you want me to do?'

Selene heard Kainan's breath speed up.

Then he spoke, his voice low and tight. 'Kage, Riv, Ki'Remi, this is an Echo 2 play. Selene, the second I call fire, you'll need to get the *fokk* out of here with your sister and Ki'Remi. Riv, you'll cover them. Kage, you know what needs to be done.'

'*Khosi*,' the shrouded man grunted.

'Once you're all at a safe distance, I'll take over. I'll keep them occupied so you can get out to Mirage before the other 50 ships arrive.

'I'll stay back with you,' Kage offered.

'*Nada*!' Kainan growled. 'You, Ki'Remi, and Riv have to leave me be. Your job is to take Sheba and Selene back to Mirage safely. Do you copy?'

'*Naam, khosi*,' came the reluctant agreement.

'I know what I need to do and it doesn't involve any of you.'

Selene's heart dropped. She suspected what he was planning, and her knees weakened with dread.

'Kainan, is there no other way?' she asked, her voice echoing through their HUD network.

'This is the only choice, *khamila*,' he muttered. 'There is no more to be said about this. Clear?'

Apart from Selene, the helmeted team nodded. She put a

hand over her pounding heart, trying to suppress her panic and fear.

'Selene?' Kainan prompted, switching to a private HUD signal. 'Talk to me. We're on my channel. No one else can hear us.'

'I don't know if I can stand this, love,' she whispered, staring at him across the space between them. 'You're taking the worst resort. Which might harm you permanently.'

Kainan sighed. 'It's the only way, Selene. Please trust me.'

She sensed the finality in his words. 'Come back to me, *khaji*,' was all she could say.

'I will,' he grated. 'Go with the others, *khamila*. Get your sister out of here and leave the rest to me.'

Selene jerked at his words, then breathed hard to steady herself.

He was right, and she had no right or wherewithal to stop him.

She nodded, and he noted it with a jerk of his chin.

After a beat, he switched back to group comms.

'Mirage, provide cover once the rest of the team is out of this ship, and once they're on board, fly to a safe distance and keep your airlock open.'

'I'll do my best, *khosi*.'

'Ready at my command?'

'Ready,' the Sable Riders intoned.

Selene couldn't bring herself to say a word.

Tears clogged her throat as she drank at the sight of her aloof, cold man committed to his mission.

Unable to handle the agony, she sliced her eyes away, tamping down her terrified feelings and bracing herself for what lay ahead.

Kainan jerked his helmet. 'We are GO.'

In seconds, Kage's hidden rifle spat out a series of rounds. The guard crats reacted.

They swung their rifles towards his stealth position and fired.

One shot hit Kage in the chest, but his armor repelled the bullet.

At the same time, Ki'Remi shoved Sheba behind him.

Selene ran towards the pair, and they fled the bridge room, ducking fire as they moved as fast as possible.

Selene fired a few shots, providing cover for the unarmed pair, coming between them and the action.

Seeing the fleeing group of humans, the crats fired at them from the bridge level below them. Riv pumped lead, and a barrage of gunfire blazed in the space.

Riv, Selene, Sheba, and Ki'Remi took cover where they could. Kage picked off the crats one at a time, holding them off as best he could.

Then Kainan began his diversion.

He fired from his position on the lower level. The crats responded and swung away from the crouching group.

'Move!' Riv shouted, sensing their break.

The group ran outside the large doors and into the long corridor.

One plucky droid followed, trying to cut them off as they advanced down the corridor. Kage took him out.

The group barreled forward through the long, lone halls, heading towards their marker – the same panel they'd slipped through onto the command deck.

Still cloaked, Kage provided cover from behind and put down a few crats who dared try to ambush them.

Shortly, they reached the human-sized ventilation panel. They stopped just outside it when Selene had a thought.

'We don't have suits for Ki'Remi and Sheba. So how are we going to do this?' she panted, staring at Riv.

'Kage will take Ki'Remi, and Riv will carry your sister,' the Edenite responded.

Kage re-materialized before them. 'I've got three or four bogeys behind me. Our weapons fire has slowed them down, but they're still blasting. Let's get the fokk out of here. Selene, Kainan would kill me if he heard this, but you'll need to act as rear guard.'

Selene nodded and gestured for him to rush through the panel. 'Whatever it takes! Go!'

Kage eased through the panel, activated his suit thrusters, and reached out to grab hold of Ki'Remi. He then let himself and his friend fall to the lower decks.

Riv did the same, grabbing hold of Sheba, who'd been nervously watching from the sidelines all this time. She waved to her sister.

Then she and the ghostly Rider were away.

Selene heard the rush of footsteps in her direction, and she launched herself through the panel opening, heart pounding.

Shots flew towards her, and she fired back, then ducked, disappearing into the enormous vent where she reversed her jets downward in pursuit of her friends.

KAINAN

On the bridge, Kainan was battling crats whose heavy blasters were assaulting his position.

Behind the dozen guard crats still standing were the gold-cloaked Eminences, who'd filed out to watch the assault as it unfolded.

When the Riders, Selene, and her sister were clear of the bridge, Kainan shot at the door controls to keep the crats with him from following them.

Twas all in vain.

The fluctuating output throughout the ship's systems meant the doors tried to squeeze shut, but the massive power needed to close them was unavailable, so their motors died down with a grunt.

The silver guard crats kept trying to rush his position.

He kept them back, working his weapons to keep them from overwhelming him and catching up to the rest of his crew.

'Mirage,' he breathed. 'I need an update on the boarding party. Are they onboard and safe with you?'

There was a short pause during which Kainan took a hefty blast to the chest. He fell back, dropping to take cover.

He almost choked from the hit.

It felt like a massive punch to his system.

He paused, firing as his suit rushed to give him more air and repair itself from the damage of the droid's fire.

'Mirage!?' he panted, ducking more shots.

'*Khosi!* I see them. They're running towards me.'

'All of them?'

'Yes, all of them.'

'Fokk yeah,' he breathed, skulking along a fallen bulkhead

on his haunches while firing back toward his attackers. 'Let me know as soon as they're on board and you've high-tailed it. And also, an update on those fifty Technocracy ships?'

'Two minutes away.'

'Hurry. Get the team onboard.'

'I am.'

With no warning, the crats stopped engaging in their crossfire.

An eerie silence fell across the destroyed bridge.

'My favorite Edenite?' he heard a familiar voice call out. 'We've stopped firing because we will have the absolute advantage in less than 90 seconds. So we're wondering if you'd like to rethink your surrender or lack thereof?'

Kainan activated his external mic. 'Not in a million years.'

'Why are you so adamant? Rise to your feet when you speak so we can discuss this, Technocrat to Edenite, face to face.'

Kainan took a deep breath, then rose. He moved to a spot above the bridge floor where the Eminence stood, looking up at him from below.

'Ah! There you are,' the high Technocrat stated. 'Now tell us, why is there a delay in giving up our stolen tech and the AI you took from us?'

The Edenite crossed his arms over his enormous chest. 'Because I need you to understand how much you ripped away from my life. And from the lives of my men. You stole our chance at a normal existence. As you whispered to me many years ago, you stole our forever.'

'How poetic. We do remember our conversations. But you misunderstood our intentions, then and now. We were trying to design new weapons, never-before-seen creations that would devastate our enemies forever. That was the only forever we were ever interested in. Not in yours.'

'So we were just your cheap fodder, your lab rats?'

The Eminence sneered. 'We don't like your choice of words, but yes.'

'No longer,' Kainan promised, his voice laced with steel. 'I never thought I'd ever see you again – so to have you join us is a surprise – but also a major plus because now I get to show you what I've been waiting years to share.'

'You'd better hurry then, Edenite. Our other ships will be here soon, and we'll take what we want just like we've always done. Now and forever.'

Just then, the Eminence jerked his droid head away, his attention arrested by an unseen distraction.

At the same time, Mirage's voice filled Kainan's headset. 'Update, *khosi*. The Technocracy fleet has arrived. They've surrounded the vessel you're in. The good news is that I have the team safe and sound. We've also flown several thousand klicks away. I managed to pull the Haven Mercy with me in a tractor beam as I sensed life signs in the ship. You're good to go.'

'Stay there. Keep your cargo deck open.'

'As instructed.'

Kainan stood still, waiting.

Moments passed before the Eminence swiveled his transparent carapace skull, and the strange gold orbs fell on Kainan in an unflinching stare.

'The time has come, protege. To teach you the ultimate lesson. No one steals from The Technocracy, and no one denies us anything. We are here to retake what's ours.'

'You don't say,' Kainan shot back.

He pulled off his helmet and then unzipped his meta suit.

He stepped out of it carefully.

'What are you doing?' the Eminence called out, pointing a gold arm to the man undressing before him.

The Edenite ignored the demand, removing every article of clothing until he stood before the bemused crats in his shorts and nothing else.

He tossed his meta-suit and helmet to the level below. They fell at The Eminence's feet.

'Have at it,' Kainan drawled. 'All our secrets, technology, and all the *fokk* we've been up to for the last twenty-odd years. It's all in there. In the metanoids, the chips, and the neural network. You'll find it all.'

The Eminence jerked its skull in a triumphant cackle. 'At last! You've realized they were ours all along!'

It gestured, and two of its fellow crats grabbed hold of the suit and helmet.

The group turned as if to walk away, pausing mid-step when Kainan spoke again.

'Wait, I'm not done,' he said. 'There's one more thing I wish to share with you. The ultimate prize. What your experiments turned me into. The technology you poked and prodded me for, that you tortured and twisted my body for, causing me years of unbearable pain and misery. You could never have known how much of what you pumped into me would mutate and produce new, immeasurably powerful structures in my DNA. It's all right here. Inside me. It's this gift that I want to share with you.'

The Eminence's gold orbs lit up with eagerness and greedy joy. 'Excellent, protege. We will take it all. Show it to us.'

'With pleasure,' Kainan murmured.

He extended his arms out.

Tendrils of white, red, gold, sapphire, and silver stirred under his skin. The white-hot, red, and sapphire heat spread across his entire body.

Then it leaked onto his hair, fingers, and feet.

His molten eyes blazed just before his entire body combusted.

The extreme temperature sucked the oxygen from the room, searing the air.

'What are you doing?' The Eminence shouted, panicking at the sight of the unexpected transformation. 'Stop this now. We've seen enough.'

A whisper came from the whirlwind of fire that was Kainan. 'I cannot be stopped. In case you forgot, you denied me, my continued existence, and my choice of what forever would look like. So I'm going to deny you yours.'

A whirlwind began to form under and around the resulting form of flame and blazing tongues of energy.

The crats crouched to escape the intense rising heat that scorched their carapaces.

The pair who'd clutched his meta suit and helmet combusted when their nuclear batteries heated to over 2000 degrees.

The sudden increase in temperature caused a radioactive explosion that consumed them in an instant.

The rest of the crats swiveled their gold and transparent skulls in horror at witnessing the obliteration of their fellow beings.

They tried to escape, but a turbulent wind kicked up, forming whirling eddies of air that turned into a tornado-like vortex that sucked them to it, an energy so powerful they couldn't escape it.

The vortex began to move across the bridge like a fire tornado. Howling, the crats were sucked into the whirling, burning core and rotating flames.

Bulkheads were uprooted, stations sucked in, and spawned into blazing spouts of energy.

The Eminence tried to hold on to a handrail, but it melted in his hands. He screamed before he was caught up in the mesocyclone-like updraft rotation of the plume and disintegrated into it.

The super blaze spread with speed to the rest of the ship. It ignited the temporary nuclear batteries the crats had used to shield themselves on Deck 3.

They exploded, adding to the high heat. It burnt entire decks to a crisp, traveling swiftly down the gigantic air draft. Before long, it reached engineering. When it touched the antimatter drive, it melted. Seconds later, the ship's engine imploded on itself.

The core of the pyrocumulonimbi on deck three flamed against the bridge's view screen, melting the thick sheet of alloy glass.

This pushed the flaming supercell into space, where 50 Technocracy capital ships hovered.

They fired at the fiery nebula rushing toward them, but to no avail.

The pyroclastic storm tore through space, taking out ship after ship.

They ruptured, blew apart, and exploded like fireworks against the dark void of space, reducing into microscopic energy atoms.

For a moment, it seemed space contracted due to the massive energy being parsed through it.

The atmosphere flamed until, after a time, its vacuum contained the furnace.

The furnace roiled into a smaller cloud of flames, hovering mid-firmament between a sea of ashes, churning debris, and a deep, almost reverent stillness.

20

Now You Can Have Your Forever

SELENE

On Mirage, the entire party on board watched the fireworks with wide, horrified eyes through the giant holo screen.

Kage, Ki'Remi, and Riv shared long, worried looks.

Sheba held Selene as she wept, staring at the glowing, roiling, pyroclastic form.

Then it was all over.

All 51 of The Technocracy ships were gone.

Disappeared. Scorched into oblivion as if they'd never existed.

All was dark except the cloud of flames still floating in space.

Then it moved towards them.

'He's coming!' whispered Selene through a ragged, hurting throat.

The three Sable Riders onboard rushed down to the cargo deck doors.

Selene, too, followed by Sheba.

They crowded at the view window of the blast doors outside the cargo hold, waiting.

A bright light encompassed the cargo hold, sparking with flames and embers.

They all stepped back, holding their arms over their eyes to shield them from the brilliant cluster of heat and luminescence.

The light fell, and they heard a thump.

'Mirage, doors!' Kage ordered.

The external cargo hold entry closed, and the internal doors slid open as soon as their seams were joined.

There he was.

He stood inside Mirage's airlock, merged into his meta-human form, covered in hideous burns and bruises.

Kainan swayed, and Selene leaped forward, catching him as he slumped onto the floor.

The journey back to Eden II was a somber affair.

Kage and Riv sat on the command deck, guiding the Phantasm back home.

A deck below, Selene sat by Kainan's bed where he'd lain since being carried in by his brothers after falling unconscious on Mirage's storage deck.

After docking in the battlecruiser, they'd taken him into the Phantasm's gleaming white medbay, where Ki'Remi had placed him into a med-scanner bed and induced a coma.

Two hours into their return flight, Selene sat glued to his bedside, watching as Kainan's vitals spiked up and down.

She wouldn't let go of his hand.

Ki'Remi and Sheba worked in the background, but she hardly acknowledged them. All she could do was stare at her man, stricken by despair.

She only stepped back to let the pair administer medical care.

Casting aside the shock of her recent capture, Sheba had stepped into her natural nursing role to assist Ki'Remi. The pair moved flawlessly in a dance of professional precision.

Their patient was gravely ill. Silent. Unmoving.

The hiss of the high-tech ventilator in the room was the single sign that Kainan was still alive.

His skin was scorched in swathes of peeling, blistered black char with full-thickness third-degree burns. His face, too, had not escaped the blaze.

His magnificent hair was shaggy, short, and burnt in places to the scalp. His eyebrows and lashes were gone, his beard ragged and seared.

His metanoids were giving up the fight, Selene thought. *He looked so vulnerable.*

She wanted to run her hands through his thick hair, which was now sparse and matted. She longed for his strength, his love, his heat.

She missed him. Period.

After a few hours, she found her voice, speaking to the Riders' medic. 'What are his symptoms?'

Ki'Remi threw a glance at her from the other side of the bed. 'He has many.'

His voice, or a close approximation, came from the med bay's speakers.

Selene jolted at the sound, unused to the lost Rider's selective mutism and his brusque substitute vox, even though Sheba had told her he controlled it via his neural node.

'Injury to the lungs from smoke inhalation. Loss of fluid from burnt skin. Shock, heat loss, and an inability to regulate body temperature.'

'How bad is it?'

Ki'Remi shook his head and frowned. It was unclear whether he was uncomfortable speaking or with the question itself.

Sheba, adjusting Kainan's IV bags, glanced at him, and her gaze softened.

'He's free of infection for now,' she told her sister, taking over from the Riders' medic. 'His altered chimera cells are fighting his normal metanoids and DNA. Should they win, they'll shut down the entire body.'

'Which could result in death. In milliseconds,' Ki'Remi's sub-vox said. 'A swift death. Like being vaporized by a nuke or a supernova.'

Selene breathed in. She knew the clinician meant well, but she'd been unprepared for his blunt answer.

'What are you doing about it?' she whispered.

'The med-scan bed is on full power, analyzing the criticality of his burns,' her sister told her. 'It uses a high-tech

411

laser to identify Kainan's weakened meta-human cells that need to be discarded. It's also re-programming the healthy metanoids to accelerate the cell multiplication process to cover and heal entire sections of the lost muscles, tissues, and organs. In other words, it's scanning his body and neural networks to identify the rogue cells. Eliminating them and trying to repair the normal metanoids being killed off by the chimera effect.'

'It's a band-aid,' Ki'Remi interjected coolly. 'This last combustion has reduced his life span. The rate of damage and attrition because of the chimera cells is higher than the replication of his healthy meta-human cells and neutrons.'

'How long does he have?' Selene ventured, afraid of what the answer could be.

Ki'Remi's response was curt and clinical. 'Weeks.'

Selene felt the gut-punch response throughout her body. Eyes burning with tears, she turned her face away and walked to the med bay's windows.

Outside, a rush of swirling colors and flashes of occasional bursts of light greeted her.

But all she could see was a sky full of darkness through her tear-soaked eyes.

One without Kainan in it. Without him, she would be nothing.

A soft hand fell on her shoulder. 'Sel,' Sheba said. 'Don't mind Ki'Remi. He's just blunt, as I've come to find out. Know this, hon. We haven't given up. So please don't give up as well.'

Selene folded into her sister's arms. 'Sheba, I just got you back. We just lost Father. I can't lose anyone else. He is my light. He is my chimera, and I need him so much.'

Sheba held her tighter, and they stood in each other's arms.

'My sky is falling, Sheba,' she said as tears clogged her throat. 'You two are everything. You're all that matters to me.'

'Then, whatever happens, I will hold up half your sky,' Sheba murmured. 'And with the half you hold up for me, that should keep our world from falling apart.'

The instant the Phantasm docked at Eden II's orbital space station, Kainan, already transferred onto Mirage, was whisked away to Dunia.

Selene had insisted, knowing that one of her planet's few advantages over Eden II was its medical facilities.

They flew straight down onto the landing pad at New Malindi's Macion Hill Hospital.

The facility was one of the most sophisticated hospitals on the planet, offering leading-edge inpatient and surgical care and a System-wide famous program in regenerative medicine and body reconstruction.

They whisked him into a private med-scan room.

More high-tech equipment was pulled closer around his bed. Galvanized by the Prime's presence, a team of reconstructive specialists went to work 24/7 on their new patient.

Selene was permanently by his side.

Sheba had accompanied her for the first day, but after

seeing her sister's exhaustion, Selene had ordered her sibling to be whisked away to the Prime's Residence to get some much-needed rest.

In her gyrfalcon form, Mirage was also present by Kainan's bed, watching from her new perch on the sill of the hospital window.

Ki'Remi had stayed on as Kainan's physician at his insistence and with Selene's approval. He spent just as much time as Selene at the hospital.

As had Riv and Kage. They were soon joined by Zane and Xion, who'd flown in from Eden II the moment they'd heard about Kainan. The Riders stalked through the hospital's waiting rooms, pacing its corridors, unable to relax.

Their presence had scared some Dunian patients and visitors.

Hence, hospital staff transferred the entire party into the nurses' large breakout room adjacent to Kainan's private hospital chamber, which suited many nurses just fine.

Rina was still acting as Caretaker Prime, allowing Selene to focus on Kainan and Kainan alone.

Apart from short breaks to shower, check her messages, and take small snacks, Selene's energy was all about him.

She read to him, spoke to him, and prayed for him. She made promises to the planet's power. She begged Dunia for its benevolence. For healing and Kainan's full recovery.

What she didn't do was sleep. Kainan was still in a deep coma three days later, and she was exhausted.

It was mid-afternoon.

Light rays filtered through the room's blinds, falling in shards on the floor.

The room was empty except for the bot nurse, who monitored the patient's vitals.

Selene placed her head on the pillow above Kainan's and slid a hand over his shoulder. She could hear him in her mind telling her she needed to sleep.

She huffed with weary amusement at the memories of his past attempts to get her to rest.

She felt hot tears leak out of her eyes.

They fell on the pillow.

One of them trickled downward until it fell against Kainan's resting cheek.

He shuddered.

She reacted, sitting up straight.

Then, one thick arm reached up and tried to pull the ventilator mask off his face. He thrashed in the bed, and it rocked dangerously.

'Kainan, relax,' Selene cried out.

She stood, trying to push down on his massive shoulders.

This just enraged him further.

The bot's red indicators flashed as it rolled up.

'Code 3!' it repeated mechanically.

In seconds, the room filled with medics rushing to aid the patient.

She felt a strong arm move her away and looked up at Ki'Remi's commanding face. He nodded at her, and she sagged in relief as he took over.

Selene stepped back as Kainan's ventilator mask retracted, and Ki'Remi and the medical team tried to control the brawny, muscled Edenite.

She saw one of the burlier doctors bury a long needle in Kainan's thigh.

He flailed, but soon, his body relaxed into smaller lashes

of movement. His eyes, however, flew open and then around the room wildly. Only when they met her own did he calm down.

'*Khamila*,' he rasped.

'I'm here,' she called out to him, placing one hand over her heart.

His eyes never left hers as more medics swarmed around him.

Then his gaze flicked up to Ki'Remi, and they spoke silently.

After a few moments, his eyes glazed over as the medicine took hold of him.

They fluttered as if to close, but not until he dragged them back to Selene.

He drank her in. Then they shut as he fell asleep once more.

It took another two days for Kainan to wake again.

This time under his own steam and breathing for himself.

It was a gentler waking than the last, and he opened his eyes as Selene read from a book in her comm tab's library.

'*Khamila*,' he whispered roughly in his deep voice.

She looked up, joy spreading across her face, throwing down her reading device.

Their hands met in the space between them.

'How are you feeling, *khaji*?' she murmured, smoothing her other hand over his brow.

'I can't feel most of my body,' he rasped. 'What have they done?'

'They had to sedate you and give you a shipload of meds. There was no other way you could have withstood the pain.'

'How bad is it?' Kainan insisted, glancing at the med scanner hovering over his body.

'I think it's best to let the doctors or Ki'Remi tell you more. Shall I get them?'

'Not yet,' Kainan whispered. 'I need a few moments with you.'

She smiled but knew he could see the agony and sadness in her eyes.

'That bad, huh?' he probed. 'That's the first time I've seen you lost for words, my love.'

She answered by squeezing his bandaged hand, which drew his eyes to their intertwined fingers. His gaze traveled up his arm to the worst of the scarred injuries.

His eyes locked on them. '*Fokk*,' he breathed. 'Bad then. How long?'

She shook her head, unable to speak.

'Weeks, then,' he rasped, coughing as he did.

'Don't speculate, *khaji*,' Selene whispered.

She leaned over and kissed his dry, hot lips. 'They're doing everything they can.'

'I need to know that for myself.'

He glanced at the ceiling, accessing his neural node.

His eyes shut for a moment before he turned his bloodshot eyes back to her. 'Looks like the medics can't help me. My node is registering catastrophic failures of my normal metanoids. They're dying at a higher rate than ever before. I have days.'

'Kainan,' she breathed, the grief almost too much to bear.

All she could do was lean over and touch her lips to his.

He broke their union to lift his hand and stroke her face. 'We'll get through this, *khamila*.'

'How?' she probed. 'How?'

'Just let it be, my love,' he rasped. 'At least I put an end to the crats and their torment across the System. For that, I feel relieved, almost healed from all the pain and anguish their existence wrought on me. For this alone, *khamila*, let us be grateful.'

He wrapped his arm around her and squeezed, pulling her close.

She placed her head on his chest and cried for a long time before the heaving emotion lashing her body quietened.

'Where are we?' he growled.

'On Dunia. At a local hospital, one of the best,' Selene said, sitting up, still wiping tears away from her ravaged face.

She turned to scramble inside her bag for tissues.

'Dunia?' Kainan repeated slowly.

'Yes. We brought you here after -.'

She turned back to see Kainan attempt to rise from the med-scan bed.

'What are you doing?'

'Get me out of here,' he barked.

'What?'

'I said, get me out of this hospital room.'

She panicked. 'And take you where?'

'Zulu One,' he breathed. 'To the grotto.'

'But why?'

'Because that is where I *fokkin'* need to be.'

She blinked, staring at him, trying to make sense of his

words.

Still seeing her confusion, he tried to clarify further. 'Remember when we last visited the grotto? During the incursion?' he said roughly.

She nodded, confused.

'You left me there. Somehow, I found myself pulled to the waters. I got inside, and it did that thing it does. It spoke to me. It told me to return when I was ready for healing.'

'It what –?' Selene croaked.

He rolled towards her, his molten eyes enlarged against his ravaged face, pleading.

'Please, *khamila*, take me there. I don't know how long I have left. I have to try everything in my power to get well.'

She shook her head to clear her racing thoughts.

'You're sure those are the words it said? It spoke to you?'

'It did.'

'I thought it could only speak to certain people,' she wondered. 'It must have sensed your need and wanted to help you.'

'*Khamila* –,' he warned.

'We don't need to go to Zulu One,' she remembered. 'There's a grotto right here at the Hospital. Every major facility on Dunia, and a hospital this size, is expected to have one.'

She rose to her feet and scrambled for the call button on the silent bot nurse.

It was Ki'Remi who answered the prompt. He walked into the room and glanced at the bed, his eyes widening as they met Kainan's. He gave his friend a quick smile.

'Ki'Remi? Good,' Selene said in relief. 'I think it's best if your brother tells you what he has in mind.'

With a curious look on his face, the Riders' medic prowled to Kainan's side.

His friend clutched his arm and stared at each other, speaking neurally.

Selene watched the waves of different expressions flow over their faces as they deliberated.

After what seemed to be a vigorous debate, Ki'Remi nodded his head.

'Where is this grotto?' his sub-vox asked.

'I don't know,' Selene answered. 'Let's get the hospital med team here and find out. We need to discuss the option with them.'

'It's not optional,' Kainan grated. 'It's my wish.'

The hard line of his jaw said just how stubborn he would be about it, too.

By then, a few medics had stepped into the room, followed by the rest of the Sable Riders, who'd clued into all the sudden action in Kainan's room.

The spacious hospital room now seemed tighter than an overcrowded maglev carriage at the height of a Dunian summer festival.

The physician on duty walked in, glancing with hesitation at the glowering Edenites.

'What's going on?' he ventured.

'We need to get to the grotto,' Kainan whispered, his energy too sapped to provide more information.

Ki'Remi came to the rescue, giving the doctor a quick summary of what Kainan wanted to be done.

Appalled by the new idea, the small, tidy man turned to Selene. 'Respectfully, Prime,' he whispered, his eyes fluttering with nerves. 'The patient should not leave the med-scan bed. It's what is keeping him alive. The expiration of his healthy metanoids could increase, placing his life in extreme danger. Also, the grotto here has only ever been used as a pain relief option for our patients. But never to try and heal injuries as serious as this.'

Selene placed a hand on the agitated man's arm. 'Doctor, we hear you. But I'm not the person you need to talk to. The patient can speak for himself.'

She turned to Kainan.

'I know I have the right to request and access the healthcare and treatment that I believe will best meet my needs,' the Edenite whispered, yet his voice was laced with steely resolve. 'That includes being given access to the grotto. So please, let's respect my wishes.'

Realizing the battle was lost, the doctor bowed and gestured for his team to act as the patient had requested.

Minutes later, Kainan was bundled in an air chair, floating through the hospital's corridors. He'd insisted on piloting it using the carrier's control pad.

Selene strode on one side of him, Ki'Remi on the other.

Behind them came Sheba and the Riders en masse, followed by several medics trailing on like a bemused entourage.

Soon, they were outside, under the blue skies and twin suns of Dunia.

A soft, sweet breeze swept over them, mixed with the fragrance of blossoms and the heady perfume of lei'oia vine flowers.

The medics directed them towards a hidden paradise near the northern Milawi gate of the Hospital's stunning gardens.

They passed a pretty river lined with purple dunivillea flowers, shimmering wisteria, and cascading argonivea flowers.

Patients and families wandered through the rows of flowering and edible plants that emitted evocative fragrances.

The river led them to a cave within a rock wall.

The darkened entrance opened into a large, glowing pool, flanked by two small waterfalls, glow worms, bioluminescent fungi, and trailing vines similar to those Selene and Kainan had seen at the Enclave's grotto.

Lightning bugs flashed above the deep blue pool of water dotted with lily pads and blooming lotus flowers.

They streaked light onto the dripping stalactites to transform the cave ceiling into a twinkling nighttime sky.

There were no steps at this cave, just a tiny sandy beachhead, where Kainan directed the air chair.

He lowered it until it hovered over the sand.

'Brothers,' he called out hoarsely to the Riders. 'Get me into the water.'

His friends were by his side in an instant.

Kage and Ki'Remi lifted Kainan, huffing with the effort of hefting their still bulky brother. They swept into the depths of the pool until they were waist-high.

Selene waded in, keeping close. The rest of the group stood along the pool's edge, watching.

'Ready?' Kage asked his friend gruffly.

'Ready.'

The two Riders lowered Kainan into the deep water.

His body touched the mirrored surface, which danced and rippled against his skin.

'*Sante*. Let me go,' he choked out.

Kage and Ki'Remi stepped back and out of their *khosi's* way.

Kainan reached a hand towards Selene.

She pushed through the water to grab hold of it.

Selene watched, amazed, as his hurting body floated under the surface as he was enveloped in the cave's waters. A powerful energy appeared to hold him up with a firm gentleness.

Selene felt an overwhelming urge to intercede on Kainan's behalf, so she paused to find the right words.

'Please, Dunia,' Selene whispered. 'Heal Kainan. Restore his body, renew his power. May you find it in your goodness to avert all pain and danger so that he may enjoy fulfillment and a long life. That he may rise once more to lead with wisdom and compassion and prosper with happiness and strength.'

Kainan gave Selene a deep look of appreciation and love.

Time seemed to almost halt for a moment. Then the water's surface began to stir, with little waves that lapped at his body. They began to form into small ripples that washed over his slightly submerged form.

A whisper echoed through the cave.

'Do you believe now, Edenite?'

Kainan's eyes searched Selene's face for a long moment. 'I believe,' he rasped. On shore, the gathered group gaped in awe at the conversation and experience unfolding before them.

The whisper floated over the waters once more. *'You made the right decision, Edenite. Dunia's forests and waters are overflowing with the remedy you need. Let go so that we may renew you.'*

The rocking massage of his body increased.

It was lulling him to sleep. Still clutching Selene's hand, Kainan closed his eyes and let his body relax into the waters.

Selene leaned over him and kissed his lips.

'Sleep now, my love,' Selene whispered. 'Get well for us all.'

He slipped into unconsciousness, his head falling back.

The water covered his skull, slicking back the ragged strands that had remained since the vortex transformation.

Yet the invisible, buoyant force kept his eyes and airways above the surface.

Silence fell again in the grotto, and Selene lost all track of time. She stayed by his side, holding his hand.

The Riders stationed themselves throughout the cavern's edge, sitting on rocks nearby. Mirage found a ledge high above the waters to settle on, a vantage point from where she could always keep her eyes on her *khosi*.

Ki'Remi stood like an impenetrable and still sculpture beside Selene, his arms crossed over his chest as he monitored Kainan through his neural connection.

At one point, Selene noticed a small whirl of light under Kainan's skin. 'See?' she whispered, pointing at Kainan's upper arm.

To where a series of burns had carved charred paths into his skin.

Her eyes were fixed on a tiny subnormal energy coil that transformed the scorched surface into a baby-smooth finish.

'It must be working,' she proclaimed, looking up at Ki'Remi with expectation.

He nodded with a grim expression.

On hearing the hopeful update, the other Riders stood to their feet.

'How long will this take?' Kage called out.

Ki'Remi shrugged his broad shoulders. 'As long as it needs to,' he replied in his sub-vox so everyone could hear.

'Then we'll stay here 'til he wakes,' Kage promised.

The Riders sank back down to their perches, and Selene

smiled at them through wet eyes.

She felt uplifted by their united support, which reflected the true heart of these men and their noble loyalty.

She squeezed Kainan's hand. He needed to heal, not just for her, but for them.

Hours later, Kainan still floated in the darkened waters, deeply asleep.

Selene had just left his side. She sat on a rock at the water's edge, wrapped in a robe her best friend had placed around her.

Rina now sat holding Selene's hand. She'd offered the tired woman some food. Selene had demurred, nibbling on just a cracker, her stomach still unable to handle any rich sustenance.

All she could manage was a small sip of water as she welcomed the warmth of the soft kimono around her.

Sheba sat next to the pair, tabbing through a comm screen where Ki'Remi had patched a neural feed from Kainan's vitals from his neural node.

The Riders sprawled on the water's edge—each grim-faced and unrelenting in their commitment to remain in the cavern until their brother woke.

The pool's waters began to ripple with a small surge. They spiraled around Kainan, changing the water's surface into a swirling, writhing mass.

The group rose to their feet as Selene inhaled in panic and tried to take a step forward. But Sheba pulled her back.

'Sel, wait,' she insisted. 'Something's happening with his vitals.'

She gestured to the comm tab.

Selene dived for the screen.

'What does it say?' she demanded, flicking her eyes between the screen and the pool where Kainan lay, unaware of the turmoil in the waters that held him.

'The replication of healthy metanoids is increasing fast.'

'Indeed,' Mirage called out from the ledge above. 'They're powering down his rogue chimera atoms. They're being neutralized.'

'His other systems are also healing fast. So fast!' Sheba breathed.

The five Sable Riders exchanged glances on the other side of the cavern.

Then, as one, they waded into the water, fighting its powerful waves to stand in a circle around their still-sleeping brother.

'What's happening?' Selene said.

Sheba lifted a hand to pause her sister's worried outburst. 'Ki'Remi is speaking with me. He says he's almost sure he knows what's happening. This is the final stage of the healing process. We need to let it happen. He also says the Riders will protect Kainan should anything unexpected happen. Which is why they're surrounding him.'

Selene took a shaky breath. Then she scrabbled for Rina and Sheba's hands, and the women held on to each other.

Around them, the cavern seemed to have come alive. Sparks

from swarms of agitated bioluminescent bugs zipped above the water.

A wild wind flew into the cave, whipping at their clothes and hair. A column of whirling air and mist formed over the water's surface, agitated by an unseen energy.

While they all watched, the column formed a vortex.

It whirled with such intensity that the three women almost fell back.

A powerful funnel formed over the rocking body, rising higher and higher towards the cave roof.

The tail of the water spout then bent until it touched Kainan's body, and they saw it glow as it sucked up a wild luminescence from his body.

The liquid vortex expanded before suddenly holding form midair. The column fell back to the surface with a loud splash before dying away.

A hush fell over the cavern.

It was broken moments later by Kainan, thrashing in the water. The Riders surged to hold him steady, but he pushed off their efforts.

He rose out of the pool, swaying as he opened his eyes to the astonished expressions of the group surrounding him.

'What are you all staring at?' he grumbled.

'At you, *khosi*! Damn!' Kage blurted. 'You've risen from the dead looking ten years younger. Damn, I need some of this healing water too!'

Kainan glanced down at his reflection on the wet surface and drew a sharp breath. The man he saw there was indeed a reborn version of himself. '*Fokk* me,' he breathed.

Seconds later, he almost fell back into the pool as Selene launched herself at him.

He wrapped his arms around her, shaking his head as if to clear out a nightmare.

'Is this real?' he rasped.

'It's real,' Sheba called out, brandishing the comm tab with Ki'Remi by her side. 'Ki'Remi confirms what the comm tab is saying. All indications are that your metanoids are now regenerating at a healthy pace! And there's no sign of the rogue DNA assaulting them.'

The gathered group sagged in deep relief.

The Sable Riders clapped hands around each other while Rina and Sheba fell into a hug.

Even Mirage lost her cool, flying around the cavern in mid-air dips and rolls.

Still standing in the grotto pool, Selene looked up at Kainan with wonder.

She traced her hands over his brow, cheek, and chin.

She touched the new, smooth skin and the pulsing kaleido-scope of nebula tattoos on his shoulders.

Moments later, she returned to his face, pressing her fingers against his cooled lips.

Even his hair had regenerated, falling back to his shoulders once again.

'You've never looked healthier, stronger, and more hand-some, *khaji*,' she murmured.

He stared down at her, the familiar sapphire gold gaze lighting her on fire like always.

Then he captured her lips with his.

'I feel amazing, *khamila*,' he said against her mouth.

'Thank *fokkin*' Dunia!' she breathed, holding him tighter.

'Language, love,' he said with a laugh.

'*Fokk* language when I have the love of my life back in my

428

arms.'

'Forever,' he whispered, kissing her with renewed emotion. 'Now you can have your forever, *khamila*.'

'And as long as our souls fly together, never apart ever again, we shall love forever,' she said with a small smile.

He held her for a long moment, then he turned, his eyes searching for his Riders, his brothers. His family.

'They never stopped believing in you,' Selene said, stepping aside as the five men moved forward to embrace their brother.

Kage reached out to him first, and Kainan folded into his arms in a close hug.

'We *fokkin*' love you, big guy,' Kage murmured, clapping Kainan's back.

'Appreciate it, K. Love you too,' his leader said, burying his face in his friend's shoulder.

'So good to have you back,' Riv said, his usually calm voice breaking with emotion.

'You've always had our back, Kai,' Zane added, throwing his long arms around Kainan. 'You burnt the stars for us, and we could never repay you for the sacrifice. Not even in this lifetime.'

Ki'Remi dipped his head, his solemn face wreathed in a smile.

'I did it for you all, and I'd do it again,' Kainan said. 'In a heartbeat.'

The six Riders wrapped arms around each other until Kainan looked up and extended an arm to Selene, Sheba, and Rina, who stood by, watching, with tears running down their faces.

They joined the men and stood interlinked together for a long while.

As the bioluminescence of the underwater lagoon around them pulsed with an incredible cerulean glow that lit them all up from within.

Epilogue

SELENE

'While we are gathered in grief, we are also in celebration. Of a great man, a great leader, and a caring father. Kei'Lano Munene III is remembered today as a visionary man who led the planet of Dunia from strength to strength.'

The words of the Dunian cleric soared above the crashing waves below.

He was used to raising his voice against the maelstrom of waves far below his feet, having conducted many ceremonies at this very same spot.

Selene felt Kainan squeeze her hand. She squeezed it back.

Her other arm was wrapped around Sheba's shoulders.

They stood on a bridge that spanned a narrow strait between the islands of Carpe and Evera, off New Malindi's wild southern coast.

Below the bridge, a frenzied eddy surged.

The whirlpool created waves up to twelve meters high, and the roar of the churning waters could be heard miles away.

A cool breeze flapped jackets and threatened scarves.

The bridge swayed in the wind, yet the three stood steadfast and rock-solid in their support of each other during their collective grief.

In the skies above, birds wheeled against a bank of gray clouds that threatened rain. Yet the storms held off with an almost sentient reverence for the ceremony below.

The Dunian cleric continued the short eulogy.

Secured between the trio and himself was a simple coffin.

Kei'Lano's body, which had been in the state morgue since the uprising, was now housed in an ebony black sarcophagus.

A simple floral wreath of Kei'Lano's favorite blossoms lay on its cover.

Kei'Lano's ceremonial guns finished the ensemble, laid over a woven cloth featuring the crest of the Munene family.

Onshore, a group of Kei'Lano's work colleagues and allies, the Sable Riders, and loyal staff members Selene retained under her employ were gathered.

They were the only invitees to the closed ceremony, intended for just friends and family. They stood on the edge of a cliff, their dark clothes in keeping with the somber gray sky.

They'd come from far and wide to say goodbye to their friend, who'd gone too soon.

The cleric's voice carried across the windswept landscape. He spoke of Kei'Lano's life, his accomplishments, and his legacy. The mourners listened intently, tears streaming down their faces.

Their private, quiet grief contrasted with the broader planet's shared and recent mourning.

Days before, a public funeral service had taken place in the vast halls of Dunia's Parliament House. It had begun with a procession of the coffin from his home, which lay on a floating open flyer.

Three hundred military guard members, including the Sable Riders, had been included in the procession through the streets of New Malindi.

They'd marched to Dunia's soaring Parliament House, where just over 500 foreign and local dignitaries and guests had assembled to farewell their former leader.

Armed guards and military personnel had been deployed throughout the capital to ensure peace.

At the same time, millions tuned in from all over Dunia to watch the live holo stream of the service screened across homes, streets, and parks.

It had been a majestic send-off for a well-loved leader, led by a eulogy that their new Prime and her sister read out.

The media had reported how calm the two sisters had been, and their elegance and composure had been praised for days across all networks.

Only after the period of public mourning did Selene and Sheba feel free to put their father to rest privately.

However, they couldn't bring themselves to reread the eulogy today, so they requested the clergy to take on the gut-wrenching task.

'May he rest in peace,' the cleric said, his words rising above the wind.

The heartfelt tribute ended.

The two sisters, who had publicly said what they needed to over the last few days, bowed their heads.

A clutch of drones, attached to the coffin with thick steel ropes, lifted the coffin into the air. Away from the bridge and towards the cliff's edge. Kei'Lano had always loved the ocean, and it was fitting that he was laid to rest within its endless, liquid majesty.

The coffin hovered before the drones lowered it into the churning spray of the waiting whirlpool. Their clamps released, and the coffin fell.

It floated briefly before the powerful eddy sucked it inside itself, claimed by the sea.

The mourners stood silent, watching the waves crash against the cliff below. It was a beautiful, fitting tribute to a life well-lived.

Above, thousands of Dunia's colorful birds wheeled in the air, keening in a fond farewell. Then, they flitted between the clouds, joined by a silver-feathered gyrfalcon that also paid its respects by dancing in the wind.

The funeral attendees watched as the coffin vanished, and Dunia took back one of her own into the depths of her massive, watery core.

As they turned to leave, Kei'Lano's friends and family took comfort in the fact that their father, colleague, friend, and mentor, was now at peace.

Surrounded by the beauty of the natural world.

They would never forget him, and the memories of the good times they'd shared would stay with them forever.

KING AUBAN, RHESUS

'We have news.'

The handsome, golden-haired King of the Rhesian Realm of Nations looked up from a report on his comm tab. He watched as his closest advisor shuffled into his office. The man looked somewhat shaken.

'What news?'

'About The Technocracy. Their fleet - over fifty ships in all - is no more. They were wiped out in an attack. In an uninhabited part of the System.'

'What do you mean, wiped out?'

'Decimated. Gone. No trace of their fleet has been found. We have a long-range satellite drone in that sector. Although all we can see is from a distance, the telemetry it picked up showed that a Technocracy ship arrived at a certain position. They proceeded to attack a medical vessel in the area. Unprovoked, might I add. Some other party arrived days later, presumably to aid the medical vessel. More Technocracy ships jumped to the same position, and within minutes, all fifty crat ships exploded in a great fireball. One so great it seemed like the stars were on fire.'

'And who destroyed the crats' ships?'

'We're not sure, but we also detected the signatures of several ships in the area simultaneously, all of Edenite bearing.'

'You think the Edenites did this?'

His advisor shrugged.

The King was skeptical. 'You're saying that ships from Eden II were responsible? I don't believe it for a moment.'

'Your Highness, I beg to differ. The Sable Group has worked secretly on its ship-building technology for many years. Who knows what they've been up to?'

'I respect The Sable Group, and Kainan Sable is a good friend to us. He's a retired soldier, now a businessman. He and his Group are more interested in making major schills and enlarging their bank accounts than waging war. At least, that's my estimation.'

The other man in the room didn't look quite so convinced. 'Regardless, we need to find out exactly who did this. The repercussions could be disastrous if we don't have the intel.'

'Then do it,' the King ordered. 'We need to know if there's another force out there that's more powerful than The Technocracy.'

'Yes, Your Highness.'

The advisor bowed and backed out of the royal rooms.

He nodded to a second man sitting waiting in the lobby outside the King's offices, who leaped to his feet and moved to walk alongside him.

'What did he say?' his new companion asked.

'He asked me to find out who wiped out The Technocracy. Whoever they are, the bastards eliminated our advantage just like that!' The first man's voice wavered with a mix of rage and disbelief.

'Keep it down,' his companion said, lowering his voice as they swept past a gaggle of ministers on their way to court. 'We will prevail. Auban's authorization is all we need.'

'I hope so. Our trackers show that the attacking ships did indeed have Edenite bearings. The King doesn't believe they have the capabilities for this. I think they do. We've watched them take over the shipping world by storm. Their vessels are faster and better than our own. So is their tech. The operation on Dunia to retake the planet was cloaked in secrecy, but I believe they may have played a part. Perhaps in exchange for xentium, the very same thing we seek. This is probably why we couldn't increase our stake in it, no matter how much we tried to twist the arm of their new Prime. The Edenites must somehow be involved in Dunia's sudden revival, given that planet's sudden confidence at the negotiating table. And if The Sable Group is indeed beginning to stand in the way of our progress, we must cut them off at the knees.'

'Agreed. I'll put the Rinnax brothers on it straight away. But how about the xentium we need?'

'We can't get the amount we require without force. Worse, we don't have the resources to fight for it. So let's enact Plan B, my friend. It's time to find out if what Massimo Makori claimed - that there's new tech being developed that could upset the xentium equation - is already in play. Getting our hands on it could help rewrite the imbalance of power.'

'Sounds feasible. What will The Klatsch say about this delay when they find out? They've invested schillions into this endeavor.'

'Pah!' scoffed the King's advisor. 'They've no choice but to invest in us; otherwise, they'll become obsolete. They're desperate for xentium because our depleting orhial stores already impact their manufacturing output. They're also facing crises because their factories are shutting down due to power failures, leading to unemployment and mass strikes at their collective manufacturing plants. The waves of discontent are rising, and they're demanding answers. They need us to exert our political influence to access xentium while protecting their monopolized power and manufacturing output. They hoped Dunia would be a shoo-in, and they'd have access to untapped xentium by now. But Selene Munene has proven to be quite the adversary and a strong leader. With overwhelming support from all of Pegasi's governments, especially after Dunia's victory over the crats. I'm unwilling to push her to the brink or anger our neighbors by going anywhere near her again. And neither should The Klatsch. So we'll need to find another way to gain what we want.'

'You still haven't told me what we should say to them.'

'We'll play The Klatsch as much as they're playing us. We'll tell them we had no idea who these new rogues on the playing field were. We'll also tell them that we're working on finding out. But we'll hold off on sharing any intel until you and I can determine how to use it to our best advantage. And remember, neither the King nor the Prime Minister is to be told a thing. We'll tell Auban when I think he's ready to hear from us.'

'As you wish,' the second man said. 'Always as you wish.'

'To the Triumv.'

'True and sure.'

SELENE

Selene sat at her father's desk in the Prime Residence in New Malindi the evening after his funeral.

It had been a long day, from the private send-off to the small wake after. Kei'Lano had never been one to make a fuss, so they'd kept the ceremonies simple, including the wake, which they'd hosted here at the formal residence.

It had ended up being a tear-filled afternoon of laughter

and memories as those closest to him shared anecdotes from his long and wonderful life.

Selene and Sheba knew their father's life had been tragically cut short, no matter what anyone said.

He would never see them flourish in their chosen careers, smile with them when they partnered in love, or hold their babies, his grandbabies, in his hands.

The consolation she took was that his passing had freed his soul to join the love of his life, Selene's mother, Astrea.

As the Dunia's twin suns cast a beautiful dusky light, Selene gingerly touched the beautiful ebony wood desk in the expansive library, a place that she'd avoided since his passing.

Apart from storing away his medals a few weeks ago, she'd not stepped into the room since.

Strangely enough, it was only after saying her final farewell to him earlier today that she felt comfortable in his most personal space. She settled back into the worn leather chair and breathed in.

She was flooded by the lingering scent of her father's cigars that had announced him before and after he left a room, followed by the menthol-like balm of the ever-mint sprigs he'd chewed to mask his secretive love for the skinny cheroots.

She smiled, remembering how he'd tried to hide his bad habit from her for years.

And how he'd failed each time, finding refuge in his library and office where he'd withdrawn to find peace and inspiration for his work and calling.

This was the place he'd often invited Selene to discuss the most difficult questions they had faced while governing

Dunia.

This was where they'd read together or play a game of cards with Sheba and friends. Most of the time, however, it'd just been the two of them these past few years.

Seated in his chair, she missed him terribly, her eyes misted with emotion.

She whispered the words she'd waited all these long weeks to say. In the most private and intimate place her father had inhabited.

'Thank you, papa, for the shared laughter, the wisdom, and the unfettered love. Thank you for your guidance and wise words when I was lost and for loving forgiveness when I made my mistakes. And there were many. You taught Sheba and me how to love unconditionally. The greatest gift of all.

The silver lining of this tragedy is that I've now met my life's love. He's a good man – a man you knew and a man you cared for like your son. He respects you, too, which gives me so much joy. He is wise, kind, and strong. He fights for what he believes in and supports me as the next Prime of Dunia. I know he'll be a great father to our children if we choose to have them.

Farewell. Don't worry about us. I think Sheba will be OK. I'll be OK most days. But, other days, I may miss you so much it'll hurt. I promise to keep your work and legacy alive. I promise to love and live as you did. I promise to keep making you proud.'

It was all she could manage. She turned her chair to view the expansive gardens and twilight ocean beyond, and wept into her hands.

The storm of grief passed after a few minutes, and she used the cuff of her sleeve to wipe the moisture away.

When she finally felt back in control, she half-turned the chair again.

Her eyes caught a movement and saw Kainan's silhouette in the lounge room across the corridor.

He was pacing to and fro, deep in a silent conversation she assumed was with one of the Riders.

She smiled at seeing him, feeling a lift in her spirits. She didn't know how she'd have survived these past weeks if it had not been for his support.

He'd been such a fantastic help, flipping the duty of care in their relationship from her hands to his. Because since his miraculous grotto experience and rapid recovery, she hadn't had a moment to breathe.

The minute Kainan left the hospital, both Sheba and herself had been thrust into preparing the official state funeral service for her father.

Kainan had offered to stay on Dunia, by her side, as she, her sister, and Rina worked with the Council and relevant authorities to oversee the events.

She'd had to alternate between being a grieving daughter and the planet's leading diplomat for the ensuing weeks, which had drained her immensely.

Sheba and herself were wrecked, caught up with planning for both the service and funeral, managing the expectations of hundreds of people who all wanted to pay respect to the former Prime in their own unique and sometimes ridiculous way.

Kainan and Ki'Remi had stepped in, nourishing both sisters with food, rest, listening ears, and for Selene, tender kisses and sensible advice from her man.

The Sable Rider's medic checked Kainan often and reported his healing progress.

When he did, Selene caught moments of intensity between

Sheba and the silent Edenite clinician.

If anything had happened or was happening between them, Sheba was not sharing. And Selene wasn't one to pry - for now.

She had so many other things to think about.

There was the case of preparing for her inauguration in two months. In between re-establishing the shaken confidence of her people and guiding the planet as it reflected on recent events.

She was determined not to let any Dunian citizen slip into disillusionment, cynicism, or despair, especially when the patriotic frenzy of celebrations died off.

To do so, she needed to take charge of evolving any long-held assumptions and presumptions that had led to the coup.

Which began by renewing their planet's internal and external defense capabilities. She was committed to establishing Dunia's security and increasing its bargaining and strategic power in the System. To do that, she needed a Defense Head to take full responsibility.

She approached Kainan and asked his thoughts to persuade him to step into the role and work with General McKenzie to design a credible deterrence strategy.

He'd mulled over it, and they'd negotiated a temporary agreement. One where he would travel between Eden II and Dunia as required.

He'd still head The Sable Group, and if the arrangement worked for everyone, he was willing to look at balancing both roles long-term.

He'd also given her invaluable insights into rebuilding Dunia's cities battered by recent violence.

Speaking of violence, her thoughts strayed to Massimo

Makori and his shattered legacy.

The One Dunia Alliance had been disbanded, and its leaders were caught and sentenced to long prison terms. Massimo's wife and fellow traitors were now secured in Gineliv III's maximum holding facility.

His adult children had scattered, having fled Dunia for parts unknown. Except, of course, Mirage, now back with the rest of the Riders on Eden II, had tracked them down and found them hiding out on the pleasure planet of Zanyria.

Selene chose to hold off from pursuing them further. The shame they'd experienced was punishment enough, for now, she hoped.

The government sold Massimo's lands, properties, and holdings to compensate his victims.

At Selene's request and after a high court secured and an Elder Council endorsed Order, the Makori extended dynasty, friends, and families had lost all of their shares in the mining industry, especially the xentium fields.

Xentium production, however, was back in full swing. One of Selene's dearest friends, Harlow, was on the cusp of a breakthrough technology that would harness the most potential from Dunia's most precious resource.

Selene hoped the commercial profits from the new technology could fund Dunia's rebuilding efforts and ensure its future by investing in its people, creating social safety net programs, and providing security for each Dunian on and off the planet.

The Technocracy, for whom xentium had been such a boon, had been decimated for the most part.

The Sable Riders' nano-virus payload had reportedly even reached their exploration and mining ships on the galaxy's edges, causing them to fail. Their armadas were wiped out, and their dominance of the System diminished.

However, a few days ago, a curious message had been intercepted from a far-flung corner of the Omegaverse.

It stated how The Technocracy would rise once more. It also vowed that they'd return to destroy Eden II, Dunia, and the entire Pegasi system in vengeance once they did.

Selene sighed.

'That's the sound of a woman with the weight of a planet on her shoulders,' she heard a deep voice say. One that would always send shivers down her spine.

She swiveled her father's chair forward and smiled at the sight of her man.

He stood leaning a muscled shoulder against the office door jamb.

'Hi,' she said, taking all of his magnificence in.

Barefoot. Chest bare, from his broad, glyphed shoulders to his thick arms and the whirl of hair below his belly button.

His long, new locks fell to his shoulders, giving her the urge to run her fingers through their silken lengths.

He wore loose, soft pants that hung low on his narrow hips. She squeezed her fists tight, longing to tear them off him. Instead, all she could do at this moment was savor his beauty.

'Hey,' he drawled. 'You OK?'

'Better now that I've seen you.'

'How much more do you want to see?' he said hoarse and low, his voice cascading over her body with heat.

'Everything. I've missed you so much,' she breathed.

The air between them electrified.

Missing him was an understatement. She yearned, thirsted, and was slaked for his touch. She longed for his lips on hers.

His chest against hers, his heavy thighs pressing down on hers. His thickness moving deep inside her.

Yet yearning was all she was allowed. They hadn't made love ever since he'd left the hospital for a few reasons.

One was her busy schedule. The other was Ki'Remi's strict order that Kainan remain under observation for a few weeks in case his recovery stalled.

According to the medic, sex was out of the question, given its ability to intensify his metanoid activity.

So they'd remained impatiently celibate, reduced to sleeping in each other's arms in Selene's bed, aching for more.

He'd tried to get her off, and she'd forbidden it, telling him that if he couldn't get off, neither could she.

They'd since resorted to drawn-out make-outs and even longer, colder showers.

'I have news,' Kainan announced, a smile dancing around his lips. She felt the air spark even more between them. *Damn, they were so ionically aligned.*

'Tell me,' Selene said, rising from the chair and rounding the desk towards him.

'Ki'Remi just gave me the all-clear,' he said, raising an eyebrow.

Selene's body reacted with heated anticipation at their endless attraction and explosive polarity. 'Is that right?'

Kainan launched himself away from the doorway and stalked towards Selene.

'Where's Sheba?' he asked, stopping before his woman.

Selene looked up at him, bracing herself for the onslaught of molten passion in his eyes. 'She went out for dinner with old friends. She said she won't return until tomorrow. I think she thinks we want some alone time.'

'She is a brilliant woman.'

With that, Kainan bent over. He nabbed her around the thighs and into his arms, launching her over his shoulders.

She laughed aloud, a sound that fast became a moan as he worked his free hand under her skirt, ripped her panties down to her thighs, and began stroking her oversensitive mound.

She held on to his shoulders as she melted.

'Kainan!'

'Should I stop?' he teased.

'Holy Dunia, don't you ever stop!'

'As you wish, my love,' he ground out, charging out of the room.

He took to the residence's stairs, one pair at a time.

While he did, his fingers stroked her clit that was so deliciously accessible to him.

He kicked in her door and strode in, throwing her to the bed.

They tore their clothes off with abandon.

Naked, Selene scrambled back to the headboard as she watched Kainan move to the windows and shut the blinds.

He strode back, and that's when she noticed the strobing flashes of wildly hued energy under his skin.

'Should we? Can we?' she panicked, sitting halfway, pointing one finger at his body.

He glanced down and gave her a soft smile. 'All clear. It turns out I still have some of my chimeric potency. However, the new balance in my body means I now control their power and replication, rather than them being out of control after I transform. I'm still me, *khamila*, but a much more contained version.'

Selene fell back onto the bed in relief but also in anticipation. 'You're sure?' she continued, wanting to be safe.

He paused with a slicked-raised eyebrow. 'Fokk, woman. Shall I give you a detailed breakdown of my medical prognosis? Or shall we get back to where we were?'

She parted her legs provocatively in response. He shot her an appreciative smirk and crawled to her, pausing between her thighs, dragging his sapphire gold eyes over her lush curves.

'You're so beautiful, woman. Maybe you were the one killing me all along.'

'It goes both ways, lover.'

He leaned over and, with a grin, dived. He took possession of her core with his lips, tongue, and power to draw deep into her center. Her clit fired, and she bucked, trying to jack herself against his mouth.

He pushed her hips back and continued his lashing.

She blew, jerking so hard she felt her back crack with the energy and passion coursing through it.

He continued his assault until she came again, flooding his mouth with her essence. He lapped it up as she mewled and thrashed across the bed, soaking in her sweat.

Sated, Kainan rose and crept over her, dragging his thick cock over her skin. She reached for it and stroked him long and slow. He moaned, his lips finding hers in a deep, sensual exchange.

'*Khaji*,' she invited, sliding the tip of his cock across her clit and into her slit, flushed and heated for him.

He lifted himself off her, flipped her over, and caressed her satiny cheeks, sinking long fingers into wet readiness.

She cried out. 'Please, Kainan! I need you.'

It was all the encouragement he needed. He positioned himself, then sank into her, first slow and achingly tantalizing, before driving into her.

She bucked with passion as he rode and made electrifying love to her.

The chimeric colors of his body flashed against the bedroom wall, in cadence with his impaling power.

They imploded, falling together as the maglev train of ecstasy they were chasing hit them with a power so intense they both roared.

Later, they lay heart-to-heart, wrapped in each other's arms.

'*Khamila*,' Kainan whispered, 'I found out something from Mirage just the other day. She discovered the name '*Selene*' is an old Earth and ancient Greek word for the moon. In Greek and Roman religion, she was the personification of the lunar goddess. According to Hesiod's Theogony, her parents were the Titans Hyperion and Theia; her brother was Helios, the sun god; her sister was Eos, the dawn. Her lover was Endymion, with whom she bore fifty daughters. One version of the story says that Selene placed Endymion in eternal sleep to prevent him from dying and to keep him forever beautiful.'

Selene smiled against his lips. 'So you're my Endymion.'

'A version of him, it would seem.'

'How true,' Selene said, amazed. 'I stood beside you in Dunia's waters and begged for your healing. You went into a deep sleep, which brought you back to us whole.'

'And for that, I'll be eternally grateful,' Kainan murmured, nipping her mouth.

Selene laughed. 'The myth is right about one thing. I could live like this forever,' she whispered with a sweet smile.

His mouth softened. '*Naam*. I could, too. Given the myth

also says you're the mother of fifty, what can I look forward to? A gaggle of curly-haired, honey-skinned babies?'

She pulled away from him and sat up, eyes wide with joy. 'Really?'

'Of course, *khamila*,' he growled. 'I want babies with you. I want to create my forever with you.'

Selene felt her womb clench with longing. She traced a finger from his forehead to his lips. 'Can we order them with sapphire and gold eyes?'

'I bet if we ask Dunia nicely, we may even get our wish. As it happens, we're both in favor. Of an entire planet.'

'It might just work,' she said. 'Dunia can be generous.'

After a beat, she spoke again. '*Khaji*, this may sound sweet and sentimental,' she whispered. 'But you are truly my forever.'

He gave a small laugh and pulled her even tighter to him. 'I'll give you even more sentimentality, *khamila*. If this is my forever, I'm glad I almost had to die for it.'

They fell into silence, chest to chest. Their lips brushed, occasionally dipping into full-blown sensuous kisses.

As the night wore on, they fell asleep, foreheads touching as an inky, velvety night sky fell over a sentient star-lit world filled with the promise of a forever yet to come.

THE HAPPY EVER AFTER OF ONE BEAUTIFUL STARLIT
STORY

AND THE BEGINNING OF ANOTHER

The Sable Rider Series continues with
BOOK 2: STARS AT DUSK

Harlow is a brilliant, sassy scientist who's wary of Kage Sable's moxie and full-on intensity. But he slowly draws her in, one delicious moment at a time. Together, they'll fight for the relationship they want while keeping their top-secret breakthrough from a ruthless and secret galactic organization. Together, they'll fall into a dusky twilight of heady love and impossible starlight.

NOW AVAILABLE
GET YOUR COPY NOW

One more thing, lovely.
Your reviews matter.
A LOT.
Reviews are truly the lifeline for authors like me; they not only boost visibility but also help other readers discover these fantastic stories.
A few words can make a huge difference!
If you loved 'Stars on Fire,' please leave me a kind review on Amazon or Goodreads.
I thank you, kindly.
💋 *Sky*

Bonus Chapter - Forever Under The Stars

Selene and Kainan's promise of forever took time, but it was right on time.

It took Selene a year after her father's death before she felt the guilt ebb away at his death.
Only then did she feel strong enough to say yes to Kainan's gentle yet insistent request that they bind their souls together in a Kwavi wedding union.

Read all about their incandescent wedding now.

**Visit my bonus content, freebies, and extras chapters page to read about
their happy-ever-after nuptials.**

https://skyovereden.com/bonus

Also by Sky Gold

I am a best-selling author, writer, and lover of all things delicious, fun, and courageously life-affirming. I look to my gorgeous husband, my kids, my wonderful extended family, my friends, my sweet Russian Blue cat, and the stars themselves for my inspiration.

You can connect with me on:
   Website: https://skyovereden.com
   Or via Facebook (join my readers group for freebies and giveaways!), Instagram, TikTok, Goodreads, and Bookbub.

The saga of the Sable Riders continues with Kage and Harlow. Get Your Copy Now!

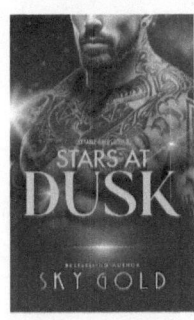

Stars at Dusk

''Your brass is ballsy, Kage Sable.'

She's **sassy-smart-strong ...** A genius, generous, confident scientist.

He's a master builder, an ex-warrior, a kick-ass engineer and ... **her new ballsy and sometimes grumpy 'boss'.**

They fight their feelings for each other ... while keeping their top-secret breakthrough from a ruthless and secret galactic organization.

Together, **they'll fall into a dusky twilight of heady love and impossible starlight.**

NOW AVAILABLE TO PURCHASE OR FOR FREE ON KINDLE UNLIMITED.

Stars of Gems

What happens when a wildfire siren meets a soul of cold, hard metal?

Illanna Merani is the wildfire volcano to Zane Sable's icy tundra. She's the meteoric stardust to his deep, dark, frozen depths. She's the savage steel to his cold metal.

Ne'er, the two should meet. Until they do - and **the wild connection between them goes OFF.**

Cool, calm and always in control, Zane Sable is yearning for something he can't quite articulate. Wild and bold, Illanna Merani is seeking freedom in her star-based career and love for music. **Their needs, moods and personalities clash, but could they discover precious gems of true love within the stars?**

Their journey to an explosive, magnetic and alchemic happily ever after becomes a metaphysical contradiction, **a co-existence of two mighty opposites** who become enamored with each other while caught in a love-hate web of major tension.

Battling their feelings, their psionic reactions, sabotage and a series of mysterious forces lurking around their project, **they face off against the stunning backdrop of a lunar star-lit plain.** Where the much-awaited Eden II Twin Rings waits to rise, a construction of astronomic proportions that will rival anything else seen in all of Pegasi.

Together they'll set off a meteoric tsunami of epic proportions, a kinetic explosion of attraction and sensuality that will sear the stars above into gems of incandescent light.

If you love an enemies-to-lovers HEA, and a paranormal, urban fantasy saga packed with spice, steam, sass and plenty of starlit adventure, get 'Stars of Gems' today!

NOW AVAILABLE.

Stars in Mist

She's the love of his life. The one that got away. They shared a love so deep and eternal. Until she mysteriously disappeared. Now endlessly searches the galaxy for her, only her. Convinced that neither time nor space can keep them apart.

Over twenty years ago, **Riv Sable's girl and the love of his life went missing** in mysterious circumstances.

He's dedicated his life to searching the outmost reaches of Pegasi to find her. Just as he's about to give up, he gets a glimmer of hope.

Could this be the HEA he's scoured an entire universe for? And what stands in the way of reuniting with the woman who captured his heart many years ago?

Together, their souls will find each other among 'Stars in Mist'.

Get enamored by this transcendental second chance romance. Get your copy today!

Saber Blade

Book 1 in the seductive 'Hawkstone Realm' trilogy, the new series from Bestselling Author Sky Gold, is an epic, soaring adult fantasy romance.

An assassin with a lethal oath. A King with no throne. A fierce love that will unravel their world.

She seeks vengeance for what she and her people lost, no matter the price. He aims to outplay the dark, powerful forces seeking to use their *u'chawi* sorcery to destroy him.

He can only trust a few, not, at the very least, the shikari. When he's forced to make her his fight master, their proximity descends ... Into a battle of *sābər*-edged wits and insults and - a fight for love against all odds.

Welcome to the wild Desolation of Katánē, the Thousand Mile Lands, where fierce winged *Sābər* Hawk warriors collide with witchers, bladers, and assassins in a dark, intense, sweeping, addictive fantasy romance saga set in a court mired in mysticism, magic, betrayal, and intrigue.

Binge read 'SABER BLADE' now.

Dragon Domini - A Forbidden Dragon King Romance
PRE-ORDER NOW FOR ONLY $0.99

Beta readers are saying:
  'Dark, spicy, delicious and intense!''
  'If you loved The Sable Riders, this is your next binge!'

Steal from a Shadow Dragon King, and he won't kill you. He'll claim you.

Lumi De Veil is a siren dancer, a slave, and a rule-breaker who commits the ultimate sin: stealing a star-shattering jewel from Zavier Phanos-Draquis, the most powerful Shadow Dragon King alive.

Instead of destroying her, Zavier traps Lumi under his roof and forces her into a dangerous alliance against enemies clawing their way from an eternal realm.

Forced proximity ignites forbidden desire.

Zavier is ruthless, possessive, and terrifyingly controlled. Lumi is defiant, sharp-tongued, and hiding a secret royal lineage she has no clue about. He is immortal and barred from giving her forever and eternity. She believes she is mortal, and falling for him could destroy them both.

Because if they fail, worlds fall. If they surrender, immortality is rewritten, and loving each other may shatter the stars.

From bestselling author Sky Gold comes the angsty, spicy start to the interconnected standalone 'Dragon Shadow Kings' paranormal romance series, with forbidden romance, forced proximity, and a ruthless Shadow Dragon King.

Order Your Copy Today

www.ingramcontent.com/pod-product-compliance
Lightning Source LLC
Chambersburg PA
CBHW030542020726
47494CB00005B/1457